THE DRAGON CHOKER

THE DRAGON CHOKER

A Cracked Slipper Novel, Book 2

STEPHANIE ALEXANDER

Second edition printed January 2020

Cover and Distribution by Bublish, Inc.

ISBN: 978-1-64704-038-3 (paperback)
ISBN: 978-1-64704-039-0 (eBook)

To my husband, Jeffrey Cluver

The ring is on my hand,
And the wreath is on my brow;
Satin and jewels grand
Are all at my command,
And I am happy now...

...And thus the words were spoken,
And this the plighted vow,
And, though my faith be broken,
And, though my heart be broken,
Here is a ring, as token
That I am happy now!
> —Edgar Allen Poe, Bridal Ballad

Seldom, very seldom, does complete truth belong to any human disclosure; seldom can it happen that something is not a little disguised, or a little mistaken.

> —Jane Austen

PART I

CHAPTER I

COME WHAT MAY

ELEANOR BRICE DESMARAIS DID not often pass an afternoon mucking out stalls. She had no aversion to hard work. Eight years of living under her stepmother's roof as the maid in her father's house had left her accustomed to the aches that came along with a vigorous day's labor, but all that was nearly two years behind her. It was hardly becoming for the wife of the Crown Prince of Cartheigh to haul hay bales and wield a shovel, even if her hauling and shoveling benefited not a mere cow or horse, but a unicorn.

The unicorn in question peered into the stall. Her white mane fell over the edge of the half door leading to the paddock. "This is unnecessary," Teardrop said. "Let me call the groom."

Eleanor shook her head. The grooms had lingered, embarrassed and confused, until she snapped at them to take their leave. Her own rudeness irritated her. As one who had spent much of her life in servant's shoes, she always treated the help with respect.

"I agree with Teardrop," said her parrot, Chou Chou, from his perch above her head in the rafters. "It's frightfully warm. You might expire."

"Hush, Chou," said Eleanor. "I'd rather be out here in pants than inside in a petticoat and corset."

3

"Why don't we take a ride?" asked Teardrop. "We could visit the beach at Porcupine Bay."

"No," said Eleanor. The thought of Porcupine Bay brought memories of his pale eyes reflecting the sky. She attacked the hay with her pitchfork.

Three festive weeks had passed in the resort town of Solsea, full of the usual summer diversions: parties, tournaments, picnics, hunts. At every event Eleanor stood beside her husband, Prince Gregory, smiling and laughing and dying inside. Only her newborn daughter, Leticia, brought her any real happiness.

Leticia was over two months old. Two months since she was accused of the theft of an enchanted national treasure and her husband abandoned her. Since she'd exposed Ezra Oliver, the king's chief magician, as the true culprit, and sent him into magical oblivion.

Two months since Dorian Finley had sworn he would find a way to love her.

Eleanor knew one false move on her part or Dorian's would send them both to the scaffold. Gregory was the heir to the throne, the keeper of the Great Bond. The living legacy of three hundred years of good fortune wrought by a mystical synergy between unicorns, dragons, and the Desmarais family. He would hardly suffer an affair between his wife and his best friend. Eleanor and Dorian had not spoken more than pleasantries since their last night together during her exile at Rabbit's Rest Lodge.

The misery of their separation in plain sight finally drove her to the physical exertion of cleaning the unicorn barn. An ocean breeze drifted over the cliffside and across the rolling grounds of the royal compound, Trill Castle, but it stopped short against the walls of Willowswatch Cottage. The modest moniker belied the mansion's heft. Its Fire-iron and granite walls blocked any hint of moving air that might have found its way to her sweaty forehead. The unicorn barn, with its stone facade and dazzlingly white interior, was cheery, but a stable is a stable. Wide un-paned windows let in both sunlight and flies, the latter of which buzzed around Eleanor's face. Heat bore down on her from all sides. She ignored the headache pounding behind her eyes. She'd barely managed a full meal a day the past few weeks.

She brushed a few strands of damp blonde hair behind her ears. Sweat dripped down her face, and she wiped it away with the tears that snuck out of her mismatched eyes. One blue, one brown, both stinging with cooped-up frustration. At least the perspiration provided a disguise, let the tears flow without suspicion.

"What in the name of holy HighGod is this?"

Eleanor straightened, only to be confronted by both sources of her misery. Gregory and Dorian, in their riding clothes, stood in the barn's entrance. Gregory walked to her, but Dorian stayed framed in the passageway.

"Sweetheart," continued Gregory. "What are you doing? Let me call a groom."

"We tried to convince her, sire." Chou Chou flew down from the rafters and lit on the handle of her pitchfork. As he flapped around in an attempt to maintain his balance, a few red and blue feathers floated down amidst the hay. "Talk some sense into her before we have to call a witch to revive her."

Eleanor wiped at her face again and forced a smile for the millionth time since her return from Rabbit's Rest. "I don't mind. The exertion will help me fit into my dresses again."

"Hardly. I think you slighter than ever before. Don't disappear on me. I need something to hold onto." Gregory ran a hand down her arm and her skin crawled.

She glanced at Dorian, but he was examining a stirrup. He turned it over in his hands, and the silvery Fire-iron threw reflections of sunlight against the walls in jolly rainbows. Eleanor wished he would look at her.

"Where are you boys going?" she asked, turning back to the hay.

"Just taking Vigor and Senné for a ride down to Porcupine Bay."

Porcupine Bay, again. The hay crinkled and crackled as Eleanor flung it about Teardrop's stall.

Dorian finally spoke. "Would you and Teardrop join us?"

"I must return to Ticia." Eleanor probably would not have joined them anyway, but her breasts ached after two hours away from her daughter.

Gregory scowled, and a line appeared between his light brown eyes. "Again? What about the wet nurse?"

Dorian opened Senné's stall door. He eased the black stallion's silver horn aside and disappeared inside.

"Gregory," Eleanor said. "I can't stay away from her all day."

"Hasn't this gone on long enough?"

She swallowed her pride and sidled up to him. "Oh, stop. Don't you want me to come along to the Harper's dinner tonight?" She touched his cheek.

To her surprise he grabbed her around the waist. He spoke in her ear again. "I want you to enjoy yourself. Have a few glasses of wine. Relax."

She knew exactly what he meant. As she whispered her reply, she caught Dorian watching them over Senné's stall door. "You know I have to see a witch first, husband. The birth—I need to know all is healed."

"Well call one. Soon." It was a command, not a request. He kissed her nose and strode into Vigor's stall.

Vigor and Gregory followed Dorian and Senné into the courtyard. The grooms rushed around them, handing off bits of tack and hoof picks, happy to be allowed to do their duties. Senné and Vigor stood beside each other, black and white, like two giant chess pieces.

"Enjoy the ride," said Eleanor, as Dorian swung into the saddle.

"We'll miss you, and Teardrop," he replied. She cringed at the distance in his voice. He could have been speaking to his butler.

Gregory kissed her again. This time she felt the flick of his tongue. He mounted and she held Vigor's bridle. The unicorn nuzzled her with his velvety lips. She stroked his nose and squinted up at Gregory.

"Dorian and I have been called to Point-of-Rocks to meet with the Ports Minister," he said. "There's a shipment of raw Fire-iron coming down from the Mines. A big one."

"Bigger than usual?"

"Early summer yields are always good. The dragons burn hot in the spring months. Mating season," he said with a laugh. Eleanor ignored the reference to mating and attributed his mirth to the thought of copious amounts of money. Fire-iron, the light, wondrously versatile result of a dragon's body heat and fiery breath, was the lifeblood of her country.

"We leave the day after tomorrow."

"How long will you be gone?"

"Oh, nine, maybe ten days."

Eleanor's heart sank. It must have shown on her face, because Dorian teased her. "Don't be glum, Eleanor. With Gregory gone you can hole up with Ticia all day and night if you choose."

She tried to join him in their old banter. "I hope the Ports Minister has stored up on whiskey and wine if he's to entertain you two for ten days." It was a sorry attempt, but Gregory didn't seem to notice. He grinned.

"Don't worry, Dorian will bring me back to you with my brains intact." He leaned down. "Now go send for that witch. I don't want to wait another two weeks."

She watched them go, across the grounds toward the steep path leading from Neckbreak Cottage to Porcupine Bay. Gregory didn't look back, but Dorian did, although he didn't wave or smile. Eleanor felt warm breath on her neck and rested a hand on Teardrop's silky neck. Chou Chou lit on her shoulder. Neither spoke, but their silent understanding comforted her. She kept her face from crumpling. When Dorian and Gregory disappeared she walked up the stone path to Willowswatch to attend her daughter.

The next evening Eleanor sat on a blanket on the south lawn with her beloved stepsister, Margaret. They passed Eleanor's daughter and a basket of grapes between them. Ticia smiled and cooed and enjoyed the attention. Eleanor missed the company of her other dear friends, Anne Iris and Eliza, but with Anne Iris recently married and pregnant (under speculation that the two had not necessarily happened in that order), and Eliza busy with her second baby, neither had made the trip to Solsea this year.

"I wonder how Anne Iris is getting on," said Margaret, as if reading Eleanor's mind.

"I wonder how her husband is getting on."

"True," said Margaret. She ran a hand over her kinky brown hair, made kinkier by the summer humidity. "Perhaps pregnancy will distract Anne Iris from flirtation."

"Doubtful. She'll have more cleavage to flaunt than ever."

"Poor man, he'll be a jilted husband before he even has a chance to be a jilted father."

They laughed, and Eleanor felt a prick at the reference to jilted husbands. She'd enjoyed a brief respite from guilt in the weeks following her return to Eclatant, but lately her conscience had been hanging on her skirt like an insistent child. Although she had been a jilted wife for the entire duration of her marriage, she couldn't fully embrace her husband's comfort with deceit.

Gregory, Dorian, and Raoul Delano crossed the lawn. Raoul sat on the blanket beside Margaret and kissed her cheek. A blush lit Margaret's face, and Eleanor marveled at her friend's happy beauty. She only wished her stepmother could see it. *How Mother Imogene thinks her homely I'll never know.*

Gregory pulled Eleanor to her feet and took Ticia. He held the baby high in the air and blew on her belly. He snuffled at the fat rolls around her neck and she tried to suck on his chin. Eleanor laughed. Gregory's love for their daughter always elicited a genuine reaction from her. He rested the baby on his shoulder. She seemed no larger than a kitten against his broad chest. His auburn hair melted into the fuzz of the exact same shade on her head.

"Did you find a witch?" he whispered.

"I did, but she cannot come until Friday."

Gregory exhaled, hard. "Well, we can both think on it while I'm away." He spoke to Dorian. "I'll need something to distract me from my loneliness."

"You can drink alone," said Dorian. "You've done it before."

"Alone?" asked Eleanor.

"Dorian's sister changed the dates of her visit. She's arriving tomorrow with her family."

Dorian looked out over the cliffs. He pulled a flask of whiskey from his pocket and took a long drink. "Gregory generously gave me leave to remain at Trill with Anne Clara and Ransom and the children."

Eleanor feared her voice would shake, so she waited a moment to speak. "How kind of you, Gregory."

"Ah, Dorian only sees Anne Clara a few times a year. It was the least I could do for keeping him locked in the Council Room at Eclatant." Gregory gave Ticia to Eleanor and sat on the blanket.

Eleanor smiled casually at Dorian. "Are you anxious to see Anne Clara?"

"I am." His eyes, so light they were at once the color of the grass and the water and the washed out sky, were fixed on the Shallow Sea.

Eleanor strained for some hint, for some acknowledgement from him. He sat on the blanket beside Gregory. He tapped his fingers on the hilt of his father's Fire-iron knife, the one he always kept in a sheath along his right boot. As she looked down at his dark hair a terrible thought struck her. Dorian had changed his mind.

Gregory left the next morning with several Unicorn Guards. Anne Clara and her family arrived a few hours later. Eleanor drifted through the next two days in a fog of false happiness. She planned picnics and tea parties. She took a long nap with Ticia. She spent a floury afternoon in the kitchen making cakes with Anne Clara's children.

One of the Finley cousins hosted a dinner in honor of Anne Clara's visit, and Eleanor took an hour determining which of her gowns Dorian would find most enticing. Her choice, soft blue silk with lace trim around the bodice, emphasized her nursing-enhanced cleavage. She hovered beside Dorian throughout the party, hoping he'd ask her for a dance. She had watched with disdain for two years as countless other women desperately maneuvered around him. Her efforts were just as soundly ignored. She called for her carriage before the clockworks struck ten. Raoul and Margaret accompanied her back to Trill. She rested her head against the rocking window and closed her eyes; both to give Raoul and Margaret privacy and to avoid the passionate looks flickering between them.

On the third morning of Gregory's absence she made her way to the unicorn barn again. The grooms must have assumed her unsatisfied with their supervision of her mare's care. She could hardly detect an errant piece of straw, and could see her own reflection in the Fire-iron trough of clean water. She sat down in the scratchy straw with the pitch-fork over her lap. Chou Chou and Teardrop refused to leave her alone.

"The weather is fine, is it not?" asked Chou.

"Lovely," said Teardrop. "Though I do feel thunder on the horizon."

Eleanor opened her mouth to reply; then shut it. She dropped the pitchfork and hung her head between her knees. Her stomach clenched as she held back the sobs that had been hopping around her mid-section for three days, searching for a way out. Teardrop snorted. She nibbled at Eleanor's hair and her wide hooves rustled the straw. Her mane rested on Eleanor's back like a comforting blanket on a cold night. Chou lit on Eleanor's head.

"There, there, darling," whispered Chou. "Please, don't—"

"Eleanor?"

She lifted her head. Dorian looked down at her over the stall door. She wiped her eyes and stood. Chou left her head for Teardrop's back.

"We could ride down to Porcupine Bay," Dorian said.

A few wordless minutes later and Eleanor and Teardrop were following Dorian and Senné across the grounds. They passed Margaret and Raoul as they set up a game of lawn bolls.

"Off to Porcupine Bay?" asked Raoul.

Eleanor nodded. "If only you could join us."

"If only we had unicorns we might," said Margaret. "I don't fancy hiking down that cliff in my dancing slippers."

Dorian and Eleanor waved goodbye and continued on their silent way. Eleanor did not fear the incline. She only feared what Dorian might have to say when they reached the beach. She ignored the breathtaking view around her, and the chattering of the cliff lemurs. As they descended, the wind picked up and blew the smell of salty water and damp seaweed into her face. She imagined his explanations: the danger, the immorality of lying to Gregory, the pointlessness of continuing an affair with no hope of ever being anything but just that. She heard herself trying to rationalize with him, and then screaming and crying, then agreeing with the hopelessness of it all. Her imaginary dialogue so engaged her that she lost her balance when Teardrop stopped behind Senné at the edge of the blood-colored waters of Redwine Falls.

"Let's go this way." Dorian pointed past the falls and back up the cliffside. She nodded. As they began the ascent Eleanor took hold of Teardrop's mane. She could see the falls behind them, but the path had already faded to nothing but a jagged edge along the rock. There was no beach below, only boulders reaching their scarred faces out of the tossing waves like drowning sailors gasping for air. She waved at the gulls screeching and hissing around her head. Teardrop nicked one with a swing of her horn and they retreated.

"They're protecting their nests," shouted Dorian over the wind, waves, and protesting birds.

She looked down, her face blanching with dizziness, and counted no less than ten twiggy brown nests full of fat yellow eggs in the rocks around Teardrop's hooves.

"Teardrop, are you sure you can do this?" she asked.

"No," said Teardrop, "but I will try."

Eleanor gritted her teeth. "I'll leave you to it."

They climbed for half an hour. Teardrop slipped twice and dislodged several loose rocks. With each jolt Eleanor shut her eyes and muttered prayers.

Senné stopped and waited for Teardrop to catch up. Dorian pointed out a long, dark patch in the blue water. "There's a reef out there. No ships can get within half a mile, not even the villager's fishing boats."

Teardrop's footing improved with each step. Eleanor relaxed and watched the sea. She wondered how many living beings, other than the gulls and a few bats, had ever taken in the view.

She faced forward again and her heart stopped. Dorian and Senné had disappeared. She looked down, searching for Senné's black form against the gray rock.

"Do not fear," said Teardrop. "Here we are."

Eleanor slid from Teardrop's back. The mare ducked into what at first seemed nothing more than extra darkness amidst a host of cast shadows. Eleanor could just make out the flash of Senné's horn and the light in his liquid eyes. Teardrop walked the three paces across the cave and stood beside him. He puffed in her ears and she nipped his shoulder. Both settled into quiet watchfulness. Teardrop glowed softly white against Senné's black bulk.

As Eleanor walked further into the cavern she could see her hands again. She turned toward the light, and climbed through another opening in the rock. She wondered how Dorian, with his height and breadth of shoulders, had contorted himself to fit.

He stood in a chamber made from a space between the cliff wall and a pile of boulders a hand span above his head. Sunlight streamed through the haphazard cracks between the rocks and struck the hard-packed dirt floor.

"I thought this place…we could come here…"

Eleanor threw her arms around his neck. His mouth found hers and they both tumbled to the ground.

She sat astride him and pulled his tunic over his head. Their arms collided as he repeated the favor for her. He buried his hands in her hair, then scraped them down her back. She wrapped her arms around his head and arched her back. He kissed both her breasts and his tongue flicked over her skin. He rested his head against her chest and squeezed her until she couldn't breathe.

"High God, Eleanor," he said. "How have I survived the past two months?" She hated herself for it, but she started crying. He looked up at her. "My love, what is it?"

She shook her head and bit her fist. She spoke around the sobs. "I thought—you changed your mind—you didn't want to—"

His impossibly beautiful eyes widened. "Changed my mind?"

"Yes. You've been so cold—we haven't spoken in weeks—"

He took both her hands in his. "I've been cold because I'm afraid anything I say will give me away. When Gregory told me about the trip to Point-of-Rocks I wrote Anne Clara and asked her to come right away. I've spent weeks searching this place out."

Eleanor swallowed. "I'm sorry—"

"I made my decision at Rabbit's Rest. Come what may, I'm here, in this with you."

Ten minutes later she had finally cried herself dry. She nestled in the crook of his arm as they lay in the dirt. She ran her fingers over his forearm, and lifted his hand. She kissed the knuckle that should have ended in his smallest finger, had a giant bird not snipped it off during her exile last spring. He curled his remaining fingers into a fist and then tugged at a lock of her hair. "Will you spend all of the time we have together sobbing? I'll have to store handkerchiefs up here."

Eleanor punched his arm, and rolled on top of him. "There's one more thing."

He sighed and blew her hair out of his face.

"I'm afraid this won't be enough for you. Since we can't…as we said at Rabbit's Rest…the risk of a child…"

"I told you I understand your fear. I've already considered it."

"And what conclusion have you reached?"

"Well." He laced his hands behind his head. "We can find enjoyment other ways. Not to belittle the pleasures of the most holy act, but it's not the only dance at the party."

"What do you mean?"

He could not hide his confusion. He cleared his throat. "I assumed you would be familiar with…that you had some experience with…"

She blushed. In this cave she fully planned on pretending Gregory Desmarais, Crown Prince of Cartheigh, did not exist. Unfortunately, all her experience of the intimate sort came from her association with him. For a moment it felt as if her husband had peeked through one of the cracks in the rocks above them.

"My education in this subject has been basic and…not particularly… inspired."

Dorian sat up on his elbows. "Indeed?"

"Indeed, sir."

He smiled, and looked much like an eager schoolboy about to impress his teacher with the wealth of his knowledge. "Let us get right to it."

He sat up, and once again she wrapped her legs around him. He touched her nose, then ran his fingers down to her lips. "We'll go slow."

She followed his lead and traced her own hands down his face. His fingers wound across her breasts and circled each nipple. She shivered, and stroked the smattering of dark hair covering his hard chest. She reached his belt, and then let her hands drift down further.

He sucked in his breath, and she joined him when she felt what waited for her beneath his calfskin riding leggings. She had noticed something through the fog of Rabbit's Rest, but within the span of a few days she had faced execution for treason, nearly died in childbirth, and finally heard Dorian proclaim his love for her. She'd been in no frame of mind to dwell on particulars. She'd been too overcome to fully understand his…girth.

"Dorian?"

He opened his eyes. "Yes?"

"I… Never mind. What were you saying?"

She shivered again at the color in his pale cheeks, and the shimmering dots of black in his green eyes. She had seen that look on his face before, in a broom closet, a lifetime ago.

"I said we'll start at the beginning." He loosened the buttons on her leggings. His big hand slid below the waistband and she gasped. "And we'll go to the end."

CHAPTER 2

THUNDERHEADS

TWO DAYS LATER ELEANOR sat on the edge of her bed in her nightgown. She'd asked Margaret to stay with her while the witch did a quick examination of her nether regions to determine their readiness to resume marital relations. Margaret handed her a cup of water. Eleanor always felt a bit lightheaded after such awkward sessions. Her maid, Pansy, bustled around the room, no doubt waiting to bring out the smelling salts should she keel over. Once Eleanor's head cleared she asked the witch for the verdict.

"Your husband may return to your bed," said the old woman, "but I would advise you to go slowly. It must have been a difficult birth, and a difficult recovery. Excuse my familiarity, Your Highness, but have you and your husband been intimate...in other ways?"

Color rose in Eleanor's cheeks as she thought of Dorian's gentle explorations. "I've experienced some intimacy, but it hasn't been painful."

"It may take some time to readjust to true relations."

As the witch gathered her tools, Eleanor asked if she might have a few words alone. After Margaret and Pansy left the room Eleanor called the old woman to the chair beside the bed. "Are you sure I'm ready?" she whispered.

The witch nodded. "It may indeed take a few tries, but with care you'll be fine."

Eleanor took the woman's hand. "I think myself not healed. I think I'm not ready."

Comprehension dawned on the witch's face. "Your Highness—"

"Please. Can't you just say—"

The witch shook her head. "Lady, I understand your plight, and your fears. Others have said the same to me—"

Hope leapt into Eleanor's chest. "And you helped them."

"I have, in the past, stretched the truth—"

Eleanor squeezed her hand again.

"—but in this case I cannot. I cannot lie to the prince."

Eleanor let go and hid her face in her hands. The witch made more excuses but Eleanor did not hear them. She had three days until Gregory's return. She dismissed the witch and called for Chou Chou. She sent him to Dorian's room with a message.

Dorian tugged at Eleanor's leggings.

"Lift your seat. They're stuck," he said. She giggled and did as he asked. She lay on her back, watching the sunlight flicker through the cracks between the boulders. She caught sight of a gull or two flashing past. Her heart was light, the witch's visit blissfully out of her mind.

Dorian kissed her navel. "Are you ready for lesson number two?"

She ran her fingers through his wavy hair. "I'm always prepared for any lesson, at any time."

"We'll see." His kisses trailed down her belly. He pushed her right leg to a gentle bend. His hand wrapped around her thigh, and he bit the inside of her leg. She exhaled hard as his mouth crept lower. She looked down at him.

"Dorian, what are you doing?"

"Shhh."

She felt his tongue and gasped. "Oh! What are you—"

"For once, Eleanor, please, don't ask me questions."

She didn't ask him anything else, but a few minutes later all her questions were answered. She cried out, with such gusto she heard Teardrop whinny in alarm from the exterior cavern.

She stared up at the rocky ceiling, her chest rising and falling. "HighGod above," she finally said. "It's no wonder you have to beat the women off with a stick."

He collapsed against her, laughing. She reached for his shoulders and pulled him toward her face. "Thank you," she said. "That was quite enlightening. However, I don't see what was in it for you."

"On the contrary, your pleasure is mine."

She touched his lips. "How can I reciprocate?"

His mouth curled at the corners and her pulse quickened again. "There is a way, if you're keen."

She kissed him and pushed him onto his back. "I have a notion of how to proceed, but I may need some direction."

He murmured his agreement. She unbuttoned his leggings and took his quiet instructions. As always, Eleanor was a quick study.

Eleanor counted Margaret Easton her dearest friend. As for her other stepsister, Sylvia Easton Fleetwood, Duchess of Harveston, there was no love lost between them. Margaret and Sylvia's mother had married Eleanor's father when all three girls were in the realm of ten years old. Within a month Cyril Brice had unexpectedly gone on to HighGod. Imogene Brice had wasted no time dismissing Rosemary, the witch who had been Eleanor's tutor for as long as she could remember. Imogene promptly designated Eleanor as the maid in her own father's house, and generally harassed and abused her for the next eight years. Thankfully, Rosemary provided Eleanor with clandestine tutoring, for Eleanor was unsure if she would have survived life under Imogene's harsh rule without the solace of learning and letters. Sylvia followed her mother's lead in all things, from her hatred of Eleanor to her scrambling up the social ladder. While Eleanor had softened to Margaret long before her unexpected elevation, the enmity between herself and Sylvia only deepened with time and good fortune.

Regardless of her personal opinions, Eleanor knew Sylvia was not the most famous hostess in Cartheigh for nothing. Never had a lady taken the social calendar by storm so quickly. No other hostess was so beautiful or gracious. No one else provided such lavish food and drink or music so lively. No one else could attract quite the caliber of guests, or boast such a fabulous setting as The Falls, the most magnificent estate on the Solsea cliffs. When Sylvia offered to host the Waxing Ball the other ladies agreed it was a fine idea, although it was unheard of for a hostess in her second season to take responsibility for the climax of the weeklong Waxing Fest.

Eleanor wondered if some of the smiling, simpering women secretly hoped the party would fall as flat as the chest of a six-year-old girl. They did not realize that Sylvia was never without a plan. According to Margaret, she'd come up with this one last winter, over several long, hopelessly boring months in Harveston with her mother, her baby son, and her ancient, doddering husband. She'd planned at least ten parties' worth of themes, many of which she'd already unveiled this summer. She had saved her greatest vision, however, for the Waxing Ball.

Throughout the ball Eleanor watched Sylvia with begrudging respect. Her stepsister stood on the outskirts of the party all night, directing the magicians. She swept past Eleanor and Margaret as the servants passed morsels of shrimp and sweet cheeses.

"Sister, here. Take this." Sylvia thrust her wine glass at Margaret. She pushed her dark hair off her shoulders. "Where are the damn servants?"

"Passing the shrimp, Your Grace," Eleanor said to the top of Sylvia's head.

Sylvia's eyes were the same shade as her hair. She squinted up at Eleanor, but ignored the comment. She seemed to have bigger shrimp to skewer. "That damn apprentice set off a drizzle beside the chocolate fountain. He'll never conjure at a party in Solsea again."

Eleanor watched a young magician frantically waving his arms in an attempt to dissipate what appeared to be a miniature rain cloud. "A bit harsh, perhaps?" asked Eleanor.

"Hardly. Better to make an example of one magician and keep the attention of the others on their spells and their pay." Sylvia pranced off in the direction of the hapless apprentice.

By the end of the meal, the temperature in the ballroom had dropped, and a light breeze picked up. Leaves on the enchanted pear trees dotting the room showed their pale undersides. The willow trees shed a profusion of enchanted pink petals. The petals drifted amongst the dancers, never seeming to feel the need to meet the floor. People pointed at the thick clouds swirling against the ceiling. The unmistakable scent of impending rain filled the air. Eleanor saw Sylvia wave at the magician in charge, and the storm broke.

The candles dimmed to a faint glow. Everyone gasped as the first fingers of lightning shot through the clouds. Rain pelted from the sky, but it disappeared above the tallest guests' heads. On cue, the musicians started in with a boisterous reel, and the flashing lightning kept perfect time to the music. The dancers stampeded the floor.

Gregory appeared at Eleanor's side. They joined the swirl of faces and colors leaping out from the darkness. He pulled her embarrassingly close, but she supposed it didn't matter, as no one could see her properly anyway. Sylvia had draped herself across one of the handsome Fleetwood boys, a cousin of her own decrepit husband.

She deserves a bit of a lark after so much effort, thought Eleanor.

The energy in the room seemed to flow not only from the lightning, but the dancers themselves. Eleanor would have lost herself with the rest of them had she not been so preoccupied. She looked for Dorian in the jostling, sweaty mob.

"Amazing, isn't it?" Gregory yelled. "Leave it to your stepsister to reinvent the Waxing Fest!"

She abandoned her search and smiled at him. "Yes, it's—"

He interrupted her, but she couldn't hear his words over the thunder, or read his lips through the flashing lightning.

"Pardon?"

He shouted into her ear, "Tonight you return to me. A most wonderful night!"

Eleanor joined Margaret and Chou Chou in her stiflingly warm carriage. Gregory and Dorian had brought Vigor and Senné, as they often did on summer nights. Eleanor opened the windows and tugged at the bodice of her gown. As she wiped her sweaty neck, she silently blessed Pansy for suggesting an upswept coiffure. She envied her husband and her lover their pants and their cooling breeze. Eleanor and Margaret chatted about the ball.

"Astounding," Eleanor said. "A monsoon, in the Duke of Harveston's ballroom."

"Sylvia's always loved storms," said Margaret. "When we were very small she'd strip off all her clothes and run naked through the rain. You can imagine it drove Mother mad."

Eleanor laughed. "She would have liked to do so tonight."

"The male guests would have approved, if not the ladies."

Chou Chou joined the conversation. "Sylvia was particularly interested in the opinion of one male guest."

Eleanor pinched Chou's beak. "Not her husband, I assume."

"No, yours."

"That's nothing new. Sylvia thought herself halfway to the crown last spring during my exile. She needs to keep herself in Gregory's sights in case I'm accused of treason again, or choke on a chicken bone."

Chou landed in Eleanor's lap. His round yellow eyes fairly bulged from his head. "Don't you want to know what she said to him?"

Margaret leaned toward him. "Chou, were you spying on my sister?"

He nodded.

"Well, tell us what you heard!" she said.

Chou's scaly toes curled and uncurled. "I took a few turns around the ceiling while we waited for the carriage. As soon as you ladies left Sylvia made a line for Gregory. I clung to the tapestry behind them for a listen." He cleared his throat, and the voice of Sylvia at her most coyly charming slipped from his beak.

"Are you having a nice time, Your Highness? Can I get you anything?"

Gregory, with a hint of impatience: *"Lovely time, yes. I'm afraid I must be going."*

Sylvia again: *"So soon? Why? If you leave the party might as well end. I'll just call off the storm and send everyone home."*

Margaret scowled. "Must she be so obvious?"

"Shhh," said Chou in his own warble. Gregory returned. *"If it were up to me we would be the last to go, but I'm afraid Eleanor must return to our daughter."*

Sylvia again: *"You could send them on and stay. I'd love the company."*

"Gregory obviously wanted to follow you. He started to walk away but Sylvia grabbed his hand. *"It must be difficult for you, Your Highness, with the princess so dedicated to your daughter."*

Gregory: *"Of course she's dedicated to our daughter. As any mother should be."*

Sylvia: *"Oh, don't I know it, as I'm also dedicated to my own dear son. I've heard nothing but praise for the princess's mothering."* At this kind sentiment Margaret coughed into her hand. *"But I think some women forget. We must remember the needs of our husbands, lest we never become mothers again."*

Chou laughed Gregory's rumbling chuckle and ducked his head under his wing, in what Eleanor assumed was a reference to Gregory's habit of swiping his hands through his hair. *"Indeed, Your Grace, I think you're correct."*

Chou paused. "Now this next, I hope I can do it justice. Sylvia sounded…unlike herself. Like…an old friend offering advice. *"In all seriousness, Your Highness, Princess Leticia is young. I'm sure Eleanor will learn. Just give it some time."*

Gregory again: *"I appreciate your concern. Now I really must be going. Thank you for another memorable night."* Chou pecked Margaret's hand, in a birdie goodbye kiss. "Once he left Imogene appeared out of no-where, like one of those enchanted lightning bolts. She grabbed Sylvia's arm and whispered a lot of somethings in her ear. I couldn't catch a word, but it didn't appear to be a pleasant conversation. Sylvia stormed off, and I had to make a swoop for the carriage."

"I must get a parrot," said Margaret.

"Thank you, Chou," said Eleanor. "How comforting to know of Sylvia's concern for my marital felicity."

Margaret put a hand on Eleanor's knee. "Don't worry, darling. I'm sure Gregory has no interest in my sister."

Eleanor squeezed her hand and smiled. She rested her chin on the window ledge and inhaled the salty Solsea air. Let Margaret think what she would, but Eleanor's disquiet had nothing to do with jealousy or concern for Gregory's fidelity. She'd lost interest in both subjects long ago. The same could not be said of the topics of her stepmother and Sylvia. Eleanor remained convinced of Imogene's involvement in Ezra Oliver's ill-fated plot to bring her down, although she'd never uncovered any proof. Imogene's discouragement of her daughter's solicitation of Gregory's affections could mean only one thing. Imogene had heeded the warning Eleanor had given last spring. *I'm the future queen of Cartheigh…I won't forget.*

She must not want to draw attention to herself, Eleanor thought.

Apparently Sylvia did not share her mother's newfound modesty.

Eleanor had chosen Letitia's nursery herself. The spare bedroom, connected to Eleanor's own chamber in the south tower of Willowswatch cottage by a narrow passageway, had a lovely picture window overlooking the gardens surrounding Speck Cottage. She thought someday Ticia would enjoy looking out at the wood-planked cottage with its pink shutters and cozy front porch. Speck had always reminded Eleanor of a doll's house.

Darkness hid the soft yellow rugs and the carved silver suns the servants had hung from the ceiling. She couldn't see the heirloom Fire-iron cradle with its rabbit fur dragon robe, or the embroidered purple rabbit stationed beside Ticia's silk pillow. She dared not light a candle, as experience had taught her the flickering lights would rouse the baby from her milk-induced sleep. Eleanor would have a time getting her back into the cradle, however, after Sylvia's outlandish Waxing Ball that did not seem such an awful prospect. The more time she spent in the nursery, the more likely her husband would give up and returned to his own chamber.

She'd lifted Leticia from her cradle, sat in the rocker, and put the baby to her breast. Leticia responded with sleepy obedience and set about nursing in her sleep. Eleanor tickled her chin and her feet to keep her going, but after half an hour the poor child was so full and tired her head flopped to one side and her lips locked. Eleanor held her upright for a few minutes to give the air a chance to escape her belly, and laid her in her cradle.

She pulled the straps of her nightdress back over her shoulders. She waited in the dark for a while, listening to Ticia's soft breathing and the distant crash of waves through the propped windows. Sweat beaded on her forehead. She might have stood there all night had she not heard a voice calling her from beyond the closed door.

"Eleanor? Are you not finished?"

She found her husband sitting on her writing desk, a glass of wine in one hand and a wooden jewelry case in the other. She assumed Gregory must have dismissed Chou. Last summer he'd usually stayed with Teardrop on such nights, but tonight she wondered if he'd gone to Dorian.

A voice in her head screamed at her to go to Gregory, but she couldn't. She sat on the dainty pink coverlet. He crossed the room and slid the strap of her nightdress over her shoulder.

"I had the witch's report. I'm glad you're well again. I brought you something from Point-of-Rocks."

She opened the box. A necklace, one the likes of which Eleanor had never seen, lay on a velvet pillow. The chain itself, Fire-iron links interspersed with tiny diamonds, was a wonder, but the center stone captivated her.

It was carved into the shape of a dragon, standing on its hind legs, its teeth bared and its tail curled high behind it. Tiny lights shifted and flickered inside it, like handfuls of sand lit ablaze and come to life. As Eleanor watched, the stone turned from midnight blue to canary yellow to a deep blood red. The red remained for a while, before giving way to rose petal pink, then a bright green, so it seemed like a tiny, living lizard. The green must have been satisfactory, because the color held as she lifted the necklace.

"Fascinating," she said. "What is it?"

"It's called spectite. I picked it up in the Point-of-Rocks bazaar. Some traveling Mendaens found the stone in abundance on the south-ernmost islands. Where men and women go naked day in and day out, even magicians and witches, and they know nothing of learning or true magic."

"I've heard of those places," Eleanor said, as the green became a snowy white. She forced herself to look at Gregory. It was hard to believe that less than two years ago his very presence had been enough to fix a smile on her face. "Thank you."

Gregory sat beside her on the bed, and she lifted her hair. "I thought of you when I saw it." He hooked the clasp. "It's been so long. I've ached for this day."

"As have I." The fewer words out of her mouth the less likelihood of her bursting into tears.

He pushed her back on the bed and lifted her nightdress. She grabbed at his hand. "Gregory, the witch said we must be careful. Go slowly, because the birth was so difficult. She said it might take several—"

"Yes, sweetheart, I understand. She said something about it."

"Gregory, I'm—"

His mouth cut her off. He unbuttoned his leggings. She turned her head when he pushed against her. It started out slowly enough, but then his pace quickened. She gasped.

"Gregory!"

He must have misread her meaning. He bore down hard, once, twice, three times, and groaned. There was no mistaking the meaning in her cry this time. She rolled away from him before he had a chance to do so first, as he always did. She curled on her side and tucked her hands between her legs.

"Eleanor?" He shook her shoulder.

She pressed her face into the coverlet. Every fiber of her being wanted to hit him. Scratch his eyes out. Rip every auburn hair from his head.

Ticia, Dorian, Ticia, Dorian. The names formed a protective circle around her temper and her sanity. She faced him. The tears on her cheeks showed him her opinion of their reunion. She had assumed him drunk, but his eyes were surprisingly clear.

"Maybe a few attempts would have been a good idea," he said with an awkward laugh. He stood, and tucked himself back into his leggings. He stood at the end of the bed with his back to her.

"I'm sure next time will be better." He walked to her side of the bed and kissed her forehead. "I'll leave you to get some sleep. I'm sure Ticia will have you up with the sun. Goodnight, sweetheart."

When he was gone she took up two pillows and dragged the pink coverlet from her bed. She crept into her daughter's room and spread the blanket on the floor. She rested her head on one pillow and put the other one over her head, but try as she might she could not sleep. She finally gave up and sat in the rocker until the sun crept over Neckbreak and Walnut Cottages on the eastern side of Trill Castle, and the bitterbits began screaming their morning wake-up songs.

Chou Chou returned with the dawn. He flew into Leticia's open window. "Darling," he whispered as he lit on the back of the rocker. "What are you doing in here? And awake?"

"Where were you?"

"I stayed with Dorian."

"I see."

"I told him of the return to…the former state of affairs," Chou said, his voice even lower. "He was quite disturbed."

Eleanor felt as if she were listening to her own voice from outside her head. "Disturbed. Yes, aren't we all."

CHAPTER 3

WHAT IT'S LIKE FOR A MAN

"Damn."

"What is it?" asked Gregory.

"Damn, damn, damn!" Dorian threw a few extra damns in for good measure. "My bow. It's cracked."

Gregory took the bow from Dorian and ran his fingers along the polished wood. He flexed it and it bent at a decidedly sharp angle. "Damn is right, man. It's done in." Gregory turned on the two stable boys they had brought from Trill, and his own manservant, Melfin. More servants came and went across the dirt and grass courtyard, if it could be so called, of the Egg Camp. They loaded pack animals with food and drink to sustain Gregory and his friends during their long day's hunt. The Egg itself cringed behind them, a three-story oblong stone house embarrassed by its own architectural awkwardness. "Which one of you fools cracked Mister Finley's bow?" Gregory asked. "Fess up, now!"

Dorian dropped the bow and fixed a look of supreme irritation on his face. The stable boys, each of whom clenched the bridle of a skittish hunter, exchanged panicked glances. Dorian thought the younger of the two might hide behind the horse if only he could convince the animal to stand still.

Dorian took hold of the feistier horse and swatted the animal's neck. "Stand, you bloody fool."

The horse threw up his head and chewed his bit. "Sorry, sir," the horse said.

"Now boys," Dorian said. "Did either of you damage that bow and fail to inform me?"

The younger boy looked at him with damp brown eyes and let his older friend answer. "No, sir. We didn't, I swear—"

"I forgive you. It must have been a sad accident." Dorian hardly wanted to torture these poor children, since he had in fact broken the bow himself before they left Trill. A pity to sacrifice such a fine weapon. The older boy started to thank him but he turned back to Gregory. "Looks like I made the ride out here for nothing."

"I'd say use one of mine, but they're all too short for you. So are Raoul's. Too bad Brian's not here."

"Ah, Smithy. He got more than he bargained for when your father made him Duke of the Northcountry."

Gregory laughed. "He has a castle and a fortune and a title to make the Smithwick family proud—"

"But he won't be enjoying life on the edge of the Dragon Mines like he enjoyed Solsea summers. More rain, fewer beautiful women."

"He'll be back next year, once he's settled into his responsibilities. He'll need to find a wife. But we could certainly use his long arms right now."

Both men fell silent, and Dorian could see solutions rolling through Gregory's mind and being dismissed. "I'll ride back to Trill for a spare," said Dorian. "I should have brought one in the first place."

"It does seem the only option. Senné can get you there in a few hours."

"You and Raoul go on without me." Dorian held up his left hand. "Between the ride and a meal and stringing a bow with nine fingers, I won't be back until this evening."

"Too bad, friend."

Dorian clapped Gregory on the back. "Ah, you know Senné and I always enjoy a long ride. Besides, I'd rather have two days of good hunting than three sitting on my ass in the Egg."

"I have some feminine entertainment joining us after dinner."

Dorian doubted Gregory meant women of musical persuasion. "All the more reason to hurry back," he said.

"I told Melfin to make sure they're lively." Gregory tugged at the back of his neck. "I enjoy lively women…enthusiasm…" he muttered to himself as he wandered to his mount.

Dorian waited around the courtyard with a cheerful, aching smile plastered on his face. He called out wishes for a pleasant weather and slow quarry. He waited until Gregory, Raoul, and their attendants disappeared over a low hill. He'd never seen fine Desmarais hunting horses move so slowly. If he pushed Senné they could make it back to Trill Castle in under two hours.

"Bring Senné," he said to the older of the two stable boys. The boy did not dally.

Just over three hours later, in the cave above Redwine Falls, Dorian wrapped his arms around Eleanor's shoulders. She sat between his bent knees, chattering about this and that, but he scarcely heard her. He grunted answers to her questions. He ground his teeth, all the while cursing himself for the anger that simmered beneath his monotone responses.

Excitement had turned to anxiety as he picked up the bow he'd strung two days ago, left Trill, and backtracked up the cliff to their cave. To his surprise, once he started the ascent towards a seemingly successful rendezvous, tendrils of irritation wrapped sneaky fingers around his mind.

Dorian pulled Eleanor closer, like a selfish toddler hiding a favorite toy in his lap. He buried his face in the flaxen thickness of her hair, and then bit the side of her neck. Another childish gesture. Next he would stand up, stomp his foot, and shout *mine!*

"What's wrong?" she finally asked.

"Nothing." He pulled her around to face him and kissed her.

"Maybe we should talk about—"

He kissed her again, and snipped off her words before they could spread through the cave like the roots of a stubborn weed. She returned his kiss, but for the first time he sensed her holding something back.

Her reluctance added to his frustration. His hands chased themselves over her body, trying to wipe the past two weeks away and take them back to that last meeting, before Gregory returned from Point-of-Rocks. His need for her, the need that sat in his groin and in his heart as if his blood had turned to hot Fire-iron, made him reach a hand under her tunic, then thrust it down the front of her leggings.

She did not respond as she had before. There was no gasp of delight, no exhale of hot sweet breath on his neck. She grabbed his hand. "Dorian, please."

He turned away from the sorrow in her mismatched eyes, like bits of earth and sky trapped in her face. "I'm sorry. You don't want...you don't want me to...I understand."

"No, that's not it...I just...I'd hoped to avoid this topic."

"Say it." He walked to the wall and leaned his forehead against the cool stone.

He closed his eyes as her halting words floated over his shoulder. "Gregory...he's been very...attentive..." The noise of his teeth scraping together in his own head sent chills down his back. "...and not very patient. I have some...pain."

Dorian's lungs seized in his chest. The breath he finally drew in fairly sucked all the air out of the cave. "Motherfucker! Mother—motherfucker—"

Dorian rarely swore, but even the shock on her pale face did not silence him. Senné's silver horn poked through the cave opening. "Is something wrong?" he asked, with the calmness of a servant asking after an undercooked steak.

"No! Everything is just fucking perfect!"

Eleanor climbed through the hole. Dorian waited a few minutes, and then followed her. She stood between Senné and Teardrop, her face hidden behind the swirling black and white silk curtains of their manes.

Dorian spoke to Senné first. "Peace, old friend. No anger justifies my rudeness. Pray, forgive me."

"I have never known you to speak so," said Senné, "and I feel only worry at the pain that would bring forth such words from your mouth. You have my forgiveness."

Teardrop eyed him with less understanding. He spoke to Eleanor through a protective layer of shiny white hair. "Eleanor, come back. Please, I pray you will also forgive me."

She stepped out from behind Teardrop. Teardrop snorted her concern but Eleanor silenced her with a few quiet words of reassurance and a squeeze around her arched neck. She wiped her wet face on the mare's mane. Teardrop muttered to Senné and kicked the rock wall behind her. The sound of her agitation followed Dorian and Eleanor into the chamber.

Eleanor sat on the dirt floor. He sat before her, as if in preparation for an imaginary game of poker. She broke the silence. "I understand your anger."

"What if we were careful, Eleanor? I've never, not in all these years, had one woman lay a claim of a child on me. You know I can control—"

"Is that what this is about?" Her face went from white to fiery red.

"Of course not, but it…you don't know what it's like for a man… for me…knowing he can have you whenever—"

He knew as soon as he said it he'd crossed an un-crossable line. Her anger made his seem kitten-like in comparison.

"For a *man*? For you? *You don't have to bed him!* You don't have to feel him jabbing and scraping away at you—feel your pride and heart and your soul shriveling up like a…a bunch of grapes left out in the sun!"

Teardrop whickered from the other chamber, but both unicorns must have assumed there would be no peace in the cave this afternoon.

"So the fact that you've gone ten or twelve or however many years without spawning any *bastards* with the *hundreds* of women you've bedded is supposed to make me risk my daughter and any poor child we might beget and even your own stupid neck?"

He grabbed her arms. "Eleanor, please—"

"I won't. I'm leaving—"

"I'm so sorry." An unfamiliar burning ran from his eyes to his nose. "I'm afraid I might very well kill Gregory with my own two hands for causing you pain. I'm so jealous and angry I don't know if I can live with it."

She swallowed with a small chuffing breath. He let her pull him into her lap, as much of him as would fit without squashing her. He rested his head against her chest. "I'm sorry. I'm sorry," he whispered.

"Shhh, dearest. Don't. I love you, Dorian. I forgive you."

As she stroked his hair some of the anger ran out of him. He could not say all, but it relieved some of the pressure.

"We always knew this would come," she said.

"I didn't imagine he would hurt you."

"Darling, we must speak freely, or every one of our meetings will end like this. We return to Maliana in less that two weeks. It's unlikely we will be able to meet here again, and we have no safe haven such as this at Eclatant."

The impending return to the capital city and the shining Fire-iron monolith of Eclatant Palace had loomed in Dorian's mind for weeks. He spoke from the vicinity of Eleanor's breast. The weight of his head pulled the collar of her tunic low, and his breath bounced off her skin and back into his face. "If we can find a hideaway we may have an easier time of it. There are so many people about and our duties keep us from much leisure. More excuses to come and go. You have your charity work—"

"—and your Council duties and unicorn training."

Dorian nodded. "With the Paladins adding Senné to the breeding program we'll be spending even more time in the stables. Perhaps if I was put out to stud it would ease this ache in my poor neglected personals and I'd not be such a mouthy ass."

She flicked the end of his nose and kissed his forehead. "In that vein I must address another dragon in this cave. It brings me the same pain you must feel in relation to my…my marital arrangements. You cannot go on leading a seemingly celibate life, darling. You were hardly thus before. It will only raise suspicions."

Dorian sat up from her lap. "Gregory is full of questions. I said I've been bedding a girl from the village, but I don't know if he believed me. With honesty, in this regard my past history is not serving me well."

"Please…believe me," she said as she wrung her hands. "I would not expect you to live like a magician for the rest of your life. If you must take your pleasure elsewhere I won't begrudge you."

He started to rebuff her, and then stopped himself. He wanted no one else, yet he could not deny the need to keep his reputation as a wonton womanizer somewhat alive, if only for the sake of their secret. Nor could he ignore the tiny hated voice in his mind, the one that asked a simple question. *Never again?*

He flinched at the pain in her furrowed brow and downcast eyes, but when he squeezed her hand she squeezed back. He put a finger under her chin and made her look at his face. "I love you Eleanor. I'll never lie to you. If anything I do causes you pain you must tell me, and I will cease and desist. Soldier's honor."

She gave him a weak smile. "So it's come to this, that I would tell the man I love to bed another woman." Before he could respond she cupped his face in her hands. "Enough, all of it. We've spent most of this beautiful afternoon screaming at each other."

"I must return to the Egg. It will be nigh dark before I get back."

"Then make me forget, Dorian Finley. Give me something to take from this cave and hold onto in my bed when the sun goes down."

So he did just that.

CHAPTER 4

HIGH GOD'S WORK

MALIANA, THE HOME OF the Malian kings who ruled Cartheigh for eight hundred years before the Desmarais came to power, was a city that had leaked into being. Streets and squares and neighborhoods flowed willy-nilly down the hill from Eclatant Palace. Not long after he sealed the Great Bond and drove the Svelyan invaders from the Dragon Mines, Caleb Desmarais razed the original castle of the Malian kings. By building his own palace on the ruins of his forbearers' fortress, Caleb claimed the center of the greatest city in Cartheigh. Every house in Maliana had at least one window with a view of Eclatant's buttresses and turrets.

Eleanor never tired of admiring the palace, and she did so now through the rear window of her carriage. She watched the receding Fire-iron gate, as imposing now as it had been on the morning Ezra Oliver had delivered Eleanor and the cracked slipper into Gregory's keeping.

Who was that man I fell in love with? Did he even exist? Or was he just the fantasy of a lonely, naïve girl?

"Dearest, what are you thinking?"

"Hmm?" Eleanor turned to Rosemary, her teacher and her oldest companion, seated across from her on the green silk carriage cushions. She had a brief picture of Rosemary's face in the garden of her father's house, on that night when the witch had suddenly reappeared to send her off to the Second Sunday Ball. The night Rosemary had made all her dreams come true, or so Eleanor had thought at the time. "Just daydreaming. Pardon, what were you saying?"

"I said I should have warned the healing witches to meet us in Meggett Fringe, lest anyone teeter over from the shock at the sight of a unicorn in a slum. She may keep the crowds at bay. Your adoring public."

"Hush," said Eleanor with a wave of her hand. She shifted until she had a clear view of the shops and taverns of Smithwick Square. Teardrop paced beside the carriage with Chou Chou perched between her ears. They avoided the crush of Pettibone Lane, where drivers seated atop elegant carriages shouted curses and angled for the open spaces closest to the boutiques and confectioners and frilly teashops. Their mistresses tiptoed between the coaches and the doorways, their skirts modestly raised in an effort to avoid the street mud.

On the west side of the square Eleanor's carriage turned down a narrow street. No signage named it. Citizens of Maliana referred to the street and the cluster of bars, gambling houses, and bordellos lining it by the same handle.

"Down Pasture's End," the locals said.

The sidewalks came alive with women. Thin and fat, dark-haired and light, some impossibly young and some so worn out Eleanor could not have guessed their ages had her life depended on it. While Pasture's End offered ladies to suit every taste, she found commonalities in their presentation: painted faces, garishly dyed dresses, and exposed cleavage. Eleanor's mouth went dry as her stepmother's old threats rang through her head. She'd spent much of her childhood in terror of being abandoned in this damp corridor. She pressed her nose to the windowpane. The women on the street watched her carriage go by. Unlike the other townsfolk, none of them waved. They met her gaze through the glass with empty eyes.

When Eleanor could look on them no more she turned her attention to the architecture, and found it surprisingly grand. One house in particular, stone with a wide front porch and painted a pristine white, rather reminded her of her father's house in its better days. Flowerpots filled with red tea roses lined the stairs. A butler in a crimson uniform stood beside the door.

"The Red-headed Hussy," Rosemary said. "It's owned by Pandra Tate, the only woman in the End who wholly runs her own establishment. Only the wealthiest gentlemen patronize her house. No one else can afford it, and they know Pandra is the soul of discretion. She's known to have the most beautiful girls in town. And the cleanest."

Eleanor scowled. "Suspicions would indeed be raised if those fine gentlemen gifted their wives with the weeping pox."

"Perhaps." Rosemary tucked her chin-length white hair behind her ears.

"I'm sorry," said Eleanor, embarrassed she'd let her own bitterness drive her to such crudeness.

"No, it's a frustration to any thinking woman." She pointed at the Hussy, and the houses surrounding it. "I feel most sorry for the ones that find their living inside those places. Although the girls in the Hussy have a far more pleasant go than those out on the streets. Or those that work the houses further down the End."

As the carriage clattered on, stone gave way to mismatched brick and then wood, and finally boards reinforced with mud and topped with straw roofs that looked likely to burst into flame at the first sign of smoke. While not a single woman had been visible in any of the Hussy's wide windows, in these ramshackle buildings they spilled from every crevice. They called out to the men stumbling about on the sidewalk and swigging beer from tin tankards. Eleanor cracked the window. The exchange of a tattered crone and a potential customer rang loud and clear.

"—give ya a tumble the likes of which you ain't never had."

"Nah, lass. You're too skinny for my likin'."

"Skinny! I'd flatten ya, I would."

"You crazy bitch! No funds today."

"You've the funds for that beer and smokin' weed."

"Right, so I'm too drunk for your mess."

"Never! Just toss me two pence and I'll take hold of yer—"

"That's enough of that." Rosemary closed the window. Eleanor wordlessly blessed her for doing what her own morbid curiosity would not allow. She leaned against the cushions and closed her eyes as they continued on to their real destination, the slums of Meggett Fringe.

The coach stopped in a block of relatively empty space surrounding a bucket-less well. An abundance of weeds sprouted from the well's cracked brick walls. Eleanor opened the door, took hold of her skirts, and stepped down the two Fire-iron stairs. She lit on the muddy ground before the startled doorman could offer her a hand. Rosemary followed her, and Chou Chou landed on her shoulder.

"A square in Meggett Fringe," Chou said. "Now why are we here?"

"A third of this city lives in the Fringe, Chou," said Eleanor, "and I've never set foot here. That's reason enough."

"Hmph. By the time we return to Eclatant, Teardrop and I will be the same color. Soot gray and mud brown. I'll have to ask Pansy to draw me a bath, and then sit in the window like a cormorant and hope the sun dries my poor feathers so that I might once more take flight."

"You *can* wait in the coach," Eleanor said.

Chou left her shoulder for higher ground on her head. "Never. I might miss something interesting. The view is better from up here." She could feel her hair tangling as he turned in a circle. "Although it is a sad view, indeed."

Eleanor had to agree with him. One-story buildings crammed against one another and the street's edge. Eleanor could not tell where one shack stopped and the next began. Some were little more than glorified tents. She could not imagine the fuel that could produce the noxious smoke spewing like airborne grease from holes in the thatched roofs. The smog mingled with the equally harsh odors of rotten food and an unseen something, recently dead.

Water ran in rivulets around Eleanor's feet. Years of emptying wash buckets and chamber pots left her uncomfortably aware of the source of the flow. Barefoot children ran past without pausing or leaping over the little rivers of their own piss. Mud splashed up from their pounding feet. They called out to anyone who would listen.

"Ma! Ma, look! A fancy buggy!"

"Jack, a unicorn. A real one. Didya see it? Hey Jack!"

"—a rich lady—"

"Just look, ya stupid bastard!"

Soon Eleanor could discern no meaning, just a jumble of harsh Maliana gutter accents. If the houses blended together, so did their occupants. All thin and dressed in the same brown and gray clothes. The women's simple dresses ended mid-calf. Bare feet on most of the adults, and all of the children. She couldn't determine anyone's hair color. Most of the women and girls appeared unacquainted with a brush, while the men and boys had shaved their heads quite bald. Mud and soot coated everyone.

The children stared up at Teardrop with eyes like empty soup bowls. The women hugged themselves, weeping and calling out to HighGod. The crowd did not seem bent on either attacking her or clearing a path for her to pass, so Eleanor raised her arms. The people hushed.

"People of Meggett Fringe," she called. "I've come to see the state of affairs here, and report back to my husband, Prince Gregory, of your condition."

Little sparks of conversation lit in the crowd.

"I have a gift for each of your children." One of the two soldiers stationed beside the carriage held up a wooden chest with a heavy Fire-iron lock. Chatter burst into flame and raced through the crowd.

Parents pushed their sons and daughters forward, and mothers came to Eleanor with babies clutched in their arms. A dozen or so children, ranging in age from a girl of twelve-ish down to the toddler whose hand she clutched, huddled beside a towering pile of garbage and castoff furniture. The youngsters lining up in front of Eleanor were positively well kept in comparison with that rudderless bunch.

"Can you tell me, young sir," Eleanor said to the first boy in line, "who are those children?"

"Aye, Mistress Lady," the boy said around a mouthful of moldy looking teeth. "Them's the street sleeps. One's ain't got no mum or dad or even grannie to take care 'em."

"I see. Excuse me for a moment, please."

Teardrop followed Eleanor across the square. Chou Chou bobbed along on the mare's head. Eleanor stopped in front of the oldest girl. She squinted up at Eleanor as the other children clung on each other, giggling and sniffling. Her gray eyes held the solemnity of a soldier on a long walk home from battle.

"What is your name, girl?" asked Eleanor.

"Jan."

"Is this your sister?" Eleanor pointed at the little girl clutching Jan's hand.

"No."

Jan blushed at Eleanor's silence. She lifted her right arm, the one with no toddler clinging to it. It stopped at the elbow. She wiped the stump across her face and continued. "I found her, by herself, a few months back. Thought she'd snuff it if I didna' watch over her, so here we are."

"Where are your parents?"

"Don'know. Had this bad arm when I was born, see, and Mum thought it an evil sign. She let me stay on for a while but I left when I's five."

41

Chou whistled in sympathy. Teardrop whispered in Eleanor's ear, "A strong child."

Eleanor held four gold coins. "Here. Can you take care of it? And promise me you'll use it for food?"

Jan looked at the coins with the same wonder she might show if Eleanor dropped four dragon eggs into her hands. "Yes, Princess Eleanor. I promise." She picked up the skinny, scraggly-haired baby at her feet with a practiced one-armed scoop. She whispered something in the little one's ear and pointed at a clutch of men selling bread and hard cheese from rickety wagons. The baby smiled. For a moment, both were beautiful.

Eleanor passed out money to the other street children. They yelled and raced away, holding the coins above their heads. She returned to the line and her slightly more respectable subjects, and spent the next two hours handing out money and listening to complaints. She peered over the bushy and scabby heads for Jan, but she and the baby had disappeared. When she finally reached the end of the line Eleanor addressed the crowd again.

"I must leave you now, and visit with Brother Marcus. Thank you for your welcome and your honesty. I will take your words with me to Eclatant."

They called out blessings.

"Sweet lady, thank you!"

"HighGod carry Your Highness!"

As Eleanor walked across the square to the Godsman's school, the one substantial building in sight, she realized not one of those people had recognized her carriage. It dripped with Desmarais purple and green and flew the national banner five times over, but no matter. A few miles from Eclatant Palace itself, and no one even knew her name. No one, that is, except Jan.

As Teardrop could not fit through the narrow doorway of the clapboard school, she stood sentry outside with the soldiers. Brother Marcus welcomed Eleanor, Rosemary, and Chou Chou into the Brother Lawrence School for Boys with the hand clasping and blessings typical of any Godsman.

Eleanor had never before seen a man who would look down on Dorian Finley. Everything about Marcus was huge, from the width of his shoulders to the blockiness of his head to the span of the hands that engulfed hers in greeting. He wore his grayish hair nearly as short as the poor boys he taught, perhaps in the hopes of deterring the stray louse that might migrate from the heads of his pupils to the sleeve of his long brown robes.

He ushered them from the front hall to a cozy office. The room fairly bulged with stacked books and threadbare furniture. Eleanor took a seat in a ragged chair beside Marcus's paper-covered desk. Rosemary removed a boy-sized bow from the cushion before taking the next chair. It was too warm for a fire, but a candelabra in the hearth cast a peaceful glow over the office's pleasant mustiness.

Marcus returned with a tray of sliced apples, water cups, and crackers. Eleanor handed a cracker to Chou. He muttered his thanks and promptly began dropping crumbs in her hair.

"Pardon," he said, through a mouthful. "All those poor, hungry people aroused my appetite."

"So this is Larry's," Eleanor said, using the moniker the Fringers had bestowed on the school. "I'm honored to visit such a landmark."

"Thank you, Your Highness," said Marcus. "I'm honored to meet you. The woman who
bested the most powerful magician in history."

Eleanor squirmed at the reference to Ezra Oliver. "I didn't really best him...much of it was luck..."

"You turned his own magic on him. Sent him tumbling into a

magical vision, did you not? I've studied Ezra Oliver—fascinating man. I'd love to hear more about—"

"Pardon, Brother," said Rosemary, "but the princess must return to Eclatant."

Marcus blushed. "Of course—your interest in our little school flatters me. What can I tell you?"

Eleanor rummaged through her mental history stores. One hundred years ago a wealthy young scholar had heard the call of HighGod and joined the Godsmen. He'd left a fortune to keep Larry's running in perpetuity. The Godsmen taught Fringe boys who showed intellect and motivation, and enough gumption to resist the temptations of the streets. The curriculum consisted of basic literacy and mathematics, religion, and trade skills. Many former Larry's students had left the Fringe as assistants to cobblers or butchers or bakers. Some eventually started their own endeavors on the decent side of town.

"Brother Marcus," Eleanor asked, "Do you think there's room for another school here in the Fringe?"

Marcus's broad face split into a grin. "Of course! We never have space for all the worthy boys—"

"Pardon, but I am not speaking of the boys. While I wish more of them had the opportunity to study at Larry's, there are those with even fewer options."

Rosemary grabbed her hand. "You mean—"

Eleanor nodded. "A school for girls. For the poorest girls of Meggett Fringe."

"Oh, Eleanor! Oh, what a wonderful idea!" White light leaked from Rosemary's ears in her excitement.

Marcus sat back in his chair. "I heard you were a forward-thinking woman, Your Highness, and now I believe it." For a moment Eleanor thought the Godsman might renounce her idea, but then he let out a hearty laugh and slapped one beefy hand down on the desk. Eleanor could almost see that sorry piece of furniture wince.

"It's a fine suggestion! I've always believed HighGod smiles on all learning, boy or girl…" He waved up at Chou Chou on Eleanor's head. "…or perhaps even fowl!"

"I'd like to have the school here, beside Larry's, so the witches will be able to learn from your vast experience. That is," Eleanor said to Rosemary, "if Afar Creek Abbey would do me the honor of stewarding this endeavor."

Rosemary took a handkerchief from her pocket and wiped her black eyes. "Must you even ask? We would assume this task a hundred times over."

Eleanor rattled on for a while about her plans for the school; the building, the lodgings she wanted to include for the poorest girls, the curriculum. "The girls will learn practical skills of course, but I want to teach them more. Literature and history. Art."

"This all sounds wonderful," said Marcus, "but you know what I must ask."

"Money," Eleanor said, and the Godsman nodded. Eleanor rested her elbows on the desk. "Don't worry about that, Brother. The crown will cover the cost."

Chou landed in the middle of the desk. His blue head waved from from side to side like a tsk-in finger. "Doubtful. King Casper, HighGod bless him, has no care for the combination of women and learning."

"I'll not take it up with the king. Gregory will."

If Chou had possessed eyebrows they would have crept up his feathery forehead. "Do you think he'll agree?"

Eleanor thought of the embarrassed guilt that lingered behind Gregory's eyes with every conversation and nighttime visit. She fingered the gorgeous spectite necklace he'd brought her from Point-of-Rocks. She'd become fond of it, and wore it daily. Gregory nearly always commented on it, as if to remind her of his attempts to buy her forgiveness.

"I believe he can be convinced."

At dinner Eleanor did the unthinkable. She set down her fork, leaned toward her husband, and in a whisper asked him to visit her chamber that night. He didn't answer, and she had the hilarious thought that he might refuse her. If that had been the case she might have taken up her fork and brained him there at the table, crown prince or not. Finally, he swallowed a gulp of wine. Once his Adam's apple had returned to its proper position he turned to her with what looked like a blush and told her he would be honored. She grabbed her own glass. Some aged member of the High Council had engrossed Dorian in conversation. The man had a horn to his ear. Eleanor hoped the fact that Dorian had to shout to be heard prevented him from noticing her invitation to Gregory.

He would have come on his own, and I just made him think he was wanted. He must think thusly at times anyway. At least tonight it's for good reason.

Gregory excused both of them before dessert, and as she stood Eleanor could not avoid Dorian's eye. They were accustomed to these sad goodnights, but tonight the pang was worse than usual. She prayed everything she felt would be conveyed in two blinks and a casually given hope for a pleasant evening.

Pansy helped Eleanor undress. She emerged from her dressing room in her frilliest nightdress. At the sight of Gregory under the coverlet, up to his chin in powder blue silk, she swallowed a peal of hysterical, anxiety-induced laughter.

"Come," he said. "It's freezing."

"It is unusually chilly for LowAutumn," she said, as she climbed into the bed. He pulled her close, then leaned over her and yanked at the curtains.

"Pansy!" he yelled. "Stoke the fire!"

Normally she would have chided him for his rudeness to her

servant, but tonight was not the night. She wrapped her arms around him, rested her face against his fuzzy chest, and listened to the maid shuffling around the room. The bright burning fire outlined Pansy's stocky form against the curtains. She curtsied to the bed, and then her shadow disappeared in the direction of her own tiny bedroom outside Eleanor's chamber.

"Better," Gregory said. He kissed her neck, and she forced herself to respond to him. When his arousal was sufficiently obvious she pushed him onto his back and rolled on top of him.

"Gregory."

"Yes," he said, through a mouthful of her hair.

"I must ask you something."

"Now?"

"Yes, please, darling. Now." She tucked her hair behind her ears, revealing his reddened face and hungry brown eyes.

He batted at the silk ribbons hanging from the collar of her night-dress. "Speak your piece, but when you're finished, so is this nightdress."

She smiled down at him. "Of course." And out it came. The school, the witches, Marcus, all her plans. Gregory didn't interrupt her, although at one point he rubbed his eye with a closed fist.

"My father won't like it."

"You can convince him."

"How?"

"We'll think of something, together. Perhaps we can take a ride tomorrow, just the two of us, and discuss it? Maybe down to that grove of pecans on the other side of Afar Creek." She ran her fingers over his lips. "Don't you remember? Just after the wedding…my plaid riding habit ended up in a puddle…and you and I on that fallen log?"

He took her arms and rolled her onto her back. "It means so much to you?"

She nodded.

"Then you shall have it." Something fierce crept into his voice. "Father won't refuse me."

"No one can refuse you, Husband. No one."

CHAPTER 5

A SWORD OR A ROSE

DORIAN WATCHED GREGORY'S FATHER over the shining expanse of His Majesty's Fire-iron desk. Gregory sat beside Dorian like an animated portrait of King Casper's youth. The same square jaw, chestnut eyes, and shock of auburn hair. Time had added a potbelly, a few grays, and a bristly mustache to the older version. Casper listened to Gregory's request with tight lips. "A school for girls…in Meggett Fringe."

"Yes," said Gregory. Dorian could see his hands itching to float to his hair. It usually needed a good comb-through after a session in his father's office.

"A waste of money," the king said.

"Not necessarily," Gregory replied. "Eleanor hopes to give these girls a way to support themselves. Teach them to read and cipher. More Fringers feeding themselves will result in fewer coins going to the Godsmen."

"Why would anyone hire a peasant woman with one foot in Pasture's End? Just because she can cipher? And you know none of the tradesmen will hire women. It's against guild law."

"Maybe they'll be servants. A servant who can read a task list is always valuable."

Casper looked unconvinced. To Dorian's surprise Gregory didn't pout or plead. He stood, and paced the marble floor.

"The commoners love Eleanor, but we can't parade a Desmarais princess about the city like a theater performer. Any showing of compassion on our part reflects well on the crown, and it will allow her to be in the people's sight while maintaining propriety."

Casper nodded. "Hmmm."

"The witches will oversee the building and then the operations. All we need to do is provide money and send Eleanor out every few weeks to smile and pass out a few more coins."

"Well spoken, my son," Casper said. "Don't you think so, Finley?"

"Indeed. I couldn't have said it better myself."

"Thank you, Father. I'm glad you approve." Gregory punched Dorian's arm. "And you, too."

"I don't know if approve is the right word, but I'm willing to let you make a go of it." The king sank back into the fuzzy embrace of his purple velvet armchair and rested his hands on his belly. He tapped his fingers on the rows of Fire-iron buttons on his tunic. "You say the witches will manage the place."

"They'll manage the students and their lessons, and report back to us on the finances."

"Witches are notoriously honest." Dorian hadn't anticipated the king's quick acquiescence. He knew how much the school meant to Eleanor, and Rosemary, and he'd come prepared to argue.

"Very true," said the king, "however, I do think we need more oversight."

"You don't mean Eleanor herself?" asked Gregory. "I'd rather not encourage—"

"No, I mean Sir Maxmilon Faust."

Gregory crossed his arms across his chest, and Dorian scowled. Eleanor had no warm feelings for Faust, one of the oldest and most conservative members of the High Council. Two summers ago, Eleanor instigated a vicious political argument with the late Ezra Oliver during one of Faust's lamentably boring dinner parties. Rather than thanking her for enlivening the atmosphere, Faust hadn't spoken to Eleanor since.

"Father, I don't think—" Gregory began.

"You'll take him or leave this endeavor. Besides, he'll have a partner."

"Who?"

The king pointed in Dorian's direction. "Mister Finley."

Gregory took a moment before speaking. "Faust dislikes Eleanor and the witches. He's as old-fashioned as they come. Yet you share Eleanor's progressive thinking, and count her a great friend. A sister."

Dorian swallowed at the astronomical inaccuracy of Gregory's last statement.

"So why do they make fine overseers of her new school?" asked the king.

"Because Faust will always challenge her, and Dorian will always support her."

"Therefore?"

"The truth will be somewhere in the middle." Gregory rapped the back of Dorian's head.

"Admirable logic, Your Highness." Dorian took a swig from his flask to avoid grinding his teeth.

Casper stood and walked around the desk. He put a thick hand on Gregory's shoulder and led him to the office's wide window. Dorian followed at a polite distance. Father and son looked out over the court-yard of Eclatant Palace. Servants, guests, soldiers, and vendors scurried around fine carriages and clunky wagonloads of supplies. Eclatant never rested. The open window let in the LowAutumn breeze, and Dorian inhaled the familiar busy smells of the palace: horses, rose bushes, and baking bread.

"A fine evening," Casper said to Gregory. "Will you spend it with Eleanor?"

"I suppose," Gregory said. The confidence leaked from his voice. He shuffled his feet.

"It's wise to keep one's wife happy when one can. Especially since you chose one with such strong opinions."

It seemed the king waited for a response, but Gregory had none, so Casper went on.

"Perhaps she deserves a bit of placating after the unfortunate events of last spring, but don't make a habit of letting her use your guilt against you."

Redness crept from the tip of Gregory's nose to the ends of his ears.

"I hope she's making you happy as well. My sweet little granddaughter is in want of a brother, and soon." The king returned to his desk. The sound of two laundresses fighting over a basket of spilled bed linens drifted through the window. "You may go."

Gregory faced his father, bowed, and walked to the door. Dorian followed him, but once they stepped into the hallway Gregory dismissed him.

"You may go," he said in a voice eerily similar to his father's. "I'll tell Eleanor her request has been granted."

"Come…this way, Your Highness…Larry has quite a show for you." Marcus steered Eleanor out of his office and down the hallway toward the library. "Now—now stop!"

Eleanor paused in the doorway, her toes in the library and her heels in the hall. She smiled at the student body of the Brother Lawrence School, some fifty boys crammed into the tiny library like skinny books on a shelf. She waved to Jan, the only girl in the bunch. Jan blushed and lifted her good hand.

"She's a hard worker, that one," whispered Marcus. "A great help in the kitchens. And bright as a dragon's eye. She'll be a credit to your new school."

"For her keep, and the baby's, until the new dormitories are ready." Eleanor handed Marcus a bag of coins. "Have you spoken with the carpenters about—"

A door slammed behind Eleanor and her heart leapt in her chest like a drop of grease in a hot pan. Two boys pushed past her and ran to join their fellows in the library.

"Boys! Excuse yourselves!" Marcus's face flamed. "So sorry...the bellringers—"

"It's not a problem—"

He shook his head. "No, it's inexcusable—these Fringe boys—I doubt teachers have such problems in the academies—or at the Covey..." Marcus clomped across the library and berated the children until the younger bell ringer burst into tears. Marcus's anger couldn't stand against the child's mortification. He offered the boy his own handkerchief and turned to Eleanor with a sheepish smile. "He's sorry."

"Please, it's forgotten." Eleanor stepped into the library. "Now, you all have something to show me?"

The children hushed. On Marcus's cue Jan called out in a high, quivery voice, "We'd recite for Your Highness, *The Ballad of the Bond*."

Fifty childish voices chanted the simple poem that had been teaching Carthean children their national creed and most beloved history for three hundred years.

"In the mountains of the North,
dwell the dragon and the unicorn,
In the marshes, safe from harm,
beneath the mountains, Caleb's farm.
A foundling foal, a gentle man,
A friendship forged by Caleb's hand.
The dragon loves the unicorn,
A beast calmed by a single horn.
Farmer first, then Great Defender,

Sword and horn will lead to splendor,
When first began the Bond, we sing,
Between dragon, unicorn, and king."

Eleanor clapped and congratulated the children on a fine recital. She spent an hour quizzing them on the history of the Great Bond. Boys as young as five explained the delicate mystical balance between unicorns, dragons, and the royal family. How Caleb Desmarais had raised the orphaned unicorn foal Eclatant, and how Eclatant's decedents had been loyal to Caleb's ever since. How the unicorns somehow calmed the dragon's rage, therefore allowing Carthean miners relatively easy access to the vast Fire-iron treasures of the Dragon Mines. Lastly, how Caleb's army had driven the Svelyan forces from the Mines after a five-hundred-year occupation.

"Once the unicorns came to our side the Svelyans got clobbered," said the puffy-eyed bell-ringer, "and so Caleb Desmarais became king of all Cartheigh. Forever and ever. Or until the next Desmarais king."

"Well spoken, son!" Eleanor said. "Every Carthean must thank HighGod for the Bond. We pray for the Desmarais kings, and the unicorns, for they hold the key to our security, and our happiness."

Eleanor climbed into the carriage after her teacher. Rosemary closed the window and leaned back against the worn carriage cushions. "Surely we are doing HighGod's work, child," she said.

While Eleanor met with Marcus and his students, Rosemary had spent the afternoon on the grounds of the new school. Eleanor smiled and recited the old prayer Rosemary had whispered when she tucked a tiny Eleanor into bed in those cherished days before her father's death.

"Praise ye, HighGod above.
May my hands play your music

May my lips sing your songs
May my scythe reap wheat in your name for your people
May I gather eggs only to share them
May you hold my mind in yours."

"You remember," said Rosemary. "You would. You've always been an old soul."

They sat in comfortable silence for a few moments. Rosemary closed her eyes and hummed a lullaby. Eleanor hated to disturb the peace, but she'd never get a better opportunity. "Rosemary, I need your help."

The hum stopped. "Yes, I know."

Eleanor didn't have to explain. Rosemary had given Eleanor and Dorian her blessing on the day of Ticia's birth. Eleanor knew she'd carry their secret with her to the grave.

"We need a meeting place, and a way to arrange meetings without speaking of our plans, or HighGod forbid, writing of them."

"I know the city like my own face. I'm sure I could find a safe location. As to a way of coordinating your visit, I've had a few ideas, but I keep finding holes in them."

"I'm at as much of a loss." Eleanor's stomach grumbled, and she realized she'd not partaken of a midday meal. Rosemary opened her beloved green satchel and pulled out a small burlap sack. She arranged a light lunch of apples, carrots, and a bright blue bubble squash on the cushion beside her.

"Don't lose hope, darling. We'll think of something." Rosemary said a quick prayer of thanks. "How HighGod creates such colors I'll never know. Perhaps something in the palette speaks to a hungry body in need, or hints of some nourishment particular to each fruit."

"Hmm," agreed Eleanor as she picked up an apple. Swirling colors, like the colors in her lovely spectite necklace.

Eleanor's mouth fell open, and she nearly lost a bit of her apple.

She set down her carving knife. *My necklace. Changing colors.* Within moments, she'd formulated the elusive plan.

Eleanor and Margaret climbed the stairs of the Brice House. The door opened a crack, then swung back on its hinges. The maid gasped. She ran down the passageway, as if a dragon had come to call and would burn the house down if she did not inform her mistress. "Madam! A royal coach! Purple and green, in our drive!"

Eleanor nodded at Margaret, and since they both knew the way they let themselves in. They crossed the front hall. Eleanor peered around the sitting room door. The maid frantically whacked the pillows together. Eleanor stepped back into the shadows.

"Damn and blasted fireballs!" Imogene Brice's voice floated into the hallway.

"Is it her?" Sylvia's whine joined her mother's.

"Of course it's her. I knew she'd interfere. Well, stand up. Stand up!"

"Why should I? Eleanor Brice once emptied my chamber pots, and now I'm meant to leap at her presence?"

"Hold your tongue, girl! If I've said it once I've said it ten-thousand—"

The maid ran into the hallway and almost collided with Eleanor and Margaret. She gushed apologies and opened the sitting room door. "May I present our esteemed visitor, Her Highness Princess Eleanor Desmarais, wife of—"

"Yes, yes," said Imogene.

The maid giggled and continued. "Ahem, and your daughter, Mistress Margaret Easton."

When Eleanor entered the room she was struck, not for the first time, by the fact that there could not be two women in Cartheigh more different in appearance than herself and her younger stepsister. She thought of her own tall, willowy form, her white-blond hair, her long face and nose, her pale brows, and queer eyes. Sylvia was petite, curvaceous, voluptuous. Her face was full and heart-shaped, her hair and eyes and brows darkly dramatic. Eleanor might dislike Sylvia, but she didn't deny her beauty any more than she denied her possessing prowess.

Sylvia's mother had to be afforded the same credit in respect to her looks. Eleanor often wondered how Imogene managed to retain such a face at near forty years of age. A cavernous line between her eyebrows was the one flaw in her visage. Sylvia had yet to replicate that scar of repetitive rage, but otherwise they were identical, from their tiny waists to their not-so-tiny bosoms.

Imogene curtsied. "To what do we owe the honor of this visit?"

Eleanor did not remove her gloves, and she shook her head when the maid offered her a glass of pear juice. Her eyes swept the room. Since her last visit Imogene had not only added a few new vases and oil paintings, she'd turned the house into a veritable shrine to all things Fleetwood. A banner emblazoned with the Fleetwood family crest hung from the window. She displayed the Fleetwood family tree in a Fire-iron frame on the sitting room wall.

"To what indeed," said Eleanor. "Why, just this morning I met with Mister Francis Delano at his lovely jewelry shop, Talessee Master Craftsmen. You must know it. You've always been fond of baubles, and it is the finest jeweler in Maliana." Imogene opened her mouth but Eleanor spoke over her. "I stopped in on a business matter but the discussion turned to personal topics, as they often do. The Delanos are distraught, for their son's proposal of marriage to the girl he loves was denied by her mother."

"Your…Highness," Imogene said. "This matter is best left between my daughter and I—"

"To quote the soldiers that escorted us here, Madam, bollocks to that."

Margaret stepped out of Eleanor's shadow. Her brownish eyes, already on the smallish side, were puffy from a carriage ride's worth of tears. "Yes, Mother, bullocks to that!"

Sylvia crossed her arms over her chest. "Can't think of your own response, Sister? You've been spending too much time with Eleanor's parrot."

Eleanor turned on her. "As one who was forced into a marriage with a man you don't love, I hope you'd wish a bit more happiness for your own sister."

"How dare you...how dare you suggest..." For once Sylvia could come up with nothing else.

"Why on this green earth would you deny Margaret a marriage to Raoul?" Eleanor asked Imogene. "He's from a wealthy, respectable family. He loves her."

"Because he's a foreigner! And his family may be wealthy enough, but they're still tradesmen! My grandchildren won't be half-breed laborers! Margaret can find a Carthean nobleman to marry—a powerful match, with her position—"

"You mean by friendship with Eleanor?" Margaret asked.

The hair on Eleanor's arms stood on end in indignation. "You should be happy your daughter found such a good, loyal man. He's the one I pity. Marrying into this family!"

"With all respect, Your Highness, this has nothing to do with you."

Eleanor narrowed her eyes. "It has everything to do with me, because Margaret is my dearest, oldest friend. The only sister I have. Raoul is nearly the same to my husband. You will apologize to Raoul and his family. You will start planning the wedding tomorrow. Prince Gregory will hear of this, and I know he will support me. Am I making myself clear?"

Blood rushed to Sylvia's face, but Imogene put a hand on her arm before any profanities could pry open her lips. "As glass. Congratulations, Daughter."

"Thank you," Margaret said.

Eleanor dipped a shallow curtsy, and Imogene and Sylvia had to follow her. "I look forward to assisting with the wedding plans. Have a delightful afternoon." She left in a swirl of green and purple silk with Margaret trailing in the wake of her beaded skirt. Once they cleared the front door Eleanor burst into giggles and embraced Margaret. "We should visit my father's house more often, dearest. Such fine company, and stimulating conversation! Now…about your gown…"

That evening, Dorian excused himself after dinner with a claim of too much whiskey and an aching head. He sat at his desk in his bedroom and made a weak attempt at catching up on delayed correspondence. He found nothing particularly inspiring to say to his brother Abram, so he set the quill on the desktop beside the miniatures of his sister and mother. He wished he could keep a painting of Eleanor, but of course that was out of the question.

He selected a poetry collection from the many volumes lining his bookshelf, but its lovelorn prose only depressed him. He stripped off his tunic and tried to work up a sweat with several sets of rigorous push-ups and some hefting of the furniture, under the assumption it would make him sleepy, but to no avail. At dusk he called for a simple dinner of bread and dried fish, but it tasted of salt and sawdust. He finally sprawled on his tall bed, atop a bearskin dragon robe that was too warm for this time of year but too valuable to be tossed on the floor.

He shut his eyes against the candlelight flickering across the arched ceiling. He'd brought the candle from Harper's Crossing. It smelled of lake lilies. The scent of his childhood comforted him, and he drifted off.

"Someone outside," said a croaking voice by Dorian's ear. Frog, his cantankerous raven, pecked at Dorian's forehead. Frog was so taciturn, sometimes even Dorian forgot he was there.

"Hmm? What?" Dorian asked.

"At the window." Frog flapped his wings, his shiny black pinfeathers pointing as clearly as any finger.

The reflection of the room on the windowpanes made it difficult to see what was on the other side, but Dorian caught a flash of red. He stood and opened the window for Chou Chou.

"Good evening, Dorian." Chou waved his head in Frog's direction. "Frog."

Frog just shook his tail. The two birds were not fond of each other, as they had nothing in common but a beak and feathers. Chou found Frog an unpleasant curmudgeon, and Dorian knew Frog thought of Chou as a flippant gossip.

Dorian closed the window. "Crackers by the perch. I suppose you've been ousted from Eleanor's room." Since Gregory returned to Eleanor's bed, Chou divided his nights between Dorian's room and Teardrop's stall in the unicorn barn. While Dorian had nothing but affection for Chou, he dreaded the parrot's nighttime appearances.

"Yes, but I'll have none of your dour face tonight. You'll be glad I came, I tell you." Chou dropped his voice to a whisper and stretched his impossibly long neck in Dorian's direction. "Is anyone else about?"

Dorian sat on the bed and shook his head. He could not afford a valet, and the chambermaids had all come and gone for the evening. The last one had cast appreciative and hopeful eyes at his bare torso, but he dismissed her.

Chou hopped into Dorian's lap. "I must speak quickly. Frog, come down here."

"Hmph," said Frog from the glass ball on the end of the bedpost. Dorian threw a pillow at him. He squawked, and joined them on the bed.

"I have something for you," said Chou. He uncurled the scaly toes of his left foot, and a Fire-iron ring dropped onto the dragon robe. Dorian picked it up. The small center stone blinked at him. Red…green… brown melted to a soft lavender.

"Spectite," said Dorian.

"Expensive gifts are hardly Eleanor's style," said Chou. "She prefers to show her affection in more genuine ways."

"I know it," said Dorian, who indeed knew it better than anyone. He slid the ring onto his finger. It went pale, until it matched his skin tone.

"Rosemary has found a place for you to meet. And in this ring, a way to plan your visits."

"How?"

"It is complex, my friend," said Chou. "There is a spell on this ring, and a spell on Eleanor's dragon choker. A memory is trapped inside them both. A memory only you and Eleanor share. If you think on it, the two pieces, ring and choker, will connect. The choker glows red." Chou tapped his curved beak on Dorian's ring. "This one will glow blue, a dark blue, like the sea before a storm."

"Indeed." Dorian held the ring in front of his face.

"This is our plan. You and Eleanor will only be able to meet once, maybe twice a month. When either of you think it is time, you must call to each other with the spectite. Yours will glow blue, hers red, and you will know one or the other is in need. She will give a meeting time to me, and I will deliver it to Frog. You can do the same. The two of you must never speak of it, of any of it, to each other."

Frog joined the conversation. "Our own discussions must be succinct. I'll not have you blathering."

Chou hissed at him. "Don't question my dedication to my mistress's safety."

"Quiet, both of you. We all know what's at risk," said Dorian. He knew something of the workings of magic from his studies. "I don't understand how we will set the spell in motion. Eleanor and I are not magical folk."

Chou paced the bed. "The magic is in the memory, and in the jewels, not in you or Eleanor. Since only the two of you share the memory, only the two of you can set the spell in motion. Rosemary conjured it, but she cannot work it. It tried all her skill perfecting it, as she is a teacher by nature, not a conjurer. She even hid the spell so other magical folk will not notice it."

Dorian clenched his left hand over his right. The ring dug into his palm. "How do I call her?"

"You must focus your soul on the memory."

Dorian nodded and closed his eyes. He felt Chou land on his shoulder. The parrot whispered in his ear. "She said to tell you this. Broom closet."

Dorian turned his mind back to that summer day over a year ago. He saw her walk through the door of Walnut Cottage, her hair a sopping mess and the delicate white lace of her bodice plastered to her breasts and stained with red punch. He remembered his hands on her waist steering her into the broom closet, heard the bang of the door as he kicked it shut behind them. He saw her strange, lovely eyes widen. He felt the glorious, frantic pressure of their first kiss.

Cold fire crept up his arm. He looked down at the spectite ring. It smoldered in deepest blue.

Only Afar Creek Abbey could spread arms wide enough to touch both Meggett Fringe and Eclatant Palace. The witches had always held the thousands of acres between the richest and the poorest, even in the cloudy days before the Malian kings, when the Maliana had been a mere ford on the Clarity River. They had never bought or sold a plot, and never held a title, yet no one disputed their claims. The Abbey was, and the Abbey always would be.

Afar Creek, that fickle body of water, ran over the eastern fields. It had changed course many times over the centuries, through floods and droughts. Rich planting and grazing land had turned to cracked dust or damp clay. So it was with a low-lying field abutting the outer pastures of Eclatant Palace. A drab, marshy meadow ill-suited for growing, sur-rounded by a stand of scrubby tupelo trees. In the days of Rosemary's childhood, a small herd of cows had grazed the field, but the grass had gone sour after several long-gone flooding seasons. These days, only magpies and passing foxes on their way to raid the rabbit warrens vis-ited. Seventy-five years of neglect had seen the stone granary fall into disrepair. A few remaining fence posts intervened between battling cat-tails and blackberry brambles. Much of the shingled roof had collapsed, but somehow the thick wooden doors remained upright and securely on their hinges, as if they had been awaiting Eleanor's arrival.

She slid from Teardrop's back, all the while casting terrified looks over her shoulder. The trees, the cattails, and the clouds above her head in the HighAutumn sky suddenly had prying, spiteful eyes. Birds must have been singing, crickets may have been chirping, but she heard only the sound of her own shallow breathing and Teardrop's gently clopping hooves. She pushed through the brambles and a few remaining red daisies. They clung to her leggings, demanding she return to Eclatant and put this foolishness behind her once and for all.

Eleanor had balked at a hideaway so close to Eclatant, but Rosemary's logic persuaded her. They needed somewhere close to the palace, as nei-ther Eleanor nor Dorian could be seen traipsing across the countryside on unicornback. The granary was far enough from the palace for safety, and near enough to provide easy access and an explanation of a longer-than-usual ride if one or the other was ever seen.

"A new path has been forged," said Teardrop.

Eleanor squinted and saw what Teardrop saw. Something had tram-pled the weeds. Not a fox or the visiting ghost of a long dead cow. Something much larger.

"Senné." Eleanor picked out a few hoof prints in the flattened grass. The door had scraped a shallow trench in the dirt.

Eleanor yanked at the door until it opened wide enough for Teardrop to pass. She heard Senné's whickering hello. She shut the door behind her and stepped into the shadows of the granary.

A family of barn swallows flew from cracks in the walls, circled Eleanor's head a few times, and settled on the exposed beams of the remaining roof. They hopped from beam to beam, chattering in irritation. As Eleanor followed the swallows' angry progress above her head she noticed there were no windows along any of the four walls. The place must have been dark as a coffin when completely enclosed. Sunlight streamed through the uncovered half of the rectangular building, and lit the dust eddies thrown up by Teardrop's wide hooves. Teardrop and Senné stood nose to tail with waving ears, quiet sentries.

Eleanor took a few tentative steps along the plank floor. It shifted and squealed under her battered riding boots. At one point her heel pushed through a moldy board. At the crack her heart nearly leapt from her chest.

She stood in the shower of sunlight, but she could not make out the far wall through the blinding, disorienting white. She finally shielded her eyes with both hands, and it all made sense. She was not looking at a wall of light, but a wall of white sheets strung across the granary on a laundry line. The corners knotted over the line made each sheet droop in the middle, giving the impression of spirits strung up by spectral arms. She pushed one of the sheets aside and peeked into the sanctuary Dorian had created for them.

His back was to her. He fussed over several dragon robes he'd laid out on the slowly disintegrating floor. Red flecked the dark brown. She smiled at the thought of him outside the granary, stripping fading red daisies from their stalks. He tossed a few more flowers on their makeshift bed, and shifted three flickering candles. When he seemed satisfied with the lighting, he straightened and pushed his hair back from his face. To her amusement he tugged at his tunic. He shifted it up and then back again and straightened the sleeves. He stomped the mud from his boots.

"As handsome as ever, love." She stepped around the curtain. New-burning candles, laundered sheets, and cut flowers overpowered the smell of damp wood.

He turned, and his obvious embarrassment touched her. "I wanted to clean up some…try and make this place…well…"

"This place is wonderful, because you and I are in it." She crossed the little room, knelt, and ran her hands over the thick fur of the dragon robe. It pulsed with warmth under her fingers. She straightened and tucked one of the daisies into his collar. "But you're a dear for all this."

Dorian pointed at the candles. "Thankfully any leftover hay was eaten or molded away in the last century." She stepped into his arms. They stood there for a quiet while, swaying slightly, as if an imaginary flutist serenaded them from the dark rafters.

He finally broke the silence. "You're not crying. Should I be alarmed?"

She smiled up at him, as always marveling at how far she had to tip her chin to meet his eyes. "I'm here with you. There is no happier woman on HighGod's earth."

CHAPTER 6

A FACE LIKE A STONE

THE SENTRY DID NOT speak as he led Dorian and Gregory through the equally silent passageways to Pandra Tate's private parlor. The king himself could have been taking his pleasure down the hall and no one would be the wiser. Pandra had long since perfected the art of keeping her clients away from one another. She personally coordinated everyone's movement throughout the Red-headed Hussy, therefore insuring no one ran into his father-in-law after leaving the embrace of a whore or two.

Dorian and Gregory kept their faces hidden beneath heavy cowls anyway, as they had on the ride into Maliana from Eclatant. It was nearing ten o'clock, and they had come on horseback, but on those rare occasions the prince traveled without the company of his guards he took every precaution. Both men waited until the sentry had closed the door behind them before removing their hoods.

Dorian went to the bar. He poured Gregory's wine and his own whiskey, and then settled into a red velvet armchair. The soft cushions closed in on him like the bosoms of a smothering auntie.

Gregory swirled the wine in his glass. "What if I wanted white? I forgot and all this bloody red in here."

Dorian chuckled, and found there was some real feeling behind it. Lately he had doubted he'd ever again be able to look at Gregory without wanting to punch him. He pointed around the room. "A bull would have a fine rage in this place."

Pandra loved her red hair, her red-garbed staff, and her red décor. Layers of crimson wall coverings, draperies, and upholsteries gave Dorian the morbid feeling of being inside a beating heart. Even the cinnamon-scented red candles followed Pandra's pallet. He supposed it was meant to put heat in a man's blood, but Dorian found the whole place nauseating. Not that any of Pandra's clients complained. She'd simply stop serving the goods, and many an unhappily married man (and perhaps just as many happily married ones) depended on Pandra's goodwill for his worldly delights.

"I'm surprised you accompanied me here tonight," said Dorian. "It seems risky given your recently repaired relations with Eleanor."

Gregory shrugged. "I was surprised myself when you suggested it. After all your blather about how we're too old for this nonsense."

Dorian's newfound ability to plaster any number of false facades on his face impressed even himself. "I have something I want to tell you. I've been lying to you, for a long time now."

Gregory finished his wine, and his damp fingers in his hair made it stick together in clumps. "I think I know what it is."

Dorian's stomach clenched. "What is your speculation?"

"You've been odd since the summer before last. Moody. Tiresome, actually."

"Beg pardon." Dorian gripped his whiskey with a sweaty hand as Gregory poured himself another glass of wine.

"When I bestowed Senné on you it must have seemed like an inevitability. These things just take time."

"What takes time?"

"A title, of course. I'm sure your financial situation is intolerable. I promise, I'll rectify it as soon as I can. It will be worth your wait."

The tension bled out of Dorian's shoulders. "Greg, this has nothing to do with titles. I've told you umpteen times. I'm grateful for the position I have now. It's more than I should expect."

Gregory scowled. "So why have you been so sour the past year or so?"

"I've been in love, Greg. With someone I should never have fallen in love with."

"You? In love?" Gregory's surprise irked Dorian. "Who could possibly cause the great ideal of every female in this kingdom to check his prick?"

Dorian drained his glass, just for an excuse to wait a few moments before speaking.

"Who is this amazing woman?" Gregory asked. "I'd like to meet her."

"A month ago you could have met her here, in this room."

"No. A whore?"

Dorian glared at him.

"Sorry, Dor. I'm just surprised. You could have any woman at court, and you fall in love with a whore?"

Dorian's mind silently screamed what he wanted to say. *I can't have any woman at court because you got to her first! You stole what was meant to be mine before I had a chance to know it!*

"Where is she now? Have you hidden her somewhere?" Gregory asked.

"She's dead. She died in a difficult pregnancy, well before the child could have lived in the daylight."

Gregory didn't speak for several long minutes, and Dorian let him stew. "I'm sorry. Terribly sorry, and I'm sorry for my disrespect. If I lost Eleanor, and a child…it's too much for any man, even one such as yourself…" He trailed off. For some reason Dorian felt the prick of tears at the fact that this man could elicit both rage and camaraderie from him in the span of a few minutes.

How am I going to do this? Be his friend and his enemy, love him and hate him? It will be the death of me. He ran a fist over his eyes, glad that his ruse made it seem a natural response.

"Why didn't you tell me?"

Dorian shrugged. "Ashamed, I suppose. I'm telling you now. So you'll understand my melancholy."

Gregory leaned forward and rested his elbows on his knees. His rear end had to be near scraping the red and black rug below the absurdly pillowy couch he sat upon. "I'm in no way trying to diminish your pain, but…you should get married."

"I hardly think it's the time."

"Why? You're twenty-six."

"I'm also without funds to support a wife."

Gregory's face hardened. "I've told you, that won't always be the case. Start looking now. A distraction."

"I can't have the woman I love."

"Dragonshit, Dor. Plenty of men marry women they don't love."

"Did you?"

"No, but I might have if Eleanor hadn't come along. Besides, love changes. Those first months are fleeting and then you have…" Gregory cleared his throat. "It's just different. You could find someone suitable. Nothing stopping you from continuing this"—he pointed around the red room—"or any of your other dalliances. You just have someone to return to when it's over."

That short speech explained more to Dorian about Gregory's marriage than two years of observing it. He shook his head. "I won't begrudge you your own methods, but I have no desire to saddle myself with someone merely suitable. Or saddle that suitable someone with a man in love with an impossibility."

"Damn. There you go getting all poetic on me. Suit yourself." Gregory leaned back and splayed his legs in front of him.

Dorian gave him a wan smile. "I'll spare you any more of my ruminations. Just spare me your matchmaking."

"A deal, friend. What will you do?"

"For now I'll find my outlets here, as I have been doing. It seems the simplest way."

It was all too much of a profound, heart-wrenching discussion for two men, even those who had known each other as long and been through as much as Dorian and Gregory. They shifted into their usual manly dialogue of unicorns and hunting and weaponry. Dorian was about to ring the bell for the butler when there was a soft knock at the door.

"Come," called Gregory. Dorian and Gregory stood, out of respect for the woman who had ushered both of them into manhood, albeit in different ways.

The door opened and Pandra Tate swept into the room, born on a wave of her own red velvet trappings. She curtsied before Gregory. Dorian took a measure of her layers of thick red hair and her tiny waist. She rose and offered him a hand shrouded in a black glove. He looked into her bright blue eyes to keep from glancing at the alabaster cleavage that drew a man's eye like a raven to a shiny coin. Pandra was twelve years his senior, but she was amazingly well preserved for all her years of use.

"Mister Finley, it's been too long. Since the sad demise of your lady love."

Dorian had visited Pandra just last week to explain what he needed of her. She'd grudgingly agreed, as she had agreed to every request he'd ever made of her.

"I've had difficulty returning," he said, and kissed her hand.

"Please, shall we sit for a while? I can have my man bring us some cake. Red velvet."

Gregory and Dorian exchanged glances, and once again Dorian felt that frustrating twinge of solidarity. He stifled a snigger as Gregory spoke. "It's been too long since I've sampled your wares, and regrettably

I can't stay all night. I'm not the carefree sixteen-year-old you once knew, although I would sometimes like to be."

"Of course, Your Highness." Pandra rang the bell. "I have a lovely young lady in mind for you tonight. New."

"Not too new, I hope? Schooled in the arts?"

"Oh, I'm hurt you would even ask." She gave him a wicked grin. "I school all my girls myself."

Gregory returned her enthusiasm. "Damn, Pandra, there's something to be said for quality." A butler appeared at the door. Gregory turned to Dorian. "It's true we can't dally. Does midnight give you time?"

Dorian laughed. "That's more than enough time these days."

Gregory saluted him and followed the butler out the door.

The door shut and Pandra asked Dorian to sit awhile. She offered him another glass of whiskey. He took it and admired how she managed to appear poised while perched on the same ridiculous couch that had nearly consumed Gregory.

"Here we are again, after all these years," Pandra said.

"Thank you for your help," Dorian replied.

She pursed her painted lips. "Come now, won't you allow me a bit of reminiscing?"

Dorian considered her over his glass of whiskey. Indeed, the two of them could reminisce for hours and never cover the same ground twice, but the memories hardly made for polite conversation. Dorian had first visited the Hussy at the age of nineteen, with a sixteen-year-old Gregory and the king's blessing. He'd had five years of conquests under his belt by then, and Gregory was far from innocent, but it was under Pandra's roof that they'd expanded their knowledge. Gregory had sampled all of Pandra's fine fare (and according to Eleanor he had not retained much), but the Madam herself had taken a particular interest in Dorian's education. She'd taught him things about her body and his that he could never have learned in a thousand years of his own experimentation. For two boozy, hazy years he'd visited her several times a week, until she stopped charging him and he stopped offering to pay her. He continued his effortless pursuit of women at court, and now looking back he could hardly believe he'd managed to avoid death by duel, disease, or simple exhaustion. At the peak of his fascination with Pandra he supposed he'd some feeling for her, but she was a whore and he was full of himself and his newfound virility and sudden importance. He cringed at how he must have treated her, and countless others.

Those who think me arrogant now should have seen me then, he thought.

She'd finally cut him off when he asked her to bring another woman into one of their trysts, or maybe two. Even through his drunkenness he'd recognized a flash of hurt on her face, but it disappeared just as quickly. She'd offered him two other girls. He accepted, and he never lay with Pandra again. It had not bothered him. If anything, he respected her for it.

He could not help but compare those two years of unfeeling, unrepentant carousing to the past two of constant, aching heartbreak. No matter the pain, he much preferred the latter over the former. He said a quick prayer of thanks for his own maturation.

"Fond memories, but no need to dwell on the past."

"Shall we talk about the present? Tell me, Dorian, who is this woman who has captured your heart? That you would lie to your prince and your oldest friend? And put me in a tight spot, honestly."

"I told you, I appreciate your cooperation. I don't need much from you. Just a room and the appearance of using it." He held out his glass and she filled it again. "Perhaps I will use it someday, but I'm not yet that desperate."

"I want to know who she is. She must be married, and important, for you to go to these lengths."

"Don't ask me again. I won't tell you."

She rattled off the names of a few well-known court ladies. He did not respond in the negative or the affirmative.

"Sylvia Fleetwood? I've heard the good duchess is quite lovely."

Nothing.

"Ah, you have a face like a stone. She must be wonderful, this woman."

"She's the most amazing creature I've ever beheld."

To his surprise Pandra's face reddened. "And you've beheld many, for sure." She stood. "I don't think this is a wise idea. If the prince finds out I deceived him—"

"If he ever finds out, I'll take the blame. Please." Dorian stood and took her arm. He towered over her. "Gregory harasses me constantly about my lack of interest in…the interests I used to have. I need him to believe I'm too lovelorn over this imaginary dead woman to pursue anyone else. Anyone else I don't pay, anyway."

Pandra's enviable chest heaved. "If this woman is married it's just an affair. It will die. Why go to such effort?"

He bore down on her arm and spoke through clenched teeth. "You have been in this business so long you've forgotten how to love."

She tried to shake off his grip. Her own voice was fierce. "No. I haven't forgotten. I knew five years ago, when you were just twenty-one, and I know now."

He let go of her. "I'm sorry if I ever hurt you. It was not my intention."

She laughed, and then peered up at him from under her long lashes. "Silly boy," was all she said.

"Will you do as I ask? I'll come a few times a week."

"Yes, yes. I said I would, and I will."

"I have one question. How do I know the girls won't…notice…that nothing actually happens in the rooms I take?"

She poured her own glass of whiskey and sucked it down with the precision of an experienced barkeep. "My girls, and the rest of the staff, never speak of anything that happens here. No one knows who lies with who. If I catch so much as a word, I toss them out of this house immediately. I've done it before, and they know there are no second chances."

"You're a hard one."

"How do you think I've stayed in business so long? Every pretty peasant in this city wants to work for me. I don't have to suffer fools, nor do my customers."

She sat again, and rubbed her eyes. When she looked up at him the light caught smudges on her polished veneer. "Before I show you to the room you won't use I would say something else, only because you're an old…friend."

He sat, and dangled the empty whiskey glass between his knees as she continued. "I won't ask you the name of your lady again. Best I don't know, although I have my suspicions."

He opened his mouth but she held out her hands. "Don't. I don't want to hear it. I only know if you must lie to Gregory, whatever you're doing is placing you in danger. It must be doing the same for this woman. You must be wary. When you think you're being careful, take more precautions. And ask yourself if it's really worth it."

"Nothing is worth more to me, Pandra. Nothing."

She smiled. For a moment he was reminded of his sister Anne Clara, although the two women looked nothing alike. "I envy her, your lady. I envy her and I pity her."

CHAPTER 7

THE LOAD YOU CARRY

HARVESTON ERUPTED FROM THE flat expanse of the Western Plains like an out-of-place volcano, a looming stone aberration amidst endless fields of wheat, oats, and barley. The steeples of the Chapel of the Autumn Reap, Second Covey of Harveston, and Godspell Abbey jabbed the empty blue sky above the three-story stone wall encircling the city. Not one of those monoliths, however, could outreach the stone turrets of Buckhill Castle, the sprawling domain of the Duke of Harveston.

Buckhill covered ten city blocks, an oasis of trees, grass, and fountains hidden behind a wall within a wall. The estate reclined amidst the bustling city like a matronly queen at a Fest party. As the Duke of Harveston liked to say in his increasingly infrequent lucid moments, Buckhill was a grand dame before Caleb Desmarais laid the first cornerstones of Eclatant Palace.

Harveston's aristocracy sniffed at the arrogance of Malianans, with their kings and unicorns and ridiculously beautiful palace. They welcomed any opportunity to prove that Maliana did not hold sway on sophistication in Cartheigh. In the pursuit of social equilibrium, they fully embraced the marriage of Margaret Easton, sister to their beloved Duchess, to Raoul Delano (short, swarthy foreigner that he was).

The royal family, complete with wet nurse and several nannies, arrived a week in advance of the wedding. Eleanor hoped to assist Margaret in the management of her mother and sister. Imogene rushed around Buckhill as if being pursued by a pack of angry fairies. She gushingly welcomed each guest and screamed at the kitchen staff over bland soup. She placated Raoul's mother by dragging that unfortunate woman from the mansion to the chapel several times a day. Sylvia floated from room to room, all tranquil gorgeousness, as if planning a birthday party for a favorite servant.

After seven days of chaos the wedding day arrived. Eleanor sat at the head of the chapel on a raised throne beside Gregory during the ceremony. Margaret practically glimmered with joy, while Raoul stopped several times during his vows, lest he be overcome with emotion. Eleanor cried throughout the entire hour, until Gregory ran out of handkerchiefs.

Tears of joy, and tears of sadness. Eleanor remembered Dorian's pale face in the crowd at her own wedding. She cursed herself for not running to him then and there, in her heirloom Desmarais wedding gown. She inadvertently slipped into one of her favorite fantasies. Dorian had been at the Second Sunday Ball. She imagined him asking her for a dance. She saw understanding on his face as she told him of her love of learning, rather than the apprehension with which Gregory had met the same revelation. In her mind she danced with him, fell in love with him, and ran from him. He always came for her the next day at the Brice House, on Senné's back with the glass slipper in his hand.

"Eleanor…Eleanor!" Gregory's hissing whisper brought her back to reality. Eleanor stood with the rest of the congregation. The Godsman sent the bride and groom down the aisle. She wiped her eyes, and blew Margaret a kiss.

The décor of Buckhill's Grand Ballroom obviously predated Sylvia's arrival. The floors and walls, all stained a dark mahogany, called attention to white marble pillars covered with carved antlers. Painted horses and a pack of hounds chased a beleaguered fox across the vaulted ceiling. Surprisingly, Sylvia had not provided any frilly magical diversions to distract from the manliness. She'd stuck to flower arrangements, lace banners, and glass vases of sparkling Fire-iron beads.

All six hundred guests sat at long tables. Servants rushed to and fro, offering second helpings, filling wine goblets, and cleaning spills. The king sat at the head of the longest table, with Eleanor and Gregory on his right side and Margaret and Raoul on his left. Eleanor shouted across the table to Margaret. She immersed herself in her friend's good humor.

Eleanor's confusion over the lack of magical entertainment didn't last long. Silence fell when the king tapped his goblet with his fork. Orvid Jones, the new Chief Magician, rose from his place at the far end of the table. Eleanor smiled and waved. She'd always liked Jones, the youngest chief magician in recorded history, and she knew his position weighed heavily on him. Eleanor said a quick prayer as he positioned himself in the middle of the ballroom and raised his arms. His pointed nose and bucked teeth coupled with the dangling sleeves of his dark magician's cloak gave the impression of an abnormally large bat. A sheen of nervous sweat shone on his forehead.

Eleanor always looked forward to the magical entertainment, but most of the guests had witnessed enough of these performances to render them all unoriginal, Sylvia's thunderstorm not withstanding. As Gregory had once said to Eleanor, "If you've seen one swirling fireball, you've seen them all."

Jones muttered a few unintelligible words. The creamy mist swirling out of his palms became blindingly white. His arms shook, and with a resounding crack the white light shot toward the ceiling.

It split, and the dogs and horses and the unfortunate fox could no longer be seen against the ceiling. Rainbows, as perfectly hued as any to grace a springtime sky, swirled over the guests' heads. Jones pointed and one shot across the room. It ricocheted off the marble pillars, the candelabras, and the chair of Raoul's arthritic grandmother. Eleanor's hair blew back from her face as six more miniature, multicolored cyclones spun across the dinner tables. Others rolled into balls and bounced across the floor and over the tables like a bunch of lawn bolls gone berserk. Eleanor's mouth hung open in astonishment. She looked around the ballroom and found she was not alone in her amazement. Ezra Oliver could hardly have put on a better show.

Jones's face twisted into a snarl as he summoned the largest rainbow. It hovered in front of him, a soldier at attention. His right arm shot out, and the rainbow split. A purple rope leapt from its place in the spectrum, twisted, and burst into thousands of violets. The tiny flowers floated lazily to the table and landed in the water glasses. Red became a rain of silk hearts, yellow fat rolling suns that burst like happy soap bubbles. Orange fireballs blinked and crackled before exploding. Green leaves gave way to a last spray of bright blue hummingbirds. The flittering creatures buzzed Margaret's head before disappearing in a puff of azure smoke.

One last rainbow remained. Jones snatched it from midair and threw it in Raoul and Margaret's direction. Margaret leaned back in her chair. The rainbow popped and fizzled in front of her before forming a dark gray rectangle. A Fire-iron money chest appeared on her plate. It sprang open to reveal a pile of gold coins, and then disappeared with a thwack.

"A gift from the crown, to be collected upon your return to Maliana," said Jones, as the guests applauded. Jones blinked, as if shocked by his own performance. He looked as if he might like to disappear into his cloak. He made a hasty bow and returned to his seat.

Gregory whispered in Eleanor's ear, "That's talent."

The toasts began as their host, the elderly duke, bumbled through a speech of welcome Eleanor assumed Sylvia had written for him. Raoul's father stood next, then Raoul himself, and so it went for an hour, until everyone had spoken his piece. King Casper spoke last. He raised his glass to the health and happiness of his son's old friend and his bride, and then called for everyone's continued attention. "We have one other announcement. I ask my son to rise again and deliver this message."

Eleanor exchanged raised eyebrows with Margaret across the table. Clearly she wasn't in the know.

"Thank you, Father," Gregory said. He addressed Raoul with that surprising eloquence Eleanor had heard from him on several occasions, including her own wedding. "In the spirit of friendship, Raoul has agreed to let me momentarily cast the torchlight on one we both hold dear. This person has served me, as a friend and adviser, through dark hours and light. He is the epitome of a Carthean gentleman. Gracious, loyal, and learned. My father will rule us for many years to come, but someday when I am king, I will count myself fortunate to have him at my side. So that every Carthean will recognize the value the crown places on his friendship and his counsel, my father has decided to bestow an honor on him usually reserved for those of the blood or close to it. This man has come to this place through his own merit. An example to all of you."

By now there was no question about whom he spoke. Dorian watched his goblet through the entire speech.

"Dorian Finley." Dorian looked up as Gregory continued. "My father would give you domain of the Lake District. Duke of Brandling, with all the privileges that name entails."

The tables burst into frenzied whispering, although propriety and a standing prince dictated silence. Eleanor had never seen Dorian flummoxed, but he appeared as surprised as anyone. His eyes across the table sought her approval, and she smiled her congratulations. He blinked, and stood. "I am honored, Your Majesty, and humbled, as I have always been by the friendship of your son. I can only hope my actions will do justice to the faith you place in me." He sat, and the crowd applauded again.

Gregory lifted his glass. "To new beginnings!" he called down the table. "To the joy of the new husband and wife!"

"Here, here! To Mister and Missus Delano!" came the replies from around the ballroom.

Gregory hoisted the goblet further. Wine slipped over the edge and splattered on Eleanor's bare arm. It ran over her skin in a thin red stream, and then plunked onto the silk tablecloth. A red stain spread around Gregory's dinner plate. "To you, Your Grace," he said. "Dorian Finley, Duke of Brandling."

The new Mister and Missus Delano were too modest and enthralled with their own happiness to care that the focus of their wedding had shifted away from them. Guests swarmed Dorian and Gregory, complimenting the prince's generosity and congratulating the newest member of the peerage. Eleanor thought to leave Gregory and Dorian to it, but she had trouble finding anyone else upon whom she could latch. She desperately missed her old friends, Anne Iris and Eliza, who were eternally ensconced in their respective country homes with their growing broods of children. She longed for the old days of their messy, girlish camaraderie. Eleanor always had difficulty conversing with those with whom she was not well acquainted. She found herself drifting back to Gregory and Dorian.

She stood between her husband and her lover, ignored the irony always inherent in such positioning, and admired Dorian's modesty and easy elegance. After a half an hour, however, discomfort set in, and then outright anxiety.

She noticed that many of those offering their congratulations were wealthy fathers with daughters in tow. The women seemed younger and more beautiful by the moment. They smiled and bowed before Dorian, a parade of potential duchesses. Dorian finally excused himself. Gregory and Eleanor followed him into a corner by one of the ballroom's few windows.

"HighGod, I thought my face might freeze from smiling," Dorian said. "I prefer a dour countenance, you know."

"But you're so much prettier when you smile," said Gregory.

"Ha. I'll ruin my reputation."

"All of those women are well aware of your reputation. Now that you'll have the funds to shore it up, you'll have no choice. The ladies of this kingdom won't allow you to remain a bachelor for long."

Eleanor swallowed and joined the conversation, because she could see no other option. "They were quite eager. I thought that last girl likely to climb into your lap if you sat."

Hurt flashed in his eyes but he joined her. "Notice I remained standing."

Gregory laughed and drained what must have been his tenth glass of wine. He squeezed Eleanor's waist and looked between his wife and his friend with slightly crossed eyes. "Get yourself an innocent, like I did. You're an old hat at all this now, Eleanor. You could teach Dorian's new wife how to survive marriage to a man at the whim of his country. Come, who would you pick for him?"

Sweat ran down Eleanor's back. She said the name of the last eager young woman, as it was the only one she could remember. "Patience Palmer was quite lovely…and…amiable."

In truth, Patience had been an obvious dingbat. Dorian nodded. He spun his spectite ring around his finger with his thumb. At that moment the orchestra struck up a reel. "Perhaps I'll ask her for a dance. Will you excuse me?" he addressed Gregory. "Thank you again, Your Highness, for this amazing honor."

Gregory and Dorian clasped hands, and Dorian took his leave. Gregory dragged Eleanor onto the dance floor. Fortunately, she knew the steps, for she hardly heard the music or noticed her own feet. She danced for an hour, and then took her seat to pick at a piece of wedding cake. She chided herself for her feelings. This was a night to celebrate for Margaret and Raoul, and now for Dorian, not drown in her own insecurity. Besides, what right did she have to deny Dorian a wife and children? How could she expect him to continue this lonely existence, with a few clandestine meetings a year in a cave or a rotting barn?

I'm damning him to a life of misery and deceit.

Trumpets blared and she stood with everyone else as Margaret and Raoul left the ballroom. She shouted Margaret's name, but Margaret did not hear her over the rest of the crowd. When she scanned the packed ballroom she found Dorian, as she always did. Three laughing young women surrounded him, but he didn't seem to notice them. He clapped and watched Eleanor over the heads and hands of the cheering guests. She willed herself to look away.

With the bride and groom gone, most of the partygoers began offering goodnight kisses and handshakes, but a hundred or so diehards remained to continue the celebration. As midnight loomed, Eleanor sought out Gregory. She planned on being fast asleep in her room before he had the chance to remove his boots. She circled the ballroom several times and finally found him outside on a balcony. At least twenty men surrounded him, Dorian included. She caught Gregory in the middle of some raucous story. Eleanor winced when he stumbled against Dorian and dropped his goblet.

"Sweetheart!" Gregory shouted as she eased through the gathered courtiers. "Come, join us. Some would say it's not a conversation for ladies…but your ears are not as tender as they seem."

"I came to say goodnight," Eleanor said, "so I will do so. Goodnight, Your Highness." She swept a low curtsy.

"The night has hardly begun!" He took her arm and led her away from the crowd. "Don't leave. I'm not ready."

She exhaled her anger and tried to explain. "It's been a long day. I'm so tired. You stay. I don't mind. Enjoy yourself."

He bore down on her arm. "I don't want to stay without you."

The anger crept back. "I said I'm tired."

His nose brushed hers. She could almost taste the wine on his breath. "I don't care. I'm tired of your excuses. Tired of you only calling me when you want something. Tonight it's about what I want, and I'll have it."

"We can talk about this in the morning, when you're sober." She grabbed his hand and tried to pry his fingers loose. "I said I'm leaving." She looked over his shoulder at Dorian. His back was to them. Even through her anger she recognized this as a good thing, for she could not predict his reaction to Gregory's heavy hands. "Gregory, let go. Let go!" He only squeezed harder. Real pain sliced through her arm.

"Don't make a fucking fool of yourself!" he said. The crowd of men behind them went silent.

"You drunken slob, you've already made us both the fool!"

Gregory took her other arm. She struggled against him. He released her arms, but he leaned into her face until his nose brushed hers. "You're not leaving."

She turned and stalked away.

"Eleanor! Damnit, you come back here!"

Someone must have held him off, but she couldn't say for sure because she never turned around. She did not stop until she reached her room. She closed the door, pushed a chest of drawers against it, and drew both latches. Chou Chou had retired early, after an overindulgence of wedding cake had left him with a bellyache. She ignored his greeting and collapsed on her bed with her hands around the dragon choker. Her parrot did not question her. He lit on her pillow and whistled a lullaby.

The next morning Gregory called for Dorian before breakfast. The prince returned to the location of the disaster, like a thief drawn back to the scene of a crime. They stood on the balcony and looked out over the manicured paths of Buckhill Castle's gardens, flowerless this time of year, but impressive nonetheless. The cone-shaped trees reminded Dorian of the dunce caps the magicians had placed on the heads of his fellow students back in his school days. He mentioned the resemblance to Gregory.

"No one would dare place a dunce cap on the head that would one day wear the crown, no matter how I might have deserved it," Gregory said. He dismissed Melfin, and then waved away three more servants that appeared in an effort to meet any need he might have. Gregory's limited supply of patience had run out by the time a fourth butler offered him a buttered scone.

"Bugger off, for fuck's sake!" he shouted at the hapless man.

"Feeling it this morning, are we?" Dorian asked.

"Horns and fire. What do you think?" Gregory rubbed his eyes and pointed into the morning sun. "Forgot to close the bed curtains last night and that damn yellow ball about bore a hole into my forehead. Couldn't get back to sleep."

"Hence my own early wakeup." Dorian hadn't slept much himself. The bestowal of the Dukedom overwhelmed him, in a way comparable only to his parents' deaths and his love for Eleanor. He'd spent the night in spasms of guilt. Gregory's words haunted him.

Gracious, loyal…grateful to have him by my side…an example to all of you.

I'm lying to you, Greg. I'm betraying you in the most heinous way, and you make me a duke.

And then, just as powerful, his anger over Gregory's harsh handling of Eleanor on this same balcony. A sour stew of emotions.

A soft voice behind them interrupted his musings. Gregory turned with a scowl, no doubt to tell the encroaching maid he did not, under any circumstances, require a glass of pear juice. He stopped mid-command at the sight of Sylvia Fleetwood, her low-cut pink gown, and her tray.

"Good morning, Your Highness. Mister Finley. Would either of you care for a glass of pear juice?"

"Just what I was waiting on, Your Grace, thank you." Gregory took the glass from her. He drained it in one noisy, un-princely slurp. "I'll have another if you don't mind."

She obliged him, and he drank that glass halfway through before pausing and putting a hand on his stomach. Sylvia offered Dorian a glass, but he demurred.

"Are you hungry?" she asked him. Her dark eyes darted from his boots to his face, with a barely perceptible pause at his groin. "A man of your size must have quite an appetite."

"My appetite is shockingly poor, Your Grace." He'd never been able to stand Sylvia's form of simpering, two-pronged flattery.

They passed a few minutes talking about the wedding and the weather before Sylvia lowered her voice. "Do tell if I'm overstepping my bounds, sire, but about the trouble out here last night—"

Gregory's jaw jutted. "Who has the nerve to gossip about my private affairs?"

"I was on the upper balcony"—she pointed to a rounded terrace above them—"and I couldn't help but overhear. I just wanted to be sure you resolved the argument."

"Why do you care?" Gregory leaned his elbows on the railing. "Certainly not for Eleanor's benefit."

Dorian wondered the same thing. Sylvia faced the castle and leaned against the railing herself. Her elbows behind her pushed her bosom into pleasant prominence. "I'll not pretend, Your Highness. Eleanor and I have never been friends. It's doubtful we will ever more than tolerate each other."

"Then why the concern over the harmony of her marriage?" asked Dorian.

"Two people are involved in any marriage, sire." Sylvia kept her eyes trained on Gregory. "While I have no great love for Eleanor I do wish you…happiness." She cast her eyes to the ground and color touched her white cheeks. "I can't imagine the load you carry. The weight of this country on your back."

Gregory swelled. Dorian looked out over the gardens again to cover his own rolling eyes.

No one spoke for a moment. Sylvia seemed to want Gregory to break the silence, so he did. "Nothing I do is good enough for her. I never know what will anger her, or make her happy. I wanted her to stay with me last night, but she wouldn't, even when I asked her with kindness." He hung his head. "So then the kindness was gone. I lost it."

Dorian knew when he'd been cut out of a conversation. He drifted a few feet away, but the early morning quiet carried their voices.

"In all honesty, sire, she's probably still smarting from the humiliation of last spring's accusations. She will make you suffer for it. It's the way of a woman."

Gregory slammed his fist on the railing. "Ah, that! Can't we just put it behind us? One week, to ruin a lifetime?"

"I'm only saying what I believe to be the truth. If I were you I would try to ignore it. If she sees she can make you miserable, she will only continue. Treat her kindly, but don't fall into those traps of remorse."

"You sound like my father."

"He's a wise man, after all. I will tell you, from the first I met Eleanor, when we were but girls of ten, I could see that she would have one way. Her way." Sylvia laughed. "Perhaps that's why we never got on. I have my own methods, you see, and I don't like to stray from them."

"Your mother should leave you be. You're far more enjoyable without her standing over your shoulder."

Sylvia's mouth set in a hard line. "She means well, in her way. She only wants the best for me."

"As she wanted the best for Eleanor?"

Sylvia did not respond. Dorian watched them out of the corner of his eye. He'd been Gregory's constant companion for over eight years, and he'd never known Gregory to speak so candidly with anyone else. He wouldn't have believed Sylvia Fleetwood capable of eliciting honesty from her own mother, let alone Gregory.

What a wily bitch, he thought. *Eleanor should know.* Vague ideas shuffled around his head, despite Eleanor's distaste for Sylvia. *Would it be so bad for Gregory to take a mistress? A distraction from his marriage?*

They'd have to discuss it in the granary. If they could spare time to talk. It had been over two weeks since their last meeting. Dorian could hardly walk for the ache in his groin. He relieved the pressure himself, but it returned as soon as it left.

Once again Gregory reignited the conversation. "Let's not spoil a lovely morning with unpleasant memories."

Sylvia's face lit up just as quickly as it had clouded over. "Pooh on unpleasant memories! I'd rather make some pleasant ones." She stepped away from the balcony and held out her hands. "Your wife left you last night before the dancing ended. Let us make up for it. Might I have this dance, Your Highness?"

"What, here? There's no music."

"Who needs music?" She swung her skirts and spun, all the while humming a popular waltz.

Gregory grinned at her. "How can I refuse such an offer?"

He bowed and took her hand. She was right. Not every dance requires music. Dorian left them to it.

CHAPTER 8

A Fine House, No Doubt

SENNÉ'S FEATHERED HOOVES DIDN'T disturb the leaves covering the forest floor. Despite their prodigious size, he and Vigor caused less stir than Dorian and Gregory would have on foot. Dorian breathed in the mossy smell of LowSpring. He'd been unsure of this little diversion, but now the hunter in him took over.

Gregory, Dorian, and Eleanor had embarked on an impromptu three-day voyage to the Lake District to visit Dorian's new holdings. This morning, miles of flat, deserted land had finally surrendered to thickening forests. Eleanor hung her head out the carriage window. She admired the oaks and maples as if she had never before seen a tree. Throughout the journey Chou flitted between the windows and Dorian's head. Dorian avoided the carriage. He always preferred to ride, and he did not relish the idea of being cooped up in the carriage with an untouchable Eleanor.

A distraction had appeared in the form of a Great Woolybuck on the side of the road. It regarded the travelers with mild interest from the bushes. It peered at them from wide dark eyes and shook flies from its giant antlers. Its copious winter coat was sloughing off in shreds of brown wool.

Gregory nearly toppled from Vigor's back at the sight of the rare beast. He called the procession to a halt and Dorian to attention. He instructed the sergeant in charge of the forty soldiers accompanying them to stand watch over Eleanor. Dorian had balked. With Teardrop at home in the Paladine, he didn't want to leave Eleanor on the side of a deserted road, soldiers or not. He needn't have worried, however, as Eleanor wasn't keen herself. She wanted to come along.

To Dorian's surprise Gregory agreed. She relieved the sergeant of his mount and swung astride in her traveling gown. Dorian wondered what she would have done with Ticia had the baby not been sent home to Eclatant with her nannies. Perhaps Eleanor would have tucked her into the saddlebag.

The buck found them much more interesting when they rushed him. He gave a lowing hoot and disappeared into the forest. The chase passed with shouts and laughter and much dodging of low hanging branches, until nature tricked the pursuers by planting an unexpected river in their path. The river, swollen with a recent northern rain, churned past them on its way toward Lake Brandling. The buck covered it in four wet leaps and disappeared up the steep embankment.

Gregory pulled Vigor to a halt but Eleanor pointed at the two guards who had accompanied them. "Go, before he escapes!" she shouted. "We'll wait here."

Gregory nodded and clucked to Vigor. Dorian cast a look at Eleanor over his shoulder before giving Senné his head. She smiled and waved. She'd been somber the past few days, and her happiness encouraged him. Both unicorns followed the stag with ease, and another mile had flown past before Gregory reined Vigor in. As they plodded along Dorian tried to guess the birds above him by their songs.

"Ach, we lost him." Gregory hung his bow over the carved pommel of Vigor's saddle. "Too bad, that rack would have just fit on the wall over—"

Senné stopped, his ears swinging wildly. "Listen," he said.

Vigor slowed and raised his silky muzzle toward the treetops. "The birds."

Dorian listened. The birds had gone quiet.

"There is a vulpine smell on the wind," said Senné.

"Blackjohns?" Dorian asked, in a reference to the black foxes that hunted in packs in the dry grasslands south of Maliana.

Gregory turned in his saddle. "This far north? It's just a red fox creeping up on the sparrows."

"A pack of blackjohns wrecked havoc on the villagers' sheep five years back in the Crossing. They follow the deer and wild donkeys toward the mountains. The rains have been sparse until the past two weeks. It's wetter up here."

"Ah, I doubt—"

"Shhh," hissed Vigor, and for once Gregory obeyed.

Dorian looked back the way they had come, and suddenly he heard it. A yip, yip, yipping carried by the same light breeze that had already brought the blackjohns' scent to Senné' and Vigor.

Eleanor stood in racing water up to her knees. Her full skirt, with the wet creeping up the heavy wool toward her bodice, outweighed the rest of her. At least thirty blackjohns, drooling dark gray creatures the size of setters, stood on the shore. They snarled and snapped at each other as if arguing over whether she was worth the risk of entering the river. Their red tongues flashed between needlelike teeth the length of her thumb.

They'd appeared out of nowhere, a silent, coordinated mass of hungry fur. The horses had spooked and tipped their riders in a few confusing seconds. Eleanor made for the water before remembering she would not get far in this skirt, but it had still saved her. Both guards lay in bloody heaps beside the swords they had used in an attempt to protect her. One had thrown her a short knife before a blackjohn ripped out his throat. She brandished it, all the while cursing the social niceties that had sent her on a cross country trip dressed for an afternoon tea and provided her with the skill to wield a sewing needle but not a blade in her own protection. The blackjohns worried the bodies, dragging them across the pebbled beach. As one of them met her eyes over a soldier's bloody neck, Eleanor found her voice. She screamed for help and prayed Dorian and Gregory had lost the woolybuck.

She turned at the sounds of her own name. Senné filled her eyes, a black avenging tornado, all blasting breath and rolling eyes. He didn't pause at the bank's edge. Dorian let go of the reigns and grabbed Senné's mane with one hand. He clutched his sword in the other. In her mind's eye they hung suspended for a moment before crashing into the rushing water.

Gregory and Vigor followed close behind, and both men leapt to the ground before the unicorns cleared the river's edge. The blackjohns darted at the unicorns' feathered hooves. One leapt into Gregory's face. He gripped it around the neck, flung it to the ground, and sliced its head clean off.

Senné tossed his head to loosen a furry body impaled on his horn. Dorian darted around the stallion. He ran at the five blackjohns surrounding the body of one of the downed soldiers. The noise that came from his mouth sounded something like *"GRRRAAAGH!"*

His sword fell, left, right, left again. Back above his head and straight down. All five blackjohns lay in a heap at his feet like so many cuts of hairy meat. The others tucked their tails and ran for the woods. Gregory followed them. "Get out! Fuck off, you giant rats!"

Eleanor stumbled out of the water and Dorian gripped her arms. She looked up into his frightened eyes. His wet hair splattered across his forehead and lines of muddy water and fox blood ran down his face. He grabbed at the base of her neck. "I shouldn't have left you. Are you hurt?"

She pulled his hand away, but as her legs trembled beneath her she reached for him. He caught her and lowered her to the ground. Her mutinous hand would not let go of his. Their fingers intertwined and locked together. "I'm fine," she said. At the sound of Gregory's boots on gravel their hands darted apart at the same time.

Dorian stepped away. "She's not hurt," he said to Gregory. He turned his attention to dispatching the few blackjohns that still writhed against the rocks. She cringed at the ching of his sword on the stones.

Gregory knelt at her side. Shock kept her tears as bay, as a mere twenty minutes ago she'd been sitting on horseback chatting with two living soldiers about the fine weather. Gregory pulled her into his lap. The brown water skipped over his boots. He whispered in her ear.

"Sweetheart. I'm here. It's all right."

"I know," she said. "I know, Gregory. I'm fine."

"Nothing can hurt you." He rubbed her arms. She winced at the pressure on the yellowing bruises of their balcony altercation. "I won't allow it. I swear it."

As was the case with all estates in the Lake District, the road to Dorian's house led to the back door. Most of Harper's Crossing's gentry did their visiting by boat, so they saved the ornate entryways for the lake frontage. The inbound view by carriage consisted of a drive lined by ancient oak trees leading to a stone mansion. Chimneys anchored each corner of the bulky rectangle. Wooden outbuildings and stables coated in decades-old layers of peeling red paint dotted the property like molting hens.

The old history books referred to the estate as Laurel Leigh, after the first family to hold the Dukedom of Brandling, over five hundred years ago. Generations of locals and their lake drawl had corrupted the name to Laralee. When the last duke died, the estate had passed to the crown. The servants employed to keep up the place had done so, but Laralee had the feel of a forgotten grandmother. Eleanor had a quick glimpse of dark paneled walls; vaulted ceilings hung with the drippy crystal chandeliers popular in the last century, and faded furniture, before Gregory swept her into one of the guest rooms to recover from her trauma.

Eleanor felt no physical ill effects. She desired only to leave the bedroom and ascertain Gregory's mood. She couldn't sleep in the strange bed. She lay awake clutching her choker, listening to Chou Chou's whistling snores and willing her husband to be as emotionally dense as always.

The next morning, she met Dorian, Gregory, Anne Clara, and Anne Clara's husband, Ransom, at breakfast. Gregory went on at length about the size and number of the blackjohns he'd dispatched. He made reference to Dorian's bravery and that of their unicorns, and even Eleanor's strength in fighting the swollen river, but he took the lead role in the play. He'd either missed those few tense seconds as he chased off the remaining foxes or simply misread Dorian's concern for that of a soldier coming to the aid of a distressed civilian. As was often the case, Gregory was most concerned with his own performance.

The servants cleared their plates and Gregory pulled out Eleanor's chair. "Come, sweetheart. Let the duke show you his new domain."

The hall, painted a bright white with ornately carved moldings and high ceilings, could not have differed more from the rest of the house's dark interior. A butler opened a door that seemed nothing more than a giant window, and they stepped out onto Laralee's wide veranda.

"Oh, Dorian," Eleanor said. "It's beautiful."

The massive lawn rolled toward the lake in three terraced levels, each acres wide and divided one from the other by a stone balcony built into the hillside. Marble unicorns and dragons capered in a circular fountain. Jets spurted from their horns and showered the water lilies. Clumps of mountain laurel bushes lined the flagstone pathways, and Eleanor could imagine their blossoms pervading the air in springtime. Thick forests buttressed either side of the grounds, but with the width of the lawn she had an unobstructed view of Lake Brandling. The dark water winked at her in the morning sunlight, and she pointed out a flock of lakegulls playing on the currents. A few other mansions lined the far shore of the lake, beyond the wooden boathouse and dock. Two skiffs with bright yellow sails waited to transport Dorian wherever he might need to go. Anne Clara and Ransom's boatman wandered the dock, tinkering on their own little craft.

For once, Dorian did not have a clever remark. "I've passed this place by boat a thousand times. HighGod knows I never thought I'd be standing here."

"Enjoy it, man!" said Gregory. "You deserve it." He put a hand on Eleanor's shoulder.

Dorian lowered his eyes and murmured his thanks, while Eleanor flushed with guilt, bruised arms or not. Anne Clara suggested she give Eleanor a tour of the house. Gregory, Dorian, and Ransom left on a long ride to examine the state of the property.

To her relief Gregory never came calling that night. His evening carousing cumulated in a midnight dip in the fountain. He was frankly haggard at breakfast, and his wobbling steps led Eleanor to believe him still drunk. He made a brave show of it in a game of lawn bolls, but he returned to his room to nap off the booze when the servants arrived with the lunch basket.

It was warm for the first week of LowSpring, and Eleanor relished the sun on her face. She joined Dorian, Anne Clara, and the children in a game of hide and seek while Ransom held his squirmy youngest son on his lap, lest the toddler fall off the terrace wall. His big brother and twin sisters wrestled their uncle to the ground. Chou flitted around the children's heads, doing passable imitations of their parents' drawling reprimands. Their shrieks of glee carried over the grass. Eleanor could almost feel Laralee's sigh of relief at the laughter that once again graced her acres. The afternoon blew past, and soon Ransom was escorting the younger children to the house for their naps.

Walter, Anne Clara's oldest boy, was not agreeable to losing any time with his uncle to sleep. Anne Clara agreed he could stay with them on the lawn if he desisted in running, jumping, or harassing Uncle Dorian. The child frowned from under the fringe of dark hair falling into his eyes.

"What else shall I do, Mother?" he asked.

Dorian patted the spot beside him on the blanket. "Come, Walt. Shall I tell you a story about a grouchy dragon?"

Apparently four-year-old boys are partial to such stories. Walter sat beside Dorian, and then climbed into his lap. Dorian lay back and laced his hands behind his head. His nephew sat astride his stomach and peered down at him from wide blue eyes. Dorian launched into a tale from his days at the Dragon Mines. Eleanor had heard the story, albeit a more adult version, about a dragon the miners called Spit, who came down with a rotten tooth. Walter laughed at the idea of a grumpy dragon, but when Dorian reached the part where the magicians cast a spell to make the great beast sleep, and he led the miners up to its massive jaws to extract the fiery tooth, Walter's fingers drifted to his mouth. He lay on Dorian's chest. Dorian whispered the rest of the story in Walter's ear with his arms around the boy's thin back.

Eleanor thought her heart would burst as she watched them. All her doubts, stifled by Gregory's potential suspicions and happiness over Dorian's good fortune, came flooding back.

That should be his child. It should be his wife watching him, not his sister and the woman keeping him from a normal life.

She watched the lake for a while, lost in her thoughts, until Anne Clara nudged her. Walter's head slumped against Dorian's chest, and his mouth hung open. He rose and fell lightly. Dorian's own gentle breathing rocked him. They had both fallen asleep.

The doubt would not be suppressed again. It followed Eleanor through five more days of picnicking and pony rides until Chou Chou confronted her.

"I'm just missing Ticia, that's all," she said. This seemed to satisfy him, and he let her be.

To her relief, Gregory suggested they return to Eclatant. Dorian would follow along with Senné in a week.

Eleanor and Gregory visited Dorian's study on a rainy Tuesday morning to bid their host goodbye. Gregory stopped to chat with Dorian's new valet. Eleanor peered around the cracked door.

Dorian sat in a high-backed cowhide chair, behind a wooden desk in desperate need of refinishing. He leaned on one elbow with a hand in his hair and a charcoal pencil between his teeth. She watched him, solid and still against the rivulets of rain running down the windows behind him. He must have felt her gaze. He looked up from his ledger, removed the pencil, and smiled.

Gregory pushed past her and she followed him into the study. The three of them chatted about the journey home and the fine time they'd had together. Eleanor walked to the window as Gregory instructed Dorian on the servants' wages, documents to be filed with the local magistrate, and the date of his official entitlement once he returned to Maliana. Rain blurred her view of Lake Brandling.

Dorian and Gregory joined her. "A fine house, no doubt." Gregory punched Dorian's arm. "A good place for a boy to grow up."

"Or a girl," Eleanor added. "A girl would find it just as enchanting."

"I suppose you're right, sweetheart. We'll have to bring Ticia for a visit. She'll need playmates, Dor. Just as this place will need a hostess!"

"Just getting the house aired out and refurnished will be enough of a challenge for now."

"You, redecorating? You definitely need a wife, friend."

Dorian changed the subject. "Thank you again, Greg. I still—"

Gregory waved him off. "The topic of your gratitude is hereby declared put to rest, by order of your prince."

Dorian laughed, but Eleanor didn't sense real joy behind it. The two men clasped hands, Dorian kissed hers, and they all exchanged wishes for safe highways and dry weather. Gregory strode out of the room, eager to be on the road as always.

She looked back once over her shoulder before closing the door behind her. Dorian stood at the window and rested his forehead against one of the Fire-iron panes. One arm above his head, the other hand splayed across the glass. She fled from the sadness in the set of his shoulders, and the solitude she'd forced upon him.

CHAPTER 9

HIS OWN MASTER

DORIAN CALLED TO ELEANOR with the spectite the day he returned to Eclatant, but she asked Chou Chou to demur. She claimed ill health and spent an afternoon crying on her bed with the necklace glowing red under her hand. Three days later she set the time herself. After the unicorn's blacksmith checked Teardrop's shoes she rode past the Paladine toward the granary.

She'd barely pushed the draping sheets aside before Dorian embraced her. "Thank HighGod," he said, as he lifted her off feet. "It's been a lifetime."

Eleanor bit her lip as he pressed his head against her chest. She kissed the top of his head. "Dorian, put me down."

He dropped her gently, then fell on his knees on the dragon robes and took both her hands. She turned away from his beckoning eyes. "There's something I must say."

"Please, speak. I won't have you distracted." He ran a hand up her leg, but she walked to the curtain.

He crossed his legs at the ankle and rested his elbows on his knees. "What is it? I'm afraid I won't like what you have to say."

She spit out the words before they could stick in her throat. "We can't continue as we have been." She turned around. "This. Us. It has to end."

He snorted a laugh and stood. "Is this about the riverside? We salvaged it. You were nearly killed. Extenuating circumstances. HighGod willing it won't happen again."

"We both accepted the danger a long time ago. It's just...I...I won't do this to you anymore. Everything you've worked for...and yet...you have no one to share it with."

"I share it with you."

She shook her head. "That's not enough. No family. No legacy. I won't let you ruin your life."

He strode across the rotting floor and it groaned under the force of his boots. He put a hand under her chin but she couldn't meet his eye, lest she lose her resolve. "I told you, I made my choice. Nothing could match the happiness I feel when I'm with you."

"You deny the loneliness? The hopelessness? You can't tell me you didn't imagine your own children when you held Walter or the twins."

"Of course I'd love to have a child of my own someday, but not enough to let you go." He put a gentle hand on her shoulder. "I have my nieces and nephews. I have Ticia, and whoever else comes along."

"No," she said, fighting tears. "I can't let you do it."

"It's not your choice to make for me."

"I can't choose for you, but I can choose for myself."

"Don't do this," he said. To her horror her Dorian was gone and he resembled a desperate servant who'd just been dismissed. "Eleanor, don't do this to me."

"I'll try to find joy with Gregory. It's what I should have done from the beginning."

He drifted to the dragon robe and sat down, hard. "You're serious."

She nodded, and the silence in the granary went on for a small eternity.

He looked up, and she saw some of his strength return in his clenching jaws. "I'll not beg you if this is the path you choose."

She swallowed, but there was no moisture in her mouth. The hollow pit in her stomach was sucking everything out of her. "This is the right thing to do. I know it."

He covered his eyes with his hands and did not reply.

She wrenched the curtains aside, then ran across the granary and shoved the door open with both hands. Teardrop snorted and followed her. Eleanor grabbed the braid woven into her mane and climbed onto her bare back. They pushed through the brambles and pounded across the boggy field towards the woods.

She reined the mare in several miles later, in the middle of a nondescript stand of oak trees, and slid to the ground. Teardrop was blowing hard but Eleanor read her meaning as clearly as if they were sharing an apple back in the Paladine. "What has happened?"

"I don't know how I did it, but I did." Eleanor paced the forest floor kicking up dead leaves and a few springtime sprouts. "I let him go, Teardrop. I let him go."

For a moment she thought she would be sick. She leaned forward with her elbows on her knees, but she hadn't eaten anything in two days and nothing came up. She wrapped her arms around herself and sat on the damp ground. Her leggings soaked through, but she did not feel it. Teardrop snuffled her hair and whispered in her ear, "It's time to go home."

Eleanor nodded and mounted. She waited to feel some sense of peace, or relief, but the forest breeze blew right through her.

Every morning Eleanor woke and lay in her bed with her eyes closed, testing her heart to see if it had mended in the night. The witches had an old adage, *with time even a broken bone will set crooked.* She could not find the truth in it.

She spent all her free time with Ticia, or Teardrop, or at the building site of her new school. She tried to love her husband, HighGod knew she did, but she could only manage intermittent fondness for him. She discovered theatrical skills she never knew she had in her attempts to make him believe her passion genuine. She was no longer the naïve girl he'd inducted into conjugal bliss.

With Margaret and Raoul ensconced in a townhouse in Maliana, Eleanor found herself sadly lacking in distractions. Margaret visited weekly, but Eleanor did not keep her from her husband. She hadn't forgotten the affection of newlyweds, even if she'd sadly lost any hint of it. Eleanor longed for the company of Eliza and Anne Iris.

Dorian hibernated in the Council Hall. When he did emerge, he stood beside Gregory like a solemn watchdog. He never spoke to Eleanor about the end of their affair. They fell into a ghost of their old friendship in Gregory's company and then drifted apart, falling seeds born on different breezes. She watched him when she could, but he didn't meet her eyes across a ballroom or jousting pitch or chapel aisle.

One HighSpring afternoon, when Gregory stopped into the nursery to observe Ticia's first attempts at walking, she casually asked him about Dorian's melancholy.

"He does not seem himself these days," she said.

"He's weighed down with his new responsibilities," Gregory said, as Ticia gripped his fingers with her tiny hands and put one unsure foot in front of the other. With her long arms and legs and dueling ginger pigtails, Ticia resembled a tiny antelope trying for its first steps. She squealed and grinned and drooled for her parents.

"Father has assigned him specific tasks…like gathering information on rumors of a plague in the far south." Gregory let go and Ticia plopped on her bottom. She laughed at the noise of her own padding hitting the wood floor. "And he has other…trials. There are things you don't know about Dorian Finley, Eleanor. I'm not at liberty to enlighten you."

She nodded, all the while fighting a snort of frantic giggles at the last. She moved onto a safer topic. "The school opens before we leave for Solsea. Two weeks from today, after Ticia's birthday."

"Have you decided on a name for the place?"

"Queen Camille's School for Girls."

"After the first Desmarais queen?" he asked. "Ticia's great-great-great…"

Eleanor nodded. "She was a brave woman, who overcame many hardships. An inspiration." She lifted Ticia and rested the baby on her hip. "Do you like it?"

Gregory kissed Eleanor's cheek. "It's a fine name." Ticia grabbed his nose. "Let go, little princess."

Eleanor smiled and removed the baby's hand. "I know it wasn't easy for you…convincing your father about all this. I want you to be proud of the school, and I thought giving it a Desmarais name—"

"Of course, sweetheart, it's very nice." He planted another kiss, this one on Ticia's palm. "Now ladies, I must run. Rumors of a woolybuck in the southern fields. I lost one. I won't lose another."

As he closed the door behind him Ticia burst into tears. "Hush, baby." Eleanor rocked her until her sobs turned to snuffling. "Poppa always comes back."

Ticia's breathing became heavy in Eleanor's ear, soft baby snores. She walked to the window and looked out over the west courtyard. Dorian, Gregory, and Raoul waited for the grooms to bring their mounts. She paused, hoping Dorian would look up at the nursery window, and to her surprise he did. She lifted a hand. For one happy moment she thought he might smile or wave. He merely tipped his head and turned away, so she did the same.

"HighGod is smiling on us!" Rosemary said.

Eleanor stood between Rosemary and Marcus in front of Queen Camille's. A crowd had assembled before the stone and wood school-house, with its wide front porch, hand-lettered sign of welcome, and sparkling windows. Dorian and Sir Maxmilon Faust stood behind

Eleanor like two dour bookends. The new pupils huddled around them in a nervous mob of gray skirts and bare white feet. Rosemary and Marcus had scoured the Fringe for the cleverest, most virtuous, hardest working girls. Their finds ranged from twelve-year-old Jan down to a four-year-old who was rumored to have a memory to rival the Abbey's Oracle herself.

Eleanor raised her hands. "People of Meggett Fringe. Today we celebrate the first free school for girls in Maliana. How blessed are we to see those farthest from the wealth and beauty of this city gifted with the chance at learning?" The crowd cheered, and she had to shout to quiet them. "Your daughters will need your help in their new endeavors. Mothers will have to carry more water. Fathers will have to help with the little ones. But hear me, citizens; your support will lead your daughters on a path to fruitful work later. Someday, these girls will walk past Pasture's End and return honor and honesty to the women of Meggett Fringe!"

The Fringers applauded again. Eleanor took a short knife from Sir Faust and cut the green and purple ribbons strung between the white picket fence posts. She threw coins at the mob and led the girls into the school. The obedient procession walked down a narrow hallway to the small but well-stocked library. The girls sat in a semicircle on the cheap wool rug. Their eyes darted between Eleanor's face and her gown and the rows of books lining the shelves.

"Girls," Eleanor said as she hunched on a child-sized chair before them. "I know many of you are frightened. Perhaps you have not often left home." She glanced at Jan. "Perhaps you do not have a home to leave. No matter, little ladies. This is a safe place. Mistress Rosemary and Brother Marcus picked each one of you because you are smart and good. You must promise me you will work hard, and listen well. Show all of Meggett Fringe, and indeed all of Maliana, that girls can learn just as well as boys." The girls nodded and whispered affirmations. "When I was young I had some trouble. I kept learning, and I kept my friends close to me. I never gave up, even when I was tired and sad and lonely. You may feel those feelings, but you must help each other, and all will be well."

Fifty childish voices said, "Yes, Princess Eleanor. Yes, Mistress."

"Well, that's enough of that! I would have each of you tell me your name."

They stood and came to her, some shy, some giggly, and introduced themselves. Halfway through the procession Jan and her tiny ward had their turn.

"Mistress Jan," Eleanor said with a smile. "I hear you have been a great help in the kitchens at Larry's!"

"Yes, Your Highness. I try," Jan said. With her hair braided and her face washed and plumped out with good cooking she had transformed into a pretty little thing.

"Good. And now you will have your own bed here, and a bed for your little sister."

"She ain't my sister—"

"Hush, child. She's as good as, and you've earned the title. Will you work hard for me? For her, and for yourself?"

Jan's wide gray eyes held hers. "I swear I will, Your Highness."

Eleanor rested a hand on the baby's white cheek. "And what's her name?"

"Don't know," said Jan. "I call her Ruby, and she answers to it."

"Ruby it is, then."

Dorian saw Eleanor and Rosemary into the royal coach. Eleanor had not had the heart to tell Rosemary of the sad state of affairs. The witch smiled and slipped into the carriage, granting Eleanor and Dorian a moment of relative privacy Eleanor could hardly stand.

"Thank you for coming," she said.

He looked at his boots, down the dirty street, anywhere but in her eyes. "I came because the king asked me to come." She winced, but his voice softened. "But it is an honor. You're doing a great thing here."

She started to reply but he continued. "I won't see you at dinner. Could you please tell Gregory I'm engaged in the city?"

She nodded. Dorian bowed and walked to his horse. He flipped a coin at the boy who held the horse's reigns, mounted, and trotted past the cracked well and across the square. Down Pasture's End, as the saying went. The boy tossed the coin in the air and ran to show his mates.

Eleanor delivered Dorian's message to Gregory, and then took her supper on her own in her room. Gregory did not argue with her, as he was chin-deep in reports and requests from the High Council, and in a foul mood. Pansy helped her into her nightdress. She opened a book, and then closed it. She moved her chair to the window and watched the sun set over the stone wall of Eclatant. She tried not to think of what Dorian was doing in the city.

He's his own master, she thought. *I have no claim on him. I never did.*

Chou lit on her shoulder, like her feathery conscience. "Why are you doing this?"

"I won't hash it over again."

"You didn't eat anything. You haven't eaten anything in weeks." Chou hopped onto the arm of the chair. His neck tilted to an angle only parrots can achieve without detaching their own heads. "He looks like a walking corpse. You might as well just confess to Gregory and let him kill you both quickly, rather than drag out this agony."

"No. This is how it must be. Dorian will thank me for it someday. I know he will."

Chou's head popped upright. He shook his feathers. "I'm sure he will. If either of you survive the lesson."

CHAPTER 10

SUFFER ME

Two weeks before they were to leave for Solsea, Eleanor woke to find Margaret sitting at her picture window.

"Margaret, sister, what a pleasant surprise!"

Chou climbed out of Margaret's lap and stretched his wings. "We thought you'd never wake."

Eleanor laughed and checked the clockworks beside her bed. "It's just past seven, Chou. Don't accuse me of sloth just yet." Eleanor wrapped a shawl around her shoulder as she slid out of bed. The polished wooden floor was slick and cold beneath her feet, but her friend's unplanned visit warmed her. She took a pear from the bowl on her desk and joined Margaret at the window.

"To what do I owe the pleasure?" Eleanor said as she tucked her feet beneath her nightdress. "Has Raoul started snoring?"

Margaret gave her a wan smile, and Eleanor noticed the puffiness around her stepsister's eyes. She took Margaret's hand. "What is it, dearest?"

Margaret bit her lip. "I lost a baby."

Eleanor's face crumpled with Margaret's, and the two women cried in each other's arms for a longish time. Chou bounced from one head to the next, whistling and chortling in sympathy and picking at one or the other's hair.

"I know your pain," Eleanor whispered in her friend's ear, for, as she'd lost a baby herself, she did indeed. "How are you feeling? Are you well...bodily?"

Margaret nodded. "It was very early. I've had some pain...but it's passed."

"And Raoul?"

A smile twitched on the corners of Margaret's mouth. "As dear and kind as ever...it's...well..."

"It's Imogene, the old bitch," said Chou. His black tongue flitted back and forth like an agitated snake.

Margaret inhaled in a chuffing sob. "She's angry with me...says it's my fault...now that I've saddled myself with a foreigner I must at least produce a few sons to keep the jewelry business in the family line."

"She didn't—" Eleanor couldn't finish. "The old bitch, indeed!"

Chou whistled. "They say mimicry is the highest form of flattery."

Eleanor stormed around the room. "How dare she! Her own daughter—and no concern for your health or your tender emotions." She flung her shawl on the bed. "I'm calling Pansy to dress me. We shall ride to the Brice House this afternoon—"

"Eleanor, no," said Margaret.

"No? Whatever do you mean? Of course I'm going. She won't dare speak to you so if I tell her she can't."

Margaret stood and wrung her hands. "I didn't come for that... only the comfort of your understanding. You needn't go to Mother—"

"Oh, it will be my pleasure."

"But—"

"She shall hear it straight from—"

"Eleanor—"

"And I won't mince words, I tell you—"

"No!" Margaret threw up her hands.

Eleanor froze with the bell she used to call Pansy in mid swing. It let out one solitary, tinkling ding and went silent.

"I don't *want* you to go to Mother."

"Listen to Margaret, Eleanor," said Chou. He fluttered, bouncing in place between the two women like a flag at the start of a horserace.

"I know you want to be…of assistance…and I'm grateful for the times you've stood up for me in the past. To Mother. To Sylvia. But I…" Margaret swallowed, as if she were telling Eleanor of some unmentionable sin. "I think it's time I fought my own battles."

Eleanor sat on the edge of the bed. "Well…of course. I suppose, if you feel it's best—"

"I do…you've been my rock these past few years. Perhaps I'd not be married to Raoul if you hadn't had the gumption to tell Mother what she needed to hear…but I'm a grown woman now. I need to stand in my own skirts, not hide behind yours."

Eleanor took Margaret's hand. "I'm proud of you…but…you know I only want to see things turn out well for you. To advance your happiness."

"In the end, darling," said Margaret, as she leaned her head on Eleanor's shoulder. "You can't make my happiness for me. Only I can do that."

Her words rang in Eleanor's ears and made her stomach turn, like a damning sermon during fasting season.

Oh, dear HighGod, what a mistake I've made.

It took two days for Eleanor to summon the courage to approach Dorian. She watched him, as she had these long months, and grieved. He wandered the parties and picnics like a lost shadow. Women flocked around him, but he paid them no more mind than he did the early summer mosquitoes. He laughed with Gregory, but the smile slipped from his face as soon as the prince sought another distraction.

Twice she almost called to him with the spectite, but she couldn't stand the thought of hours waiting for a red glow that might never come. She finally decided to seek him out at the Paladine, the sprawling conglomeration of barns, storehouses, and fields that housed the Desmarais unicorn herd. The Paladins, or unicorn keepers, had sequestered Senné.

"Stallions at stud are always mean. And dangerous," Gregory told her over breakfast. "Particularly the first time around. He won't tolerate any visitors but Dorian."

Senné paced the paddock in front of the one-stall stud barn as Eleanor approached. He alternately blew long blasts of air and slammed one feathered black hoof into the fence rail. He whinnied in the direction of the larger barn that housed the mares in season. Eleanor assumed him driven mad by the scent.

The stallion's ears slicked against his head when he noticed her. "You're not welcome," he said.

"I mean no harm."

"Leave." He whacked his horn against the rail and she stepped back.

"Please, Sen," she said, "let me pass. I must speak with him."

Senné snorted, and made a few circles of the paddock at a stiff trot. He stopped before her. "Go. He's inside. In the hayloft."

"Thank you." She glanced over her shoulder at the deserted yard. Senné's rage had indeed deterred any other visitors. She didn't call out as she entered the barn. The warm smells of dung and hay met her at the entrance. She stepped over a sack of carrots and a pile of sliced apples beside Senné's feed bucket. Full to the brim with untouched oats.

She followed a rustling above her and a few drifting bits of hay to an opening in the planked ceiling. As she took hold of the hayloft ladder a queer feeling came over her. She'd climbed a similar ladder a thousand times, to reach her bedroom in the barn behind her father's house. Three years and a lifetime ago, it seemed.

She crept up the rungs and peered into the loft. Dorian had stripped off his tunic and undershirt. Sweat ran down his back. He hoisted the hay around the loft with a pitchfork, his ferocity reminiscent of hers in the unicorn barn at Trill Castle the previous summer. He'd lost weight. He'd not had any extra to lose in the first place, but he was no less beautiful in her eyes. Every muscle stood out in stark relief.

She put an end to her gawking, swallowed, and spoke. "Dorian?"

He spun around with the agility of a startled rabbit. He brandished the pitchfork in her direction. As the shock drained from his face he lowered it.

"Might I come up?" she asked.

He shrugged and returned to the hay. She climbed into the loft and folded her hands in front of her stomach. She tried to find a way to begin. "How are you?"

"Fine."

"Are you looking forward to—"

He jabbed the hay. "Just say what you want to say, Eleanor."

She took a step closer. "Very well." The words were stuck in her throat. If she said them and he denied her, she'd have lost her best chance. She opened her mouth and prayed for the best. "I was wrong. I made a mistake."

He paused his assault on the hay, but he didn't speak, so she rattled on. "I'm so sorry. I realize it now. I thought I'd make you happy by setting you free, but I've only caused us both the worst kind of pain."

He chuckled. "Smart girl."

"I don't expect you to forgive me—"

"Good, because I don't." He dropped the pitchfork. "You can't just say you're sorry and erase the past three months."

"I know—"

"You have no idea what I've been through. I've questioned every decision I made." He kicked the pitchfork and it skittered across the wood floor. "I swore. Come what may, I swore, and you threw it all away."

"I didn't! I thought I was doing right by you!"

"I betrayed my best friend for you. For all his faults, he's been nothing but generous for nine years. I've spit on his friendship...and my loyalty to my country...for love of you!"

"I'm so sorry." A few tears escaped her eyes. She swiped at them. She couldn't think of anything else to say. "Please, just promise me you'll think on it."

The loss of weight only accentuated his eyes. They fairly leapt from his face. "I've thought of nothing else, day and night, for three months."

"Do you think it's been easy for me?" she whispered. "Hoping you'd take another, and dreading it? Waiting to see my wish for you to be happy without me come true?"

He hung his arms at his sides and looked to the ceiling.

"I love you," she said.

"I don't know. And keep your voice down."

She put a hand on his bare chest and said it louder. "I love you, Dorian."

"Quiet! Sound carries out here."

"I won't stop saying it—"

He grabbed both her arms and pinned them behind her back. His grip tightened around her, and he kissed her. She returned the gesture, for this kiss had been waiting in the back of her throat since she'd left him in the granary. They wrapped around each other like creeping vines. He lifted her by her seat and she clutched at him with her legs. He stumbled backwards and sat down hard on a few stacked bales of hay.

He pushed her to her feet, and scraped his hands down her body. When he got to her leggings he wrenched them down without loosening the buttons. He kissed her stomach and her thighs.

"Yes," she whispered. "Yes."

She tugged him upright and put a finger to his lips. "I said yes."

Eleanor unbuckled Dorian's belt. He took hold of her right thigh, but as her leggings were draped between her riding boots she couldn't lift her leg. He spun her around and she dug her fingers into the hay. He ran his hands over her bare bottom, and up her back.

"Do it," she said. "I want you to do it."

She felt a moment of heat between her legs, and then he thrust into her.

She cried out at the fullness of him. He clamped a hand over her mouth, and his other arm across her breasts. His hand muffled her cries to moans. He drove her hard into the hay. His breath came in hot, harsh blasts against her ear.

Just when she thought she could take no more Dorian shuddered and pulled away from her. She followed him, trying to regain his solid warmth. A noise escaped him, something between a growl and a sob. A hot stream gushed across her back.

He collapsed on top of her. She rested her face against the hay. It scratched her cheek, but she didn't care. She felt only the wonderful weight of him, heard only their quick breathing. He rested his forehead between her shoulder blades.

Before either could speak a whinny sounded in the paddock below them. Dorian stood, and buttoned his leggings.

"Senné," he said. "A warning."

Eleanor pulled up her own leggings. Dorian tossed her a burlap sack. "Clean up."

She wiped her back and straightened her tunic. *Please, say something,* she thought.

He looked out the window. "It's Welkie. Stay up here, behind the hay, until we're gone."

"Your Grace!" Eleanor recognized Welkie's voice. The Paladin had overseen her training during her early days with Teardrop. "Your Grace! Are you about?"

Dorian pulled his tunic over his head. "I'll be down in a moment, Welkie." He took up his pitchfork and disappeared down the ladder without looking back.

Eleanor hid behind the hay until she was sure they were gone. Then she climbed down the ladder, said goodbye to Senné, and returned to the palace.

Ten agonizing days later, in the granary, Eleanor turned at the whisper of sheets pushed aside. Their sanctuary had gathered dust these three months, but Dorian had strung the sheets well. He stepped into the chamber he'd created for them. She smiled, but he looked at the floor. Her heart sank. "Tell me you've made your decision."

"All right. I've spent the past week hashing it over."

"I understand. I do. If I were you—"

"Eleanor, might I have a moment? Before you decide what I'm going to say."

She hid her face in her hands. She heard him cross the floor. "I forgive you," he said.

"What?" She removed her hands.

"I know you meant well. We shared the same pain. No one could inflict such upon themselves for anything but love. But I have to say something else. I'll only forgive once. These past three months…I can't do it again."

"You swore," she said, "and now I'll do the same. I'll go to the scaffold with your name on my lips." She rested her head on his chest for several quiet minutes. The swallows yelled at them from the rafters.

He rested his hand gingerly on the back of her head, as if he were afraid her hair might throw sparks at him. "There's something else. It won't leave my mind. The…the hayloft…I didn't mean to…after what Gregory did to you…" It seemed he could hardly say it. "Did I hurt you?"

She looked up at him. "No! No, it was…different from anything I've…and it was more…it was wonderful."

He exhaled. "Thank HighGod. I've been so worried...it wasn't how I'd imagined our first...how I imagined I'd make love to you."

She smiled. "You don't have to imagine any more."

"Eleanor, if you—"

She shook her head. "I'm finished with that foolishness. We must take care, but if I'm to be yours, and you to be mine, then so we shall be."

They sank into the dragon robes. Once the last bit of cotton or calfskin had been tossed aside he pushed her onto her back. It seemed his mouth touched every corner of her body before he entered her, slowly this time. She cried out, as she had in the hayloft, for it seemed she had already forgotten the length and breadth of him. He moved against her, and she matched his rhythm.

Without warning he rolled over and pulled her on top of him. She gasped, and stifled a laugh, for from this angle she sincerely felt his member might jab her heart. His hand went between her legs. He touched the tiny button, the one he always paid so much mind. She arched her spine and leaned back to give him room. Between the feel of his fingers and the feel of his shaft she thought she might explode from pleasure. She looked down at him, his empty pale eyes, his flared nostrils. The color had seeped from his face to his chest. Her hips bucked, once, twice, and she fairly screamed as she collapsed against his chest. He slid out of her, and groaned his guttural release as he spent himself between them. They panted against one another.

"Did I make that noise?" she asked.

He wrapped his arms around her back and laughed, and at the sound she knew it would be all right. She bit his shoulder.

"You did," he said. "I must say...you put my fantasies to shame. And I've had three years of fantasies."

"You mean you thought of this—"

"The first night I met you. I was very drunk, and you weren't officially married, so at the time it seemed acceptable."

She laughed. "I thought of you that night. All night. I couldn't sleep." The memory, the lost opportunity, made her throat constrict.

"Shhh. Let us think of right now."

She swallowed her tears. "Yes, now. Dorian, can you…do it again?"

"Can I do I it again, she asks!"

"Well, can you? Is it possible?" Eleanor had never known such from her husband. She'd never been particularly keen to extend their intimate sessions, and he'd never shown an inclination for anything but sleep post-coitus.

He ruffled her hair. "I'm not the most arrogant man in this kingdom for nothing."

"The most insufferable man."

"Please, suffer me."

"There's been enough suffering. I'll have only joy in this granary."

"Ask anything of me, my love, and you shall have it." He rolled on top of her and proved why he was indeed the most arrogant man in Cartheigh. He proved it then, and again in the granary, and in the cave above the Shallow Sea. Again and again he proved it. Three months of agony faded to a memory, but some nights Eleanor woke in a cold sweat, from a dream where Dorian had not forgiven.

CHAPTER II

UNGODLY DOINGS

THINGS CHANGE, THINGS STAY the same, and four years flew by before Eleanor had a chance to count them. On LowAutumn the seventh, in the year Desmarais Three-Hundred Twenty-eight, she celebrated her twenty-fifth birthday in her riding leggings.

"Is it coming?" she asked.

"It is, Your Highness."

"Male or female?"

"I can't yet tell, but it's dark—and a wee lady!"

"Smashing!" said Dorian. He beamed down at Eleanor.

Eleanor stroked Teardrop's head in her lap. "You have a daughter, dearest. All mothers should have a daughter."

Teardrop hadn't made a sound through the tricky birth, even as Eleanor encouraged her and fought to keep from biting her nails. The foal had to be positioned just right to avoid piercing its mother's birth channel with its tiny horn. Welkie had been brutally honest about the danger.

The taciturn unicorn-keeper smiled as he wiped down a dark, wet bundle of pointy ears and spindly legs. He sung an old tavern song.

"Come, come, drink to the dragon
Never a sharper horn been born

Come, come, a glass to the dragon
But loveliness is the un-ilia-corn..."

Teardrop rolled onto her chest. She nosed the filly, and then set about licking the afterbirth from her fuzzy coat. Eleanor walked to the stall door on tingly legs.

Dorian's grin matched Welkie's in its shit-eating proportions. "A black filly. There hasn't been one in the Paladine in—"

"Fifty years. You mentioned it...once or twice...or twenty times."

He laughed. "I'll tell Senné. He shouldn't be the last to know he's a father."

"Uncle!" came a high voice. "Mother! Has the baby come?"

Ticia ran down the corridor of the brood mare barn, five years old and as tall and spindly as ever her mother had been at the same age. Her auburn hair hung down her back in two long plaits.

"Darling." Eleanor stepped from the stall. "I told your father to wait until we called for you!"

"I didn't want to wait." Ticia put her hands on her hips.

"And your father saw fit to bring you." Eleanor couldn't hide her exasperation. "Where's Poppa?"

"He's coming, with Nathan."

Gregory rounded the corner with a red-haired boy in his arms. Eleanor kissed Ticia, and then took her two-year-old son from his father. Nathan rested his head on her shoulder. "Mama," he said.

"Hello, love," she said, and then to Gregory, "did you wake him?"

"Boy can't sleep all day, Eleanor. Not with this excitement! How's she progressing?"

"A live birth," said Dorian. "A black filly."

Gregory shook Dorian's hand as if Dorian had sired the filly himself. "Congratulations, man! Smashing!"

"That's what I said."

Eleanor wondered, as she always did, just what Dorian felt as he clapped Gregory's shoulder. Dorian was honest with her in all things, including his desire to keep his feelings about Gregory to himself. He'd gently rebuffed all her efforts to discuss the relationship between the two men.

"I was just going to visit Senné. Please, excuse me." Dorian walked out of the barn, and at the sight of his retreating back Eleanor felt a familiar twinge in her stomach.

She opened the stall door for Ticia. "Very quiet, now, Tish. You mustn't disturb them."

Ticia's mouth hung open as she watched the tiny black unicorn. The filly had already mastered her rickety legs. She nuzzled her mother's milk bag.

"Gregory," Eleanor said. "You shouldn't have brought them."

He leaned over the stall door, the look on his face a mirror of his daughter's. "Oh, I knew it would be fine. Welkie in charge—"

"Teardrop's first birth. What if something had gone wrong and Ticia had seen…you didn't need to bring Nathan, anyway."

Gregory patted his son's back. The child had his father's hair and his mother's pale blue eyes, minus Eleanor's infamous birthmark. To her relief, Nathan's eyes matched perfectly.

"He's the future king of Cartheigh! He should be in the Paladine, not in bed."

"He's two, Husband. He's a long way from the crown."

"Never too early," said Gregory. He pulled Nathan's fingers from his mouth.

Eleanor sat on a bale of hay with Nathan in her lap. She rocked her sleepy boy, closed her eyes, and let he mind drift over the past few years.

Nathan's birth had followed a miscarriage. That pregnancy had gone along just long enough to be noticed by everyone at court, and then ended in a rush of blood and pain on a rainy Sunday afternoon. She'd caught again soon after, and spent the next nine months in fear of both a fruitless pregnancy and the successful delivery of a dark-haired, green-eyed baby. When Nathan arrived, just as red-haired as his sister, she'd said a prayer of thanks to HighGod for all their sakes. The kingdom rejoiced in the new prince. Nathan's birth promised the continuation of Caleb Desmarais's bloodline, and therefore of the Great Bond. Eleanor teetered between relief at her son's obvious parentage, pride in his destiny, and terror at the responsibility heaped on the baby by his very name. It seemed that Nathan held the Dragon Mines themselves in his tiny hand from the moment he emerged from her womb.

He was a tender child, but serious, and she saw much more of herself in him than she did in her lively daughter. Ticia was her father's child, from her hair to her eyes to her high spirits and chaotic charm. She'd inherited but one trait from her mother: a tendency to voice her every opinion regardless of her audience. Ticia sassed her esteemed grandfather in a manner that bordered on sacrilege. She fidgeted whenever Eleanor read to her, while Nathan brought books to his mother and Rosemary and his Uncle Dorian and anyone else who could be persuaded to flip pages with him. To Gregory's annoyance, he was as content sitting on his mother's lap in the library as he was at swordplay. Nathan's budding scholarly proclivities pleased Eleanor. She hoped Ticia would someday follow her little brother's suit.

"...have arrived from Harveston." Gregory's voice brought her mind back to the brood mare barn.

"Pardon? What's arrived from Harveston?" she asked.

"Not what, who." Gregory leaned on the stall door. "The Duchess and her mother."

"Wonderful. Did Sylvia remember her husband this time? Or her three sons?"

"Must you be so unpleasant? Sylvia's been cordial for years. As has her mother, she's as meek as a stewed rabbit, the old biddy—"

"What's a biddy?" asked Ticia.

"Biddy, Biddy," said Nathan. "Tweet. Tweet."

"Hush, now," said Eleanor. "I don't understand why you insist on putting on a show every time they appear at Eclatant, Fest or not."

He squatted in front of her. "I've told you, sweetheart. You've no need for jealousy. Sylvia is but a good friend. She's been nothing but gracious—"

"I'm sure." Eleanor set a now wide-awake Nathan on his feet. He passed the time in proper two-year-old boy fashion, by leaping from a stack of grain sacks into a pile of loose hay.

Gregory took her hand, but Eleanor didn't speak. Let him think her jealous. In truth, Gregory's philandering bothered her no more today than it had four years ago. She'd long since agreed with Dorian that a mistress for Gregory would do no harm to their cause. She wholeheartedly opposed, however, the idea of Sylvia Fleetwood as that mistress. The fact that neither Eleanor nor Dorian had ever been able to confirm Sylvia's status in relation to Gregory drove Eleanor mad, as did her husband's tendency to go to great lengths to entertain the visiting Duchess. Eleanor couldn't argue with Sylvia's lack of obvious malice in the past few years, or Imogene's gradual retreat to dignified matriarch of Sylvia's growing brood of young Fleetwoods. No matter. Eleanor still believed both mother and daughter to have the most un-familial of intentions toward her person, and her own children.

Gregory gave Eleanor a sly smile. "Let me prove my undying devotion to you. This afternoon?"

"Gregory, please, the children." Eleanor stepped into the stall with Ticia. "Isn't she lovely, Tish? What shall we call her?"

Ticia's reddish brown eyes widened. "I can choose?"

Gregory squeezed through the door. "You can. Do you know why?" Ticia shook her head. "Tell her, Welkie," said Gregory.

Welkie squatted in the straw. "You're a Desmarais princess, Your Highness. Like your mother. And your father's dear departed sister, Princess Matilda. HighGod bless her."

"But why do I get to name the baby?" Ticia wanted the point, as her mother always did, but she used her father's charm to get it. "Do tell me, Welkie. Please, pretty please?"

"Well, the only girls allowed their very own unicorns are Desmarais princesses. Your Poppa decided that if this one was a girl, she'd be yours."

"Mine?" Ticia squealed. She clapped, and Teardrop snorted. Ticia put a hand over her mouth and repeated herself in a whisper. "Mine?"

Gregory joined Welkie in the straw. Eleanor couldn't help but smile at the seriousness on his face as he addressed his daughter. No matter how dubious his devotion to herself, she'd never doubted his fidelity to his unicorns and his dragons.

"It's a great honor, Leticia. You must learn to speak with the baby, and understand her. She will be your friend, and your protector, if you show her you're worthy."

Leticia nodded, just as unusually solemn as her Poppa. "I must think of a proper, good name," she said. Eleanor could see ideas flashing around her daughter's lively mind. "I know! Cricket."

"Cricket?" repeated Eleanor, Gregory, and Welkie.

"Yes," said Ticia. "Crickets are black, and they jump high and fast. And they sing those lovely songs. I like to listen to them in my bed."

Gregory took Ticia's hand. "Tish, I'm not sure—"

"It's perfect," said Teardrop. "Her name is Cricket. Come, Ticia."

Ticia looked to Eleanor, who nodded her on. Cricket pricked her ears in Ticia's direction, but as the child came closer she retreated behind her mother's tail. Ticia stopped and held out her hand. Eleanor had never seen her daughter stand so still for so long. Cricket peeked around Teardrop's legs. She took a few wobbling steps in Ticia's direction. Ticia laid one white hand on the filly's dark muzzle.

Gregory smiled at Eleanor and took her hand. For the first time in longer than she could remember she returned his squeeze.

Two days later Rosemary called a meeting at Larry's. She referenced Queen Camille's, but asked that Dorian and Eleanor leave the estimable

Sir Maxmilon Faust behind at Eclatant. Eleanor climbed into her carriage and took the seat across from Dorian. As they rolled through the palace gate he closed the curtain. Eleanor's heart slammed against her ribcage as he moved to her side of the coach. In five years they'd never been alone outside the granary or the cave on the Solsea cliffside.

"How long is the ride to Larry's?" Dorian's hand rested on her thigh. He fingered the rose-colored silk of her gown.

She lifted her skirt and slid his hand beneath it. "An hour, give or take, this time of day."

"Plenty of time." He kissed the side of her neck. "We're going to see a Godsman. We might as well give him reason to absolve us of our sins."

Marcus shuffled them into his office with his usual profuse blessings. Eleanor found she could hardly look into his earnest, ruddy face without blushing. Dorian was sublimely aloof as always.

"You had a pleasant ride, Your Grace?" Marcus asked.

"A most enjoyable ride, for sure. A bit bouncy—"

"Tea, Marcus?" Eleanor asked. "I'm parched."

"Understandable," said Dorian. "Unusually warm in that carriage. Hot, frankly."

"And cakes?" Eleanor kept talking. "I could use a cake or two... didn't eat much this morning..."

Marcus rushed out to collect the refreshments. Eleanor threw a stray piece of chalk at Dorian. It bounced off the end of his nose.

Marcus returned, with a tray of cakes in hand and Rosemary trailing behind. As Marcus poured tea, Rosemary took the chair beside Eleanor. "Thank you for coming, both of you. You must have found it odd—this meeting—but Marcus and I thought it of utmost importance—"

"—Rosemary, you cannot speak for the both of us—we're in agreement on certain—"

"—and disagreement on others," finished Rosemary.

Eleanor's brow lifted. "I have wondered why you needed to see us in private, and now you've further confused me."

Marcus opened his mouth, but Dorian asked Rosemary to explain.

"Very well," Rosemary said. "I must speak to you about a...problem...a situation...Sir Faust wouldn't like it, and it doesn't reflect well..." She trailed off and worried her thin fingers over the rickety desk.

Marcus folded his hands on the desk. He sounded more preacher than teacher. "There are rumors about. Ungodly doings connected to Queen Camille's. Several of the older girls have left the school. Disappeared. No one's seen them for two weeks."

Eleanor paled. "Do you suspect foul play?"

"Foul," said Rosemary, "but not in the way you're thinking. The girls are said to have left the school and joined one of the bordellos."

Eleanor felt as if someone had poured a cup of icy water down her back. "That's not possible."

Marcus sighed. "It is. The girls who work the pricy whore—err, bordellos never leave the premises. No one can enter unless he's a paying customer. A mother from the Fringe can bang on a door, but no one will tell her if her daughter is inside."

"With their skills, the girls don't need to—"

"I'll be frank, Your Highness. They can read, and cipher, but nothing's changed in Cartheigh. Rich women are wives; poor women are servants. Those in the middle are both wives and servants to their husbands' trades. I mean the cobblers' wives, the bakers' wives. These Fringe women don't even get that chance. If they can get into one of those fancy hothouses they earn more, eat more, and work less."

"A servant has some honor," Eleanor said, "...but those places..."

"If I may," Dorian said. "Some of those places...the women are better taken care of than the servants at Eclatant."

Eleanor's temper flared, both at Dorian's sentiments and his admitted familiarity. "Speak for your own servants, sir," she said.

"Peace, peace," said Rosemary. "As of now, we're can't be sure of the truth. I pray those girls just ran off...but I wanted to make you aware of the stories floating around the Fringe."

"I grew up in the Fringe, Your Highness," said Marcus. "I know how Fringers think. There's a lot of pride. There's not a soul on those streets who doesn't long for a way out, but still, we protect our own."

"I didn't know you grew up—how did you—"

"I'm a graduate of Larry's, of course," said Marcus. "Other opportunities didn't...come to fruition...so I enrolled here."

Eleanor found it odd that a boy from the Fringe would have had opportunities better than a spot at Larry's. She said so.

Marcus cleared his throat and glanced at Rosemary. "I spent some time...at the Covey...but it was not meant to be."

"You were a magician?" Eleanor paused. "Wait, one can't be a magician and then not..."

Marcus blushed, and Rosemary seemed inclined to save him from some sort of embarrassment, argument or not. "Marcus and I disagree on this next point."

"We do," said the Godsman. His massive jaws clenched. "Rosemary is spooking at shadows."

Whatever solicitude Rosemary felt must have floated to the ceiling with the faint white light drifting from her nostrils. Her face darkened. Eleanor had known Rosemary her entire life. She could count the witch's displays of temper on one hand.

"I've lived a hundred years, Marcus. I've outgrown any spookiness I might have once had." She crossed her arms across her chest. "I've seen a man. Maybe five times. At night, wandering in front of the school."

"Obviously something about him bothers you?" asked Dorian.

Rosemary nodded. "Just last week, I was returning to the school from a visit to the Abbey. We passed within two feet of one another. I said a loud good evening, yet he said nothing. You know the deference we witches are accorded. Even the crudest Fringe thugs return my greetings."

"What does he look like?"

"I've never gotten a proper look. He seems of average height and build, but he wears a dark cloak and pulls it around his face."

"Are you sure it's a man?" asked Eleanor.

"No, but something in his walk...I'm fairly certain."

Marcus waved his hands. "There are hundreds of scoundrels in the Fringe. I worry about the lost girls, not some rude drunk. Perhaps he hangs around the school...because he is..." Marcus blushed. "...a perversion..."

"If he is a pervert, all the more reason to watch out for him," said Dorian.

After a few more mundane updates Eleanor, Rosemary, and Dorian excused themselves. A smallish hoard of soldiers followed them across the block to Queen Camille's. They left Rosemary in the library after a quick visit with some of the students.

Eleanor walked down a dim hallway, out the back door, and into the tiny garden. The girls grew all manner of vegetables in the warm months, from carrots to cucumbers. A few juvenile pumpkins peered shyly at her from between their leafy fingers. She opened the door of the wooden shed that served as the school kitchen. The scent of baking bread and squash soup met her at the door.

"I thought I'd find you here!"

Jan, now a lovely, petite young woman of sixteen, looked up at Eleanor's voice. She dropped her rolling pin, brushed her brown hair from her eyes with her good hand, and swept a curtsy. "Good afternoon, Your Highness."

Eleanor hugged Jan. The girl turned sideways to avoid dusting Eleanor's gown with flour. Eleanor asked after Ruby.

"She's learning Svelyan," said Jan. "Mistress Rosemary says she has an ear for it. Not sure how, since she's been listenin' to Fringe talk her whole life."

Eleanor laughed. "And how are you?"

"I'm well. I've been writing a story, about a maiden who falls in love with a—" She stopped as Dorian entered the kitchen. Her face flamed and she fiddled with her apron. She appeared to have forgotten what she meant to say. She curtsied again. "Your Grace."

"Hello, Jan."

At the sound of her name Jan's face burned brighter. Eleanor thought of herself at the same age, with a head filled with romantic notions and a scarcity of male company. "I'd love to read your story, when you're ready to share it with me."

She's growing up. Eleanor squeezed Jan's hand and thought of the missing pupils.

"Jan, have you thought of what you will do? When you leave Queen Camille's."

Jan's gray eyes widened. "Shall I go soon?"

"You have time to think on it," Eleanor said, although in truth, at age sixteen Jan was fast approaching adulthood.

They said their goodbyes, but as Eleanor opened the door Jan cleared her throat. "Besides writing stories…and reading 'em…I don't know, Your Highness."

"Don't worry. We'll find something for you," Eleanor said.

Apprehension followed her across the courtyard. Jan could cipher. She could recite the history of the Desmarais kings backward and forward. She might be writing the next great chapter in Carthean literature. What would it do for her?

She could bake a lovely cream tart, but no matter. The men of the guilds hired only male apprentices. Booksellers, bakers…any women working in those shops were wives and daughters and the occasional sister.

Eleanor had thought to give her girls a chance at a better life, but as Marcus has said, nothing had changed in Cartheigh. How could she expect her first student, her brightest charge, to be thrilled at the prospect of emptying chamber pots in a rich man's house?

CHAPTER 12

THE ART OF LOVE

ELEANOR WATCHED THE CITY of Point-of-Rocks slide past the carriage window. It had none of Maliana's grandeur or Solsea's quaintness. The people sagged along with the buildings. From the few scrubby trees to the warehouses to the jostling crowds to their tiny wooden houses, everything fought for space. The gray LowWinter sky hung over it all like dingy laundry on a limp line. It was a place of function, not beauty.

Gregory had, for some unfathomable reason, insisted Eleanor accompany him on this latest trip to Point-of-Rocks. She'd balked. She hadn't wanted to leave her children, or the school. The missing girls were just as lost as they'd been on the day of Eleanor and Dorian's visit with Marcus.

She'd yet to hear anyone speak of the mystery at court, and to her great relief, the strongest links in the ladies' gossip chain had quit the palace. After two weeks, numerous uncomfortable dinners, and long embroidery bees that slipped into the realm of torturous, Imogene and Sylvia returned to Harveston. As Imogene took great pains to announce, the Duke's health had taken a turn for the worse, and he would soon meet HighGod. Sylvia seemed unconcerned, as long as her husband decided on life or death in time for the Waning Fest.

Eleanor had looked forward to a bit of snooping around the Fringe before the Fest preparations began in earnest, but Gregory wouldn't take no for an answer. She'd brought along several books, and he spent most of the two-day voyage to Point-of-Rocks engrossed in reports from Port's Minister. They'd disembarked at the Desmarais's drafty monstrosity of a townhouse in what passed for Point-of-Rock's most refined neighborhood. Gregory promptly abandoned her to the servants and commenced with two days of meetings with merchants, ministers, and port security.

On this fifth morning she'd insisted he take her with him. The carriage dropped Eleanor and Gregory in the midst of the Point-of-Rocks dockworks. She gaped at the merchant ships towering over her head. Flags of a dozen countries whipped from masts that seemed likely to prick the low-hanging clouds and bring on a late morning shower. Eleanor and Gregory had to yell to be heard over the shouts of the dockworkers, the lowing of cows, and the slamming of crates and barrels across at least twenty gangplanks. The smell of vegetation gone rotten turned her stomach.

Gregory noticed her wrinkled nose. "Trips to Point-of-Rocks are never pleasant, but they are necessary," he said.

Eleanor nodded. The Clarity River met the Shallow Sea in the Point-of-Rocks Harbor, and most of the goods coming in and out of Cartheigh passed through the City Dockworks. The Ports Minister led Gregory and Eleanor from ship to ship. Dockworkers transferred hunks of raw Fire-iron, already bought and paid for by foreign kings, builders, and artisans, from barges to sailing vessels. Watchful soldiers froze and saluted as Gregory maneuvered around them. A merchant organized more crates of Fire-iron furniture, jewelry, and fighting metal. He offered Eleanor a tiny bracelet for Leticia. Gregory smiled behind the handkerchief he held over his nose. Eleanor sensed his pride in the wealth of his kingdom.

She noticed three ships anchored in the harbor. She shouted into Gregory's ear as a flock of renegade chickens burst from a broken crate in a noisy, mutinous cascade of white feathers, "Are those ships waiting for space at the dock?"

Gregory yelled back at her, "They're in quarantine! Rumors of plague across the Shallow Sea. It only takes one infected foreigner to start an epidemic."

"What's the nature of the—"

But Gregory and the Ports Minister had already moved on. Eleanor chatted with a few Kellish dockhands. Once Gregory completed his business they returned to the carriage. Gregory pointed the driver in the direction of the Port City Bazaar, Point-of-Rock's one attraction. The constant flow of goods through the port enabled the vendors to collect all manner of exotic wares.

"Some of it is stolen, and it's all overpriced, but the bartering is part of the fun," Gregory said. He opened the window and yelled to the coachman to halt.

Eleanor and Gregory stepped from the carriage into the market square. Five soldiers flanked them. As word of their presence spread the shouts of the vendors subsided to a hopeful buzz. Men and women lowered their heads and curtsied, all the while holding up piles of rich fabrics or pieces of silver and porcelain. A few young women smiled at Gregory and waved flowers. Gregory blew them kisses and they held their hands to their hearts and clung on each other.

"I once had that effect on you, sweetheart," he said, as they wandered the stalls.

Eleanor selected a few kamelcow hair paintbrushes for Ticia and a puppet with an uncanny resemblance to Chou Chou for Nathan. A magician offered her a Fire-iron backed mirror.

"It flatters the viewer, Your Highness," the magician said. "I swear by all the scales of the North Country it shall never repeat the same compliment twice."

Eleanor peered into the mirror. "A vision!" the mirror said, as ardently as any young suitor to his beloved. "Green becomes you. Your lips are like two pink pillows upon which I long to rest mine."

"You don't have lips," Eleanor said to the mirror.

"Your hair is like the setting—"

"I'll take it." She smiled at the thought of Chou Chou basking in the mirror's adulation. With enough use, the mirror might indeed run out of things to say.

She longed to purchase something for Dorian, but it didn't seem appropriate, so she turned her attention to Rosemary. She left Gregory haggling with an old lady. The woman clutched a Fire-iron sword that surely outweighed her. She hemmed and hawed, as if she sold weapons to the future king every day of the week.

Eleanor stopped at a bookseller's stall. The man behind the table was tall and broad-shouldered, with closely cropped white-blond hair. When he opened his mouth she heard echoes of her old friend Christopher Roffi. The man who had sent her into exile just before Ticia's birth, and then helped Dorian save her life.

"Your Highness," said the Svelyan. "Can I be helping you with finding something?"

Eleanor smiled at him. "Are you from Nestra, sir?"

"No, Madam. I am hailing from a village outside the city. Are you knowing our fair capital?"

"Only from a friend's description." She picked through the volumes spread across the low table draped with a neat red silk sheet. "I'm looking for a gift. For a scholar."

"What kind of scholar is he?"

"She."

The man waved his hands. "Ah, such a fool am I with my assuming. What does she study?"

"All manner of subjects." Eleanor crossed her arms over her chest. "Hmmm…have you anything from Svelya? She's a witch, by the way."

His face lit up. "A magical lady! I have just the thing." He disappeared behind a curtain for a few moments and returned with a book bound in thick reddish brown leather. He handed it to Eleanor and she read the title, *The Warrior Witch of C'adda*.

"Have you heard of Penelope Sessa?" the bookman asked. "Our most famous witch. She led the witches of the C'adda Abbey through the Ogre Wars of five-hundred—"

"Eleanor, what are you doing?"

She held up the book. "I've found a gift for Rosemary."

"No, you haven't," said Gregory. "You know we don't use crown funds for Svelyan goods." He took the book and tossed it to the vendor. The man lowered his eyes and set the book on the table.

Eleanor laughed. "He's a bookman. He'd hardly filling King Martin Mangolin's royal coffers."

"Still, it's the principle. We haven't received their ambassador since the Roffi incident, nor any trade goods. This man shouldn't even be here."

The bookman didn't raise his eyes. "Pardon, Your Highness. I have been in Point-of-Rocks for twenty years."

"Did I ask you to speak, Svelty?" Gregory leaned across the table and the red silk sheet slid sideways. Books landed on the muddy cobblestones with several wet smacks.

"Bit players like you are tolerated here, and in Smithwick Square, but that doesn't mean I'll spend crown gold on your wares."

Eleanor retrieved the books herself and set them on the table. "This is absurd. It's been nearly six years since Roffi's death, and we've had no further problems from King Mangolin. Why punish a vendor?" She touched the Svelyan's sleeve. "I'd like to read that book myself."

The bookman stepped back. Gregory grabbed Eleanor's arm and forced it to her side. "Inappropriate, Sweetheart. Come, we're leaving."

"I want that book, and there are other stalls I'd like to visit."

Gregory took a step closer and his mouth brushed her ear. "I would advise you to let it go, for the sake of your Svelyan friend here."

Eleanor spoke through clenched teeth. "Please, sir," she said to the bookman. "Forgive us for wasting your time."

Dessert arrived and still Eleanor did not respond to Gregory. He'd joined her in painful silence during the carriage ride back to the Desmarais townhouse. They'd made for their own bedrooms at the door. By the dinner hour, however, he seemed keen to put the argument behind him. Eleanor had no such notions. She flatly ignored him through four courses.

He made another attempt. "This tart is rather dry; don't you think?"

Silence.

His jaw jutted in her direction. "Damnit! Say something." He slammed his fork onto his plate. Splashes of cream stood out in white speckles against his eggplant-colored tunic. "Will you ruin this trip over one disagreement? I brought you with me so we could be together—"

Eleanor's nostrils flared. "Please. I had to beg you to take me with you today."

"And look what it got me. An embarrassing scene and an unpleasant dinner." He drained his wine glass. "I don't know why I bothered. I thought if we could get away from the children—but we might as well be back at Eclatant. I may not be able to compose sonnets, but I can tell when someone's pretending to sleep."

Eleanor fumbled with her napkin. Gregory had never revisited the humiliating vulnerability of Raoul and Margaret's wedding night. He did not discuss their conjugal relations; his presence in her bedchamber declared his intent.

She paled. "I never heard you come in."

He snorted. "For one who can detect your children's sneezes from the other side of the palace, you have questionable hearing when it comes to your husband."

"Forgive me if I'm not satisfying you."

"You're not satisfying me at all."

She stood. "Goodnight, Gregory."

His chair scraped across the floor. He strode around the table and squeezed her arm to the point of pain for the second time that day. "This conversation isn't over. I'm tired of how things are between us."

Eleanor felt a prick of fear, but she lifted her chin and looked him in the eye. "Well, find your comforts elsewhere. As you always have."

"I'm almost twenty-nine years old, Eleanor. Every year I'm closer to the crown. It's a heavy honor. I want to find my comfort in my home. In your chambers."

Eleanor's mouth hung open for a moment. She hadn't expected that response.

"We were so young when we met," he said. "I know I wasn't always...and now the children—I'd hoped we could..."

Eleanor sat again, and he sat beside her. She rested her forehead in one hand.

"Pray," he said, "what can I do to make you happy?"

"I—well, you could ask me...about the school—or maybe we could—take more trips like this..." He nodded, and she felt like the most heinous liar. *Set me free, Gregory.*

He took her hand and she fought tears. "Wife, may I come to your chamber tonight?"

She nodded. He rose and led her from the dining room. He made love to her in his usual abrupt way, although to his credit he tried to draw it out, tried to caress some tenderness out of her. She couldn't tell if he believed her reaction genuine, not after his revelation of the transparency of her sleep feigning. She felt numb, detached, as if she were sitting beside the bed watching a stranger bed an unnamed whore.

Once she was certain he slept deeply himself she rolled toward the window. She ached for her children. She ached for Dorian's arms and his big hands in her hair and on her face. She longed for an hour without guilt and lies. For one day of honesty.

Dorian waited for Pandra as he always did, in the bloody sitting room. He'd returned from a visit to Harper's Crossing in advance of Eleanor's own return from Point-of-Rocks. He'd waited two days, in the hope that Eleanor might appear early, and then given in to the ache of their four-week separation. He drummed his fingers against the velvet arm of his chair and checked his pocket clockworks. The sooner he commenced with this sad production the sooner he could put it behind him.

He poured his second glass of whiskey as Pandra opened the door. She wore her usual layers of crimson lace and wide smile. "Dorian, it's been too—"

"I've been waiting." He dumped the whiskey down his throat.

She took the empty glass, refilled it, and returned it to him. "Tsk, I know that voice. You're in need of service. Real service."

He grunted his agreement. Pandra gave him a commiserating smile. "Missing your lady, are you?"

"You mock my pain."

"Of course not, darling. I want to ease it. I've only had the chance, what…" Pandra bit her bottom lip and her subtly painted brows crept towards her bright red hair. "…six times in four years? Since your great reconciliation, I mean."

"Nine," Dorian said. Nine times, in four years, he'd found long separations from Eleanor too much to bear. He'd arrived at Pandra's as he had tonight, with a hollow stomach and a perpetual stiffness in his leggings. Eleanor had never asked after such encounters, and he never mentioned them.

"I'm so pleased," Pandra said. "In fact, you've saved me the trouble of cajoling you tonight. I have a new girl. Young. She's hesitated to join me."

"You've never had difficulty attracting employees."

"This girl is different. I have plans for her." Pandra crept close to him. "She's innocent. A virgin. A rarity in the End." She traced her fingers along his belt. "If I could convince you to introduce her to…the art of love…she might be persuaded."

He grimaced. "You'd give her false expectations of what her duties will entail."

"Just something to remember when she's draped across some fat old man. I'm asking you for a favor. You do return favors, don't you?"

He rubbed his eyes. *A virgin.*

"Come now. It's not as if I'm asking you to do something unpleasant."

He refilled his glass, but the whiskey disappeared before the bubbles had a chance to dissipate. "I'm hardly in a position for moral grandstanding. Take me to her."

Pandra slipped her arm through his, and led him up the stairs to a room at the end of the hallway. She kissed his cheek before leaving. He stepped inside and closed the door behind him. He'd bedded Pandra herself in this room. His eyes swept over the high wrought Fire-iron bed, with its scarlet sheets and layered curtains. Numerous oversized, overstuffed pillows dotted the bearskin dragon robe rug. The scent of cinnamon hung in the air. Cinnamon always brought Dorian back to Pandra's, even in the kitchen corridors of Laralee. A guilty smell.

A young woman stood at the window. She faced the crack between the draperies and clutched the thick velvet in one hand. She was naked, save for a shawl covering her back and shoulders. A mane of chocolate hair spilled over the delicate lace. Her bare ass peeked at him from the scalloped edges of the shawl. His insides clenched with lust.

She didn't turn, but he saw her grip on the draperies tighten at the sound of his footsteps. He stopped behind her.

"Pandra sent me," he said.

"I know. I've been waiting."

He took her arm and she let go of the curtains. He ran a hand from her shoulder to her wrist, and then down her naked hip. His thumb traced the swell of her buttocks. She leaned into his hand, soft skin covered in gooseflesh. He touched her other shoulder, but as his hand went lower he suddenly met nothing but empty air.

His heart dropped into his chest, and he whirled the girl around. It was Jan.

Dorian draped a fox fur dragon robe over Jan and bade her sit on the edge of the bed. He rang the bell for Pandra and took a chair across the room from Eleanor's favorite student. She tugged the robe around her shoulders. Tears tracked down her face. His skin crawled with mortification whenever he looked at her, so he watched his spectite ring. It blinked at him with an accusing sapphire hue, just a shade away from what he thought of as Eleanor's blue.

Jan's soft voice drifted across the room. "Your Grace?"

"Yes, Jan."

"I'm sorry...I...Pandra said a gentleman of repute...I didn't know—"

"I should hope not."

She wiped her eyes and held her chin a little higher. "But the truth is...I'd have said yes even if she told me it was you coming. I'd just have said it quicker."

"Child—"

"I ain't a child. If you don't think I'm pretty...or my arm—"

"Jan, this is absolutely not about your obvious attractiveness. What would the princess say if she knew you were here? It would break her heart."

"Does Her Highness know *you're* here? I think she'd be disappointed in you, too."

"Watch yourself."

"I'm a grown woman." She stood and the robe slipped to the ground. "I'll show you."

He crossed the room. Jan sat down again at his advance, a look of mixed fear and hope on her face. He grabbed the robe from the floor and threw it to her.

"Cover yourself, girl." His pulse beat an angry rat-tat against his temples. "After all the faith Eleanor put in you—" He stormed to the door, yanked at the knob, and shouted down the hallway. "Pandra! Pandra!"

Pandra rounded the corner at a bouncy trot. "HighGod, stop your howling," she said as she slipped into the room.

He pointed at Jan. "Why is this girl here?"

Pandra glanced between Jan and Dorian. "For the same reason they're all here."

"She's from the school, Pandra. From Queen Camille's."

"Yes?"

"I oversee the school with the princess!"

"Oh...I'd heard you were involved in some way...but..." Pandra shrugged. "Why does it matter?"

"Because I've known this girl since she was twelve—and I just touched her—"

"I'm not twelve anymore!" interjected Jan.

"—her...her—and because the princess will be most displeased to know she's here!"

Pandra's hands curled into fists and disappeared into the layers of poufy silk covering her hips. "Why does the princess have to know?"

"You think I won't tell her? Eleanor has poured her soul into that place. She's not schooling those girls so they can be whores!"

"*Eleanor*, now, is it?" Pandra sat beside Jan and put an arm around the girl's shoulders. "You can tell *Eleanor* that Jan has a bright future here—"

"Bright future my ass!"

"—I need a smart girl, one that can take my place someday. Someone who can keep things running smoothly, so I can think about rest. I've not had much rest in twenty-five years, you know."

Dorian knelt in from of Jan and her face bloomed like the red blush of a new tulip. "Jan, please. You can't do this to Eleanor. She loves you."

Jan's forehead wrinkled. "Pandra said she'll take care of me. This great big lovely house will be all mine. Money and fine dresses."

Dorian shook his head. "But no honor. You could find a husband, Jan, have children—"

"Who'd want me, Your Grace?" She held up the stump. "My own mum didn't want me."

"Eleanor wanted you. She saw the smarts and beauty in you. Don't hurt her."

"It's you that will hurt her by telling her," said Pandra. "You don't want to hurt sweet *Eleanor*, do you? I'm sure she'd be more hurt to know just how you found Jan…here…naked…what were you saying? You touched her—"

"Shut your fucking mouth."

Jan gasped, but Pandra just smiled. "I thought so. Why hurt her? Why does *your lady* need to know?"

"Your lady?" repeated Jan, her eyes widening. "Your…lady?"

Dorian stood and backed away from the comprehension in Jan's bright eyes. "I will tell her, Pandra. Jan, it would behoove you to return to Queen Camille's."

Dorian bowed and left the room. He collected his cloak from the butler, let himself out the back door, retrieved his horse, and rode hard in the direction of Eclatant. The cool air seared his nostrils and dried out his throat, but he couldn't get enough of it after the sickly warmth of the Hussy. His mount scattered chickens, children, and old women on the clattering ride down the Hundred Herald's Street. A few townsfolk recognized him and called out blessings, but he didn't slow down to give alms as he often did. He wanted nothing more than to soak away his shame in a hot bath. The guard waved him through the Fire-iron palace gate. He pulled his horse up short in the main drive, at the sight of an ornate carriage parked beside the larger-than-life statue of Caleb Desmarais astride the great unicorn stallion Eclatant. Gregory and Eleanor had returned.

CHAPTER 13

THE PRICK BEATS
THE WASHTUB

ELEANOR AND DORIAN WAITED for Pandra in a stand of oak trees two miles from the granary. Eleanor sat on Teardrop's back, listening to the scritchy-scratch of winter branch against winter branch. The weak LowWinter sunlight wound through the bare limbs on its way to the forest floor like a flood searching for lower ground.

"Do you have any pain?" Eleanor asked Teardrop. She'd worried about taking Teardrop out so soon after the birth, but the mare had insisted. Teardrop's recovery provided a sensible reason for Dorian and Senné's company. Normally, they would have made a straight line for the granary.

Senné nuzzled the base of Teardrop's tale. "Should Her Highness dismount?" he asked.

Teardrop exhaled her breezy laugh. She backed up and gave Senné an affectionate nip. "I carried Cricket for four seasons. I can carry my mistress for a few miles."

Teardrop's change in position left Eleanor and Dorian side by side. They hadn't spoken much on the ride. She sensed his mortification, she was less certain about her own emotions.

Chou Chou had brought her the news of Jan's fall two nights ago, before she's had a chance to unpack her trunks, or properly greet her children. The parrot relayed Dorian's tale with harsh honesty.

"He's most distraught," Chou had said as sweat began to bead on Eleanor's forehead. "Not only about Jan, but about the circumstances in which he came to find her. He begs your forgiveness."

"Tell him we'll discuss it on the ride to meet Pandra."

She'd spent an endless, sleepless night rolling about in her bed. By the time she met Dorian at the Paladine she still did not know how to address the situation. She'd eased Teardrop in front of Senné as they made their unusually plodding way through the forest. She could feel Dorian's anxious eyes on her back. For some reason she couldn't find any words, angry or accusing, forgiving or reassuring.

When Teardrop fell back, Dorian took advantage of the new proximity. "Eleanor, please, won't you say something?"

Say something, Damnit! Gregory's words at the dinner table at the Point-of-Rocks townhouse echoed through her mind. She closed her eyes and pictured Dorian, a bedroom, and a naked, pretty girl. She saw that hungry look in his eyes, the one she'd convinced herself was for her and her alone. *For Jan. For my little street sleep.*

"I wish I could...I just don't know—"

"I told you I'd never lie to you."

The sound of shifting leaves forced a pause in the conversation. "A rider—no, two riders," Senné said.

Two horses, a gray and a bay, picked their way through the trees. The bay carried an enormous, unusually ugly man who reminded Eleanor of a furless bear. The streaming sunlight glinted off his bald head. His tiny dark eyes swept the branches, as if he expected the squirrels to attack his mistress.

The lady in question, dressed in red velvet from her feathered hat to her pointy riding boots, sat a pretty sidesaddle on her gray hunter. The saddle was red, as were the bows entwined in the animal's mane and tale. The monstrous guard and his mount also appeared dipped in raspberry jam for the outing. Human and horse, they clashed horribly with the orange and yellow leaves littering the forest floor.

Dorian dismounted, and Eleanor, Pandra, and her guard joined him on the ground. Pandra's white teeth flashed between painted red lips. "Good afternoon, Your Grace. What a fine day for a ride. I so rarely venture into the country."

"The girl, Jan," Eleanor said. "You will return her to Queen Camille's. You won't approach her again, nor any of my other students."

"Your Highness," Pandra said to Eleanor. The smile remained, but if the bright blue of her eyes had been water it surely would have turned to ice. "I've heard you're not one to trouble yourself with formalities."

"A rumor with basis in fact."

Pandra laughed. "I've found that to be the case with most rumors. Tell me, Princess, why haven't you brought your husband? One word from him and I couldn't come within a hundred paces of your school."

"My husband has more pressing responsibilities."

Pandra danced a little sashay step. Her kick sent the smell of moldering vegetation into the air. "Or maybe His Highness wouldn't approve of crown money funding a school for whores. Now, how would the HighGod-fearing citizens of his realm feel about that?"

"Enough coyness," Dorian said. "The princess has stated her piece."

"Very well, I'll state mine." Pandra took two steps in Eleanor's direction. Teardrop snorted a warning, but Pandra didn't flinch. "I need that girl. I could use a dozen like her. Smart, independent thinkers. I won't apologize for it, any more that your husband would apologize for sending his best lieutenants off to war."

Eleanor closed the bit of space still left between them. "You've lived your sad life, yet you entice those with a chance for better to join you in your misery!"

"You silly girl—"

Dorian grabbed Pandra's arm. "Your princess."

She shook him off. "What great opportunities do you have planned for your pupils? You've schooled them. You've taught them reading and ciphering and history. So they will be well-read chambermaids? Poetic kitchen cooks? Maybe a few lucky ones will land as dressmakers' wives and spend their lives hunched over a needle until they go blind. My girls may be whores, but they're safe. They live in comfort and leisure compared to what awaits your students."

The guard broke in with his Fringe gutter-speak. "Ach, right, Pandra. The prick beats the washtub, I reckon."

Dorian pulled his sword and pointed it between the man's eyebrows. The guard watched the sword with crossed eyes. "Pardon, sir. Paaar-don."

Eleanor laid a trembling hand against Teardrop's warm neck. She repeated her message. "You will return Jan. You'll stay away from my school."

"You, madam, are hardly in a position to make demands of me." She put a hand to Eleanor's cheek. When Eleanor jerked her head sideways Pandra whispered in her ear, "Nor is your lover."

Eleanor felt the blood drain from her face and down her neck. It seemed to pool in her bladder. Dorian was right. Pandra knew.

"I'm quite certain I don't know what you mean," Eleanor said.

Pandra took Eleanor's hand, and then took Dorian's. "Isn't it treason to wish the death of the prince? You two have surely died more deaths than an alley full of cats!"

Pandra's banshee-like grin wobbled. Eleanor looked down at the madam's hand in Dorian's grasp. Pandra's fingertips had gone bright red. "Don't make me repeat the sentiments I expressed at the Hussy two days ago," Dorian said.

Pandra giggled. "He told me to shut my fucking mouth. Right in front of your innocent little doll! That was just after he grabbed her naked ass."

Dorian twisted Pandra's arm and she cried out. He slapped her across the face with his free hand. Her guard grunted in surprise and took a step forward, but Senné's horn stopped him. Pandra stumbled and sat down hard. She scrambled away from Dorian. Her rear end dug a trench in the wet leaves. The heels of her red riding boots left two wiggly trails in the mud.

Eleanor didn't let Dorian reach the whore in the leaves. She grabbed him around his waist.

"Dorian," she said, just loud enough to be heard over the crackling leaves. "Stop, now."

He planted his feet, and gave another half-hearted shrug. She rested her head against his back. She could feel the hardness of his spine through his wool cloak.

"Eleanor, how can I—"

"Shhh," she said. "It's all right, love. It's forgotten."

Can it ever really be forgotten? She pushed the thought aside. *It is. It is. It is.*

Pandra shifted in the leaves. Eleanor let go of Dorian and knelt beside her before she could stand.

"I assume you've suspected this for a long time," Eleanor said. A single tear had skipped through the splotches of mud on Pandra's bruised face. Eleanor wondered how many men had struck Pandra during her illustrious career. "I understand the danger we put you in. I hope you know your help in our...endeavors...has been invaluable. Since you obviously have no love for me, you must have had some for him, at some point anyway."

"I have no feeling for you, Your Highness. My trade does not allow me to be free with my emotions, good or bad." When Pandra's left eye twitched Eleanor noticed the deep wrinkles creasing her otherwise perfect white skin. "As for him...I see why he...I understand now."

"I respect that. Now, I ask you to respect me, as your future queen. You must do as you will for your survival, but I ask that you stay away from my students. If they come to you when they've finished with

Queen Camille's, well…they will be grown women who have made that choice. It will be my responsibility to address openly the temptations of your way of life."

Pandra wiped the mud from her right hand and held it out. "That is a reasonable request."

Eleanor shook Pandra's hand and then hauled her to her feet. "I'd still like you to return Jan. As a personal favor. She is…dear to me."

Pandra dislodged her hand from Eleanor's grip. She shook it, as if trying to get the blood flowing to her fingers again. "I'm no monster, Your Highness. I'll not keep any girl against her will." She mounted her horse and adjusted her feathered hat. It had barely shifted throughout the scuffle. "Besides, you don't need to worry about Jan. She must be under your spell as well. She returned to Queen Camille's this morning."

"Praises," Eleanor said to Teardrop. As she put a foot in the stirrup a grunt and a thump sounded behind her. She whirled around.

Pandra's guard lay in the leaves. Blood spilled down his neck and darkened his crimson shirt to brown. His mount jigged backwards in a tinkling of bits and stirrups and tiny Fire-iron bells.

Dorian stood over the man with his father's bloody knife in one hand. He looked up at Pandra on her bay hunter. "If you ever meet us again, come alone."

"Her Highness, Princess Eleanor."

Orvid Jones's quivery voice floated into the alcove as the doors swung open. Three scruffy commoners, Eleanor recognized them as Dragon Miners by their snake-hide boots and shaggy beards, bowed and asked for her blessing on their way out. She shook their hands, smoothed the pale blue skirts of her gown, and entered King Casper's receiving room.

The king sat on a raised Fire-iron throne at the far end of the room.

Gregory stood beside him. Gregory's mouth turned up at the corners in greeting, while the king's did the opposite.

The Fire-iron soles of Eleanor's shoes carried her across the lonely expanse of the receiving room in a nervous, clacking staccato. She curtsied, but the king waved her upright.

"Eleanor. Jones tells me you won't be put off."

"Yes, Your Majesty. I come to you...on a matter of great... personal—"

"I'm up to my whiskers in an inventory of the Dragon Mines. Vital national affairs. I haven't eaten since breakfast. Yet you have a personal matter that can't wait." The king's round belly jiggled with irritation. "Jones! Have them bring me bread, and some of that duck soup. Well, go on, girl."

Gregory took the two steps down to her level and squeezed her hand. His loyalty encouraged her. "There is a girl, sire...or, a young woman," she said. "At Queen Camille's—"

"Your school."

"Yes. Her name is Jan. She's very intelligent, one of my brightest students. She's near to finishing her courses—"

"How nice. And how does this concern me?"

"I'd like to bring her here, to Eclatant. Give her a position."

The king scowled. "I don't need to approve the employment of every kitchen maid in the palace. Just bring the girl on and be done with it."

"No, sire...I don't want to make her a kitchen maid—"

"A chamber maid, then?" asked Gregory.

Eleanor feared she might scream if either of them interrupted her again. "Not a maid, chamber or kitchen or otherwise. Gustus, the old magician in the library, is close to retiring to the Covey. I'd like to train Jan to take his place."

For a moment it seemed as if Eleanor had offered her plan in a foreign language. As if both men needed time for mental translation.

"A woman…or a girl…managing the library at Eclatant?" the king asked.

"Your Majesty, if I may…"

Eleanor had forgotten about Orvid Jones. He stood behind her, ledger and quill in hand, taking notes. "There is nothing that says a man must manage the library."

Eleanor smiled her gratitude.

"Nothing but centuries of tradition," Casper said with a snort of laughter. "You, Jones, should know that. The Librarian has always been a man, and not just any man. A magician."

Jones cleared his throat. "I only meant to say, Your Majesty, that—"

"Pah! Ridiculous! No, Eleanor."

Eleanor's hand went sweaty in Gregory's grip. "Please, sire—"

The king shook his head. "I can see it now. You bring on this girl, in this capacity, and you'll expect the same for the rest of them. You'll want me to send them off the Dragon Mines and put them up in the Paladine."

"We've taught them well, sire. I believe we have a responsibility to provide them with opportunities."

"You can bring on as many kitchen maids as you see fit."

Gregory wiped his hand on his leggings. He stepped between Eleanor and his father. "The nursery would be very pleasant. I'm sure— what did you call her—Jen? She'd enjoy being with the children."

She sensed his silent plea for a peaceful solution. "Gregory, Jan and my other students are schooled in literature, art…they can be more. Why must they settle for servitude?"

The king laughed. "Not many of my subjects would turn down a chance to serve at Eclatant. Especially a pack of Fringe wenches."

Eleanor blinked back the first prickles of real anger. "I think we should give our women new options." She turned to her husband with her own pleading smile. "Don't you agree?"

Gregory returned to his throne, a slightly smaller, less ornate version of the one supporting his father's considerable bulk. He ran a hand though his hair as he sat. "I'm sorry but…I agree with Father. You're opening a deep basket filled with rotten apples."

The king worried Gregory's knee with his meaty hand. "Wise, my son," he said. He jabbed one ring-laden finger in Eleanor's direction. "Take the school for what it is. A roof over their heads. Food on their plate. A chance to find a position in a fine house. More than they'd ever have had without your help, for sure."

Eleanor couldn't hide her desperation. "Just Jan, then. Just give me a place for Jan in the library. I won't come to you about the others. I swear it."

The king's mustached jittered like the tail of an agitated squirrel. "No. No. No."

Orvid Jones gently took Eleanor's arm. "Thank you for your time, Your Majesty." He tugged Eleanor into a curtsy.

"This request has not pleased me," the king said. "Not after the generosity and leniency I've shown you in all your endeavors in the city. I've followed you more closely than you know."

The back of Eleanor's neck tingled as the king continued. "You mistake the people's affection for agreement with all your methods. I think you'll find many Malianans aren't so inclined to embrace your… new ideas."

Eleanor did not look up. "Your Majesty."

"There's talk of useless lessons…and girls who are putting their skills to…shall we say, dubious use. Queen Camille's was meant to strengthen the people's love for the crown. Rest assured that if it fails in that mission its existence will be…reevaluated."

Eleanor dipped her head in acknowledgement of the king's threat. Jones steered her to the door. She vaguely heard Gregory say goodbye to his father. His clipping steps followed Eleanor and Jones from the receiving room. She turned on him before he could speak.

"Husband. Let me thank you for your support."

"You know I couldn't disagree with Father."

"I managed it!"

"Don't push him. He'd not think twice about closing Queen Camille's." Gregory leaned on the door behind him. Once he seemed sure that wooden shield would stop his words from reaching the king's ears he continued. "They say some of your girls have gone over to whoring. It doesn't look good."

"Don't I know it," Eleanor said with a bitter laugh. "And how shall I entice them away from the hothouses? From the wine and pretty gowns and silk sheets? I'll offer them a pittance and a glamorous life washing dishes and emptying chamber pots!"

"It's not funny," Gregory said.

"You're right, Gregory. It's most unfunny, indeed."

CHAPTER 14

WOMANHOOD SHALL BLOSSOM

ELEANOR ALWAYS LOOKED FORWARD to summers in Solsea, but in her twenty-fifth year trepidation tarnished anticipation. The six months since her meeting with Pandra had seen the situation at Queen Camille's go from worrisome to alarming. The missing girls were never found, despite Eleanor's attempts to infiltrate Pandra's competitors. None of the half dozen willing court fops Eleanor sent in search of her missing students garnered any information. Smug satisfaction, yes, a case of the pox, possibly, but nothing she could use. In HighWinter Rosemary informed Eleanor that two more students had disappeared, the younger one a chit of but thirteen. That bit of information had sent Eleanor into a volley of curses that made Margaret tisk-tisk, and Chou Chou laugh out loud.

As tensions rose, Eleanor forced weekly visits to the school into her hectic schedule. Her students greeted her with their usual affection, but their elders no longer shared the little ones' enthusiasm. The Fringers bowed, and took her alms, but fewer people called her name and blessed her. Squinty eyes narrowed when they met hers, then darted away. No one brought a daughter to her with the promise that *here, here was a bright girl that'd do well with the readin'*.

Five days before the royal family's departure for Solsea. Rosemary sent a felt envelope to Eclatant with a private courier. The note in the witch's hand had a simple message.

EBD, I woke to find these odious missives papering the houses and streetlamps of the Fringe. Where they come from I know not. R.

Eleanor gasped when she unrolled the two leaflets. Chou peered over her shoulder and whistled his disapproval.

Both leaflets were caricatures, printed with splotchy black printing press ink on cheap white paper. The first depicted three figures. A tall, thin woman wearing a crown, and a tall, thin woman in a witch's dress. They embraced the middle figure, a woman whose breast spilled out of her gown like two greased watermelons. Four girls, ranging from a toddler to a lass on the cusp of womanhood, huddled beneath them. Their eyes turned toward heaven in abject desolation. Piles of golden coins covered their feet. The legend beneath the picture read: *In our tender embrace, womanhood shall blossom.*

The second leaflet was, if possible, worse. A young woman lay on her stomach with her rear end in the air. She read a book while the man behind her lifted her skirts with a lascivious leer. This one declared: *No reading on the job, Mistress.*

Eleanor didn't give Pansy time to fluff her petticoats. She took the leaflets to Gregory in his study. When he unfolded the leaflets he laid his strikestick across a stool and dismissed Raoul. The prince sat on the edge of the game table with a glass of wine in one hand and the leaflets in the other. To Eleanor's irritation he shut one eye.

Drunk, she thought.

"Charming," he finally said. He crumpled the pieces of paper and tossed them on the table.

"I'll send some soldiers out to collect them."

"You don't seem bothered by this."

"Of course it's bothersome. Best to deal with it quietly. If we make a lot of noise it will only collect dust, like a…like a dirty stocking left under a bed." He ran both hands through his hair.

"I don't want to deal with it quietly! I want to know who's producing this filth. I need your help!" Eleanor planted her hands on her hips.

Gregory wobbled on his feet when he stood. He plunked his goblet on the table. It tipped over, but fortunately he'd emptied it with his last swig. "Of course. You always come to me for my help."

"And I don't often get it."

"My advice is my assistance. Don't get puffed up about this. It's demeaning. You'll only call Father's attention to your problems managing the school."

"So I should just stand by while my work is vilified to the people I've been trying to serve?"   "We leave for Solsea in five days. I won't have this unpleasantness hanging over our heads."

"I think I should stay here for an extra week or so—see after—"

"No, absolutely not. The school consumes you. I want my wife to myself for a few months." To her astonishment he kissed her.

She turned her head. "It's hardly the time."

He leaned on the strikestick table. "I've been trying, Eleanor. Since Point-of-Rocks."

"Gregory, the school…aside from the children…it's everything to me." Eleanor scrambled to cover her oversight. "And you, of course."

He laughed. "I've tried to take time for you, but you have none. I haven't been drinking, although, today seems to be an exception. It doesn't matter, does it? Because of the girl and the library."

"You don't understand."

"You're right. I don't." He pointed at the door. "You may go."

A week later Eleanor and Margaret met between three life-sized ice bullocks in the corner of Sylvia's ballroom at the Falls. The bulls

lowed and stomped their frozen hooves. They shook their icicle horns at anyone who came too close. Eleanor wrapped her arms around herself. "Freezing," she said. "LowSummer, and I can see my breath."

"It's Sylvia's new way of cooling the ballroom," said Margaret. "With so many people dancing and sweating like a herd of gussied-up piglets the place will reek before the ten o'clock hour."

"Clever, really," said Eleanor. "Why spend money on perfumes and flowers when you can just prevent your guests from perspiring?"

One of Sylvia's martial magicians attended a melting bull. When the magician whispered in one dripping ear it lowered its head and slurped the water pooling around its own feet. It promptly swelled back to its pre-thaw size.

Chou lit on Eleanor's head. "Ladies, are you quite mad? It's like a Svelyan Waning Fest in this corner. Frozen and full of hulking, temperamental beasts."

"Ah, Chou," said Eleanor. "I was just about to tell Margaret about Rosemary's last letter. The leaflets keep coming. The latest shows a book with two great bosoms on the cover and—"

Chou cleared his throat and hopped from Eleanor's shoulder to Margaret's. "Eleanor, it's the first ball of the season. I know you're concerned about the school, but there's nothing to be done for it now."

Margaret put a gentle hand on Eleanor's arm. "Chou is right, darling. You know Rosemary is diligent. Let her see to it."

"You've barely slept in months," added Chou. "We've missed you. Ticia and Nathan have missed you."

"I—" Eleanor paused. She looked from one concerned face to the next. She took Margaret's hands. "You're right. We're in Solsea. It's time for family and friends. I promise, no more talk of Queen Camille's. I shan't even think on it."

Or mention it, anyway, she added silently. She smiled at her parrot. "What news, good sir? What are the summer folk saying on the night of our first summer ball?"

Chou's black tongue hung out in a parroty grin. "Everyone is all a-twitter about our dear friend Missus Delano and her anniversary gift." He flapped his wings in Margaret's face. She laughed and waved him off with a hand sporting a diamond ring roughly the size of a melon.

"Less congenial sentiments are being directed at our hostess. How uncouth, hosting a ball with her husband not two weeks in the grave." Chou's tone reminded Eleanor of her own voice chastising her children for poor table manners.

Eleanor found their hostess across the room. She wore a mourning gown, but the black silk against her white skin coupled with a plunging neckline hardly put one in the mind of a grieving widow. She held a glass of wine in one hand and rested the other against the chest of a handsome young man of the Smithwick clan. Sylvia hadn't yet made an appearance on the dance floor, but Eleanor wouldn't put it past her.

Eleanor couldn't hide her envy of Sylvia's independence. "Why should she care? Her son is the next Duke of Harveston. She has a fortune at her disposal. She can tell them all to go to the dogs."

"It may seem so," said Chou, "but remember, there are many wealthy hostesses in Solsea, and many beautiful estates."

Dorian appeared from nowhere. He took Margaret's arm. Eleanor smiled at him and touched her spectite necklace. It had glowed pleasantly crimson all evening. Perhaps the quirky spirit inside the necklace sensed her anticipation. Chou and Frog had settled the arrangements of Eleanor and Dorian's first meeting in the cave. Three days from now, during Gregory's two-day private hunting excursion with the visiting Crown Prince of Talesse.

"Come, Your Highness," said Dorian. "Let us lead you from this herd of frozen beef to a flock of performing turkeys."

Eleanor laughed. "I don't follow your meaning, Your Grace."

"His Highness, Prince Philippe, brought along a few of his favorite court entertainers. The Talessees are famous for their theatrical performances." Dorian winked at Margaret. "What say you, Missus Delano? Are the rumors about Talessee performances true?"

As Margaret blushed and mumbled an unintelligible reply Eleanor pushed Dorian toward the center of the ballroom. Prince Philippe, a short, swarthy man with blindingly white teeth and a curly mustache, introduced the evening's entertainment.

"…your gracious hoospitality. It is moooch appreciated. Now, I weell present my Sheef Poet and Meenstral, Don Paul Depolo."

As the crowd applauded a ridiculously tiny man broke from the crowd. His luxurious mustache would have fit the face of a proper sized man, or perhaps an ogre. Chou whispered in Eleanor's ear, "It seems with Talessees, the smaller the man, the larger the mustache. Could it be true of other masculine appendages?"

Eleanor shushed him. Three martial magicians of similar marginal stature and copious facial hair joined Don Paul in the center of the ballroom. They pointed at the Fire-iron chandeliers lining the ceiling. As the lights dimmed Eleanor noticed Gregory beside Sylvia on the far side of the dance floor.

Don Paul raised his arms. His melodious, rather high voice lacked the overwrought accent of his prince. Eleanor found his Carthean more intelligible than the Fringe slang of her students.

"I would sing for you a song of my own composition, based on a tale that every day grows in popularity in our homeland. It passes from friend to friend, sister to sister, and mother to daughter. We find inspiration in your fair princess."

The martial magician on his right conjured a pink fireball. It floated across the ballroom and hovered in front of Eleanor. The light stained her ivory gown pink from bodice to hem. She blushed, forehead to neckline, and there was nary a difference in the tone of her dress and that of her skin.

A lutist joined Don Paul and the magicians. Don Paul wagged his jaws and cleared his throat. "I have translated from our native tongue. In Talesse we call this story, *The Cinder Maid*."

Eleanor felt the blush deepen, until she was sure she must surely resemble a ripe, bejeweled strawberry.

Don Paul folded his hands in front of his chest and gazed at Eleanor as if in prayer. His quivery voice rang out across the ballroom. The lutist struck up a minor chord. Each word increased his melodrama, and Eleanor's mortification.

"A girlchild, in the night, makes her bed in the cinders
Resoluuuuuute!
She knows her patience and her prayers, will someday bring
Redemptiooooon!
A fairy looks down upon her kind heart and quiet
Pleeeee-e-eeeas!
Transforms a dirty cinder maid into a vision,
Bli-ind-ING!"
(Here Mister DePolo's eyes bulged from his face for added effect.)
"Her Lord sees perfect womanhood in her eyes,
Love-demuuuure!
She disappears, leaves a trinket of glass
Be-hi-hi-hiiind!
He finds a girl waiting in the cinders
Deliveraaaance!
He places on her tiny foot a glass...
SHOE OF GLAAAAAAS!
(His voice dropped, and his curly mustache wilted.)
"She blesses him, her Lord and Master
Loooove the Crown, and loooove it weeeeellll..."

Don Paul's arms pinioned with his voice. He crept across the room with each verse, until he stood but a few paces from the subject of his song. At such proximity he fairly screamed in Eleanor's face. The magicians conjured a rain of visions around his head. Brooms, soap bubbles, and black clouds of ash. Tiny glass slippers, spinning wedding rings, and bursting red hearts.

Margaret covered her mouth in a poor attempt to hide a flood of giggles. Chou whispered a running commentary in Eleanor's ear. "Cinders? Who ever heard of cinders in a hayloft—a fairy? Rosemary? You were hardly demure! No mention of your fall down the stairs—tiny foot, ha! Where am I in all this? Next thing you know he'll replace me with a chicken, or a—a mouse!"

The minstrel finally trailed off, but before the crowd could decide whether to applaud, he cleared his throat again. This time he spoke in a clear poet's voice.

"So hear me, maidens where you suffer
You know not what plans HighGod has laid
For those of gentle words and humble hearts
A princess from a cinder maid."

Don Paul grinned, as if amazed at his ability to find a few rhyming words in Carthean.

Prince Philippe showed his enthusiasm for his poet's performance with exuberant clapping and much flashing of his pearly teeth.

"It lost something in translation, eh?" said Dorian. Eleanor swatted him. Gregory joined Prince Philippe in the center of the ballroom. He raised his arms and the guests (who were all clapping industriously, most in an attempt to cover the sound of their own sniggering) quieted.

"Your Highness," Gregory said to Philippe. "Thank you for that touching tribute to my wife, the flower of Cartheigh." He lifted his goblet in Eleanor's direction. She curtsied, but he continued before she had a chance to upright herself. "But let us remember another lady who has generously put aside her own pain for our pleasure this evening."

Sylvia swept a curtsy so low she seemed to have sunk into the very floor. She held the pose, eyes cast on the shiny marble, without a tremble. Eleanor imagined she herself must have resembled a stork about to take flight by comparison. She peered around the pink fireball. It had shrunk to the size of a butterfly, but hovered with an annoying buzzing beside her nose.

Gregory went on. "Your Grace, I thank you, on behalf of all your guests, for allowing us to descend upon your home during this time of grief. Your husband, the late Duke, is well remembered this evening by your graciousness."

The guests raised their cups in Sylvia's honor.

Dorian read the signs. He steered Eleanor and Margaret onto one the terraced balconies adjoining the ballroom. Chou Chou fluttered about his head as they watched the sun succumb to the pull of the horizon and disappear below the Shallow Sea. They shared a few laughs over the Talessee minstrel's misinterpretation of Eleanor's temerity before Raoul retrieved his wife. It seemed the esteemed Don Paul was some manner of Delano cousin.

"HighGod give me strength," muttered Margaret as Raoul dragged her off in the direction of Don Paul.

Dorian leaned on the railing. He listened to the gulls screaming their goodnights and the bats squeaking their good mornings. "It does make one think," he said, "if so much can be lost in a mere seven years, what shall they write about you in a century?"

"I shall be a useless ninny simpering by the fire," said Eleanor.

"A beautiful, useless ninny. That's the one part the *Sheef Warbler* had correct," said Chou as he landed on Dorian's head.

"Flattering bird," said Eleanor with a smile.

"He's right." Dorian lowered his voice, although no one would know his words to be anything more that the usual courtly flattery. Chou paced Dorian's scalp. Dorian reached up with both hands and brought the parrot down to chest-level, lest he find himself with a hairline resembling that of Marcus the Godsman. Chou squirmed in his grip.

Eleanor's brows came together, and the corners of her mouth turned down the tiniest bit. She spoke in the rational, thoughtful voice Dorian knew from their study sessions. "I think I'm more…interesting-looking than beautiful. That my early appearances were fraught with mystery only added to my appeal." She pointed past the propped open glass doors, at the scores of women spinning around the dance floor like so many gemstones tossed onto a jeweler's carving table. Eleanor was quite the opposite of the Carthean ideal of the petite, curvaceous, pillowy woman. "I'm not like those…"

"You're long where you should be short." Dorian let go of Chou and flexed one bicep. "And hard where you should be soft."

"Riding does raise unsightly muscles." She laughed and glanced at her own bosom. "I'm sadly small in the one place I'm meant to be large!"

Chou landed on Eleanor's more receptive head. "It is depressing. You'd hardly fill out one of Imogene's heirloom teacups with those bosoms!"

Dorian guffawed, but he looked up at the sound of someone else's laughter. Gregory and Sylvia descended the staircase from one of the upper balconies. Sylvia clung to Gregory's arm. When they reached the landing Sylvia paused, but Gregory plowed onward. He dragged her toward Dorian, Eleanor, and Chou.

"Good evening! Did you enjoy the sunset, sweetheart?" If Gregory found it odd to address his wife while escorting her archrival, he didn't show it.

"Husband," said Eleanor. "Lovely, but the celestial show is over. I'm sure I'll see you both on the dance floor." She curtsied and returned to the ballroom before Gregory or Sylvia could reply.

"You think she was happy to see me?" Gregory pulled a flask from his pocket. He offered it to Sylvia and Dorian. Both demurred. A good thing, because when Gregory took a drink he found it empty. He belched.

"You'd have to ask her," said Dorian.

"Later. Sylvia was showing me the grounds. We've been up. Now we're going down. Or, at least one of us will be."

Sylvia giggled into her hand. "Gregory!" she said, like a chambermaid teasing a stable hand.

"I won't keep you, then," Dorian said.

"So serious. I'm just having a laugh with you, Dor." Gregory winked, but Dorian couldn't decide where he was aiming his irony.

"Of course." Dorian smiled back at his prince. "Since you're out of whiskey, I'll fetch one inside." He excused himself, and Gregory and Sylvia disappeared down the next set of stairs. Dorian caught a flash of red trailing behind them at a safe distance, so he hovered by the doorway.

Ten minutes later Chou reappeared. He lit on Dorian's shoulder.

"Anything of interest?" Dorian asked.

Chou began whispering in Dorian's ear. As always, his mimicry was spot-on. Dorian could almost smell Sylvia's perfume and Gregory's drunken breath.

Sylvia: *"Dorian is like an overripe lemon. Sour."*

Gregory, with a laugh: *"You don't know him."*

Sylvia, pouting: *"He barely speaks to me. How could I know him?"*

"He's just looking out for me. You're a known minx."

"Sylvia swatted at him," said Chou, "then she said: '*I think his demeanor is more out of concern for Eleanor than for you.*'"

Gregory: *"They've always been close. Like siblings. It's all that scholarly, academic dragonshit."*

Sylvia: *"Don't you think it odd? How close they are."*

"Gregory took a moment. I strained so hard to hear him I nearly fell out of the willow tree. Then he laughed again. '*What are you suggesting?*'"

Sylvia: *"Only that you keep your eyes open."*

"I could hear the anger in his voice. HighGod knows I've heard it before. '*This topic is distasteful to me.*'"

"She apologized, then she said: *I'm being silly. Look at you and I. We're…friends…are we not?*'"

Gregory: "*We are. Dear friends.*"

"'*Come, then, friend. Let me show you the greenhouses.*' She led him across the lawn, and I couldn't follow. No cover."

Dorian ground his teeth. "So are they having an affair?"

"I suspect so, but we can't be sure."

"The idea of Sylvia as Gregory's mistress had never bothered me as it does Eleanor," Dorian said under his breath as he and Chou returned to the candlelit ballroom. "If she's going to hone his powers of observation, however, I may start worrying."

Eleanor and Dorian met in the cave three days later. Chou had already relayed Gregory and Sylvia's conversation to her, of course, and Eleanor had added Sylvia's suspicions to her ever-growing list of concerns. They spent a precious hour discussing it, and Eleanor promised to set Chou upon her husband and stepsister like a bad cold. They also reached a mutual decision to avoid each other socially and take a month before attempting another meeting.

"If that's to be the case," said Eleanor, in an attempt at positivity. "Should we not take full advantage of this rendezvous?"

Dorian climbed through the crack in the rock leading to the larger chamber. Eleanor heard Senné and Teardrop shifting and shuffling on the other side of the wall. Dorian dragged an oval something wrapped in strips of old leather behind him. When he propped it against the wall it reached just above his knee.

"You had that thing strapped to your saddle," she said. "What is it? Why did you bring it?"

"Always the questions." He stooped to unwrap it, revealing a mirror with a simple frame of roughly carved wooden leaves.

She knelt beside him and smiled at his reflection. "Am I to have my hair styled?"

He rested an elbow on one knee. His face was sweet seriousness. "The other night, on the balcony. You said you don't find yourself beautiful. I didn't argue with you."

She laughed. "That wouldn't have been prudent."

"I couldn't tell you then." He tugged her in front of the mirror and looked over her shoulder. "You were right about some things. Your beauty is interesting and mysterious. There's no one like you. Your hair. Your eyes. The way you walk. Your laugh." He traced her jaw line with his thumb. "No one taught you any of it. Hundreds of lovely women in a ballroom, and everyone's eyes follow you."

She leaned into his warm, dry hand. He whispered in her ear, "That's what everyone sees. Now I want to show you what I see."

She watched as he helped her out of her clothes. Every time she blushed and turned away he gently eased her face toward the mirror. He pulled his own tunic over his head. She swallowed at the sight of his bare chest and arms, his hands cupping her breasts. She'd never imagined anything like the way her own body looked under his touch. The color in her cheeks, her lips slightly parted, the light sheen of sweat on her chest. She marveled at her pert nipples and the muscles in her thighs. She put her hand over his and guided it down between her legs. In a matter of minutes, she'd left embarrassment behind in favor of fascination.

He pushed her forward on all fours and entered her from behind. She heard her usual gasp, but it was all the more compelling owing to her hair cascading over her shoulders and the way he looked to the cave's ceiling and closed his eyes. He gripped her hips with both hands, the muscles in his stomach straining, and bit his lower lip.

When the pressure on her knees became too great Eleanor flipped onto her back. Before Dorian could mount her again she scrambled sideways to ensure a clear view.

She watched the mirror as he slid her legs up over his shoulders. She couldn't help it. Even this seemingly awkward position suddenly seemed like a work of art. A sculpture to be placed in a chapel or a great hall. Tinier details leapt out at her. His hands on her thighs, the way her breasts moved with his thrusts, the flexing muscles of his...

With that it was over. She climaxed with a shout, and he was right behind her. He lay on top of her for a moment, before easing to the side so as not to crush her. Their eyes met in the mirror.

"Did you like the view?" he asked.

"What do you think?"

"I think you're beautiful."

"Maybe you're right," she said. "If I am, then I'm doubly so in your hands."

CHAPTER 15

DANCE AROUND THE FIRE

DORIAN TOOK HIS TIME making his next move. As was often the case, his precision annoyed Gregory.

"It's Rope and Nine, Dor," Gregory said. "You're not leading troops into battle."

"Hmph," was Dorian's reply. He eyed the horsehair net strung between two carved wooden poles, each about a story high. He whispered over his shoulder to the martial magician serving as his Arm.

The Arm muttered under his own breath, and a dark blue fireball floated toward the net. It joined other dark blue fireballs, some light blue ones, and Gregory's green and purple ones. Each ball hovered in one of the many square spaces in the net. Dorian's new blue ball found a spot between one of its sapphire fellows and one of Gregory's purple fireballs. The object of Rope and Nine seemed simple: four in a row of one color, and enclose three of the opposing player's fireballs with the other color. Each player directed his Arm, and the magicians rarely provided advice. The conjuring of so many fireballs in colors unnatural to one's own magic required complete concentration. Dorian had chosen his colors in an effort to ease his Arm's burden. The man's magic usually assumed a shade of blue. Gregory, however, always played the royal colors. Dorian pitied Orvid Jones, whose magic usually chose a shade somewhere in the realm of fresh butter. A line of sweat dripped down Jones's brow as he forced twenty odd fireballs to hold deep purple and forest green.

"Nice move," said Gregory. He gave Orvid a few directions and a new purple ball joined the others. "You know I only play against you so I'll have new strategies to use on Raoul."

"Have you played against the Duchess? I'm sure she's a sly opponent."

Gregory glanced at Dorian, then back at the net. "Don't dance around the fire."

"All right. Are you having an affair with Sylvia Fleetwood?"

"Hold the game," Gregory said to Jones. He took a glass of wine from one of the attending servants. "I don't care to discuss it."

"Why? You've had scores of affairs."

"I've fucked scores of hookers and chambermaids. I've never had an affair." Gregory's jaw set in a hard line. "You might see fit to discuss it with my wife. After all, she is your great…friend, is she not?"

Dorian covered his nerves with a laugh. "Of course she's my friend. I've watched her grow up. Not so different from Anne Clara."

"You've never approved of my…my…all that. You raked me over the dragon's nest about it all years ago."

"I was more idealistic then." Dorian put a hand on Gregory's shoulder. "Eleanor's a friend, Gregory, but I don't envy your marriage to her. Her strident opinions and free thinking only cause you both misery. For all my own progressive philosophy, and enjoyment of Eleanor's sisterly affections, I swear by HighGod if ever I do marry I will choose a more… manageable wife. For the sake of domestic harmony."

"I begrudge you your pondering," Gregory said after a thoughtful pause, "but you stand before me a content man." He shook his head. "Yet still, she holds sway over me. Women! The life and death of every man's happiness."

And his honor, thought Dorian. He tried to count the number of lies in his little speech. Each one damned him a little more. Over the years he'd forgotten where the truth ended and the falsifications began.

"Jones!" Gregory snapped. "Look sharp, man!"

The purple and green fireballs had faded to lavender and chartreuse. Orvid shut his eyes. His jaw jutted and the fireballs burned like little Desmarais banners again. Gregory focused on Dorian again. "Speaking of marriage—"

"Are you proposing? Need I remind you, you're already taken."

"Ho. Father and I have discussed it. You've waited long enough. You need to consider a wife."

"I told you a long time ago, I've no desire to—"

"I'll be frank, Dor. What you want ceased to matter when you accepted the dukedom. It's a position that entails alliances. I want you to consider one of Prince Philippe's nieces. You must have noticed them at Sylvia's ball?"

"Of course. Everyone noticed them."

"Luscious things."

"I'm happy as I am."

Once again the camaraderie left Gregory's voice. "The Talessees are our staunchest allies. If the Prince wants one of those girls married to a Carthean duke, and I have one on hand, I see no reason to disappoint him."

Dorian had no choice. He bowed. "I am at your service, as always."

Gregory laughed, but the rough edge didn't leave his words. "It shouldn't be unpleasant. Now, shall we continue the game? I think I have you in a tight spot for once."

Dorian realized Gregory had never clarified the status of his relationship with Sylvia Fleetwood. Perhaps it best he didn't know. Ignorance of the truth negated the need for lies. He turned his eyes to the net and plotted his next move.

The courtiers could talk about nothing but the imminent demise of Dorian's long, lamented bachelorhood. Chou Chou speculated on wedding venues, and Margaret offered to teach said duke what little Talessee she'd picked up during her marriage. As for the duke himself, only Eleanor caught the constantly grinding teeth and the subtle loss of weight that always accompanied a heightening in Dorian's anxiety.

At summer's end the royal family returned to Maliana. With no end to her separation from Dorian in sight, Eleanor smothered longing and forbidden daydreams in the problem of Queen Camille's. Two more girls mysteriously left the school, bringing the total to eight. Parents with the means to feed and cloth their daughters withdrew them. The leaflets appeared each morning, seemingly from nowhere, blowing down the streets of the Fringe in a blizzard of papery denunciations.

Rosemary whispered in Eleanor's ear one LowAutumn morning as they walked the kitchen corridors of Eclatant Palace. Circles of exhaustion smudged the delicate white skin under her dark eyes. "I've spent nights walking the streets of the Fringe, yet I have seen no one upon whom to lay responsibility. The leaflets must have a magical source, but I've shared them with the Oracle herself. She senses no spell residue."

Jan trailed behind them like a reluctant sinner on the way to chapel. Eleanor listened to the sound of three skirts swishing against the marble floor as she mulled over Rosemary's comments. "Magic does seem the only way...and yet...the Oracle can't sense enchantments? You call it residue?"

Rosemary nodded. "Spells leave traces of magic behind. Even the youngest witches and magicians can see spell residue. It reveals all manner of information. Not just about the spell, but about the conjurer."

"Why can't the Oracle find the residue?"

"Remember the Ezra Oliver affair? The theft of Caleb's Horn? Magicians and witches can hide evidence of spell work from other magical folk. But even Oliver couldn't hide all spell residue from the Oracle. She found what no other conjurer could find."

"The vision that showed us the crime. The vision that swallowed Ezra Oliver."

Rosemary nodded. "She's having no such success with the leaflets."

"But this crime is still with us, Rosemary. Every night. If we could track the magic as it happens..."

Rosemary shook her head. "If this magician, or witch, is powerful enough to hide spell residue from the Oracle we won't be able to track him. Or her. Active spellwork can also be hidden." Rosemary tapped Eleanor's spectite necklace. "I managed it, and I'm no sorceress."

Eleanor absently squeezed the dragon choker. "It's not as if we can send out a pack of hounds, or have a scouting party scour the Fringe. We need magic to track magic."

Rosemary stopped in her tracks. Jan nearly stepped on the witch's ankles. "Eleanor," said Rosemary, "darling, you've got it. We need a magical being...but not a witch or a magician."

"A magical..." Eleanor's own eyes widened. "A unicorn! Could a unicorn sense the conjurer?"

"Perhaps. Now, the conjurer could hide magic from a unicorn just as easily as a magical human, but that's a different kind of spellwork. More complex, actually. No need to go to the effort...who would expect a unicorn to be roaming the Fringe in the middle of the night?"

Jan cleared her throat for the first time. "Pardon, Mum Rosemary. No one would expect it, but it'd be right hard hiding a great beast like that in the Fringe, even in the wee hours."

Eleanor put a hand on Jan's arm. "You're right. We'll have to think on it...and Gregory will have to agree, of course. Teardrop and I can't go into the city in the middle of the night without his permission any more than we could row a boat over dry land from here to the Dragon Mines." Rosemary's scowled and Eleanor gave her a reassuring smile. "Don't fret, Rosemary, I shan't rest until he agrees."

"Everyone does your bidding, Your Highness," said Jan.

"Are you sassing the princess?" Rosemary asked.

Jan's gray eyes met Eleanor's for a moment, and then slid to the floor. "No, Mum. As they should."

"Excuse us, Rosemary, for a moment." Eleanor took Jan's good arm and led her out of Rosemary's earshot. Servants scuttled past them from both directions. They clutched cleaning buckets and serving trays and the stray chamber pot.

"Jan," Eleanor said, "I know this is not what you hoped for."

"I hadn't hoped for anything, Your Highness. Never had much right to."

"Lots of girls get a start working in the kitchens. They move up. If you work hard, I hope...someday I'll be able to find something else for you. Something in line with your...talents. This is all I can do for now. The king is not...happy with me."

"Why couldn't I stay at Queen Camille's?"

"Your courses are through. You need to make a life for yourself."

"Pardon me, Your Highness. I think that's all well and good, but you're leavin' some out." Jan paused, as if waiting for Eleanor to interrupt her, before going on. "I think you need to show everyone in this city one of your girls is on a straight path."

"There is truth in your words." She took Jan's arm. "I will find something for you. Something worthwhile. I promise. Haven't I always kept my promises?"

"You have, my lady. To me anyway." Jan curtsied. Eleanor returned the gesture, waved to Rosemary, and started back down the hallway toward the kitchen.

Rosemary breathed deep. "Cinnamon. I think you'll have an apple tart for dessert this evening. Is everything all right?"

Jan once again followed behind them with her hands clasped demurely in front of her plain gray dress. "Yes," said Eleanor. "It's fine. Now, Teardrop..."

Eleanor posed her request to Gregory in the usual manner, when he was naked. She did so because lust made him more agreeable, and he could hardly stomp out the door in a huff with his royal appendages swinging in the breeze. She waited until he had spent himself before making her admittedly odd request to take Teardrop into the Fringe overnight.

He lay on his back, his chest heaving. He ran a hand through his sweat-darkened hair. "Absolutely not."

"It's the only way to find out who's behind the slander."

"Damnit, Eleanor. A Desmarais princess, and a Desmarais unicorn, hiding out in Meggett Fringe all night? Absurd!" He stood, yanked the sheet from the bed, and wrapped it around his waist.

Eleanor followed him to the fireplace. "I've done as you asked. Quiet and dignified hasn't worked." She put a hand on his back. The sweat of their lovemaking had gone cold. "Let me do this."

"No. It's too dangerous."

"Please."

"No."

She stepped between him and the fire, and the sudden warmth raised gooseflesh all over her body. He looked her up and down, and something like a wince crossed his face.

"I've rarely addressed your...outside interests," she said, "but you must know this current...friendship...is odious to me. For grievances held long before I was princess or she duchess."

"It bothers you, then."

"You owe me this small favor."

"Does it bother you? My...friendship...with your stepsister?"

"I don't know that it is a friendship. I don't know what it is."

"Answer me." He took her wrist. "Are you jealous?"

"You answer me. Will you let me go into the Fringe?"

"You're jealous."

"Will you let me take Teardrop? Will you?"

He grabbed her around the waist and walked her backwards toward the bed. Eleanor would not have thought it possible, but Gregory was quite revived. In the end, neither of them answered any of the other's questions. Eleanor never admitted to jealousy; Gregory never admitted to an affair. He did, however, clarify his change of heart before falling asleep after the unusual strain of a second session.

"Take Orvid Jones with you."

Teardrop stepped from the empty delivery carriage. Her horn brushed the ceiling of the sundry shed behind Queen Camille's. She shook out the stiffness of a cramped, thirty-minute midnight ride.

"Hush, please," Eleanor said, as Teardrop's tasseled tail whipped against an old milk bin with a *ping ping ping*! The shed smelled of thyme and molasses and pigeons.

Teardrop gingerly lifted each hoof, as if checking her own soundness. "Beg pardon," the mare said. "I've never been contained so. It's unnerving."

"We must hurry," said Orvid Jones. "A magical being has magical senses. We could be heard, or seen, or simply felt." More and more often, Jones shed his timidity and politeness when a spell needed conjuring. He hiked up the sleeves of his black cloak. "Chou? Where are you?"

Chou crawled from his hiding place in the hood of Eleanor's gray cloak. When she stroked his head a few red feather stuck to her fingers. "Are you ready, Chou?" she asked.

He flitted to Teardrop's back. "Honestly, darling, I've never been so terrified."

"You didn't need to come. Frog volunteered."

Chou spit his opinion. "Jones, let's get on with it. Before my molting renders me flightless."

Jones addressed Chou and Teardrop. "Do you both understand?"

Teardrop nodded in her matter-of-fact way. "You will put my mind inside Chou's head."

Jones nodded. "Yes. Chou, you will be...of two minds. It may be unsettling—or uncomfortable. I will stay here, in the shed with Teardrop, and control the spell. Rosemary will keep watch for you from the attic windows." The magician ran a hand down Teardrop's shiny neck. "Do you sense anything yet?"

"Nothing," said Teardrop.

"You won't have much time, Eleanor. I can only manage this spell for an hour. Maybe thirty minutes more. Cover as much ground as you can."

"Keep well hidden in the cloak," said Teardrop. "If your husband knew you were going out on the streets without Jones's protection the consequences would be unpleasant for us all."

Chou lit between Teardrop's ears and spread his wings. "Carry on." He closed his eyes. Teardrop nodded her head to the gentle rhythm of the magician's chant. Chou began to tremble and Teardrop went still. She blinked, once, twice, and then shut her own eyes. At the same moment Chou opened his.

"HighGod," said Eleanor.

Chou's yellow eyes had gone dark brown. The voice was still his own warble, but the cadence had changed, as if Chou were doing a poor job at one of his own impressions. Chou (or was it Teardrop?) shook his wings.

"They are very light." No doubt, it was Teardrop. "I always imagined them thus." The parrot took off and sailed around the storage shed before landing with a stumble on a bale of hay.

To Eleanor's surprise the brown disappeared and Chou's own bright yellow returned. "Careful! You'll damage me!"

Brown again. "I learn quickly. Fear not."

Yellow. "I'm sure you find flying quite novel, but I don't fancy hopping about for the rest of my days. Watch the wings."

Jones spoke through clenched teeth. "Chou, please…retire!"

"Until you need me. This is all very odd."

The brown returned and Teardrop shook Chou's wings again. The parrot floated across the shed and landed on Eleanor's shoulder. "Better already," said Eleanor. "Very graceful."

"Thank you," said Teardrop. The parrot crawled into Eleanor's hood. "Now let us see what we can see."

Eleanor and her feathery excuse for a unicorn wandered aimlessly for the first quarter of an hour. Eleanor hid her face in the depths of her hood. The parrot clung to her collar amidst the draping layers of wool. She wore her riding leggings. She shoved her hands into her pockets and walked in what she hoped to be a passable imitation of a man.

As she had imagined, her fellow night strollers included the more unsavory citizens of Maliana. She brushed past mumbling beggars and ratty street children. Their voices blended into a monotonous harmony of pleading.

"Alms, sir, alms, sir."

"Blessyoublessyoublessyou…"

"A coin for me brother, sir? Just a coin?"

"Blessyoublessyou…"

She offered them all the same gruff reply. "Geddout, ya buggers."

"Bugger you, you prick!" shouted one of the children.

Eleanor recognized a few of the men stumbling through the alleyways as the carpenters who had built Queen Camille's. They sang bawdy songs and professed their love for one another. Their leather boots kicked up dirty water from the puddles that never dried out in the Fringe. One man vomited amidst the piles of garbage. A squealing cat leapt from behind an old carriage wheel. The puker stumbled backwards and slipped on his own spew. The roaring laughter of his mates, and the smells of rotten trash and an equally rotten stomach, faded behind Eleanor. She turned another corner and asked Teardrop, for at least the tenth time, if she felt anything.

"Not yet. Maybe if we—" The parrot in Eleanor's hood stiffened. "Go east. Toward the river."

Eleanor quickened her pace to a clipping walk. Suddenly Chou's voice sounded in her ear. The real Chou.

"Don't bounce so."

"I'm sorry, but this isn't meant to be a pleasure ride."

"No, I mean...you must stride. Think. Have you ever seen Dorian bounce?"

She adjusted her pace. "Point taken. Now retreat!"

The next words out of the parrot's mouth told her Teardrop had returned. "I must fly. Let me out."

"No, I don't think you should—"

The parrot slipped from Eleanor's hood with a brush of slick feathers against her neck. The bird wobbled in the air for a moment, and then Teardrop got control of Chou's wings. She (or he) disappeared into the darkness before Eleanor could finish her thought. Eleanor leaned against a damp wall and crossed her arms over her chest. She inhaled the scent of mold and smoke, and strained for any sounds or sights of note. Nothing but rows of shacks, cold cobblestones, and the occasional flicker of a lonely candle in an unpaned window. A grunting caught her attention, but it proved to be nothing more than another drunk having a last minute poke at some equally tipsy lady. Both spilled from the alleyway on her right. The man gave his beloved a squeeze and a slap on the rear and they went their separate ways. Eleanor started across the cobblestones to see if she could pick out Chou's red back amidst the thatched roofs. She didn't make it far. The parrot came flying at her head with the speed of a deftly hurled apple.

"Behind that cottage. A man, in a dark cloak. Like yours, only longer. Hurry!"

Eleanor adjusted her hood and crossed the street. She pressed against the clapboard and mud cottage. The walls were cold under her fingers. She heard one of the inhabitants snoring inside. The wind off the Clarity River skipped past her feet. It carried the smell of low tide mud, and a few flipping pieces of paper. White paper. Two, three, a dozen pieces of white paper.

She peered around the corner of the cottage. A figure walked toward her from the direction of the Clarity Dockworks, a quarter mile in the distance. She couldn't see his features, or make out his build, for he was as heavily cloaked as she. His build...or hers?

Eleanor's face went clammy as she remembered Rosemary and Marcus's argument last fall. *A man in a hood...something in his manner bothers me...skulking...*

The parrot squirmed in her cloak. Two voices jittered in her ear as Teardrop and Chou fought for space inside his walnut-sized head.

"Under the cloak, I see gray light...there is great power there...gray light."

"Ouch, Teardrop, you're hurting me!"

"Gray light. I have seen it before—"

"I'm afraid, Eleanor...we should go back!"

Eleanor peered farther around the corner and the figure stopped. She sensed his eyes on her...for now she knew it was a him.

Gray light. Gray light.

The parrot bit her ear. Teardrop. "He sees us. He knows."

Chou again. "Who? What—"

"He knows, Eleanor. Go, now!"

Eleanor heeded her unicorn. She ran.

She didn't stop until she reached Queen Camille's. Teardrop's voice had increasingly given way to Chou's terrified squawking. Eleanor blessed the light in the school's highest window. Rosemary met her at the gate.

Eleanor made a straight line for the shed. She opened the door and stepped across the threshold. As soon as he saw her, Jones sat and rested his forehead against one bony knee. She laid a hand on his trembling shoulder.

"I'm sorry. Were we late?" she asked.

"No, the spell taxed me more than it should have. There is magic here. Magic that takes up space."

Eleanor knew the atmosphere could only support so much magic in a given time and space. The more powerful the conflicting spells, the weaker some must become.

Chou burst from her hood and fell to the dirt floor, spewing feathers in his wake. "Chou!" Eleanor cried. "Are you hurt?"

"I fear my head might burst."

Teardrop leaned over him with clear brown eyes. She snuffled along his plump body. "I've left your head. It is wholly your domain again."

Chou righted himself and shook. "Lady Mare, I would rather keep my head to myself, but if I had to share it with anyone, I'm honored it was you."

Rosemary knelt beside Eleanor. "Are you hurt, dearest? I've never seen you move so fast. Not even as a child running from your stepmother."

Eleanor rested her elbows on her thighs. A thin bead of sweat trickled down her back. She asked Teardrop to stand watch in the courtyard. As Teardrop left the barn, Rosemary took Eleanor's hand. "Do we need protection? What did you see?"

"You'll be relieved to know your mysterious nighttime visitor was no spook," said Eleanor. "Ezra Oliver is not nearly so dead as we all assumed."

CHAPTER 16

NO BETTER THAN A WHORE

ELEANOR SAT ON HER bed. Hardly unusual, for she sat on it every day. Odd, however, for said bed to find itself in the middle of a meadow on an early summer morning. It was in fact the end of LowAutumn, two weeks past Eleanor's twenty-sixth birthday, and two days after her night on the streets of Meggett Fringe.

Eleanor inhaled the scent of a recent rain and ran her fingers over the damp blue coverlet. "This never fails to amaze me," she said to Rosemary in the chair beside the bed.

Rosemary nodded. "These dream visits can be unsettling. How does one know when it ends?"

"I could follow bad advice from my sleeping self." Eleanor swatted at a biting gnat. She missed and the tiny creature's buzzing filled her ears. "It's true to life, anyway. When will she arrive?"

"I am here." A witch sat in the deep grass, beside a pool of dark water. She watched ripples and reflections on the pool's surface with the intent gaze of a hungry frog after a skittering waterbug. Hazelbeth, the Oracle of Afar Creek Abbey, wrapped in the same piles of dragon robes

Eleanor had first noticed at age ten, on the eve of her father's death. Perhaps Hazelbeth had lent some of her own immortality to the furs.

Eleanor always wondered how anyone could be so old and wizened and continue to breathe, let alone interpret the messages of the Watching Pool. Hazelbeth's eyes reminded Eleanor that the witch was very much alive inside her decrepit body. Yellow where they should be white, the irises faded to a non-color, but as sharp as Teardrop's horn.

"You should have come to me," Hazelbeth said, in a voice like a blacksmith's file on a thick hoof. "I hate to disturb the pool."

Eleanor did not see how the pool could be disturbed in a dream, but she'd learned such questions never had rational answers. "Beg pardon, wise one. Rosemary keeps a connection to me, from long ago, and called to you in my sleep. Prince Gregory forbade me from visiting you. He and the king refuse to hear our story. He does not believe Ezra Oliver could return from the dead after seven years."

"He was most obviously not dead."

Eleanor couldn't hide her frustration. "Where has be been? What could he possibly have been doing all this time?"

"I cannot comprehend how he survived, much less where he's been."

Eleanor nodded. Ezra Oliver had fallen into a puddle of water taken from the Watching Pool itself and disappeared into his own vision. The Oracle, and all other magical scholars, had long since declared him dead. No witch or magician in history had ever transfered a living body from one location to another via magic. All attempts had failed. Many mortally so.

"...it could have taken him years to find a way out of ...wherever he was," Hazelbeth continued. "To make his way home. Are you sure it is him?"

"Teardrop was familiar with his magic before he disappeared. Could there be another magician who conjures gray magic?"

The Oracle sunk into the robes until Eleanor thought she might suffocate.

"No. You see simple gray, but magical beings see a rainbow as unique as your face. If Teardrop says it is Oliver's light, it must be." Hazelbeth emerged from the hood like a rabbit from its burrow. The pond whipped itself into tiny tidal waves. "How is this possible? I cannot see," the old woman said.

Eleanor had never known the Oracle to show the slightest emotion, for the good or bad. She found no reassurance in Hazelbeth's agitation.

"What shall we do, wise one?" asked Rosemary.

"He will have recognized Teardrop in the bird. He'll hide from non-human magical beings." Hazelbeth looked up and the pool quieted. "Speak with Orvid Jones. I have watched him, and heard of his goodliness. Tell him he must find a way to track Oliver. I will set my own sorceresses on the task as well. For so many seasons, I have watched the joys and sorrows of a thousand worlds in a thousand whens. I have never seen the likes of this. To enter a vision and return unharmed… perhaps more powerful than before…"

The pool resumed its restless bubbling.

"What do you think Oliver wants?" Eleanor asked Rosemary.

Rosemary squeezed her hand. "Whatever he wants, it seems to start at Queen Camille's."

"Perhaps he's trying to take revenge on me through the school."

"He's succeeding. Two more families withdrew their daughters this week."

"Dragonshit!" said Eleanor, before catching herself. She blushed, but the dark water held Hazelbeth's attention. "My tongue never ceases to waltz off with me."

Rosemary gave her a wan smile. "Prepare to catch it now, dearest. Jan has returned to the Red-headed Hussy."

The next day Eleanor rose hours before the sun, donned her riding leggings, and met Orvid Jones in the royal stables. Jones magically shortened her hair and turned it a carroty ginger. She collected a mount and paid off the sleepy grooms with a small bag of coins and a promise to take the blame should anyone discover her ruse. The grooms blessed her and swore a flock of drunken fairies could not drag her secret from their lips. One boy loaned her his cloak.

Dorian had promised to exhaust Gregory. They'd had spent a hard night at the sharpstick table after a long day's hunt. Gregory hadn't appeared in Eleanor's bedchamber. She prayed he wouldn't choose this one morning to wake early and without a hangover.

The guard noted her groom's cloak and the papers with the princess's seal and granted her easy exit. After an almost pleasant ride through cool darkness, she stood on the wide white porch of the Red-headed Hussy. Candles burned in the sconces on either side of the ornate Fire-iron door. She exhaled a foggy breath and inhaled the scent of cinnamon. She rang the bell.

A bleary-eyed guard, roughly the size of a smallish ogre, opened the door. "Watchya, boy?"

"I'm here to see Pandra."

"Pandra's sleeping! Go home to your mum!"

Eleanor put a hand on the door. "Tell her Eleanor Desmarais wants to see her."

"The princess? Where?"

Eleanor held up one hand. The Desmarais crest flashed on her Fire-iron wedding ring. "Here."

The man's eyes showed a hint of life. "Well, come in anyway, with that sparkler."

He showed Eleanor to the red sitting room and offered her a drink. She declined, and he excused himself. Ten minutes later Pandra opened the door. She cinched her crimson dressing robe and closed the door behind her.

"Your Highness," Pandra said as she curtsied. "I wish you'd prepared me for your visit. How frightful I must look!" She twirled a lock of messy red hair around her fingers.

"I hadn't planned on visiting. Ever."

"Oh, pooh," said Pandra. "So serious. You've been spending too much time with our dear dour duke." She flopped into a velvet chair and propped one bare foot on a black cowhide ottoman. "Your disgust cuts me to the quick. I could show you, if you like, just why men like your Dorian find this place so appealing. I don't discriminate."

Eleanor's temper flared. "Bring Jan to me. I know she's here." Eleanor was so angry she felt tears sting her eyes. "I told you to stay away from my girls!"

"As you said last year, once your girls are grown they can make their own choices. Jan came on her own. You mustn't have presented her with many options." Pandra pursed her lips. "Dirty dishes…or powerful men? Not a hard choice…"

"I needed time…I told her…bring her to me!"

"I'm here, Your Highness."

Jan stood in the open doorway. Her hair rolled in loose, clean waves over her shoulders. She wore a gorgeous lavender nightdress, embroidered with ribbons and Fire-iron threading. Eleanor might have worn such on her wedding night. The bell sleeves hid her stump.

"Why did you come here?" Jan asked. "The prince won't like it."

Eleanor crossed the room. "Jan, please, you must come back to Eclatant."

"The kitchen maids are horrible to me. They say I think I'm better than them…being that I can read and write." She held up her good hand, revealing an angry red blister. "One spilled tea on me. Meant it, she did."

"It will only be for a few more days. Maybe a few weeks. I'll talk with Gregory. We'll bring you into the nursery. You don't want this life."

"What do you know of this life? You say you had some troubles in your young days. Maybe you did, but you always had a roof, and food."

"I've never claimed to understand what you've been through."

"I'll be safe here. Pandra wants to teach me to run this place."

"Ask Pandra what the townsfolk whisper when she walks by. Ask her if she can hold her head high. How often she leaves this house. It's a prison."

Eleanor heard Pandra gasp from behind her. "How dare you—"

"Better a beautiful prison than a kitchen closet," said Jan, "or the underside of a bridge."

"I won't let it come to that for you, Jan. Not ever!"

"Stop it!" Jan stepped away. "Stop...acting like you care! You just don't want anyone to know your first pupil is a whore!"

"I do care! Why are you saying these things?"

Tears spilled from Jan's eyes. "You want to keep an eye on me... because I know your secret. You're no better than a whore yourself!"

Eleanor could not have been more shocked if Jan had hit her upside the head with a bottle of Pandra's best red wine. Jan had offended even Pandra's hardened sensibilities. The madam pushed past Eleanor. She took the girl by her upper arm. "Jan! Enough!"

Jan tried to cover her face with her stump, but it didn't quite do the job. She spoke from behind the curtain of her gorgeous hair.

"You have the prince. You have the palace, and your children. You have everything anyone could want." Pandra let go of Jan's arm and she brushed the hair back from her face. "Why do you have to have him, too?"

"Oh, Jan, if only I could explain."

"It's not fair."

"Come back. Please."

Jan shook her head. "I'm staying."

Eleanor's heart fell into her stomach, but she recognized the futility of arguing with Jan. She kissed the girls tearstained cheeks. "You'll always have a place at Eclatant."

Pandra gently pushed Jan out the door and closed it behind her. Eleanor's hair tickled the back of her neck. As Orvid's spell wore off, it crept past her ears. "Make me two promises," she said to Pandra. "If ever she leaves here, you will tell me."

Pandra nodded.

"And send her…" Eleanor swallowed. "…gentlemen…if there are such in this place."

"There are. You know one well yourself." Pandra backtracked. "Not that I would send him to her…or that he would accept such an invitation."

Eleanor walked toward the door. She paused at Pandra's voice.

"We will keep your secret. We must, for all our sakes."

Unlike pricy hookers, kitchen maids are not known for their discretion. Soon all of Eclatant, from the butlers to the baronesses, was abuzz with the news that Princess Eleanor's prodigy, her favorite student, had moved into the Redheaded Hussy. Chou caught Sylvia discussing the topic with a matched pair of white carriage horses. With the Harvest Fest looming and the out-of-town aristocracy descending on the palace, the news traveled across the country like a spate of bad weather. Anne Clara Finley Tavish, Dorian's sister, sent Eleanor a message via private courier.

Dearest Princess Eleanor,

I regret to say that news of your pupil's fall from grace has reached the Lake District. The tide of opinion, amongst both our own class and the commoners, is decidedly against you. I pray you take care, for the enmity does not have the feel of everyday gossip. While I would never suppose to force my opinions on you, I ask you to consider closing the school. You position is, as we both know, precarious.

Yours with love and deepest respect,
Anne Clara F. Tavish

The next day, at a lavish picnic on the south garden, Eleanor handed Anne Clara's note to Dorian.

"Ridiculous," he said. "If the king forces a closing, so be it." He crumpled the note and threw it into a fountain. It shriveled and sunk beneath the lily pads. Black ink dissipated into the water.

Chou spoke from Eleanor's shoulder. "What a mess Ezra Oliver has set upon us."

"He spread bad humor with his leaflets," Eleanor said, "but he didn't entice Jan and the other girls into the bordellos."

Chou landed on Dorian's head. "I'd not put it past him."

"Good morning, Your Highness. What a day!" Sylvia appeared as if out of thin air, as she often did. So much entertaining had taught her the art of quick conversational entries and exits. She swept a low curtsy, and bounced upright. Everything about her bounced. Her loosely curled hair, her flouncy deep purple skirts, her white cleavage.

"Your Grace," said Eleanor.

"*Your* Grace," said Sylvia to Dorian.

"Forgive me if I say hello and goodbye." Dorian walked away without bowing. Chou clung to his hair. Eleanor just caught the bird's whispered profanities, something about a nosy bitch.

"Such a charming man," said Sylvia. "Don't you agree?"

"Excuse me."

Sylvia hopped into Eleanor's path. "You're in quite a spot, sister. All of Cartheigh says you've turned our poorest girls into our richest whores."

Eleanor had tolerated Sylvia's slights to her character, and her calculated stalking of

Gregory, but she couldn't stand by while her stepsister tossed her students into the streets for spite and personal gain. ""I'm sure you've been at the helm of the ship. You think Gregory will turn against me if everyone else does."

Sylvia's face fell into a look eerily reminiscent of the monstrous

Imogene of Eleanor's childhood nightmares. "He's turned on you before."

"My son is the future king. My daughter is the princess." Eleanor leaned down into Sylvia's face. *In those days I looked up at Imogene.* The thought added strength to her words. Her voice crept up in volume.

"Gregory may be a drunk. He may be a cad. But he loves Nathan and Leticia. And I won't let anything come between my children and their birthright."

"How dare you speak so about His Highness. You're an uppity bitch. You always have been." Sylvia planted her hands on her hips.

"And I always will be." Eleanor stormed across the lawn.

Gregory stepped out from the crowd a whispering elderly woman. He took Eleanor's arm and steered her toward the dining tables. "You're making a scene. Not wise, given that everyone is already talking about you."

"Let them talk. Let them listen to your…your…whore…or whatever she is!"

Whore, whore, whore. Is there any other word in HighGod's sweet world?

"Don't direct your frustration at innocent bystanders."

She laughed, a high bitter sound, at the thought of Sylvia's persecuted innocence.

He stopped. "Don't laugh at me."

Eleanor could barely speak for her helpless giggling. "Blameless! Unsullied!"

"Take hold of yourself!"

Eleanor went to wipe the tears of hilarity that had streamed down her face, but another fit of sniggering caught her.

Gregory silenced her with a slap across her wet cheek. She sucked in a harsh breath, and heard echoing gasps rise from the little clusters of people around her.

"I told you to stop laughing," Gregory said.

She couldn't speak. In all these years, through many battles that had raged far longer and fiercer than this one, Gregory had never hit her.

He left Eleanor alone with her stinging cheek, and crossed the lawn. Sylvia still stood beside the marble fountain. The water shooting from its spout enveloped her dark head in a misty halo. She curtsied as Gregory approached. He took her arm and led her to a knot of High Council members. She smiled her beguiling smile, and never looked in Eleanor's direction.

Dorian, however, stared at Eleanor over Raoul's shoulder. His face was as stiff and white as a freshly laundered handkerchief. Margaret appeared at Eleanor's side, as if drawn by one of Ezra Oliver's infamous blood paths.

"We'll visit the nursery," Margaret said loudly. "The children will have finished lunch."

Eleanor followed her at a stiff-legged walk. Hundreds of eyes bored into the back of her head. Margaret led her to the nursery, as if she did not know the way herself.

On the second morning of the Harvest Fest, Dorian rose early, as he always did, and made his way to the Great Hall to ascertain which of the day's events required his presence. Servants had decked the walls with orange, yellow, and brown silk tapestries and banners, and a quartet of magicians plunked and whistled in one corner, but no one was about to enjoy the décor or the tunes. Apprentice magicians wandered to and fro, juggling dozens of pumpkins and adjusting enchanted, dancing scarecrows so they kept time with the ever-changing music. It seemed most of the courtiers had enjoyed themselves a bit too much at the previous evening's opening celebration.

Dorian blessed their collective gluttony and left the Great Hall behind for the library. He'd finished a recent biography of Ezra Oliver, and wanted to examine older texts on the infamous magician.

Maybe Eleanor will be there. A chance meeting.

He spun his spectite ring around his finger. She'd taken to lighting it at random times, as it had been over two months since their last liaison. Dorian had slunk to Pandra's just last week, before the news of Jan's return to the Hussy. He thanked HighGod for that small favor. He didn't know if his pride could stand another chance meeting with her.

When he entered the library, he found it deserted. Not a browser in sight, princess or otherwise. He pulled a few likely looking volumes on Ezra Oliver and the reigns of the last three kings from the shelves. He took a seat at the table he and Eleanor had once shared with the long-dead Christopher Roffi. He pictured the three of them arguing about Svelyan Fire-iron trade policy. Dorian and Roffi watching Eleanor with the same hunger. Eleanor unaware of her own loveliness.

He'd had no spark from his ring this morning, so he took a moment and sent his love her way. After all these years he could raise the broom closet memory and light the spectite with little effort. It was like breathing.

He opened the first book to a random page and read the caption beneath the engraving.

Gregory Desmarais, to be Gregory the Second, son of His Majesty King Casper and Marie Theresa Smithwick Desmarais. Based on a portrait painted in his fifteenth year, Desmarais Three-Hundred and Fifteen.

Dorian ran a hand over the portrait. Three-Fifteen, the year he'd met the prince. Bits of memories flitted around his head, most of them soaked in booze, all of them soaked in laughter. Then the more poignant ones...the deaths of Gregory's sister and mother, and the endless battles with his father...Gregory standing up for Dorian in the Council Hall, and quietly providing for Dorian's needs when Abram Finley reduced his stipend for one petty reason or another. Dorian rested his forehead on both hands.

With every passing season the weight of his deception aged him. For weeks he would detest Gregory. Want to kill him him, out of jealousy and disgust at his treatment of Eleanor. His drunken, juvenile antics humiliated the crown and wounded Dorian's considerable national pride. Dorian needed to shake him. Scream in his face.

And then, in an instant, Gregory would make him laugh, or bestow some new honor upon him. Dorian's emotions would turn, infantrymen doing an about face, and his own treachery came into stark relief.

I take what he gives me. Power. Riches. I lie to his face every day. And in a whisper, *I fuck his wife.*

Guilt turned the one sacred thing in his life seedy. He'd never been able to talk to Eleanor about his friendship (if the word could be reasonably applied) with Gregory. It was, aside from his love for her, the most complex aspect of his life. Maybe more complex.

What can I do? What can I do?

He'd asked himself that question innumerable times, and had yet to come up with any answer.

"Find something interesting?"

Gregory took the chair across from him. Dorian closed the book. "Nothing I can't recite by heart."

Eleanor's bruised face seemed to hover between them. Both men ignored it, like two polite museum patrons turning away from bad art. Dorian couldn't raise the topic. Couldn't appear to care too much.

Can't defend her. He wished he could shut out his devious, murmuring mind as easily as he'd put aside the portrait. He cleared his throat and focused on the here and now. Gregory, awake and dressed before noon following a Fest celebration. In the library, no less.

He held up a thick tome emblazoned with the royal crest. "Are you in need of morning inspiration?"

"You know better than that. I have need of you."

"I'm at your service. As long as it doesn't involve any husband hungry Talessee maidens."

Gregory humored him with a snort. "That's a discussion for another day. I need you down at the Clarity Dockworks. We've found three of the girls who disappeared from Queen Camille's."

"That's a positive development."

"One would think. However, the fact that all three are dead is distinctly negative."

Dorian slumped in his own chair. He and Gregory regarded each other across the table like overtired children. "Who would want to kill three girls?"

"I don't know. Dockmen found them under the canal bridge. Tied together. Looked to have been strangled. All three as gussied up as any of Pandra's lasses."

Dorian thought of Jan and panicked. "Are they from Pandra's?"

"No, you know all of Pandra's girls wear red corsets. Virginal white on these ladies. From one of the other hothouses, I assume."

"HighGod, Eleanor will be devastated."

"She will, but three dead girls? Turned to hookers on the crown's coin? We can't ignore it. Maybe we shouldn't ignore it."

Gregory's brush with morality annoyed Dorian, but as he needed to keep the peace (and couldn't claim the precipice of the moral hilltop himself) he let the comment lie.

"Question the dockmen," said Gregory. "See if you recognize the girls. Eleanor will want to go down there, but I won't allow it. It's not fitting, and it will only upset her further." Gregory sat straighter, and Dorian didn't like the squint in the prince's eyes.

"I'll speak with her about it." Gregory wagged a finger under Dorian's nose. "You put your mind on the crime, not on commiseration. It's not your place."

Dorian lips moved, but his teeth clenched together, like a soldier biting a leather strap during an amputation. "As you wish."

Gregory stood and Dorian followed him, as he always did. As they left the library, Gregory turned in the direction of Eleanor's room. He called one last command over his shoulder. "Take Orvid Jones with you. He has a knack for these things."

Dorian and Orvid Jones slid down the embankment beside the ancient Pontefore Bridge. The stone passageway, a relic of the days of the Malian kings, crossed the Clarity River on the north end of the Clarity River Dockworks. Wooden barges, some no bigger than horse carts and some the length of a jousting pitch, jostled each other for slips along a half mile of wooden piers. The barges deposited all manner of commerce at the Dockworks, from raw Fire-iron to raw turnips, and picked up whatever goods Maliana had to offer to the northern and southern towns. The Dockworks abutted Meggett Fringe, so the Pontefore Bridge had no need for grandeur. It got little use beyond farmers come to sell their wares, or country folk looking for work on the docks. Citizens of worth and foreign visitors came in and out of the city via Caleb the Second's Ironway, a gracefully carved Fire-iron structure two miles south of the Dockworks.

Dorian's leather riding boots didn't provide much purchase on the sliding mud and gravel. Twice he braced himself against the cold dirt. He regained his balance and wiped mud on his leggings. If he was going to smell like a dead fish, he'd rather the stench emanate from his clothes than his skin.

He and Jones reached the rocky beach at the bottom of the hill. Dorian scraped his boots along a chunk of granite, a dislodged piece of the crumbling bridge above him. Senné navigated the hill in three easy hops. He snuffed his master's leggings and his muzzle wrinkled. "A human garbage smell."

"Mister Jones!" A slight man in the dark blue shortcoat of Maliana's Constabulary called to them from under the bridge. He bore an uncanny resemblance to the Chief Magician. The same bright brown eyes, the same sharp Adam's apple, the same receding chin. When he smiled he even had the same bucked teeth.

"Hello, Henry," Jones said. "Your Grace, meet Henry Buck, my great-nephew."

The two men appeared to be the same age of roughly thirty. Henry laughed as he bowed. "Smashing to meet you, Your Grace. Quite a fine form you cut on this grungy beach. As for me, I'll look older than Uncle Orvid by next year. T'ain't fair for a sixty-year-old man to be so sprightly."

"Magic is the elixir of youth, Son," Jones said.

"Aye. What's the saying? A magician comes of age at fifty, while a common man hopes he can still cum." The constable slapped his leg at his own joke.

Jones scowled at him. "Henry, now, now. Remember your company. Not just Lord Brandling, but…" He pointed in the direction of a canvas tarp. Gray against the gray beach.

"Forgive me…forgive me." Henry shook his head and scowled. "This way, please."

Dorian has seen death more times than he could count, and had been responsible for it on several occasions, but for some reason he nearly lost his breakfast when Henry removed the tarp. Three girls rested on one another as if sharing secrets. Bluish skin. Stiff limbs. Lank hair. A purplish ring wound around each one's throat. The stomach twisting smell of death hovered around them, not yet powerful enough to override the smell of the river.

"Cover them," Dorian said as he turned away.

"Do you recognize them?" asked Jones.

"One," said Dorian. "Milla something. She has a younger sister at Queen Camille's. The others…I'm not sure. Red hair on the one girl…I'm sure Eleanor will know."

"You look pale," said Senné.

Dorian coughed, embarrassed. "I'm fine." *Girls...not even real women. And what they must have been doing since they left the school...*

"I'll feel around for spellwork," said Jones.

Dorian and Senné retreated, to give Jones room and Dorian air. Light seeped from the magician's fingers, melted butter enchantments. Henry lit a tattered brown cigarette. Normally Dorian disliked the smell of smoking weed, but it was better than the alternative. Tiny waves licked at the pebbles under his feet with a sound like a battalion of grandfathers slurping soup.

After a half an hour of magical perusal, Jones had found nothing. Dorian could see the frustration in his wrinkled brow.

"Maybe they weren't killed by magic," said Henry. "Maybe just thugs. Whores get the short end of a bad drunk all the time."

"There are no thugs in the pricy hothouses," said Dorian. "You'd be hard pressed to find better security at Eclatant. Besides, look at them, laid out like an evening meal. Someone wanted them to be found here." He wiped his damp brow with his handkerchief. "I'll send someone to collect the bodies for burial."

"Can't do that, Your Grace," said Henry. "The plague ordinance."

"Surely it doesn't count in this case."

"You know the rules. King Casper's awful worried about that plague killin' all those people in the far southern kingdoms. It could come across the Southern Sea on a boat and right up the Clarity to Maliana. All bodies found within a mile of the Dockworks—"

"Must be burned as a preventative measure," said Dorian. "Don't lecture me on the rules, Mister Buck, as I wrote the treatise myself."

Perhaps Jones sensed Dorian's irritation, for he suggested they leave Buck to the bodies and his grim duties. Dorian and Jones clambered back up the embankment. Senné passed them midway and waited on the gravel road leading to the Pontefore Bridge.

"Let me apologize for my kinsman," said Jones. He put his hands on his hips and caught his breath. "The Constabulary...are a notoriously crude...lot."

"I thought magical folk put aside their familial relations once claimed by a Covey. Or an Abbey," said Dorian.

"Most do. In my case, however, I've often crossed paths with my relations. All the men in my family have been Constables. I wanted to be one myself. Badly. I somehow hid my magical abilities until age eight. A late arrival at the Covey. Of course, magical learning proved more appealing than a life chasing murderers and thieves."

"Why should you cross paths with the Constabulary more than any other magician?"

"All those years of hiding my magic made me quite adept at it. And hence, adept at finding the hidden magic of others."

Gregory's words made sense to Dorian. "A talent the Constabulary finds useful."

Senné joined the conversation with his usual forthrightness. "Your talent for finding is not as great as Ezra Oliver's for hiding."

"You're right, my horned friend. His talents exceed mine a hundred-fold. In this case, however, I will use logic. The simple fact that I can discern no magic in this crime leads me to believe Oliver responsible for it. Do you sense anything?"

Senné took a deep breath. "I feel no magic. Not a trace."

"Yet here are these girls, from Queen Camille's, dead not a hundred yards from the spot where Eleanor saw Oliver. I agree with Jones. Whether with magic means or common violence, Oliver killed them."

"We have no proof," said Senné in his maddeningly rational way. "The king does not believe Oliver had returned."

"All the more reason we must find a way to track him. Jones, you say you have a talent. Gregory calls it a knack. Whatever it is, use it, man."

CHAPTER 17

CAUGHT PIG

ELEANOR FOLLOWED HER CHILDREN across the fairgrounds. She trotted to keep up. A corridor of soldiers framed the royal entourage. Gregory, Dorian, and Rosemary walked behind Eleanor, while Vigor, Teardrop, and Senné brought up the rear. It was like being inside a living, mobile treasure chest. Nathan and Ticia were the valuables, to be protected at all costs.

"Tish!" Eleanor called out to her six-year-old daughter. "Slow down, darling."

Ticia looked over her shoulder with a wicked grin. She ran faster. "Hurry, Nathan!"

Nathan returned to Eleanor and grabbed her hand. "Run, Mother! I want to see the goats. And the cows. And the jugglers!"

"I'm coming, Your Highness!" Air rushed in and out of Eleanor's lungs. She tried to expel some of the tightness in her chest.

She always looked forward to the annual Guild Council Harvest Fair. With the witches' help, the Guildsmen erected all manner of tents and amusements. For three days the townsfolk who could spare the few pennies admission flocked to the grassy cow pastures on the edge of Afar Creek. Change purses jiggled at the chance to sample the Guildsmen's wares and the witches' produce at Harvest Fair prices.

The fields bustled with yelling, laughing children and their dickering parents. The witches kept up a stream of family friendly magical entertainment, most of it focused on disappearing rabbits and exploding floral bouquets. The local farmers brought their finest animals to be appraised by a fat Godsman in the livestock judging. A powerful odor of cow manure wafted from the stock tent and collided with the scent of baking sweet buns. Over it all hung an achingly bright sky. Eleanor believed HighGod reserved that particular shade of blue for warm MidAutmn days in southern Cartheigh.

Fine weather or not, Eleanor had decided against the Harvest Fair outing last night when Gregory brought the news of the murdered girls. He made an attempt to comfort her, but she begged him to leave her in peace. She even dismissed Chou Chou. She bade the nanny help the children to bed, although she joyously took up that task herself on leisurely evenings. She had a good fierce cry at her desk and went to bed with the full intention of spending fair day at Queen Camille's.

Nathan and Ticia's ecstatic faces peeking through the bedcurtains with the morning sun had changed Eleanor's mind. She ached for the three dead girls, but here were her own little ones, so often at the whim of her frantic schedule. Fair day granted them a rare chance to leave the palace grounds. Run and skip and scream like other children. She rubbed her swollen eyes, hugged each skinny little body, and promised to hurry through breakfast.

Now, as she ran across the crisp autumn grass toward the banner-bedecked fair gate, she blessed her decision. Best to give it a day, to clear her mind, so she could approach the situation rationally. She'd greeted a wan-faced Rosemary with a tight embrace and a quick, *we-shall-talk-about-it-tomorrow.*

Eleanor squeezed Nathan's hand. *Today is for my babies.*

She made it so, as much as she could. She cheered Nathan through the childrens' archery tournament and held Ticia's hair as she bobbed for apples. She spent a smelly hour in the livestock barn. Nathan wandered the goat pens while she chatted with farmers and the animals with the brainpower to respond.

"I like the goats, Mother," Nathan said. "They look at me as if they know what I'm thinking."

A pair of twin goat-kids nibbled at the seat of his leggings as he spoke. "Ya got something yummy?" they asked in unison. "Yummy?"

"Ouch!" Nathan clapped his hands over his bottom.

"That's what you get, hobnobbing with those beasts." Ticia thought herself quite above goats. "Cricket would never bite my rear end."

"She might, little princess, if Nathan hides a carrot in your petticoats." Gregory leaned on the rickety fence with a mug of ale in one hand.

Vigor stretched his long neck over the fence. He snuffled at Nathan's reddish hair. "Come, Your Highness. There's no air in here. We shall suffocate on goat gas."

The kids' mother blew a raspberry at Vigor. He snorted in disgust and high-stepped it out of the barn, and so it went for several hours. Dorian searched the fairgrounds for an unbeatable game or contest. As usual, he did not succeed in not succeeding. He shot down towers of cups with a wooden arrow. He pitched lemons through a hole in a tapestry. He struck a mallet to a lever and Eleanor craned her neck to watch the marker ching off the Fire-iron bell. A fruiter flung melons into the air, three and four at a time, and he sliced them cleanly in half before they hit the ground. Eleanor lost track of which dolls and toy soldiers and sweetmeats Dorian won at each game. Ticia and Nathan thrust the prizes into her arms. The children followed their uncle and gave him pointers.

"Brilliant, as always," said Gregory.

"Hmm," Eleanor replied.

Gregory called to the fruiter, "You, man. And your lady."

The fruiter and his wife knelt before Gregory. "Take those trinkets from the princess," Gregory said. "Deliver them to our carriage."

"Yes, Your Highness, an honor."

Eleanor smiled at them. "Are you certain you can carry this load?"

Neither one responded, or looked at her. She tried again. "Do you have children of your own? Please, we have more than enough prizes. Won't you—"

"Thank you, Your Highness," the fruiter said. "You're most kind, but our children ain't in need of anything. We'll take the prizes to your carriage all right."

Eleanor handed off the toys and candies. She took her change purse from her pocket. "For your trouble."

The man and woman exchanged nervous glances. "No thank—"

Gregory stepped between Eleanor and his subjects. "Take it. HighGod bless you."

"And you, sire, bless you." The fruiter and his wife bowed and beat a path for the arched gate.

"Not the friendliest lot, those," said Gregory.

Eleanor gave him a stiff smile. The fruiter and his wife only called attention to the disturbing trend she'd noticed in the Fringe months ago. The people of Maliana, who'd always sought her blessing and shouted her name, wanted little to do with her. Their collective coldness crept around her feet and up under her skirts. During the past four Harvest Fairs she'd spent several hours clasping hands and accepting flowers, but not today. No one called out to the Glass Slipper Princess. Of course no one would ever show her anything but the utmost respect, but for the first time she sensed no love behind the deference.

Eleanor had always felt more kinship with common folk than with her well-born peers at court. The thought of life without the people's love unnerved her. She had a brief picture of a door coming loose from its hinges.

Nathan appeared at her feet. "Mother! Come! Uncle Dorian is going to wrestle a pig!"

Gregory's eyebrows shot toward his hairline. "That's something I'd like to see."

Gregory and Eleanor followed Nathan to a fenced paddock. Ticia and Dorian stood beside the gate. Ticia yanked at Dorian's tunic. "Please, Uncle."

Dorian laughed. "No, child. This is one contest I'll not take part in."

Eleanor and Gregory peered over the fence. A half-year pig, about the height of one setter and the width of four, stalked the muddy enclosure. The pig kicked up its back legs and grunted insults at the crowd. "Can't catch me…long armed monkeys…*giveitatryi'llsquashya*…"

"What's the game, Tish?" asked Gregory.

"The man who catches that pig and sticks him in that sack wins that baby goat." She pointed at the bleating white creature tied to one of the fence posts.

"You don't like goats."

"I like that one. He's small, and rather precious…and Nathan wants him, Poppa. Nathan wants the goat."

"There are goats at Eclatant, Nathan."

"Yes, sir," said Nathan. He kicked the fencepost, but he didn't complain.

Gregory squinted at the goat. "That is a fine-looking animal."

"It is," said Dorian. "Coat as white as snow."

"Horns like tiny daggers," added Eleanor.

Gregory called to the man in charge. "How many have tried to best your pig?"

"Eight, Your Highness. He's a wicked 'un. Sacks never touched him."

"Let us see about that."

Eleanor's mouth fell open as Gregory climbed into the pen. She thought he'd offer to buy the goat, but apparently he planned to procure the animal for his son the old-fashioned way.

Gregory stripped his tunic over his head and handed it to Dorian. He stood in the center of the pigpen in his white undershirt. People gathered at the flimsy fence as word spread that His Royal Highness, Prince Gregory Desmarais of Cartheigh, was about to challenge a pig.

Gregory and the pig paced in front of each other, like two dandies before a fencing match. Gregory clenched and unclenched his fists. He stretched his arms over his head, and then knotted his hands behind his back. The muscles in his broad shoulders swelled against the light cotton of his undershirt. Countless hours with a sword and in the saddle has prevented most of his overindulgence from getting the best of him. Eleanor could detect the beginnings of his father's roundness in his belly, but Gregory hadn't softened much over the years.

"Pig," he said. The crowd whispered amongst themselves. Clearly no one knew the correct demeanor for such a match. The pig grunted in response.

"I plan to insert you into that sack. What say you?" asked Gregory.

"Say good luck, prince."

"Cheeky pork!" someone yelled from the crowd. A few nervous chuckles traveled around the pigpen.

Gregory raised his hands. "Now, friends. Which of you would be willingly stuffed into a bag? Let the pork speak!"

The crowd roared with laughter.

"Talk, talk, talk!" The pig spit at the observers. Gregory took full advantage of its distraction and lunged. The animal's ears shot up in surprise at the sudden attack, but it feinted right. Gregory went after it.

He grabbed a leg. The pig squealed and slipped free. Gregory's hand slapped the mud, sending dark brown droplets into his face and hair. He spun, and his right boot slipped out from under him. His knee hit the mud with another splat.

The pig raced around the pen, kicking up mud in his wake. Gregory made a loop after it, then changed direction and met the pig head on.

He got a hold of it for a few frantic seconds, before it wiggled loose and shot through his legs.

Ticia and Nathan were jumping up and down and screaming, but it was another voice that called Eleanor's attention from the ruckus in the pen.

Dorian stood on the second rail and leaned precariously over the fence. "Greg!" he yelled. "No, left—you had him—Ah! Go for the leg—not the tail—grab the tail!" He slid from the rail and rested both arms on the fence. Hilarious tears streamed down his face. "Ha, Greg—the pig—bloody pig—is running you ragged—don't give up, man—think of your forefathers!"

Gregory grinned from the pen, his face a mask of splattered mud. He shouted to Dorian, "Kings of yore, give me the strength!"

Dorian couldn't speak. He hung on the railing, crying with laughter. He clapped Nathan on the back. "Proud of your father—" he gasped. "A fine king—"

Gregory worried the pig from one end of the pen to the other. The mud-crusted spikes of his hair pointed at the fluffy clouds above his head. The pig stopped in the corner of the ring. It stood with its stubby legs spread, blowing hard. Gregory planted his muddy arms across his chest. The delicate cotton of his undershirt molded to his chest like an extra layer of brown skin.

"What say you now, pig?"

"Fight. You eat me anyway. Fight till dead."

"So be it." Gregory cracked his knuckles. His nostrils flared, and so did the pig's. He went in low. The pig went left, then right. Gregory went right, hard.

Gregory dove, his chest sliding through the mud, and scooped up the pig in a slimy embrace. The pig thrashed, and nearly got loose again, but Gregory pushed its muzzle into the mud. He wrapped a leg over its kicking haunches. The pig man threw him the sack. He caught it in one hand, and with a few more thrusts (and a gasp for air on the part of the pig) the animal disappeared inside the sack. The sack wiggled and squirmed as if it had come to life.

"Caught pig!" said Gregory.

"Victory!" Dorian shouted.

Ticia shrieked with glee. "Poppa! Poppa caught the pig!"

Eleanor couldn't help but join them. "Good show, Your Highness!" she called. She clapped and stood on the fence rail herself. "Good show!"

Gregory let go of the sack. The pig burst forth. It stood in the center of the pen, its dirty nose to the mud. "Silence!" Gregory called. The cheering crowd hushed.

"Pig, you were a worthy opponent."

"You bested. Done."

"What is your name?"

"None."

"I'm bestowing one on you. You shall be called Wickun."

The pig raised its head. "Why? Pork need no name."

"You won't be pork. You'll live out your days in the royal stables at Eclatant. You'll be the keeper of my son's new goat."

If a pig could look shocked this one did.

"What say you now, Wickun?"

Wickun grinned. His sharp front teeth hung over his pink lips. "Fair match, sir."

The soldiers pushed the people back as Gregory climbed out of the pigpen. A sergeant appeared out of nowhere with a bucket and towel. Ticia squealed when Gregory wiped a bit of mud on her nose. Nathan gripped the rope around the little goat's neck. He stroked the creature's head and thanked his father over and over in a whisper. Gregory kissed Eleanor, and laughed when she put a hand on his muddy cheek and wiped it on the fence. She stepped away and gave him room to clean up. Dorian held Gregory's destroyed undershirt at arm's length and grinned.

"Burn it, or frame it?"

Gregory dumped water over his head and tugged on his tunic. "You try it on, you pansy. Pig was too much for you."

"You're right. I'm man enough to toss a lemon, but I leave pig wrestling to royalty."

"Breeding. It's all in the breeding."

"You, or the pig?"

"The pig, man. That is one positively perfect porkchop."

"Positively pardoned porkchop—"

Both men doubled over. Gregory leaned on Dorian, his laughter coming in wheezes and snorts.

"You sound like...the pig...Wickun!" Dorian choked out. They hung on each other.

"Mother?" asked Nathan. He looked from his father to his uncle with wide eyes.

"It's all right, love," Eleanor said. "Poppa is happy. Uncle Dorian is happy."

For a moment she knew Dorian and Gregory as they had been, before she entered their lives. She grieved yet again on this beautiful day. She loved the boys she'd never known.

Eleanor took her children by the hands. "I'll take the children to the garden. Rosemary is helping the other witches at the flower stand. You two go have an ale." Dorian wiped his eyes. She saw a flash of guilt on his face, and tried to smile it away. She kissed Gregory's cheek. "You deserve a drink, Husband, after that memorable performance. It will go down in the history books."

"A fine plan. I'm parched." Gregory draped an arm over Dorian's shoulder. The two men and half the soldiers disappeared into the crowd.

Eleanor and the children spent the rest of the afternoon selling flowers with Rosemary. Ticia arranged blooms and braided them into the hair of little girls who stopped by the flower stand. Most of them regarded her with wide, solemn eyes at first, but Ticia wasted no time charming them out of their nervousness. She's made several little friends by the end of the day. She watched wistfully as their parents collected them. Eleanor hugged her daughter.

"Ticia needs more playmates," Eleanor said to Rosemary. "She's outgrowing Nathan."

"Where does one find friends for a princess?" Rosemary wiped her wet hands on her apron.

"Eleanor! Eleanor!"

She turned at Gregory's screaming voice. Dorian and Gregory, aboard Senné and Vigor, tearing through the crowd at a full gallop. Teardrop stepped from behind the flower stand. "They will crush someone," the mare said.

Eleanor agreed. She pushed the children toward Rosemary and ran to meet the two unicorns. "What's happened?"

"Mount up," said Dorian.

Eleanor's face paled. She spun around and collided with Teardrop, already standing behind her.

"Can you mount in a skirt?" asked Gregory.

"Of course." Eleanor grabbed the braided loop in Teardrop's mane and swung onto her bare back. She took the reins in one hand.

"You must promise me you will not do anything—you won't be too—"

Dorian finished Gregory's thought. "Rash."

"Tell me what's wrong!"

Gregory swung Vigor around so he stood beside Teardrop. "Queen Camille's. It's...someone set it afire."

CHAPTER 18

HOT AND DARK

TEARDROP CAME TO A skittering stop in front of the school. Rosemary let go of Eleanor's waist and slipped from the mare's back. Eleanor waved a hand in front of her face as she dismounted herself. She squinted through the smoke. Men and women ran between the school and the ancient well in the center of the square. They carried wooden buckets, but the rope wound slowly. Most of the water sloshed over the bucket's edges by the time the would-be dousers reached the flames. Parents screamed for their children. Soot-covered girls clung to each other, sobbing, before the white picket gate. Marcus's head towered above them. He shouted directions and herded the children away from the fire. Eleanor ran to him. The whites of his eyes and his teeth stood out from his soot-stained face. Eleanor called to the crying girls, "Come, children, this way!"

They moved into clearer air. Dorian, Gregory, and Rosemary joined her in a cluster around the children.

"How long has the fire been burning?" Rosemary yelled.

"Half an hour!" Marcus said. "But it's only just caught like this in the past ten minutes. Thank HighGod you're here!"

"Is everyone out?" asked Dorian.

Marcus shook his head. "I got these girls out from the classrooms.

Some came from the dormitories with the older students. At least ten are still in the library. Ruby is in there."

"Why didn't you go back?" Eleanor asked. She coughed, and wiped at the bits of smoldering ash eating away at the fine silk of her gown like fiery caterpillars. The smell of burning hair assaulted her raw nostrils.

"I had to watch this lot!"

"I'm going in there," said Dorian.

"We can help," Senné said. "Teardrop, Vigor, and I. The fire will not harm us."

"None of you will fit inside," Eleanor said. "The passageways are too narrow! You couldn't turn around, or fit through a single doorway!"

"I'll follow you, Dor." Gregory wiped a hand across his face. Black soot covered the remnants of brown mud left on his face.

"Your father won't like it."

"Don't argue with me." Gregory strode toward the school and Dorian followed him. Eleanor started after them, but Rosemary grabbed her arm.

"Your dress will go up like a dead tree in a lightning storm!" Eleanor pulled, but Rosemary held tight. "You'll be a hindrance, not a help!"

"Well un-hinder me! You've dressed me for special occasions before!"

Rosemary crossed her arms over her chest, and then covered her face for a moment. She raised her arms. Soft white light leaked from her palms. Eleanor's legs felt warm and prickly, as if they'd both fallen asleep. She stumbled a few steps.

Her skirts clung to her legs, tighter and tighter, until she was certain her knees would give out. Then, suddenly, the pressure disappeared. A pair of green silk leggings had replaced the skirts of her gown. The ornate beadwork bunched up at her waist and knees. Leather boots took the place of walking slippers.

"Thank you." Eleanor kissed her teacher and ran into the smoke-filled school.

Eleanor couldn't see much through the smoke, but she knew the lay of the building. She crouched and scrambled down the hall. Her corset hadn't disappeared with her petticoats, and she couldn't draw a deep breath. Sweat ran down the back of her neck. She didn't see any flames. They seemed to be concentrated in the direction of the library in the rear of the building.

She jumped when Dorian appeared out of the shadows with a child on one hip and the hand of another. "Get them to the door," he said.

She nodded and took the smaller girl in her arms. "Come, sweetheart, you'll be fine," she said to the older child. The girl she held, no older than Ticia, buried her face in Eleanor's neck. Eleanor felt the child's lips moving against her skin, could smell her frightened sweat through the smoke. She steered them toward the light at the front door. Once they cleared the threshold she shouted for Rosemary, set the little one down, and returned to the darkness.

She met Gregory this time, with four more children. She heard him before she saw him. "Move on! Hurry! You must keep going!" He shoved the children in Eleanor's direction and disappeared again. These girls were older, probably between ten and thirteen. They recognized Eleanor.

"Your Highness! Your Highness, the fire—"

The heat increased by the moment. Eleanor told the girls to hold hands. "Run, children!" They heeded her, as they always did.

Rosemary screamed at her from the picket fence as the girls burst from the doorway. "I see flames on the roof!"

Eleanor took a few relatively clean breaths before she met Dorian one last time. He held two tiny girls in his arms. Ruby followed him.

"Ruby! Thank HighGod! Come, hurry." Eleanor wondered if Dorian could see through his bloodshot eyes. "Is this all of them? Where's Gregory?"

"He's still in the library! I'll go back—" He coughed into his hands. "I'll find him, Eleanor."

She hesitated, and in that moment a beam above their heads shuddered. Orange sparks cascaded around their heads like hot, pelting hail. The girls screamed.

"Go. I said I'll find him. Go, now!"

Dorian crawled down the passageway between the front hall and the library. He blessed the warm weather that had led the girls to open the school's many wide windows. On a sealed up winter day it would not have penetrated the smoke beyond the front door. The walls creaked and groaned around him, as if the building itself were calling for help. He shouted Gregory's name. On the third yell he got a reply.

"Here, Dor! By the desk!" Gregory's words came from the very air. Dorian couldn't discern any direction.

Desk, desk, thought Dorian. He shook his head and pictured the library as he'd seen it a hundred times. *Desk is in the right corner.*

The building's grumblings became a shriek. The wall of books to his left collapsed. He had a brief glimpse of daylight, and running, screaming people, before the flames roared up around him. The crackle of thousands of burning pages filled the orange and gold and black room. Dorian scrambled backward, and his hand struck Gregory's hot boot.

"There's one under there," Gregory said. "She won't come out."

"Grab her. We have to get out of here—"

"I can't—child, come out!" He reached an arm under the desk.

"No! It's hot and dark!" came a high voice.

"Greg—"

"We have to get her out of there!"

"I hear you! You must—like Ticia—Ticia after a bad dream!"

Gregory nodded. His head disappeared under the desk. Dorian caught a few words. "Come—please—safe—sweetheart—"

Gregory reappeared with the little girl's hands in his. He dragged her from under the desk. "There are two more, in the back by the wall! Two more—unconscious—"

The buttons on Dorian's tunic were searing his skin. Gregory's arm gave out from under him, and he almost dropped the girl. Her head flopped and her eyes rolled. Dorian couldn't speak through his own coughing. "We can't—the flames—"

Gregory slumped against him. "Two other girls—Leticia—is she under there?"

Dorian caught a last bit of air and shouted in Gregory's ear, "You're the heir to the throne! Your father is old and your son is a child. Your country needs you. I won't let you die!" He jerked Gregory toward what he thought was the door.

For a moment he was sure the heat and bad air had done permanent damage to his brain, for it seemed the smoke was solidifying and calling his name. Blackness rolled toward him.

HighGod's vengeance for my sins, he thought, until white joined the coming darkness, and a flash of silver.

Senné and Vigor stepped through the wall of fire.

"Are you bloody crazy? Are you out of your HighGod-forsaken mind?"

King Casper screamed into Gregory's soot-coated face, but Eleanor sensed her father-in-law included herself and Dorian in his question. The king's words ricocheted off the wall of his receiving room like crazed rats trying to escape a trap. His face, ruddy even during a peaceful chapel service, had gone a frightening purplish red. He stepped away from his blinking son and traipsed the marble floor. His boots slammed out the staccato rhythm of his anger.

"You're the heir of Caleb Desmarais and the keeper of the Great Bond! You risk yourself to save a few peasant girls? It's beyond idiotic!"

Eleanor folded her hands and tried to keep her eyes on the ground, but as usual they declared mutiny. She glanced between her husband and Dorian. Neither seemed inclined to speak, so she cleared her throat.

"Your Majesty—"

The king whirled around. His face loomed in front of Eleanor's own. His bristly mustache practically stood on end in indignation and she could smell his lunch on his breath. Ham and rosemary bread.

"Did you put him up to this?" he asked her. He jabbed Dorian's chest with one finger. "And you. I thought you had more sense. You're just as big a fool as these two!"

"Your Majesty, please," Dorian said. "I did try to stop the prince—"

"Praise HighGod! A show of brains!"

"—but only when I knew the situation to be hopeless. Gregory acted nobly, with great bravery."

"Save the bravery for the battlefield."

Gregory shifted on his feet and rung his hands, just as Nathan did when Eleanor caught him being naughty. "I couldn't just turn away," Gregory said. "You should have seen—just children—"

"Cartheigh is your child. Your crown is your first responsibility. I thought you understood that by now. Your life is worth a hundred of those children!"

"All life has value, Your Majesty," said Eleanor. "These are your subjects."

Sweat beaded on Gregory's dirty forehead. "You're right, Father. I should have thought it through. Maybe it was the smoke."

"Gregory, you did a great thing!" Eleanor took his arm but he shook her off.

"No, it's true. Needless risk, and four girls dead anyway."

"But more than that alive because of you!" Gregory wouldn't meet Eleanor's eye, so she turned to the king. "Your Majesty, this tragedy—it could have been so much worse. The school is half a block from the well—when we rebuild—"

"Rebuild?" The king paused for a moment, and then a few harsh chuckles fell from his open mouth. "Nothing is going to be rebuilt."

"Eleanor," Dorian said. "Now isn't the—"

Eleanor didn't acknowledge Dorian's diplomacy. "Someone set the school afire. Destroyed

crown property and killed four of your most innocent subjects. If we don't rebuild, the culprit succeeds."

"The school was finished anyway," the king said. "Gregory, did you not tell her?"

"I'd not gotten to it."

Now it was Eleanor's turn to go apoplectic. "How could you not get to it? The school—"

"The school was an experiment," said Casper. "It failed. You taught those girls nothing of use. History. Literature. Languages? For the love of the Bond, they have no need for it. They'll never be more than servants, and all you did was stir discontent among them by making them think. You did nothing but increase the caliber of the selection in Pasture's End! Now a whore can figure a man's taxes before she handles his cock!"

If Eleanor had been the squeamish sort she might have keeled over at the sound of the word *cock* coming from the king's mouth. She struggled to collect her thoughts. "What of the person who did this?"

"Most of the Fringe wanted the school closed," said Gregory. "The rest of Maliana, indeed all of Cartheigh, was coming to the same opinion. It could have been anyone, or a hundred people working together, who set the fire."

"I know exactly who it was, even if you don't believe it."

Gregory shook his head. "Not Ezra Oliver. Not that fairy story again."

"I saw him. Teardrop saw him. You don't even believe her."

"A unicorn, inside the head of a parrot, saw something that might have been gray light. Addled by a spell and a bird's pea brain. It's not proof." Casper's stubborn mouth disappeared beneath his mustache.

"You won't believe it until Oliver appears and smites you as you sit on your own throne!"

"Enough, Eleanor!" Gregory took her arms and walked her backwards. His eyes were wild in his sooty face. "You'll keep your tongue in your head in my father's presence!"

Eleanor stumbled, but before she could fall Dorian took Gregory by the shoulder. His voice was frozen Fire-iron. "We're all upset. We should part ways. Cool our heads."

Eleanor's heart skipped several beats as Gregory stared at Dorian's hand on his shoulder. No hint of fraternal affection could be heard in his own reply. "Wise, as always." He turned to Eleanor. "You are dismissed."

For once Eleanor's mouth obeyed her better judgment. "Thank you. I do apologize if I spoke out of turn." Her raw throat, still coated with the ashes of years of work and hope, constricted. She blinked back tears.

The king sighed. "Child, your passion has long overcome your common sense. If you were a man you'd find a means for control. On the heels of such trauma I will forgive you. But I tell you now, Queen Camille's is finished. I'll not hear of it again."

Eleanor nodded. She curtsied, and walked to the exit. Each step came a little faster. The great doors closed behind her. The tears came and she ran.

The king claimed a headache and retired to his bedchamber. He left Gregory with one parting sentiment. Dorian could almost hear the prince's pride crack.

"It's a sad day when I must berate a grown man, Gregory. A grown son of Caleb Desmarais." He called over his shoulder as he left. "And if you're going to strike your wife, have the sense to do it the privacy of your own chamber."

Dorian stood beside Gregory and waited for the prince to speak. Gregory's arms hung at his sides. His chest rose and fell. After the boisterous argument it was impossible to ignore the silence in the receiving room.

"I think I'll have a bath," Dorian finally said.

"I take it you don't approve of my discipline, either."

Dorian held his breath for a moment. "I would not use such methods."

Gregory's eyes narrowed. "What do you know of the affairs of husband and wife? You'd deem to interfere in the personal relations of your future king?"

"No. Your relations are your own."

"And you think I should ask father to rebuild the school?"

"I do. Queen Camille's was a place like no other in Cartheigh. A beacon amidst the ignorance."

"Always the poet, aren't you? Always the romantic." Gregory crept closer.

Dorian held his ground, but his heart hammered against his chest. "I only wish to offer you honest counsel. Even if my honesty draws your wrath. I seek only to help you, Your Highness."

"As you did when I asked you to marry one of those Talessee girls. It's been over six years, Dor, and still you pine for your lost whore."

Dorian's jaw clenched. Gregory smiled, and Dorian couldn't help but swallow. He hoped Gregory didn't hear it.

"In a hundred years," said Gregory, "I could never find a more loyal servant. Now go, have a bath. Cool your head."

Eleanor did not return to her chamber. Pansy would have stoked a comforting fire, and the she was quite sure that the sight of dancing

flames would incite her to scream, or vomit, or possibly seize up in a fit. She slowed to a walk, the air rushing in and out of her smoke-tender lungs. She wandered the halls, and ignored the servants, who stared at her with eyes on stalks and scuttled out of her way, like liveried crabs.

She somehow found herself in the unicorn barn, and although two hours ago she'd despaired of ever feeling cool again, the evening breeze shimmied into the scorched holes in her clothing. She looked down at her lower half, and realized the servants weren't necessarily staring at her frazzled hair and soot-stained face. Rosemary's spell had faded. She now wore a skirt from hip to knee, and pants from knee to ankle. One boot. One afternoon slipper.

Teardrop stood silently in her paddock and watched the darkening sky. Eleanor leaned against the mare's shoulder. Strands of her mane tickled Eleanor's neck and cheek, the sound of silky hair against her ear like a soft sigh.

"How, Teardrop? When we mean to do such good, how can it go so awry?"

Teardrop exhaled, her speech as airy as the wind that circled their heads, despite the heavy topic. "No one knows. HighGod has a plan. Much good was done at Queen Camille's—"

"But not enough to outweight the tragedies. Girls murdered and lost to whoring...and those four children...dead..."

"You sound as defeatist as Gregory."

"How did you know he said—" Eleanor stopped, and in spite of herself the corners of her mouth twitched. "Chou Chou."

"Some things cannot be predicted. Others..."

"Dear Chou," said Eleanor. "Dependably nosy as always."

"What shall you do now, Your Highness?"

"I will love my children," said Eleanor. "That seems the best place to start."

"It is a good start. Next steps will come. Watch for them. Signs always appear to those who look."

"Hmmm." Eleanor wound a handful of Teardrop's mane through her fingers, and tried to blink back burning tears, as if she could douse the last embers of the fire. Perhaps it had started in her own heart, and now sought to escape by scorching a path to freedom through her eyes. The princess and her unicorn watched lingering smoke drift above the city of Maliana. Smoke and clouds met, and blended. The nebulous remnants of fire and water seemed one and the same, and Eleanor could not tell where one began and the other ended.

PART II

CHAPTER 19

A BAD SICKNESS

ELEANOR SAT ASTRIDE HIGH Noon, her father's old horse, and watched her children's ponies circle the training ring at a trot. High Noon was over thirty years old, and fit for nothing but this sort of patient standing, but his height provided Eleanor with a good vantage point and gave her an excuse to spend time with him. Every so often he'd lift his head and peer around the ring with cloudy eyes.

"Jump? Jump? Jump?" he'd say. Then, inevitably, "Tired. Tired. Tired."

Eleanor patted his neck and called out instructions to her children. "Nathan, check your diagonal. Heels down. Ticia, your hands. Where should they be?"

Ticia lowered her hands. The seven-year-old's voice was as bouncy as her bay pony's trot. "It's harder for me, Mother. Why can't I ride astride, like Nathan?"

"I've told you. You'll always ride sidesaddle, in a skirt, on horseback. Astride in leggings is only allowed on unicornback."

"Can't I learn that way? On Teardrop?"

Eleanor shook her head. "Teardrop loves you, but she's my unicorn. She's not fond of carrying anyone else."

"When will Cricket be ready to carry me?" Ticia asked.

"In a year. You know that. It's good for you to learn this way. It will make you a better rider. Now, Nathan—" Eleanor turned to her four-year-old son. She started to remind him about his diagonal, but he'd already corrected it. He rose and fell easily with his spotted pony's outside front leg. She smiled. Both of her children were natural riders, but she's never seen anything like her son's comfort in the saddle. Perhaps it was his love of animals, or his Desmarais blood. "Take the fence, darling."

Nathan swung the pony's head toward the cross rails in the middle of the ring. He clucked and the pony broke into a canter. The little animal popped over the fence and continued around the ring. Nathan never wobbled.

"Wonderful!" Eleanor called. "Now you, Tish."

She leaned on the paddock rail and watched Ticia take the fence, then Nathan again. Ticia's request to ride Teardrop sent Eleanor's mind wandering. A year and a month had passed since the burning of Queen Camille's, when Rosemary had clung to Eleanor's back as Teardrop raced from the fairgrounds into Meggett Fringe. Thirteen long, difficult months.

She'd caught pregnant within weeks of the fire, but the pregnancy ended badly in the fourth month. Gregory took the news of her failure with the frozen anger that terrified her more than his shouting and cursing ever did. He visited her chamber at night, as always, but he rarely spoke of anything but the children. On a few occasions she tried to entice him into their old familiarity, but he ignored her. He saved his laughter for Ticia and Nathan, and Sylvia Fleetwood.

The Duchess had become a fixture at Eclatant. The Harveston gentry grumbled that Sylvia had all but abandoned them, and the Malianans made the point that the Duchess was a girl of the capital, after all. Eleanor burned with embarrassment at every function, for she knew everyone's assumptions about her husband and Sylvia. She sat beside Gregory at dinner, and always Sylvia sat across from him. He danced with Eleanor, returned her to her seat, and took up the Duchess's hand. Only his thinly veiled examinations of Eleanor's face following his insults betrayed any feeling for her on his part. He never transferred his attention from his wife to his mistress without gauging the reaction of the former.

If she is his mistress, Eleanor thought as she leaned on the railing.

She still had no proof of a physical relationship between Gregory and Sylvia. She'd never seen more than flirtation between them, nor had Chou, or her friends. Sylvia would not discuss it with Margaret. Gregory refused to talk of it with Dorian.

Eleanor could read the interactions between the two men like a favorite bedtime story. The spontaneity was gone. The wit and banter, checked. Gregory rarely asked for Dorian's sole company anymore. He always included Raoul, or sometimes one of the Fleetwood fops.

Eleanor knew these details, not because Dorian told her, but because Frog told Chou. She'd not had a private conversation with Dorian in over a year.

She'd been alone with him once, in Solsea, when they happened upon each other in front of the Rockwall Chapel. She'd come to deliver leftover food for the Godsmen to distribute to the poor; he was returning to Trill following a visit to a Solsea cobbler. He stopped to help her shelve jars of jam, and they'd stolen ten frantic minutes in the Chapel's larder. After he left she sat on the dirt floor of the cupboard, staring at the wooden shelves packed with canned goods, until the Godsmen finally came to check on her.

She spent the next week in the clutches of a constricting paranoia. She'd started a debate society, both as an intellectual outlet and a chance to spend safe time with Dorian. Orvid Jones, Sir Faust, and a few other academically minded courtiers and magicians regularly joined the group. Gregory dipped in and out at his father's instruction. Eleanor bowed out of the debates for a full ten days. She'd not had the wherewithal to risk a two-hour session in the library with Dorian and her husband.

"Mother, watch!" Ticia's voice called her back to the present. Her daughter raised her arms above her head. She swayed with the pony's bouncy canter.

"Wonderful, Tish, but be careful!"

"Me, too, Mother!" shouted Nathan. He followed his sister's lead. Ever determined to outdo her, he dropped his stirrups.

"Nathan, stop now!" Eleanor called.

Without picking up the reins or putting his boots in the stirrups he dug his skinny rear end into the saddle. She saw his legs tighten, and the pony skidded to a halt.

She exhaled. "That's enough for today."

The children chattered and argued as they led their ponies from the ring. They followed Eleanor and High Noon into the barn. The grooms waited at a respectful distance, for Eleanor and Gregory had always agreed on one thing: the need for both children to see to their own mounts. Ticia and Nathan tugged the saddles from their ponies' backs and dragged them to the tack room. They grabbed currycombs and rubbed down the little horses. Eleanor ran a damp cloth over High Noon's knobby knees and breathed in the smell of sweaty horsehair. She listened to her children debate the merits of various fly repellants.

Eleanor loved her children, and missed Dorian. These two emotions, along with fear, consumed her through tense days and restless dreams. In her darkest hours she cursed herself for giving in to her love for him. For damning them both to this endless worry and suffering. Those moments never lasted long. The exhaustion on his face across a table, the sound of his voice bouncing off stacks of books in the library, a whiff of his shaving tonic when he bowed before her. She clung to them all as she had clung to a young man in a broom closet eight years ago. Loving Dorian was not a predicament that lent itself to options.

Over the past year, her fears had solidified into two terrifying scenarios. In the first, Gregory killed her. This did not bother her on account of her own death, but on account of her children. She imagined them, motherless, as she had been, navigating the pitfalls of court life. The thought of Sylvia marrying Gregory, and assuming the role of stepmother, was intolerable. Ticia and Nathan under Sylvia's thumb, and therefore Imogene's, just as Eleanor herself was for all those long years. HighGod knew how Sylvia would treat them, or if Gregory would be able to protect them. She had to stay alive for Ticia and Nathan's sake.

The second situation was nearly as terrifying. Gregory killed Dorian, and let her live. She'd be around to defend her children, but she didn't know how to live without Dorian. She'd spent countless sleepless nights obsessing over both outcomes. They crept up on her when she least expected it. They did so in the barn as she rubbed oil on High Noon's hooves. She wiped her eyes on her sleeve.

"Mother? Can I ask something of you?"

"Of course, darling." Eleanor hoped her daughter's question would be complicated enough to distract her from her trepidation. She got her wish.

"Why are people dying in the city? Pansy says there is a page in town."

"Not a page. A plague."

"What's a plague?"

"It's a bad sickness, dear. One that jumps from person to person like a biting flea."

"Can't the witches find a cure? I thought they could make anyone better."

"They're trying. These things take time."

"Will the plague come to Eclatant?" asked Nathan. "Who will die? My goat? Wickun?"

"Plagues only kill people, love, sadly enough," said Eleanor. "Your goat and your pig are safe." She did what mothers have done for centuries. She fibbed. "I'm sure the witches will find a cure before the plague reaches Eclatant."

In truth, she had no such confidence. The king and the High

Council were in a tizzy over the Burning, as it was called, although it was so far contained in the Fringe. She'd heard horrible stories. The afflicted spiked impossible fevers, and then seemed to recover for a day or so, before the fever returned with a vengeance. Victims died within a few delusional, screaming hours. So far the witches had no success with a cure. Two hundred peasants had perished in the Fringe in less than two months. The king had quarantined the slum. Gregory, Dorian, and the rest of the men talked of nothing else morning, noon, and night, and Eleanor listened in whenever she could. She'd even heard ladies conversing about the plague during the Harvest Fest parties. If they could be distracted from their never-ending discussions of marriage matches and redecorating, the situation must be dire, indeed.

"I'll not have you two worrying about it," Eleanor said to the children as a groom led a gorgeous, limping white hackney into the barn. She stopped him and ran a hand over the animal's trembling foreleg. "He came up lame?"

"Aye, Your Highness. Driver noticed it as the carriage headed out the drive."

"He's not one of the crown horses, is he? I don't recognize him."

The groom shook his head. "Belongs to the Duchess. I'll just take the poor bugger to a stall and bring out old Jasper. Her Grace and her mother goin' down to Pettibone Lane. They're waiting in the Horsemaster's office."

Eleanor felt a twinge of interest. "Perhaps I'll say hello. Would you mind walking the children up to the palace when you've finished with the horse?"

"Certainly, Your Highness. But I'll warn you. Her Grace and Missus Brice are in a foul mood over the delay."

Eleanor smiled. "Don't worry. I'm familiar with the moods of the Duchess and her mother."

Eleanor trotted across the dusty stable yard. The Horsemaster's office adjoined the brood mare barn, so she entered the last stall. The occupant, a swollen chestnut mare who looked to be carrying a small herd of offspring in her enormous belly, sniffed at Eleanor's pockets. "Sugar?" she asked.

Eleanor bit back an expletive when the mare nipped her. "Hush, now," she whispered. "You hardly need it."

The mare snorted and kicked the stall door at the insult. Eleanor had not forgotten the irritability of late pregnancy. She patted the mare's neck.

"I'm sorry…just keep quiet and I'll have the grooms bring you a carrot."

The mare moved to the corner and swished her tail in a pique. Eleanor peered through a crack between two white slats into the Horsemaster's office. The straw crinkled under her feet. White flashed past the crack, then green. With such a tiny field of vision, it took a few passes before she identified Sylvia in ivory organza and Imogene in hunter and Kelly green plaid silk.

"…damned animal. Madame Fragapple's is expecting an order from Point-of-Rocks today. Mendaen silk. It shall be bought and sold, the lot, before we arrive…" Sylvia ripped her gloves off and stuffed them into a beaded handbag. "This horsiness will imbed itself in my clothing, and I won't have time for a bath before dinner. Gregory won't appreciate me smelling of sweat and saddle leather."

Eleanor's ears perked up at the mention of Gregory.

"You're so familiar," said Imogene. "Must you call him by his given name?"

"Shits and spells, Mother. I've earned the right. You were once intent on my getting into Gregory's good graces. *Must* you be so *infernally* cowed?"

"You wouldn't be so brave if you were in my position."

"You've barely passed words with her in seven years. No one cares about the Oliver affair anymore. It's time to stop worrying."

"Maybe if you kept me better informed, I wouldn't worry so."

"You know all there is to know. Nothing has changed."

Imogene muttered something Eleanor couldn't catch. Eleanor swore to herself in frustration, and pressed her face against the grimy wall. The ragged edges of the crack scratched her cheek.

"How do I know you won't make a mess of it?"

"Of course. HighGod forbid I should beat my own path." Sylvia's poufy skirts filled in the crack. Eleanor stepped back. She could almost smell her stepsister's favorite lilac perfume. Sylvia's agitated voice penetrated the walls. "I've gotten this far without your help. Although I'm sure you'll reap the benefits somehow. You always do. My marriage to Hector. Now Gregory. All of it!"

Imogene must have tugged Sylvia toward the door, because the crack cleared again. "Keep your voice down!" Imogene said. "You know she's always lingering around the horses."

"I don't care! She can't do anything to me!"

"I wouldn't underestimate her. She's a formidable enemy."

Sylvia sat on a rickety wooden chair. "Sometimes I wonder if you hate her or love her. You'd rather have her for a daughter than me, or Margaret!"

Imogene leaned into Sylvia's face. "If she'd been my daughter I'd already be the mother of a princess. She caught him in the first place. Not you."

The fight went out of Sylvia. She slumped in her chair, and Eleanor felt an odd sympathy for her. "HighGod knows I tried to be what you wanted me to be, Mother. I can't remember a time when I wasn't trying." Sylvia rubbed her eyes. "She has some kind of hold on him...I can't—"

"Your Grace? Missus Brice?" Eleanor recognized the Horsemaster's wheezy voice. "Carriage is ready for you now."

Sylvia rose. "Thank HighGod. Deliver me from this glorified paddock."

Imogene followed Sylvia out of the office. Sylvia's voice brushing off the Horsemaster's apologies faded into the stable yard.

Eleanor eased away from the wall. She'd avoided splinters to her face, but a wooden shard had lodged in her thumb. She picked at it with a piece of straw. She wasn't sure if she was more informed by her eavesdropping, or less.

"Quiet. Carrot," said the mare.

"At least you make sense," said Eleanor.

Dorian had always had a strained relationship with Brian Smithwick. Brian was Gregory's cousin on his mother's side, the son of the late queen's brother. He shared blood with the Smithwicks and Harpers, and if one had the patience to go back so far, he claimed relation to the long-disposed Malian kings. Dorian, on the other hand, was the second son of a reasonably aristocratic Lake District family. No shame on the Finley side, but his mother's father had decidedly humble origins. A former book binder, he'd somehow convinced the people of Harper's Crossing to elect him mayor. Brian had made his opinion of such class mingling known the moment Dorian made his acquaintance. Fortunately for Dorian, the king had bestowed upon Brian the great honor of Dukedom of the North Country. Brian's entitlement kept him ensconced in drippy misery in Peaksend Castle most of the time, but he couldn't be expected to resist the pull of Eclatant's food and pretty ladies and relative dryness all year.

It seemed he'd brought the northern weather with him on this windy LowWinter day. A steady drizzle had been falling since his arrival two days before. The mist blowing into Dorian's face reminded him of the perpetual dampness of the Dragon Mines, minus the smell of hot Fire-iron. For once he and Brian were in agreement.

"It's bloody miserable out here, Greg," said Brian. He pushed his rain darkened blondish hair back from his forehead. "How about a game of strikestick and a fire?"

Gregory stomped his boots in the squishy grass. "Stop whining and move around. You'll break a sweat. Dorian, draw your sword. Look sharp."

The hair on the back of Dorian's neck prickled but he obliged. Fire-iron blades met between the two men with a clang that set Dorian's arm vibrating in its socket. Rivulets of rain and sweat tracked down Gregory's face and caught in the reddish stubble on his chin. Dorian let him carry on for the sake of his pride before finishing him off. He feinted left, then spun and came down hard on Gregory's extended arm. Gregory's sword hit the grass in a splash of muddy rainwater.

"Wonderful!" Brian said. "That's over. Let's have a hot drink."

Melfin retrieved the fallen sword. Gregory made an ill-disguised attempt to catch his breath. "You two have a go while Melfin cleans my blade."

Gregory didn't let the clanging Fire-iron quell his banter. "Been down to Pandra's lately, Dor?"

Dorian grunted an affirmative over the clanking swords. Brian was a decent swordsman, but he didn't have Gregory's brute strength. Dorian dispatched him without any real effort.

"Ach, cousin. Poor showing," Gregory said. He returned to the topic of the Hussy. "Why risk the pox? Even Brian's been having luck with the latest crop of virginal debutantes."

Brian's handsome faced reddened under its coating of rain. Dorian tried diplomacy. "No lady, no matter how pure, can stand against the charms of a Smithwick." His attempts were either unappreciated or misconstrued. Brian's scowl deepened. Dorian changed the subject. "What news on the Burning?"

Gregory glowered at him. "By the Bond, I need an afternoon free of that subject."

"We should thank HighGod it's only a problem in the Fringe," said Brian. "All those dirty peasants piled atop one another in the shacks."

"Plagues always start in the Fringe," said Dorian. "They never stay there. It's impressive we kept it out of Cartheigh for so long."

Gregory swung his sword over his head. "And then a few stowaway Mendaen brats come ashore and spread the disease like a bad case of lice. Years of work, for nothing." The blade sliced into the mud again, negating Melfin's fine polishing job.

"How did they make it to land?" asked Brian. "We checked every boat."

Dorian agreed with Brian. He couldn't comprehend how seven Mendaen children, each one infected with the Burning, had avoided detection by plague containment forces. "Perhaps a lifeboat. At night. They were too ill to swim."

"No one can ask them now," said Gregory. "Dead before we could even find translators. They lived just long enough to pass on their curse."

For one who didn't wish to talk about the Burning, Gregory kept up quite the running dialogue. Brian nodded and Dorian *hmmm-ed* as he blathered on.

"The whole of Maliana is in an uproar," said Gregory. "I'd thought we'd finished with those leaflets when we finished with Eleanor's school, yet they keep coming. Why can't the magicians trace them?"

Because the most powerful magician in history conjured them, thought Dorian. He'd had that conversation with Gregory a dozen times, but a year had not warmed Gregory to the idea of Ezra Oliver's return.

"...the witches can't find a cure...blaming the crown...the bloody nerve! We've a crowd of townies banging on the palace gate. Screaming for the king to do something. I can't sleep for the racket."

"Does your father have a plan?" asked Dorian.

Brian never showed much care for matters of national security, but he looked mildly interested.

Gregory glanced over his shoulder, then beckoned Dorian and Brian closer. "We spoke of it just this morning. He's going to discuss it at the next Council meeting. I shouldn't say anything"—he looked at Dorian as he spoke—"but I believe I can count on your discretion until tomorrow morning."

"You have my word," said Dorian, and he meant it.

"Mine as well," said Brian.

"You won't be at the meeting, Smithy, so you'll have no need to feign surprise."

Brian flushed again.

"The witches have been on the outs with the people for a year," said Gregory. "Everyone thinks Afar Creek somehow profited from schooling those girls and landing them in the cathouses."

"That's a lot of dragonshit, and you know it," said Dorian.

"Father knows when he needs to throw the people a meaty bone. He's decided to take the witches off the cure and turn it over to First Covey."

Even Brian found this odd. "Do magicians practice healing magic?"

"The most brilliant magical minds in three countries conjure in First Covey," said Gregory.

"The most brilliant *male* magical minds." Dorian sheathed his sword.

"The witches will have to make magical space for the magicians to work. Any witch caught conjuring unnecessary magic will be removed from Afar Creek. Sent to one of the smaller Abbeys in the country. Not such a bad thought. We've been seeing and hearing too much from the witches these past few years."

"I agree with you, Cousin, and with your father."

"I don't," said Dorian. "Afar Creek is in a sorry state as it is. Tithing dried up months ago, even before the fire. Now you'll prevent the witches from redeeming themselves. And possibly delay the cure."

"I have faith in Orvid Jones and First Covey," said Gregory.

"As do I," Brian agreed.

Gregory sighed. "Brian, someday you will have to find your own opinions. Dorian, come. How about a game of strikestick?"

Gregory walked toward the palace. Dorian nodded a goodbye to Brian. For the first time since Brian had arrived for his extended visit, he didn't join them in Gregory's study. He seemed to have lost interest in strikestick.

Eleanor had never heard such music. The conjuring of twenty apprentice magicians filled the Covey's amphitheater. The tonal quality of their strange serenade ranged from flute-like to nasally, muted bugling. Their dark robes, coupled with the haunting notes, gave the impression of a flock of overgrown nightingales. Fireballs hovered before each man, growing and shrinking with the crescendos. Their symphony echoed from the vaulted golden ceiling to the oil paintings of venerated magicians lining the purple walls.

"Lovely," Rosemary said to Orvid Jones. "What is it?"

Jones raised and lowered his arms like an orchestral conductor. The music followed his lead. "Tonal magic," he said. He pointed at the door, closed tight behind them and swollen with a thickening spell. "It's a recent discovery. I'm hoping to unveil it to His Majesty during the Waning Fest."

One of the apprentices missed a note. *Scrrrreek!* Eleanor winced and put a finger to one ear. Jones laughed. "We're still perfecting it."

Eleanor gently turned the conversation in the direction it needed to go. "Fascinating, Jones, but I wondered if you've found a way to track Oliver?"

"I'm afraid I haven't. No time. With the Covey scrambling over the Burning cure—" Jones blushed. "Pardon, Rosemary."

Rosemary gave him a tight-lipped smile. "I wish you all the best, for the sake of the people."

"If it were my choice—we don't possess the—"

Rosemary put a hand on his arm. "Peace, Jones. I know your position, even if most of your fellows disagree with you. Mister Oliver makes his opinions clear in his leaflets."

"That's hardly fair," Jones said. "You can't blame First Covey for Oliver—or the king's decision—"

"Please," said Eleanor. "We're in the same army, are we not?"

Rosemary sniffed and shrugged.

"I've tried to make Oliver a priority," said Jones, "but with other—issues—now on the platter it must wait." He addressed Rosemary. "I'm sure you've heard. We've had the first sighting. In the Fringe."

Rosemary nodded, but Eleanor didn't follow. She said so.

"A banshee," said Jones. "The first banshee of the plague."

Eleanor paled. "I've never heard of banshees in Maliana. Battlefields, yes, but in the capital?"

"Banshees are reclusive," said Rosemary. "More spirit than flesh, really. No one fully understands where they come from or where they go when they disappear. We do know they're attracted to mass deaths. Normally they avoid cities, so if they're showing themselves in Maliana..." Rosemary shivered.

They fell into a morose silence. The apprentices played on, with only a few errant bonks and squeaks. Eleanor tried to lighten the mood. "Might I ask how it works?"

"It's complex, actually. We've long known that all magic produces a residue—the stuff Ezra Oliver has hidden from us. We've only recently discovered that residue has a sound...a tone." He conjured a ball of buttery light about the size of his head. "The fireballs we magicians use in martial endeavors are magic at it's purest form. Pure power. So the tone is pure."

Rosemary conjured her own ball of light, hers the white of glaring sunlight.

Jones smiled. "There's a knack to releasing the tone. Another spell—it doesn't require words, only concentration—" He squinted at his fireball, and it emitted a low drone. It shrunk and the drone became a trill. He silenced the sound with his voice. "The second spell pulls the tone from the first."

Rosemary murmured admiration.

"We have success with fireballs, but it's more difficult with complicated spells. Potions, transformations…they absorb sounds around them. Say, if you produced a love elixir in a chicken coop, the tone would have a distinct cluckiness to it."

Eleanor laughed. "How romantic."

The conversation drifted toward the Fest, and soon Eleanor and Rosemary bid Jones and his orchestra farewell. She tried to hide her disappointment. She understood Jones's desire to put the might of First Covey behind finding a cure for the Burning.

Still…Oliver, the fall of the witches, the Burning…Oliver, witches, plague…

The connections between them rolled around Eleanor's mind like a squeaky carriage wheel.

A leather-bound mountain blocked most of the light that streamed through the library's dusty windows. Eleanor's book, charmingly entitled *Screaming Death*, lay in the shadow of the stack of volumes. She squinted at the tiny letter.

"Horns and fire, Chou, I think I'll go blind."

Chou peered down at her from the literary precipice. "Soon you'll be needing a seeing glass. On that note, is that a gray hair I see?"

She rubbed her eyes. "With so much strife of late, it very well could be."

The new librarian, an eager young magician of no more than thirty years, appeared with a silver candelabra. He placed it on the desk beside Eleanor's ledger. Chou landed in the middle of her jotted notes like a red and blue paperweight. He ducked when the magician adjusted the candelabra.

"I found these, Your Highness." The librarian held up three small blue books. "Plagues of the last one thousand years."

She smiled at him. He'd been hovering over her all week. "Thank you, but those are the books I returned yesterday."

The magician blushed. "Oh…my goodness…of course—"

"I do appreciate your help."

"Can I get you anything?" he asked, earnestly.

"Crackers? A bottle of hot sherry? It's a might drafty," said Chou.

"Of course, Master Parrot. Crackers…sherry…stoke the fire…" The librarian set off on his mission of accommodation.

"I like him," said Chou.

"I'm not surprised."

Chou lit on the stack of books and whistled a nursery rhyme. Eleanor returned to the first chapter of *Screaming Death*.

Solitary banshees have been known to visit isolated farms following a serious injury or during a mortally unsuccessful childbirth. To draw them in great numbers, however, suffering and fear must be present on a larger scale, hence their attraction to battlefields and plague-gripped cities. Once a banshee makes its victim known, the intended succumbs in a matter of minutes. Banshees dislike Fire-iron, and can sometimes be driven from a victim by a skilled swordsman (see Chapter Eight for a retelling of General Gerald Simmons-Smithwick's fabled disposal of four banshees during the Ogre Wars).

Opinions on banshees differ widely amongst various schools of philosophical thought. Godsmen believe HighGod himself sends them to feed on our fear and pain as a reminder of his displeasure at our sinfulness. Some modern magical scholars, however, focus not on the intent of the creator, but on the intent of the creatures themselves.

"Banshees are, as much as unicorns, dragons, fairies, and even human conjurers, mystical creatures," says Ezra Oliver, Chief Magician at Eclatant

Palace, Maliana. "Perhaps they do serve the will of HighGod in some way, but I'm more interested in the motivation of the creatures themselves."

"No one can deny that banshees are powerfully magical. They appear and disappear at will. They hasten death, no matter how we fend them off with cures and spells. They're repelled only by Fire-iron, the creation of their fellow mystical beings. My latest research points to a level of personal intent in all magic, whether it be for good or evil. In order to unravel the banshee's magic, I believe we must understand their motivation."

Eleanor checked the date on the book's cover. Desmarais Three Hundred-Twenty-One. The year she arrived at Eclatant, less than two years before Oliver disappeared. The librarian delivered their sherry and crackers as she read Oliver's quote to Chou.

"Magic is endlessly fascinating," said Chou. "Who knew the intent of the conjurer played into a spell's outcome?"

"No one, it seems, until Oliver came along, but it makes sense. I imagine one's heart must be in it, whether for goodwill or ill. If Oliver is correct, the conjurer's motivation is a powerful—"

The library door burst open. Orvid Jones appeared in the doorway for a moment, before the door swung back in his face. The librarian ran to open it, but Jones did not wait on either his aid or a proper announcement. The door rebounded off the librarian's outstretched arms.

"Flaming fireballs, Monty!" cried Jones. "Kindly move! Where's Her Highness?"

Poor Monty, Eleanor thought. *Between Jones and Chou, he's not having a restful afternoon.* She waved to Jones. He dragged a chair to her desk and landed in it with a flutter of his black magician's cloak. Chou scolded him.

"Peace, Mister Jones. You'll give Monty the fits."

"I must speak with you," said Jones.

"Something pressing?" asked Chou.

Jones scowled at him. "Not *you*. Her Highness."

"We're attached at the ears."

Eleanor shrugged. "It's true."

"All right. But I don't have time to explain tonal magic to you."

Chou nibbled a crooked feather into place. "Eleanor already explained it."

Eleanor blushed. "Ah, well—Chou is a bird—musical, you know…"

Jones finally cracked a smile. "Both of you then." He beckoned Eleanor and Chou closer and dropped his voice. "It's about Ezra Oliver. I think I'm on to something."

Eleanor's eyes widened. She glanced at Monty, leaned back in his chair with a wet cloth on his forehead.

Jones went on. "I think we can track him with tonal magic."

"Do you? How?" asked Eleanor.

"You both know all magic leaves a residue, and all magic has a tone. In my orchestra we pull the tone from a spell as it's happening. I think we can also pull the tone from the residue. The leftover evidence of the spell."

Chou's eyes narrowed to yellow slits. "Hasn't Oliver been hiding his spell residue?"

"Yes," said Jones. "But you forget, he's been gone for seven years. I started my research into tonal magic just last year. I've been careful to keep it quiet. He won't *know* to hide the tone."

"Interesting," said Eleanor, "but how will you find the residue? That's what we've been looking for all along."

Jones grinned. "We've had spell residue in our hands this whole time. We just haven't been able to make sense of it."

"The residue is in the leaflets, it's just hidden!"

Jones clapped. The first sharp crack startled the cloth from Monty's forehead. The frazzled librarian called over his shoulder about more tea as he left the library. Jones giggled like a schoolboy with a naughty secret. "Yes! And…those leaflets…every day in such numbers. Powerful stuff."

"Eleanor told me powerful spells bring outside noise into their tones," said Chou. "Maybe you'll hear things…voices…something that will give a clue as to where Oliver is hiding!"

"Fabulous!" said Eleanor. "Do you think you can do it? Pull the tones from the leaflets?"

"Magic hasn't failed me yet," the magician said. "I'll give it a bloody good try."

Eleanor laughed. "That's the spirit, Mr. Jones. You're not the sheepish apprentice who accompanied me to the Dragon Mines all those years ago."

Jones's buckteeth hung over his lips when he smiled. "Responsibility doesn't lend itself to sheepishness, Your Highness. You know it as well as I."

CHAPTER 20

HIGHGOD GO WITH ME

SINCE THE BURNING OF Queen Camille's, Eleanor had greeted each Fest with the dread of a fish staring down the gullet of a leggybird. The celebrations cast a beacon on all aspects of her unhappy situation, from the disdain of her peers to the collapse of her marriage to the increased philandering of a certain pale-eyed duke.

Lately Dorian had turned his considerable charm on the noble-women of Cartheigh in doses reminiscent of the earliest days of her acquaintance with him. Eleanor understood the need to quell Gregory's suspicions. She knew how Gregory pressured him to marry. Regardless, his hands gripping another woman's waist made her want to scream. The sight of him disappearing around a corner with some gorgeous young thing incited a physical reaction that veered between nausea and a slamming headache.

Chou sat on Eleanor's shoulder at every event and whispered calming sentiments in her ear. "It means nothing…he has no choice…look away…Gregory…"

She was certain the Waning lasted for a month, but after eight days her calendar told her otherwise. Most of the courtiers went into winter hibernation. Eleanor and the servants greeted the quiet months with relief. She shut herself in her bedroom with her children and her gnawing jealousy. She tried to drive the bitterness away, but it was like the last drunken guest at a dinner party. In the end she could only offer it a spot on the couch and hope it would be gone in the morning. Instead, it got comfortable and took up residence.

She planned the first post-fest debate society meeting on a rainy Tuesday in HighWinter, the kind of morning she knew would keep Gregory in his bed long past breakfast. Eight people joined in a spirited, and sometimes heated, discussion of plague control measures in place in the Fringe. Eleanor usually led the conversation, but today she let Rosemary and Faust run away with the argument. Her own lack of contribution embarrassed her, but she couldn't focus. She finally called an end to the conversation when Faust called Chou Chou a misinformed birdbrain and Chou threatened to peck the old man's eyes from his fat face. Everyone shook hands and toasted an enlightening debate.

Chou muttered under his breath, "Faust is as enlightened as a black rat down a deep

well—"

"Your Grace," Eleanor said as Dorian stood, "Might I have a word?"

Dorian seemed taken aback for a moment, but he sat again. Chou hopped onto Eleanor's shoulder and whispered in her ear, "What—"

"Would you check on the children, Chou? Nathan slept late this morning."

Chou's black tongue wagged in her direction but he took off. The rest of the debaters left the library. Eleanor and Dorian regarded each other in awkward silence over the table.

"Jones has made an interesting magical discovery," Eleanor said.

"Yes, he explained it to me. I told him I'm at his disposal."

"Oh, well, that's what I wanted to talk...about...I..."

He pulled a quill from his satchel and scrawled a few words on his meticulously written debate notes. He slid the paper toward her.

I miss you so much.

She read the words, but her green-eyed companion from the couch did the talking. "Really?" she whispered. "You seemed in high spirits at the Fest. You found plenty of distractions."

He lowered his own voice. "I'm doing what I must do."

"And how it taxes you." She batted her eyelashes at him. "Clearly you haven't lost your touch!"

"Lower your voice," he said, his jaw working. "Why are you saying these things?"

Her rational mind told her to stop, but umpteen pretty faces swept through her mind. She yammered on. "It's ridiculous for a thirty-three-year-old man to carry on so. Undignified."

"Do you think I'm enjoying this? Do you have any idea of the pressure he puts on me to"—she had to read his lips to catch the next word—"marry every day? You know exactly what I'd be doing, and who I'd be doing it with, if I had any kind of choice." She felt the hot pressure of unshed tears as his fist hit the table between them, with a sound like a book slamming shut.

"You'd emulate his behavior in your attempts to quell his suspicions," she hissed. "Chums in lechery—just like old times. Who knew dissuasion could be so enjoyable!"

"You're irrational." He glanced over his shoulder at Monty re-shelving books on the far side of the library. "And irresponsible. I'm finished here."

"Don't you dare walk out."

"Madam, I'm doing so right now." He stood, and crumpled his notes and his sentiments into a ball. He tossed the paper into the fire and left the library.

A week later the Burning broke free of the Fringe. It wound through Pasture's End and settled into the neat wooden houses surrounding Smithwick Square. Eleanor sat by her open window each night. The winter air brought the sounds of sobbing and fever-induced delirium into her chamber, as well as traces of caustic smoke. Funeral pyres lit the darkness like morbid birthday candles on a burnt cake. Eleanor closed the window when she noticed a thin coating of ash on the sill.

The leaflets stopped appearing, which in Eleanor's mind only served to confirm her assumptions about their source. Oliver could hardly criticize the search for a cure now that the magicians had control of it. Every few days Eleanor asked after Jones's progress, but the chief magician had no luck pulling tones from the leaflets. He tried to explain over tea one somber afternoon.

"Something is missing in my spell…it lacks"—Jones made two tight fists—"cohesion…I'm sorry, Your Highness. It's difficult to explain to someone with no magical power—and I must focus my energy on the cure."

Eleanor promised patience and Jones promised to keep her informed. She retreated to the library and scoured books on magical theory and concealing spells. Unfortunately, Jones was right. The vague, esoteric theorems and descriptions made little sense. She stubbornly kept at it. The work distracted her from the specter of her argument with Dorian. The coldness stretched out between them like an ever-widening sheet of thin ice. She feared to cross it, lest she fall through and do permanent damage.

In an effort to stave off loneliness and winter boredom, Eleanor invited Margaret to stay at Eclatant. She arrived on the tenth day of HighWinter with her four-year-old daughter, Madeleine. The prince and princess rarely had visitors, and Ticia had gone wild with preparations. She'd added extra blankets to the Madeleine's bed and placed vases of paper flowers on her nightstands. She tucked drawings and sweetmeats under her pillows. She'd selected one of her old gowns for Madeleine and hung it from the bed frame. As for Nathan, he proudly displayed his collection of wooden dragons, and instructed Margaret's daughter on which ones were available for her use.

"Nathan," said Eleanor. "Maddy is your guest. You must share your dragons."

Nathan blushed. "Except Green Pea?"

"Except Green Pea," said Eleanor.

Nathan retrieved his bedraggled silk dragon from his bed and sat on it. The dragon's patched, one-eyed face peered up from under the child's bottom in a silent plea for help.

Eleanor and Margaret laughed as they settled into two rocking chairs by the window. "I'm so happy you came," said Eleanor.

Margaret's brow furrowed in squiggly worry lines. "I thought to wait out the Burning, but it's surely safe at Eclatant. So many precautions."

"Hard times, these." Eleanor sank into the rocker and watched the children. They hadn't seen each other in weeks, but their laughter and bickering already filled the nursery.

"What's wrong, darling?" asked Margaret.

"Is it so obvious?"

Margaret stopped rocking and took Eleanor's hand. "I've known you a long time. Are things bad with Gregory?"

Eleanor saw no reason to coat a spoiled fish with sugar. "We're strangers who share a bed several times a week."

"I'm sorry."

"My marriage is…a failure." Even though the children were paying her no attention she dropped her voice. "But it's been careening in that direction for years."

Margaret sipped her tea and added a cube of sugar before continuing. "If you are resigned to such, there must be another reason for your melancholy."

Eleanor chose her words carefully. "You would think I'd have learned to check my tongue, but still I let my passions run away with me. I fear I've hurt the person I hold most dear."

"Have you spoken to this…person?"

242

"I cannot. It's not prudent. Besides, what if this person won't forgive me?"

"Eleanor, your mouth runs wild, but not without reason behind it. Perhaps you're being too harsh on yourself."

Eleanor considered Margaret's speculation. "There was...validity... to my anger...but as always I went about expressing it all wrong."

"If this person holds you as dear as you hold him, he will understand that."

Eleanor raised an eyebrow. "He?"

Margaret patted Eleanor's knee and steered the conversation back into polite territory. Four days later Margaret was abed with a headache, and then a fever. The Burning came to Eclatant.

The thought of having a game of strikestick while Margaret Easton Delano hovered on the edge of death in the far eastern wing of the palace seemed absurd to Dorian, but here he stood, stick in hand. Gregory and Brian circled the table, looking for a good angle. Wooden balls pinged off each other and the three targets in table's center. Dorian rested his elbows on the back of a high stool and awaited his turn.

Bested beasts, cowhide furniture, the smell of old, unopened books. The study hadn't changed much in the years since Gregory's wedding night, when Dorian came across an eighteen-year-old Eleanor shortly after her unceremonious deflowering. He could still picture her; pale skin and hair blending with her ivory nightdress, her odd two-toned eyes leaping out from all that whiteness. No bitterness on her face. No anger. Just curiosity, and the first traces of the infatuation that had driven them both for so long.

Not infatuation, he thought. *It was more than that, even then. HighGod, how I miss her.* And then, *damn her and her slashing tongue!*

"Your play, Your Grace," said Brian. "I've got you on the defensive."

"I doubt it," said Dorian, as he leaned over the table. He aimed his stick and struck, but his shot went wide of Brian's green ball.

"He misses!" Brian pounded his fist on the table.

"One miss is hardly a game lost," Dorian snapped back.

"You *are* on the defensive today," said Gregory, from the other end of the table. "I thought you above such sparring."

Dorian grunted. *Defensive at the strikestick table...and against Eleanor's accusations.*

He ceased hearing Brian and Gregory's jabs. He sized up the table, and himself. It was becoming harder to deny it. Eleanor might have acted like a tantrum-prone child, but...the thought echoed in his head like an off note in one of Jones's tonal music concerts.

There is truth behind her vitriolic.

How had it all started? A few harmless embraces of that hazel-eyed friend of Sylvia's just before they left Solsea last summer. One of the Smithwick girls after the Harvest Fest. *Her mouth on my—does that count?* After that the faces blurred, and the lines blurred with them. He'd stopped going to Pandra's, and told himself a free fuck was no different from a paying one. Gregory's laughing, drunken face swam in and out of every encounter. And always, in the back of his own mind, *I must put him off our trail. If I can't have her, what difference does it make? I'm doing what I have to do.*

He shot, and his ball pinged off the target and struck Brian's. Brian glowered as he removed the ball from the table.

"That's more like it," said Gregory. "I need some constancy in these uncertain times. The Burning—inside the walls of Eclatant."

"One chambermaid dead, and poor Margaret..." Dorian trailed off.

"With the east wing all but cut off from the rest of the palace, I hope we've contained it. We'll know something in the next few days either way."

"Everyone is terrified," said Brian. "I've not seen a dry-eyed servant in a week."

"I received word that Margaret's fever broke yesterday," said Gregory. "If it comes back, that's the end."

"Eleanor will be crushed"—Dorian coughed into his hand—"and Raoul...how is he?"

"His parents have locked him in his own bedroom," said Gregory. "Margaret sent Maddy home and refuses to let him visit. Poor lad. He's going mad."

"Are the magicians making progress?" asked Brian. "It's been over a month."

Gregory shook his head. "It's getting worse. There are reports of banshees in Smithwick Square. Can you imagine? Banshees—"

Eleanor catapulted into the room. She wore a simple chocolate colored cotton gown. She'd twisted her hair into a messy bun. Dark circles rimmed her puffy blue and brown eyes. It seemed she'd come to continue their conversation.

"Banshee!" She gasped for breath. "In the east wing. You can hear it from halfway across the palace! Chou saw it through the hallway windows!"

Gregory paled. "By the Bond, we are in dire straights."

"Margaret's fever has returned. It's looking for her!"

Gregory crossed the room and tried to put his arms around Eleanor. "There's nothing to be done, sweetheart. Her time has come."

Eleanor shook her head. "A few have recovered. But she won't if the banshee comes to her!" She locked eyes with Dorian and pulled away from Gregory. "A skilled swordsman can drive it away. Dorian, please. If any man in this kingdom can rid us of it, you can."

Gregory stepped between them, and Dorian saw nothing but his thick red hair. "No, the banshee will attack. There could be more than one."

"Please—I'm begging you. She has Raoul, and Maddy—"

"I won't risk him!" Gregory said.

Dorian put a hand on Gregory's shoulder and eased him sideways, so he met Eleanor's eyes again. The desperation on her face made his decision. "Greg, I have to try."

"What—folly—ridiculous—" Gregory's hands raked his scalp, and Dorian had a moment to admire the tenacity of the prince's hair. Gregory's arms dropped to his side. "Let me help you, then."

Dorian shook his head. "No, sire. I'm expendable. You are not."

"Don't say that!" Both men turned in her direction, Gregory between Dorian and Eleanor, as always. Eleanor flushed a mottled red. "Neither of you are. I have faith in your skill, Your Grace, otherwise I would not ask it of you."

"With your blessing, Your Highness," Dorian said.

Gregory nodded. Dorian bowed and went to collect his sword.

"No one may pass, Your Grace," the sergeant said. "Quarantine."

"I have Prince Gregory's permission."

The man jumped as a keening wail echoed down the east wing's marble staircase. "I'd advise against it, sir."

"Peace, soldier. I know what awaits me." Dorian put a hand to the hilt of his sword.

"Then HighGod go with you, sir," the sergeant said as he stepped aside. His partner grunted in agreement.

Dorian's boot falls thudded like blunt hammer blows on the stairway's thick green carpet. His fingers squeaked along the polished handrail. As he reached the landing, the banshee's cry squelched those comforting, earthly sounds. Dorian had heard many an off-putting noise in his day. The roar of a dragon. The cries of battlefield wounded. The squeal of a tradacta, the vicious, flightless bird of the Scaled Mountains. Nothing compared to the shrieks coming from the depths of the east wing.

Something about it set every hair on his arms on end and made his eyes water. The cry went in one ear, spun around behind his eyes for a few seconds, and exited with a bang from the other side of his head.

A fat chambermaid with bushy black hair huddled on the floor beside a suit of battle armor at the top of the stairs. He knelt beside her. She opened her eyes at his voice.

"Where is it?" he asked.

She pointed down the hallway. "I've been caring for Missus Delano…" She started crying. "…but I can't stay, sir. I just can't…with that noise—"

"Shhh. You've done your duty. I'll see to it from here."

"Bless you, sir. I'll pray for ya, I will." She pointed out Margaret's door.

"Thank you." The smell of sweat and healing herbs met him when he opened Margaret's door. He saw nothing of her but a tuft of frizzy hair and a pile of squirming blankets in a four-poster bed, but her moans drifted into the hallway.

"Margaret, it's Dorian."

She didn't give any sign she'd heard him. He considered offering her a glass of water, and then remembered Gregory's final admonishment to keep back from her, for the sake of all Eclatant. He sat in a chair by the fireplace with his sword across his lap.

Perhaps he'd given the creature a clue as to Margaret's whereabouts by opening the door. The cries rose in volume. He sensed a heightened urgency. Sweat beaded on the back of his neck.

He wasn't sure what he expected. A blast of cold air, or maybe roiling smoke. There was nothing but the cry moving down the hall. Margaret went still in the bed. The banshee stepped into the room.

White skin, thick white hair flowing over its shoulders. Corpselike white. Otherwise it seemed nothing but a man, or maybe a woman, about his own height. It wore something like a pair of leggings and a tattered tunic. Its feet, wrapped in torn cloth of some kind, made no sound on the shiny wooden floor. It smelled, of all things, like honeysuckle.

Dorian stood, but the banshee didn't notice him. It walked toward the bed. Dorian gripped his sword. "Ho, you there!"

The thing's head turned with all the speed of a flower following the sun. Dorian thought it not truly male or female, but maybe a bit of both. It had fine, elegant features and bright blue eyes.

"You'll not have her," he said.

It turned back to the bed and took two steps forward. Dorian crossed the room and stood in front of it. "I said you'll not have her."

Still, nothing. The banshee stepped to his right. Dorian lifted his sword.

The effect was immediate. The sword glowed with the bright blue of the banshee's eyes. Its mouth fell open, revealing a blood red mouth and sharp teeth. It hissed at the sword, and then screamed.

It was as if someone had struck a gong beside Dorian's head. He couldn't move.

The banshee struck with one white hand and narrowly missed knocking the sword from Dorian's grip. It hissed again. Dorian took three steps back and brandished the weapon at it again. It crouched, and then leapt over his head. It clung to the ornate moldings lining the ceiling.

Fortunately, (or unfortunately, depending on how one looked at it), the banshee had no intention of staying out of reach on the ceiling. It let go of the molding and shot toward Dorian with a screech.

His sword caught its upraised arms with a reverberating crack, as if he'd struck granite, and to Dorian's surprise a few droplets of cold red blood splashed across his face. He spun to follow its leaping progress around the room, but it was too fast. It hit him between the shoulder blades with two fists. He stumbled and fell on his knees.

The banshee landed on his back, and he felt a few ribs crack. It lifted his head and attempted to smash his face into the floor, but Dorian shifted and his nose bounced off his own forearm with a meaty crack. The banshees worried his shoulders, trying to get at the sword under his body. It squealed and gibbered, and a rain of cold spittle coated his neck. He bucked his hips and flipped over. The sword came around in a flying arc and struck the side of the banshee's head. A dark red patch appeared in its long hair.

The banshee howled in surprise and wrapped its arms around its head. Dorian pedaled backward and sprung to his feet. The wounded creature scrambled onto the bed. Margaret's body bounced as it tramped across the blankets.

"Get away from her!" Dorian screamed as it knelt beside Margaret. The banshee pointed one long finger at Margaret's head.

Dorian raised his sword above his head with both hands and struck. The blade met the banshee's arm. For the meanest of seconds, it ground through hard bone, before burying itself in the blankets. The banshee's hand fell onto the bed. Blood sprayed across the room in thick gouts.

Impossible as it seemed, the banshee appeared to be struck dumb. Its sparkly blue eyes stared at the spraying stump, and watched Dorian with a gaping mouth. It clambered off the bed.

"You are bested." Dorian held the sword before his face. It pulsed with blue light. "Leave this room."

Still the banshee approached him. Still the unnatural silence.

"Leave," he said again.

"Leave," it whispered back. "Leave."

The banshee stopped an arm's width away. It held the stump up in front of Dorian like a Godsman presenting the chapel offering. The blood flow had slowed to a heavy gush. The banshee cocked the injured arm and swiped Dorian across the face with it. Before Dorian could react it repeated the favor with its good hand. Dorian's lip exploded, and he felt his right eye swelling shut. He fell to his knees and cradled his head in his hands.

Later he would wonder if he'd lost consciousness. When he raised his head again, the banshee had disappeared.

Margaret looked up at Dorian with calm brown eyes, as if he'd just awoken her from a pleasant afternoon nap. Like the rest of it, the banshee's severed hand had vanished.

"Don't come any closer, Your Grace," she said.

"Did my blade strike you? Please, tell me I didn't—"

"You did not. It would make no difference if you had."

"What do you mean—it's gone—"

"You've performed with honor and bravery, sir. I know who put you up to this. Please send her my gratitude." Margaret whispered messages for her daughter and husband. He promised to remember every word. She shivered and swallowed several times. "When I first heard it—the terror—cannot tell you—"

"Don't talk. Save your strength."

"—but when it came in the room, I—I was no longer afraid. I realized—"

She coughed. Dorian pulled his handkerchief, but she shook her head and lifted her hand in a weak wave.

"The banshees come to put a swift end to our suffering. We need not fear them." She smiled, and closed her eyes. "I must look a mess. My eyes...swollen...and my hair..."

"You look lovely," he said.

Margaret exhaled, and went still.

CHAPTER 21

TOO FAR, GIRL

"You have suffered a great loss."

Eleanor looked up at Hazelbeth's words. For an hour she'd sat beside the Watching Pool, inhaling the scent of lavender and waiting for the Oracle to notice her. Water lapped at the pool's muddy edges with the tinkle of a thousand falling tears. Eleanor held Rosemary's hand. She squeezed it whenever the grief rose in her chest like a trapped sparrow.

"A dear friend. Lost to the Burning." Eleanor's voice echoed off the cavern walls.

Dear friend...lost...lost...lost...

The Oracle didn't offer any further condolences. Her thin lips smacked together. She'd lost her few remaining teeth. She looked smaller and more shriveled than ever. "I have lived through many a plague these long centuries," Hazelbeth said. "This sickness is unusual. It enters one house and kills the entire family. In another only one or two take ill. Still others seem immune. The cure will be a long time coming. Is the Burning contained at Eclatant?"

Eleanor nodded. "It seems so. Margaret is...was...one of only two deaths. Her daughter isn't afflicted. Raoul took...her...home..." She put a hand over her mouth at the memory of Raoul urging a dumbstruck

Madeleine into the family carriage. "The king has reduced the staff. He's allowing only essential visitors in and out of the palace."

"Yet he lets you come here," said the Oracle.

"I begged Gregory to let me visit. Rosemary said she had something to share, and I needed…to escape for a few hours. I promised I'd not leave the carriage until I arrived at Afar Creek."

"Surprisingly generous of him," said Rosemary.

Eleanor felt oddly defensive. "He knows the extent of my grief. Besides, Afar Creek is as safe a place as any, what with the heightened immunity of the magical folk."

"We've had a recent death," said the Oracle. "The Abbotess, but she didn't fall to the Burning. She was over three hundred years old, and fat. Her heart couldn't take the strain of watching common folk die while we are forced to sit on our hands."

"The Abbey has never been in such a state, Eleanor," said Rosemary. "If not for our fields, we'd be starving. Without the people's tithing… and no teachers or healers bringing in fees—"

"No fees?"

"The people have been turning to the Covey for healing. They're better served there these days, anyway. Most of our healers and sorceresses have been sent into exile in the country." A rare hint of emotion crept into the Oracle's voice at the mention of her witches' rebellion. "They would not be kept from their work."

"Since the scandal of Queen Camille's, it's gone out of vogue for witches to teach young ladies." The water churning beneath Rosemary's chin cast a bluish glow over her face. Every word leaked bitterness. "Or for young ladies to learn much beyond the writing of their own names, for that matter."

"Half our numbers disbursed," said Hazelbeth. "Those that remain impoverished and dispirited. Power wanes by the day. For the first time, I feel my years." Hazelbeth's eyes closed. The water went still.

"I thought she didn't sleep," whispered Eleanor.

"She hasn't. Not for a thousand years. Until now." Rosemary called across the pool. "Wise one? Hazelbeth?"

The old woman jerked. Eleanor saw a hint of confusion on her face. The mystical heart of Afar Creek Abbey resembled someone's doddering grandmother.

"I was saying something," said Hazelbeth. "Remind me?"

"The state of Afar Creek," said Rosemary.

It was as if someone had lit a candle behind Hazelbeth's eyes. The pool leapt to life. "Afar Creek is unwell," she said, "and we have a dearth of leadership. So I have selected a new Abbotess."

"Who?" asked Eleanor.

The look on Rosemary's face was one part pride, ninety-nine parts terror. "Me."

Before Eleanor could digest this bit of unexpected information the Oracle spoke again. "Are you expecting a child? I sense a babe coming. A child who will be mentioned in the history books."

Eleanor put a hand to her flat belly. Her monthly flow had ended only yesterday. Hazelbeth squinted at Eleanor, and again the old witch's face belied confusion. "No...no. You are fair. The woman that carries this boy has hair to shame a raven's feathers."

Eleanor hugged Rosemary before climbing into her carriage. She opened the window and reached for her teacher's hand. "The Oracle and I have faith in you," she said. "Have faith in yourself."

Rosemary nodded and smiled, but the deep wrinkles between her dark eyes told a different tale. She kissed Eleanor's hand as the carriage started rolling. "Pray for me," she called.

"Always," Eleanor said.

A raven-haired woman. Carrying a son with a destiny. Eleanor could think of only one Carthean lady who could be described in such a way and simultaneously be impregnated with such a child.

She rested her chin on the window frame. Several young witches in too-short dresses clung to Rosemary's skirt. They jumped up and down on their skinny legs, sending sparks and enchanted flowers into Rosemary's face. Like all children, they wanted nothing more than to impress. "Watch me, Abbotess! No, watch *me* first!"

Rosemary shuffled them away from the Abbey gate. Eleanor's carriage rumbled through the quiet courtyard. Only a few witches hurried between the stone edifice of the Abbey proper and the dirt paths leading to the fields and outbuildings. They carried buckets, baskets of eggs, and sacks of grain. No one smiled or waved or called out the witches' ubiquitous blessings of *health and HighGod.*

No merchants arrived to barter for the witches' crops. No public teachers and healers came and went from appointments with students and patrons. Gone were the sick and injured, limping or lain out on stretchers, crying out for mercy and medicine. Eleanor could catch only the faintest whiffs of healing potions and burning incense.

The carriage left the Abbey and turned onto the Outcountry Road. Eleanor watched the townsfolk going about their daily business. They drove carts, pushed wheelbarrows, and traipsed along with baskets under their arms. They laughed and argued with one another as if nothing had changed within the gates of Afar Creek. As if the women who had cared for their illnesses and delivered their babies for thousands of years were not abandoned and destitute.

Eleanor called to the sergeant in command of her guards. "Why did we stop?"

"Crazy people, Your Highness. In front of the carriage."

She peered around the windowsill. The sergeant cleared his throat. "Your Highness, please—I'd rather you stayed out of sight."

She ignored him. Six men and three women milled around the carriage team. The eight white hackneys jibbed and snorted. Green and purple plumes bounced between their ears like feathery signal flames.

"They're of no account," said the sergeant. "Here most days. Yellin' at the witches."

Eleanor scowled. "What problem do they have with the witches?"

The sergeant scowled right back at her. "Same problem we all have."

"Watch yourself, sergeant," Eleanor said. He blushed and mumbled apologies.

The protesters were an eclectic group of ragged Fringers, shop-keeping types, and to Eleanor's surprise, a Godsman. They shouted a chorus of complaints and accusations.

"—a house of sin and false healing—"

"—my niece—dead at the witches' hands—whoremongers—"

"Does King Casper know where his colors travel today?"

Each snippet sent more blood rushing to Eleanor's head. The driver urged the horses forward, but they wouldn't budge. Passersby stopped to gawk. Soon the spectacle brought passage on the Outcountry Road to a standstill in all directions.

The Godsman shouted in his preacher's voice. "HighGod looks down on Afar Creek Abbey and weeps—"

Eleanor opened the carriage door. She jumped onto the muddy road and slammed it shut behind her. The sergeant's protests followed her up the Fire-iron ladder anchored to the side of the coach. The astounded driver slid across the bench so quickly he nearly shot off the far side.

The diatribe dwindled to a discontented rumble at the sight of Eleanor, her dark green gown, and the delicate crown atop her head. "HighGod is indeed weeping!" Eleanor called out over the crowd. "But not for the witches' treachery. They have committed none."

The mutterings picked up in volume and tempo. Eleanor raised her voice to a shout. "He weeps because the people of Maliana have abandoned their most steadfast friends! The women who have cared for your bodies and your minds! For a pittance, or no price at all!"

A woman with blackened teeth and stringy gray hair broke from the edges of the crowd. "A high price them girls in the cathouses paid! A high price for Fringe daughters burned up in your school!"

"Peace, woman," said Eleanor. People clapped the old woman's back and bellowed their agreement with her sentiments. Eleanor tried again. "Peace! The witches sought only to help—"

"Just like they helped with the Burning!"

Eleanor scrambled as the back-and-forth spun out of her control. "Afar Creek never had the chance—"

"Bullocks! Dragonshit!"

"—to find a cure! Now the Abbey is weak—"

Cheers went up from the crowd, but as the sergeant, his men and their swords moved between the carriage and the mob the heckling died down. Eleanor took advantage of the sudden quiet.

"I will forgive your disrespect, for I understand the frustration behind it. Like the witches, I wish only to help—"

"We don't want your help! Don't need it no more!" screamed the old Fringe woman. "Devil eyes! Devil eyes!"

The woman spit in the direction of the carriage. The crowd surged around her. Eleanor saw nothing but open mouths and upraised fists, smelled only unwashed bodies and unhindered anger. The horses reared. The carriage rolled backwards with a few jouncing turns of its Fire-iron wheels. Eleanor landed in the driver's lap. He yelped and held up his hands, and then must have decided he'd risk an inappropriate handling of her person over allowing her to tumble off the carriage into the screaming mob. He grabbed her around the waist and held tight.

The sergeant and his men drove their warhorses into the crowd. The screams continued, but now Eleanor heard more panic and less rage. "Sergeant, please!" she cried. "Take care!" She struggled in the driver's grip.

The crowd scattered before the soldiers' blades and the slicing hooves of their horses. People stampeded down Outcountry Road, trampling their fellow dissenters along the way. Only a few moaning, crumpled bodies remained behind. They coughed and called out for help through the road dust. The lone Godsman knelt over a pile of gray rags topped with stringy hair.

The Fringe woman would look upon her princess's devil eyes no more. She was dead.

Eleanor didn't change her dusty dress. She lay on her bed and watched a spider crawl across the blue silk canopy strung between the four posters of her bed. The tiny creature fell toward her, and then hoisted itself up on an invisible thread.

I have no line to pull me up again.

Devil eyes. In the days of Eleanor's childhood, it had been an oft-repeated mantra in the Brice House. Along with *freak, monster,* and *evil spirit. Horrid, ghastly…a bad sign…ill-begotten…*Imogene had enjoyed springing such insults on Eleanor at the slightest infraction, and often at no infraction at all.

Some people have large noses. Some have warts. I have one blue eye and one brown. I'm a grown woman, for the love of the Bond.

Still, the Fringe woman's personal insult was like hot water poured over the burns of her more substantive complaints. If she had dared speak so to her future queen, her anger ran deeper than Eleanor had imagined. She gulped down the terrifying truth she'd been sipping since the first leaflets began floating through the Fringe.

The people of Maliana hated her.

Eleanor rolled onto her side and wrapped her arms around her head. For years she'd taken comfort in the people's love. For every pair of eyes that cut her in a ballroom, she found fifty that wished her well in the city streets. She'd done her best by them, but fear and Ezra Oliver's propaganda had proven too powerful a combination.

She felt as if the floorboards had started moving under her feet. *Who am I, if not the people's glass slipper princess?*

A few tears dripped from the end of her nose onto the bedcover, turning the light blue to sapphire. She gripped her choker, dark these past few weeks since her argument with Dorian.

Stupid, petty argument.

"Your Highness!" Pansy burst into the bedroom. "Get up! Visitors!"

"I don't want to see anyone, Pansy."

"You got no choice, I'm afraid." Pansy straightened her cap. "His Majesty, King Casper! His Highness, Prince Gregory! His Grace, the Duke of Brandling!"

Eleanor scrambled to her feet as the king plowed through the door like a runaway ox. Gregory and Dorian followed him. She dropped an awkward curtsy. The king screamed at the top of her head.

"You've gone too far! Too far, girl!"

Eleanor swallowed. She'd expected the king to hear of the ruckus in town, but not so soon, and she'd hardly planned on an audience in her chamber. She didn't rise. She could almost feel the road dust coating her hair blowing away under the strength of her father-in-law's tirade.

"You climb onto the carriage? You start an argument with a mob of commoners?"

"Father—"

Casper turned on Gregory. "You let her go to the witches! We're in the midst of a plague and you let her leave Eclatant!"

"I told her not to mix with anyone—to stay in the Abbey, or the coach—"

"Dragonshit, Gregory! She's never listened to you! Why would she do so now?" The king yanked Eleanor upright. "You would bring the Burning home to my son and my grandchildren?"

"No!" Eleanor cried. "Of course not, Your Majesty—the witches are immune—I took every precaution—"

His nose was a finger width from hers. "Ha! You call inciting mob violence on Outcountry Road precautionary?"

"I only sought to show the people the error of their ways—the witches—"

"Damn and blast the witches! You risked the plague, you humiliated the crown, and you caused the death of some peasant women. They're already singing her praises in the Fringe! *And* blaspheming the Desmarais name!"

Eleanor shook her head. "No—I'm sorry—I didn't mean—"

"We've always counted on you to spread good will," said Gregory, "but you've become a liability."

"I've had a misunderstanding...with the citizenry—"

"You have a misunderstanding with your dressmaker," said the king, "not with the entire populace."

"Forgive me," Eleanor whispered. Dorian stepped toward her, then glanced at Gregory and stopped.

"We've forgiven you before," said Gregory. Eleanor knew she'd find no savior in him.

"I'm sending you and the children to Peaksend Castle," said the king. "The Burning has not reached the North Country."

"Peaksend!" Eleanor cried. "The children—in that drafty, horrible place—"

Casper's voice dropped to a dangerous whisper. "I could just as easily keep the children at Eclatant and send you to Peaksend. If you would continue to mother them, you will hold your tongue. In all instances, public and private."

"Yes— yes, sire. I will begin packing," Eleanor said.

Dorian cleared his throat. "Your Majesty, I may have another solution."

Casper grunted. Dorian spoke to the king's back. "Perhaps the princess and her children could retreat to Harper's Crossing. Plagues usually pass over the Lake District. We're too few and far apart to breed much disease."

"It would be better for Leticia and Nathan," said Gregory. "The

North Country is miserable this time of year. Or any time of year, for that matter."

"Laralee is empty. My servants would welcome the royal family."

Casper let go of Eleanor. His grip left a red band around her arm, an accusatory tattoo. "Very well. If my son wishes it. The Lake District. Let me hear nothing but silence from the east, madam."

She curtsied again, and the three men left as abruptly as they had arrived.

"Why can't we go to Solsea?" Ticia asked. She hovered around Eleanor like a nervous hummingbird.

Eleanor placed *Numbers for Young Children* atop the stack of Ticia and Nathan's other schooling books. She ran her fingers along the volumes lining the nursery's bookshelves. "I told you, darling, it's only HighWinter. It's too cold in Solsea."

"Will it be cold in the Lake District?"

"Yes, but Uncle Dorian's house is lovely."

"Will there be children to play with?"

Eleanor paused. "We must stay to ourselves, Tish. I told you that. But you'll have Nathan, and Chou."

"We can't play with others because of the Burning," said Nathan. He didn't look up from the battle scene he'd meticulously arranged on the nursery floor. "We can't die, Ticia. If I die, who shall be king?"

As always, Nathan's acute observations both impressed and alarmed his mother. "Now Nathan, don't scare your sister. No one is going to die."

"Why can't Cricket come?" asked Ticia. "Teardrop is coming. It's not fair."

"Cricket needs to continue her training—"

"I can train her!" Ticia stomped her foot. The sound ripped the weak fabric of Eleanor's tattered patience.

"Leticia Desmarais!" she said. "I've heard enough! Your grandfather wishes us to go, and your father, and we're going! Now make yourself useful!"

Ticia huffed to her bed, her red pigtails bouncing in indignation. She crossed her arms over her chest and glared at her mother. Eleanor's hands shook as she returned to the books. Only the slap of one leather cover meeting the next disturbed the silence in the nursery.

"Mother?"

Eleanor took a deep breath before she responded. "Yes, Nathan?"

"Why can't Poppa come?"

"He'll visit." She turned around. Nathan slumped amidst his army of wooden knights and unicorns and dragons. Ticia had wrapped her arms around her knees and buried her face in her purple skirt.

Eleanor knelt on the smiling sun in the middle of the green and purple rug and held out her arms. "Darlings, I'm so sorry." Both children ran to her. She tumbled backwards in a flurry of gray tulle and lace. "Goodness," she said with a laugh. "I think you both want to crush me!"

Ticia cracked a smile, and Eleanor kissed her cheek. "In truth, my loves, I'd rather not go. But it is our duty, and we shall be together. It will be an adventure. We must be strong soldiers, yes?"

As both children nodded the nursery door opened. Gregory stepped into the room with a box in each hand.

"Poppa!" Nathan cried. "Are you coming with us now?"

Gregory shook his head. "You know I can't, Nathan. Who will help grandfather?"

"Uncle Dorian. Come! We can ride in a boat on the Lake."

"Grandfather needs me here. I'll see you soon, in a month or two."

Nathan's face fell. Ticia wrapped her arms around Gregory's leg. "We'll be good, Poppa. Please come."

Gregory detached his daughter. "Stop it, now, both of you. The Desmarais don't beg." He held up the boxes. "Look here!"

The children opened their gifts, a set of paintbrushes for Ticia and a carved boat for Nathan. "Thank you, Poppa," said Ticia. "Where is mother's gift?"

"I already gave it to her."

"Children, run and show your gifts to Pansy while I finish packing."

They bowed and curtsied and did as Eleanor asked. Gregory closed the door behind them. "You're packed?"

"Yes. We leave tomorrow."

"Good." He traipsed across the smiling sun. "It's for the best."

"As you wish."

"I'm doing you a favor! It could be Peaksend."

"I know. Thank you."

"You could show a little more appreciation."

Eleanor took a deep breath. She was determined to keep the discussion pleasant. "I said thank you. I don't know what else you want from me."

"Maybe you could tell me you'll miss me. I'll miss you."

She chuckled. "You say it's about the Burning, but you need to be rid of me. Your people demand it. Your father demands it. So I'll disappear for a while."

"It's only for a few months. I'll miss you."

For some reason that repeated sentiment lit a fire under Eleanor's carefully dampened frustration. "We barely speak, Gregory, and you have others to keep you company. Although with Sylvia indisposed..."

His face reddened, and Eleanor's suspicions were confirmed. *Let it go,* said the voice in Eleanor's head, the one that always sounded like a mixture of Chou Chou and Rosemary. But she didn't. "How did the Duchess come to such a state with no husband?"

Gregory came closer, but Eleanor held her ground. "Is it yours?" she asked lightly, as if in reference to an unclaimed strikestick, or a new hat.

"You have no right to ask me such questions."

She lifted her chin. "I have a right to defend my children, and their claims."

"You impugn my loyalty to my son?"

"Sylvia's bastard won't be welcome at Eclatant."

Gregory stepped over the edge of civility's cliff. "You dare tell me"—he clenched a fist beside her face—"who will and won't be welcome in this fucking palace?"

She spoke through gritted teeth. "I'm only asking you to respect our children."

He struck her. She spun away from him, her hand to the side of her head. Her ankle rolled and she fell against Ticia's bed.

"I'll welcome a passel of my bastards to Eclatant if I choose!" he screamed down at her. He threw a crystal goblet at the wall above her head. Shards rained shards down on Ticia's pillows. "I'll grant them all titles and sup with them every night! It's none of your fucking affair!"

She covered her ears, but still she heard small fists on hardwood. Her children's voices floated through the nursery door. "Mother! Mother, what's the matter?"

Gregory jerked her to her feet. "HighGod damn you for making me do this!" He shook her. She pushed him, but it was like shoving a stubborn bull. The freckles on his nose melted into the rest of his reddened face. "I love you, damnit!"

"You've never loved me," she whispered.

"Mother! Poppa! Poppa!"

Ticia's cries cut through Gregory's fog. He let go with both hands and stepped away from Eleanor.

"Safe travels, Wife." He bowed and left through the side door.

Eleanor wiped her face and pressed her fingers into the lemon-sized welt beside her left eye. Her dark eye. Then she got to her feet and put on a smile for her children.

CHAPTER 22

A LENS OF MOTIVATION

CHOU NIBBLED ON ELEANOR'S hair. She poked him with her quill. "Stop, Chou."

He paced her head. "It's been two hours. You can't hide in here all day."

Eleanor stretched her arms over her head. Chou landed on the table in front of her. She glanced around Laralee's spacious library. The anciently aristocratic and now extinct Leigh family, Laralee's original inhabitants, had stocked the shelves for generations, and after a hundred-year hiatus Dorian had taken up that duty with a scholarly vengeance. Eleanor breathed in the comforting smells of dust and leather and ink. If not for the smudged view of the lake through the thick windows, she could have been at home at Eclatant. "I know, Chou...I..." She felt guilty even saying it.

"If you have to read *Daniel the Dragon and the Awful Ornery Ogre* one more time you might be sick?"

She rubbed her eyes. "Yes! And my scalp is sore from Ticia's braiding. I'm a horrible mother."

Chou waved his head. "No. You're a very good mother. You've just been entertaining your children all hours of the day for nearly two months. It would drive some to drink. You read."

"A few hours in the nursery without me won't hurt...Ticia has her pencils and Nathan his books...oh, Chou, I wish they could play with Anne Clara's children."

"Perhaps they can. The Burning has not reached the Crossing."

"But Rosemary says nothing has changed in Maliana. Children seem to be having the worst time of it. Ticia and Nathan are safer on their own."

"Have you heard from Gregory?"

She shook her head. "No word of when he'll visit."

"What of His Grace?"

"Nothing." Eleanor touched her choker, still dark, still cold. "All this talk of correspondence reminds me. I owe Orvid Jones a letter."

Chou hissed. "Jones! Can't find a cure for the Burning. Oliver is still at large. Some chief magician."

"Don't speak of him so, Chou. I've never met a magician like him. He doesn't care about power, or influence."

Chou crawled up the candelabra. His toes curled around the engraved Fire-iron. "Yes, yes," he said, pulling himself along by his beak. "You're right. I only wish he'd make progress. He has all the motivation he needs for a good outcome. Remember what Ezra Oliver said in the banshee book? Magic is driven by motive, both light and dark."

"No. You're misinterpreting Oliver's meaning. He never said good motive leads to a good outcome, or ill to ill. He only said one should examine motive to understand magic—" Her eyes widened. "Examine magic through motive...I wonder!"

"So do I...I wonder what you're talking about." Chou hung upside down. His head feathers brushed the table below him.

Eleanor's mind raced. "If I recall, Chou, Ezra Oliver is not a very poetic man. If he believes magic is best understood by examining it through motivation, he meant it literally."

"I don't follow."

She rested her chin on her elbows. "What motivates Ezra Oliver? What drives his spellwork?"

"I'd say anger...or vengeance...or hatred."

"Or all three. And at whom does he direct these pleasant sentiments?"

"Why, the witches. And you."

"Yes!" Eleanor cried. "And the king, I'm sure...maybe Gregory... but he's certainly intent on bringing down Afar Creek and ending my tenure as princess. Somehow Jones must use the motivation—he must insert it into the spell he uses to look for the tones!"

She stood. Chou righted himself and followed her hectic princess around the room. She talked as much to herself as to him. "The tones are there...in the hidden residue. What if Jones could use Oliver's own motives to reveal them? View magic through motivation...there's something there...something literal...physical, I know it!"

"Eleanor, you're not a magical scholar," said Chou. "Most of the enchantment theories you read at Eclatant made no sense to you."

"This doesn't make sense either, not really, but Ezra Oliver believed in the power of magical motives, and we've not seen his enchanted equal in three hundred years."

She twisted a few strands of wavy blonde hair around her finger. "I shall send Orvid Jones a lock of my hair and ask him to chip a rock from the walls of Afar Creek. I'll suggest that he use Oliver's hatred when he examines the leaflets."

"How will he do that?" asked Chou.

Eleanor shrugged. "He's the magician. He'll have to figure out that part on his own."

Peaksend Castle took shape in the mist, its towers and spires reaching out of the Scaled Mountains like the fingers of a clutching hand. Dorian had always had a deep respect for the fortress, despite its lack of architectural grace. It clung stubbornly to the mountainside through horrendous weather, bloody battles, and the odd flood. Eclatant was beautiful, but Peaksend was durable. In Dorian's mind the contrasting castles exemplified the best of his country, and the enduring power of the Great Bond. He found irony in Brian Smithwick's foppish presence at the stalwart fortress. He thanked HighGod that said Duke of the Northcountry had seen fit to extend his time to Maliana. Dorian didn't fancy the idea of a dour, drippy, diplomatic luncheon in Brian's decidedly un-festive dining room.

The frigid drizzle no longer bothered him on this sixth day of his northbound journey with Orvid Jones. He tugged at the dragon robe around his shoulders and watched the rain roll down Senné's impervious black hide in squiggly lines. Jones's sopping horse puffed along beside them, although the unicorn had taken pity on his common cousin and slowed his pace to a shambling walk. Senné kept up a stream of encouragement.

"That's a good lad. Almost there. The mines are just around the bend."

"Trying, trying," said the horse.

Dorian patted Senné's neck. "I'll be glad of a warm fire myself. Amazing. A week ago we were fat and lazy before the hearths of Eclatant."

"You can thank HighGod for the weather, and your prince for the journey. And your princess for the pleasure of our other—task." Jones shook his head. "I still cannot believe she found the solution that's eluded me for months. Embarrassing, really."

Dorian gave him a wan smile. "She will surprise you."

Three weeks ago, Jones had cornered Dorian after dinner, all aflutter with news from Laralee. He'd waved Eleanor's letter under Dorian's nose while muttering about *motives* and *that's it* and *must-get-to-work*.

"I've got it!" he shouted as he catapulted into Dorian's chamber on a bright Monday morning ten days later. He thrust a glass bottle into Dorian's hand. "Now, what is it?"

Dorian laid a volume of poetry on his desk and removed the stopper. A puff of gray smoke drifted from the bottle's neck. A familiar sound followed. Something like lowing cows mixed with grinding chains.

"Giant Buzzards," Dorian said. "The North Country."

So Jones had volunteered to visit the Dragon Mines, under the guise of addressing the mine boss's recent reports of discontent among the dragons, and requested Dorian's company on the journey. The trip north would have taken Dorian and Senné a mere two days, but Jones and a contingent of horse soldiers slowed their progress to a crawl. The soggy landscape around them crept by, rock after wet rock and cloud after dripping cloud, but Dorian didn't really mind. A saddle seat and fresh air always cleared his head.

They passed the ramshackle trading posts of Peaksend Village and the road to the castle itself. Dorian thanked HighGod the king had agreed to send Eleanor and the children to Laralee. He imagined the three of them, trapped behind Peaksend's thick walls like fireflies in a clay jar.

"Ho, what's that?" asked Jones, as their mounts crept down the narrow path leading into the Dragon Mines. As he pointed around the bend a familiar scream cut the air.

Senne´ stopped short. "An angry dragon."

Dorian nodded. A dragon's fury always sounded to him like a pack of wolves fighting with a pride of lions over the world's tastiest hunk of beef. "Maybe we've arrived during a transfer," he said to Senne´. He corrected himself. "No, that can't be right. It's nearly sundown."

"The miners move the dragons from one cave to another in the early morning, correct?" Jones clucked to his horse, and the object of mutual speculation came into view. A lone dragon hunched in the mine yard. Fire-iron chains attached to Fire-iron shackles connected the creature's legs, neck, and tail to six Fire-iron pillars. The iron reflected the dragon's sparkling dark green hide. Prismatic lights danced along the canyon walls behind it. As Dorian's party reached level ground he saw the dragon squint against the glare of its own effervescence.

"Is that a—a leash?" Dorian dismounted. Senne' followed him across the yard. Miners bowed and moved out of his path. The heat rose with each step. He stopped about twenty paces from the dragon. Three long horns revealed it as a male, one of the largest Dorian had even seen, the length of five carriages nose-to-tail. Golden scales lined its neck, rather than the usual green. They didn't lie against its neck like a horse's mane, but instead stood upright in a row of fiery sabers. Its long jaw rested in dry dirt, for its intense body heat had dried out the mud underneath it. It shuffled its front talons and opened one yellow eye.

Dorian's pulse hammered in his ears. "Thromba! Where's Thromba?"

Matt Thromba pushed his way through the crowd, his bowlegged stride and wide chest giving the impression of a walking beer barrel. The mine boss pushed his three-pronged beard over his shoulders and wiped his hands on his grimy leggings. He reached for Dorian.

"Your Grace—sir—I'm so glad you've come—"

"What is the meaning of this?" Dorian stabbed a finger in the direction of the dragon. "This abomination—if the king saw—"

"Please—let me explain—"

"—a creature of the Bond—" Dorian couldn't find the words to express his disgust. Fire-iron smoke seared his nostrils and the back of his throat. "Sacrilege!"

Thromba fell on his knees and clutched at Dorian's leg. Tears made clean tracks on his sooty face. The rest of the miners joined him on the ground. The neighs of the working unicorns ricocheted off the rock walls around them, and the chained dragon rumbled a morose reply. Senne' nibbled at Dorian's shoulder. "Speak, Thromba," said Dorian, "before I cut off your hand."

"I'm so sorry, sir," Thromba said. "We could'na think of anything else for it. Blondie—that's what we call him—he ain't been right. Like

I said in my writing, they've all been off of late. Not eating well…only two litters this year…Blondie—he's a right bull, even on a good day. Now he's fighting with the others, even the does. Runnin' up the walls. Bangin' himself against the iron. Look at those slashes on his haunches, and he's chewing on his own talons…and his tail…look…"

Dorian walked around to the dragon's rear. Its tail should have been capped with spikes, but it ended in a stub no more than ten feet front its body. Thromba rose and followed him. "I did'na know what else to do, sir. It breaks my heart to see him—like this—" Thromba covered his mouth with one hand.

Dorian recognized Tremor, the unofficial leader of the working unicorns. The white stallion walked a slow circle around Blondie. The dragon let out a soft grumble and a puff of smoke each time Tremor's horn touched his scales. Tremor seemed satisfied by his inspection. He moved off in the direction of one of the active mine caves.

"Go speak with him," Dorian said to Senne´.

Senne´ nodded. He melted into the black smoke spewing from the cave. Dorian put a hand on Matt Thromba's shoulder. His touch threw up gray Fire-iron dust and the musty smell of long unwashed cotton.

"I'm sorry, Matt. I should have heard you out first, but the shock…"

Matt rubbed his eyes. He smeared soot from his forehead down his crooked nose. "It would have been better had I prepared ye, but I didn't know how to say it."

"Have you any idea of what ails them?" asked Orvid Jones.

"No, sir. Our magicians can't understand it. Even the unicorns are flummoxed. No sickness.

Just…what's that word? Malice?"

"Malaise," said Dorian.

Thromba nodded. "I'm grateful you've come, Mister Jones. We need your expertise."

"I'll do what I can," said Orvid, "but I don't have the dragon-keeping knowledge of my predecessor."

"Ach, him," said Thromba. "Ezra Oliver talked fancy, but he couldn'a understood the Bond as he said he did. No one understands it could have turned on it. I'd pit you against him any day, sir." He peered around Dorian's shoulder. "Hey! You men! Keep that meat off the ground, now! I won't be feeding the beasts tainted beef!"

"Go, Thromba," said Dorian. "See to it."

Thromba jogged toward the bumbling miners. He threw thanks and blessings over his shoulder.

"Incurable plague," Dorian said to Jones. "Raving lunatic on the loose. Now you can add discontented dragons to your list of magical mysteries."

"I only hope I can live up to Mister Thromba's high standards."

The chained dragon groaned again and dragged its chin across the dirt and gravel. A bead of sweat ran down Dorian's back. He removed his dragon robe. The dragon's pupils expanded and contracted once, then again. Pale eyes, not so different from Dorian's own. Searching for a way out.

Jones put a hand on Dorian's shoulder, but Dorian shrugged him off. He approached the trapped dragon. It lifted its head and growled a low warning. The heat opened every pore in Dorian's body. His tunic stuck to his chest. He heard the anxious nickering of unicorns and Jones's voice calling his name, but he saw only golden eyes and smelled only hot smoky breath. He stopped. The dragon could have bitten him, or sent him up in flames, but it just spoke to him in a hypnotic, rumbling purr.

He set the robe on the ground before it, in the trench worn down by its jaw. "For your comfort," he said.

The dragon's squinted at him. Dorian backed away. It watched him until he stood beside Jones again. Then it dropped its great head on the robe, exhaled a blast of smoke, and closed its eyes.

The yard already bustled with its usual organized chaos when Dorian left the two-story wooden guest cabin at dawn. He chewed on a hunk of dried beef as he approached Jones. The chief magician stood between Senne' and one of the white mining unicorns. He held a pocket clockworks before his face, and then stuffed it in his heavy cloak. "They're late. Damn!" Buttery wisps of agitated light drifted from his ears.

Dorian responded in the same voice he used with skittish horses. "Come, lad. The sun is still behind the mountains. Who's late?"

"Our guides. I should have known. Blasted untrustworthy little bastards!" Jones's

watch appeared again. "I gave them strict instructions in Maliana. Half past five in the morning! It's a quarter to six! Why anyone employs them is beyond my comprehension!"

"Employs who?"

"Fairies, of course! Who else can lead us up the mountains to the Giant Buzzards' nesting grounds? Chalice here"—Jones pointed at the white unicorn—"generously agreed to forsake his day's work and carry me…and now here we wait. Intolerable!"

"You used magic to call them—"

"Of course, Senné!" Jones barked. "There's no other way!"

Senné's tasseled tail whipped irritably. "The magic will hold them to their promise. You of all humans should know that."

Jones blushed, but a whirring sound drowned out his sputtered apologies. A fairy landed on Senné's horn. It hung for a moment, its beady eyes glistening, and then began circling Senné's head like a girl dancing around an Awakening pole in MidSpring. A dozen of his fellows followed him. Each fairy, about the size of Chou Chou, with six arms and six legs and a round potbelly, wore a jaunty blue bonnet and matching gloves.

A grin split their leader's monkeyish face. He sounded like a singing bee. "Ready, you are? Steep goes the path."

Jones glared at the fairy before clambering onto Chalice's back. Dorian mounted, and Senne' followed the flittering cloud of fairies up the path, through the gate, and out of the Mines. The fairies zigged and zagged past Dorian's face. They bounced around the unicorns' heads and sang little ditties.

"Buzzards find 'em
Close behind 'em
Stinky birdies
Nests of turdies
Here we comin'
Can't be runnin'..."

The band of buzzard hunters crossed a boggy meadow and started their ascent into the Scaled Mountains. The wind squealed into Dorian's ears like a shrewish mother-in-law and pelted his raw cheeks with grains of granite and stray raindrops. The rising sun threw golden light on the gray mountain faces. He held his breath for a moment at the endlessness of the staggered peaks before him. It had been over ten years since his last ride up this path. Everything had changed in his life. Nothing had changed in the Scaled Mountains.

The beauty of the hard land around him reminded him of the person who would have seen it just as he did. The wind reached inside him and pulled at the longing that sat in his chest like a stubborn cough. "Eleanor should be with us," he said to Senne'.

"Call to her."

Dorian lowered his voice and leaned up Senné's neck. "What if she doesn't answer?"

"She can't if you don't call."

"She hasn't called me."

"Childish," was Senné's simple reply.

Three ponderous hours passed. The only songs on the mountainside were those of the fairies, the wind, and the sliding rocks. The path widened and flattened out sometime before noon. Dorian took loaf of dry bread from his satchel. He couldn't go more than a few hours without eating. Eleanor teased him that his ribs showed if he so much as pondered the weeklong fast at the Breaking of the New Year. He closed his eyes and thought of her laugh.

"HighGod, what stench!" called Jones. He'd no sooner said it than the smell hit Dorian's nostrils like a chamber pot dumped over his head. Senne' whickered in disgust, Dorian pulled his robe over his face, and the fairies screeched their laughter.

"You want pretty perfume? Flowers-in-a-pot?" The lead fairy chirped as he buzzed Dorian's shoulders. The Giant Buzzards' call, the lowing-creaking that had risen from Jones's bottle, sounded somewhere ahead and above them. They crested a low rise. The buzzards' rocky nesting ground spread out before them.

At least fifty buzzards, roughly the size and shape of feathered oxen, squatted over dining table-sized nests made of a gray and brown conglomeration of sticks and animal bones. The birds mooed their displeasure at their sudden company. Clunky pinkish heads, naked and leathery, bounced above their brownish bodies. They fumed at the visitors through stubby, curved beaks and flapped threats. The wind from a hundred waving wings blew feathers and putrid bird droppings into the air. Dorian coughed. "Dragon's teeth, Sen! It's worse than I remember."

"Carrion shit." The lead fairy appeared before his face again. It sniffed and grinned.

"Don't remind me, fairyman," Dorian said as he shook a few sticky brown feathers from his robe. "Can you find Oliver's hideout?"

The fairies huddled in a hovering mass with their arms wrapped around each other's shoulders before bursting apart like spraying champagne bubbles. Their high voices pierced the collective lowing of the buzzards. "Cave! This way! Cave!"

They shot across the nesting grounds and disappeared into the dark holes in the craggy mountain walls. "What if he's up there?" Dorian put a hand on the hilt of his sword.

"With this racket? He'd hear us. Disappear and appear somewhere else…how he does it…" Dorian noted Jones's begrudging admiration. Jones went on. "Why risk a fight with two unicorns and the man universally recognized as the most skilled swordsman in Cartheigh?"

"I'm sure he's warier of your conjuring than my sword. You did take his place."

Jones's face darkened. "He was my mentor. He knew a frightened novice. Not a chief magician."

"He's had nine years to observe what he wrought in you. Look."

The fairies pelted at them like a hoard of black flies going for a horse's rear end. The wisecracking leader landed on Jones's shoulder. "Found something. Man-fire-old-stuff."

Fifteen minutes later Dorian and Jones left the two unicorns on a narrow ledge and ducked into a crevice in the mountainside. Senne´ disapproved of this turn of events, but since he couldn't fit through the entryway he had no choice in the matter. His muttered protests and the thwack of hooves against granite followed Dorian into the darkness.

Dorian lit a torch, and Jones cast his own creamy magic around their feet. The fairies' glittering, whirring wings cast queer shadows on the rock walls around them. The smell of buzzard shit permeated even this deep space, but it was older and wetter and somehow more nauseating.

The passageway ended in a chamber roughly the size of Dorian's bathing room at Eclatant. Jumbled dragon robes, tin pots, and a moldy-looking cloak sprawled around a pile of dry ashes. Dorian looked up, but the torchlight didn't penetrate high enough to see where the smoke had gone.

"There must be a hole up there." Dorian knelt beside the ashes. "Still warm. We missed him by a few hours."

"He might return. I'd rather not risk surprising him in this space, without our horned friends."

Dorian grunted his agreement. Jones cast buttery light across the campsite. "Just to see if he missed anything…anything at all…no…that would be too easy." He removed a bottle from his cloak. He shook it and a few objects shifted behind the light blue glass. "An obscure magical theory Oliver began working on in the year before his…death."

"Motivation," said Dorian. "Eleanor's hair, and a rock from the walls of Afar Creek."

Jones nodded and held the bottle before his eyes. "I shall cast the spell through the bottle, and through its contents. Magical residue is hidden all around us. I must see it through Oliver's motivation. Find the most powerful spells, and the loudest tones…"

Jones's brown eyes glowed creamy white, as if his head had filled with buttermilk. Light spilled from his face and filled the bottle in his upraised hands. Jones removed the stopper, and the light raced around the cave, bouncing along rocks and robes and burnt up sticks. It swirled over the ashes as if the fire had returned to life, but now gray sparks and wisps mixed with Jones's cream. Jones called to the light. It spun itself into a tight ball, floated toward the unseen ceiling, and dropped like a saber slash into the bottle in Jones's hand.

When he replaced the stopper the bottle went dark again, but it twitched in Jones's hand. The magician's eyes drained from cream to cocoa to his usual dark brown. He rubbed them. "Forgive me." A few tears rolled down his cheek. "Whenever I conjure through my eyes I spring a leak."

Dorian touched the blue bottle with a tentative finger. "The tone is inside? How will it help us? Won't we just hear the sounds of this cave? Whatever magical tones were conjured here?"

Jones smiled. Wisps of stray light drifted from behind his buck-teeth. "That's the unexpected beauty of the thing. The power inherent in motivationally driven magic, combined with the power of Oliver's transporting spell, cause the tones to collect ambient sound not just from the original starting points, but from the *destination*."

"You mean the place Oliver is going?"

"Yes! The tones picked up the Buzzard calls because he'd conjured the leaflets somewhere near this cave. But if you listen closely you can also hear Maliana street noise. The sound of where he *ended up*."

"So inside that bottle are sounds from where Oliver went when he left this cave?" Dorian forgot about a possible unplanned appearance on the part of said enemy magician. "Open it!"

Jones twisted the stopper. Gray mist floated from the bottle's neck. Dorian listened for ambient noise over the obvious cave sounds: the crackle of the dead fire and the hiss of wet wood. "I think I hear something...yes! Can you do it again?" Jones replaced the stopper and then removed it again.

Dorian heard it clearly this time. *Creeeee---thwack! Wicka-wicka-wicka-wicka*...dying off. Then nothing.

Jones shook his head. "What, by the Bond, was that?"

"I have no idea. Someone running down the stairs? The first part put me in mind of a drawbridge...maybe a strikestick hitting a ball..."

The lead fairy leapt into Dorian's field of vision.

"Damnit, you!" Dorian said. "Stop bloody doing that!"

"What's that?" asked the fairy.

"Buzzing my face—I'm liable to slice off your nose!"

"No, stupid man. What's *that*?"

Dorian had been so focused on the sound coming from the bottle he hadn't noticed those coming from the cavern walls. The fairy's eyes widened. It grabbed Dorian's finger and worried it up and down, then did Jones the same courtesy. "Lovely day. Will come for payment. Goodbye." It zoomed down the passageway with its posse hot on its six heels.

The solid rock under Dorian's boots lurched to the right and groaned like a whore in throws of false passion. Jones stumbled. One knee hit the ground, but he held onto the bottle. He jammed the stopper into place and stuffed it into his cloak. Dorian tugged him to his feet. "An earthquake?" Dorian asked.

Pebbles and dirt rained down around them. Jones covered his head. "No! Not an earthquake! It's—"

The cave went silent, and Jones's shout echoed off the still walls.

"—much worse."

A fist punched through the rock. A carriage-sized, granite fist, complete with five grasping fingers. The gray digits stretched, rolled and then clenched again. A few small boulders shot from between its palm and fingers. They hit the far cavern walls and exploded. Dorian's raised arms blocked a hail of granite shards, any one of which could have blinded him. The stone forearm attaching the fist to the cave wall stretched in their direction.

Dorian had not lost a scuffle since he'd outgrown his older brother at age fifteen; however, he recognized a colossal ass-beating when he saw it coming. He grabbed Jones's shoulder and shoved him toward the passageway.

The fist slammed the ground. Both men tumbled, but Dorian scrambled to his feet. "Jones! Get up! Run!"

Stone fingers took hold of Jones's leg and dragged him backward. Dorian seized one of the magician's flailing arms. Dorian and the fist worried Jones between them, like two dogs fighting over a stick. Dorian slid forward until he found purchase behind a boulder. The rock dug into this chest and his arms threatened to abandon their sockets. Jones's round eyes stared at him with uncomprehending shock.

"Jones—a spell—do something! You'll be pulled apart!"

Jones moaned.

"If I drop you, the bottle will shatter!"

Jones's arm warmed in Dorian's grip, and creamy light spread down the lower half of his body.

Dorian tugged again, and Jones shot out of his leggings and boots. His forehead hit the boulder Dorian had been bracing against. He slumped beside it. As Dorian hoisted him over one shoulder he thanked

HighGod for his own height and the Chief Magician's lack there of. Jones's feet barely brushed his knees.

The fist, eyeless though it was, realized it had been left holding little more than a pair of socks. The cave shook with its rage. Dorian made for the passageway with Jones's limp head flopping against his back. The fist followed him into the darkness, punching a path for itself as it went.

The passageway couldn't have been longer than five hundred paces, but somehow in the dark Dorian returned to Walnut Cottage. Pebbles flew around his head as Eleanor walked through the cottage door...*he pushed her into the broom closet...*

He could see his own fingers gripping Jones's bare leg, and heard Senne′ calling his name. The fist slammed and cursed at him in a roar of falling rock. Senne′ screamed a warning as Dorian stepped out of the cave...*he kissed Eleanor...*and it all went black.

Eleanor's hand went to the dragon choker. She'd felt it, for the smallest of seconds, the beloved warmth. She ducked her chin and lifted the stone, but it wasn't red. It was a cool leafy green. She scrunched her eyes into slits, and willed the red to return.

"Is there a problem?" Teardrop asked. They stood in the courtyard outside Laralee's once neglected, now immaculate, stone barn.

Perhaps the sun warmed it...

"No." Eleanor let go of the choker and resumed brushing the mare's back. The sweeping circular strokes of her arm matched the thoughts chasing each other around her head.

He called...why did he stop...he called!

"Did he call?"

"How did you—" Eleanor stopped herself, for Teardrop's explanations of how she knew anything usually hinged on speculations beyond Eleanor's comprehension. "I thought he did...for a moment...but I must have been mistaken."

"It was an argument," said Teardrop. "Arguments happen between beings who matter to one another. You should call to him."

"He hasn't called to me, either…"

"Irrational."

"It's not just that, Teardrop…I told you how he's behaved."

"Hardly admirable. But remember, you succumb to jealousy, and curse him for giving into lust. Yet he's been stifling his own jealousy, and his lust, for years."

Eleanor sighed. "It seems neither of us can claim victory. If only I'd discussed it with him calmly. I'm sure he thinks me a fool."

"You should ask him if he thinks you are a fool. Then you will know."

"How will I ask him?" Eleanor leaned both elbows on Teardrop's back. "We haven't had a normal conversation in well over a year."

"You must find a way, for there is no other way." And with that Teardrop returned to tugging hay from the pile at her feet.

Eleanor touched the cold choker again.

I felt it…for a moment…I know I did…

"Your Highness? I must speak with you."

Eleanor peeked under Teardrop's belly at a pair of thin legs clad in silk leggings. No one else had knees quite so knobby.

"Hello, Abram," she said to Dorian's older brother. "I didn't know you'd arrived."

"I'm meeting with Dorian's bookkeeper. Making sure the servants aren't bamboozling him into extra pay."

"I'm sure Dorian appreciates your attention to his finances." In fact, Eleanor knew just the opposite. Dorian barely tolerated his brother, and the feeling was mutual. At the very mention of Dorian's name Abram usually went an unflattering shade of pink, and the words *Duke of Brandling* darkened cherry to crimson. In the past, Eleanor had pitied Abram, for HighGod had chosen to deposit every apple in the family tree on Dorian's branch and left Abram's quite bare. With his gangly arms and legs, protruding eyes and Adam's apple, and wispy graying hair, he reminded her of a vengeful, near-sighted artist's rendering of Dorian. She used to think him shy, and perhaps he was, but arrogance swirled through his insecurity. Besides, while Abram hated his brother, he didn't hate his brother's money.

"Someone has to keep this place running," Abram said, "but that's beside the point. You have visitors."

Eleanor wiped her hands on her leggings. "Who?" She'd given the guards at the gate strict instructions to limit guests at Laralee.

"Two young women."

"Take me to them—" She pushed her messy hair away from her face. "—no, I should freshen up first...a gown."

"That won't be necessary. They're in the tack room."

"Goodness. How rude, Abram." Eleanor started in the direction of the one-story stone and thatching hut behind the barn. Teardrop and Abram followed her.

"You should thank me," Abram said. "I can't believe the guards let them in—"

Someone had propped open the tack room door. Eleanor peered into the leathery-smelling darkness. "Hello?" she called. "Please, come out. I'm sorry Mr. Finley sent you in here—"

Two women rose from a bale of hay. The taller of the two brushed off the shorter one's skirts, and then her own. They clasped hands. Eleanor realized the shorter visitor was not really a woman at all, but a tall girl of about ten. Her older companion's dress revealed itself redder and redder as she walked into the light. "Your Highness," said a familiar voice.

Eleanor blinked. "Hello, Jan...and Ruby?" She knelt before the little girl. "My, how you've grown!"

"Highness." Ruby blushed and curtsied.

"Jan, dearest, I—" The steely-eyed young woman in front of Eleanor bore little resemblance to the girl she'd left at Pandra Tate's infamous brothel, the Red-Headed Hussy, two years ago. Eleanor wasn't sure of a proper greeting, so she hugged Jan instead.

Jan stiffened for a moment, and then gingerly patted Eleanor's back. "Your Highness...I should have written—"

"If you had, I would have been forced to refuse your visit." She shooed Jan and Ruby away from the tack room. "As it is—"

"It's highly improper!" said Abram. "Your Highness, a woman like—a scarlet woman—at Laralee? What will people say?"

Eleanor ignored him. "Jan, how did you get past the guards?"

"We've been moonin' around the gates for two days. I told the guard we're old...friends...but he wouldn't hear of it." She lifted her chin. "I offered him a favor if he'd see me in."

"See? Favors? Disgusting!" said Abram, triumphant. He licked his lips. His roving eyes led Eleanor to believe him more curious than scandalized.

"I won't give him none, o'course!" Jan tossed her chocolaty hair. "Just a ruse."

"Wait," said Eleanor. "We're putting the dragon in front of the fire. Why are you here, Jan? A hundred miles from Maliana, and your... work?"

Jan's stern façade abruptly cracked. "It's the Burning, Mistress. It's bad in the Fringe, and in the End. Ruby's been living with me at the Hussy...all those men from all around Cartheigh, comin' in and out... and children gets it the worst. I asked Pandra for a bit of time...to let me take Ruby to the country. She said yes, bless her. So here we are."

Eleanor stepped back. Her forehead wrinkled. "I brought the prince and princess here to keep them safe from the Burning. You would come to us after being exposed to the sickness?"

"No! Of course not!" Jan ran her hands over the dirty red velvet of her dress. "We've been hiding out on the roads for two weeks. Sleeping in the woods. Haven't seen anyone but my horse in days. If either of us had the Burning, it would have showed by now." Still she tugged at the red gown, pulling at her skirts and sleeves as if she could arrange them in some way that would not give her away her profession. "Please, Mistress. I just want to keep Ruby safe. She's all I have."

Eleanor rested her forehead in her hands.

"Unacceptable!" said Abram. "I won't stand for it on Finley property."

"It's not your decision to make, sir, and the man of the house is not here. If you are so desirous of salvaging the honor of Laralee, you'll keep the identity of our visitors to yourself. You are dismissed." Abram puffed and blew like an irritable Billy goat, but he removed himself. As to whether he'd keep his tongue in his head, she doubted it, but there seemed no point in worrying about gossip until it began to spread. Eleanor took Jan's hand. "You will stay another week in the stables. I'll have the grooms set up cots. I can't take a chance."

"Of course. Thank you—"

"You must understand, Prince Gregory will not approve. You can only stay a few weeks. You'll have to dress as servants."

"I can tutor the children," said Jan. "Ruby can play with the princess. They're not so far apart in age!"

Eleanor smiled. "Ticia would like nothing more, I'm sure. You cannot leave the grounds of Laralee, nor speak with anyone about why you are here, or your true home. You are servants from Eclatant. Am I clear?"

Jan and Ruby nodded. Ruby hopped around Jan's skirts. "A country holiday!"

Eleanor laughed. "There hasn't been much fun to be had at Laralee, Ruby."

"Oh, Highness, I've never had such a time! Might I visit the horses?"

Eleanor nodded and Ruby skipped to the barn. Jan tried to thank Eleanor again but Eleanor raised a hand. "Let us not speak of it anymore." Eleanor started to walk away, then paused. "Jan, the Burning is a threat not just to my children, but to the crown. We're all prisoners of our allegiance to the Desmarais family here. To the Bond itself. Servants and royalty."

"I will take care. The safety of the prince and princess will not be jeopardized on my account, or Ruby's, Your Highness."

"Please, after all this time. Eleanor."

Jan shook her head. "No. That wouldn't be fitting." She curtsied, and followed Ruby into the barn.

CHAPTER 23

LILIES-ON-THE-LAKE

IN ELEANOR'S TWENTY-SEVENTH YEAR the Awakening passed at Laralee with little fanfare. The Burning discouraged most of the Lake District's aristocracy from their usual Fest time visits to Maliana, and they hesitated to gather in large groups even in Harper's Crossing. Eleanor didn't miss the madness of an Eclatant fest, but she did miss home and the people that came along with it.

In honor of the Fest, Eleanor tried to break the children's monotony. She baked a cake with them, served a picnic lunch on the lawn, and tied ribbons to the flagpole. Ticia, Nathan, and Ruby raced around the pole under the purple and green Desmarais flag and the blue and gold banner of the Duke of Brandling. She imagined it would irk Gregory to see his son dancing around an Awakening pole with a crown of flowers pinned to his wavy red hair.

Let him show his face if he'd have a say.

Ticia had stopped asking after Gregory, and responded with sullen silence whenever Eleanor raised the name Poppa, but Nathan never tired of the topic. *Poppa-Poppa-when-will-Poppa-visit-why-isn't-he-here-will-he-come-for-the-fest-I-miss-Poppa.* When the Fest passed without a word from Gregory, Eleanor took up her quill.

Dearest Husband,

I hope this letter finds you well. We are all in excellent health in the Lake District, and it grieves me to hear tell of the continuing misery in Maliana. Your family misses you, and prays you will find time away from your duties to visit us, as it has been nearly three months since we have all been together. I am certain you could do with a few days' respite and clean air.

The children continue to thrive, although they long for their father's voice and guiding hand. Please do not keep yourself from us for too much longer.

Eleanor bit her lip as the quill scratched her closing sentiments.

Your most loving wife,
H.R.H Eleanor Brice Desmarais

Five days later she received her first letter from Gregory since her arrival at Laralee.

Eleanor—sweetheart,

I regret to inform you that my responsibilities keep me here for the foreseeable future. I am sorry to disappoint the children. You may allow them to observe Lilies-on-the-Lake. Observe by boat, not participate. It will raise their spirits.

HighGod willing I will see you soon.

Affectionately,
H.R.H Gregory Desmarais

She gave her husband credit for his honesty. Her own embellishments hadn't gotten her far, but at least an interesting outing was in order for the children. She asked the servants about Lilies-on-the-Lake, and discovered it to be an annual boat race that always followed the Awakening. Fest or no fest, distant plague be damned, the people of Harper's Crossing would not be deterred from Lilies-on-the-Lake.

So Eleanor and her children donned the requisite white on the first Sunday morning in HighSpring. Eleanor felt as if blue, green, and white had taken over the world. Blue in the sky and lake, green in the grass and trees, white in the fat clouds, billowing sails, and gauzy clothes. She adjusted Leticia's bonnet and her own, and begged Nathan to take care for his white cotton leggings. She and Ticia wore matching linen dresses. Tiny lilies embroidered on the hems, sleeves, and bodices commemorated the occasion.

Chou sat on Eleanor's shoulder. He stood out like a tomato stain against her pale skin and dress. "Don't bother with Nathan," Chou said. "He'll be a lovely springtime color by the end of the afternoon."

"What color is that? Mud?"

"Precisely," said Chou. "Or gray. Lake water on white silk."

"He won't get wet sitting in the boat with the dockmaster. Gregory's last letter was clear. Sit in the middle of the lake. Stay away from the racers."

"I'm glad he's relaxing, even a bit. There's not been one case of the Burning in the Lake District. Life must continue."

"I suppose you're right," said Eleanor. Still, she had no quarrel with Gregory's insistence that Nathan avoid the jostling line of laughing, wine swilling racers. Boats drifted into the center of the lake. The wind blew the snip and snap of fifty white sails over the chuckling waves. People called out to one another and lashed their boats together. The skiffs bobbed beside each other, a line of partygoers warming to an orchestra's rhythm before a favorite reel. The gulls swarmed overhead, screaming at one another and dropping into the water after discarded sweetmeats. It looked like great fun, but Eleanor still imagined the Burning creeping from boat to boat like a nasty rumor.

"She's not coming, is she?" asked Abram from over Eleanor's shoulder.

"No. Jan and Ruby are in the barn."

Abram sniffed his approval. Ticia looked at Eleanor with entreating brown eyes. "Please?"

"I'm sorry, Tish. You'll see Ruby later."

Nathan grabbed Eleanor's hand before Ticia could beg for her friend's company. He pointed at the old dockmaster, who was unraveling the ropes between the white-sailed skiff and the dock. "There's my boat! Can Uncle Dorian take me out on the lake?"

Eleanor laughed. "First your father, now Uncle Dorian. The dockmaster is taking you."

Nathan's lip stuck out. He crossed his skinny arms across his chest. "Why can't Uncle Dorian take me?"

"Darling, because he's not here."

"He's right there!" Nathan jabbed a finger at the mansion.

Eleanor turned around. "Nathan, don't be silly—"

Her mouth clicked shut. Dorian was walking across the lawn.

She tried to see the lanky man with the shock of dark hair as someone else, prove her eyes deceived her, but she knew his rambling stride as well as the feel of her own two feet beneath her legs.

Ticia and Nathan ran to their uncle. Eleanor willed her shoes to stay planted in the thick grass. Dorian picked up Ticia, and then Nathan. He squeezed them until they squealed for release. He held the children's hands and walked to the edge of the dock. The smile on his face was almost shy.

He bowed. "Your Highness," he said, over the children's chatter.

Before Eleanor could reply, Abram began updating Dorian on the goings on at Laralee. It didn't take him long to come to the topic of Jan and Ruby.

Dorian nodded and *hmmm-ed* as Abram ran on about the shame and impropriety of it all, and then the duke gave his verdict. "Those who spare a thought about such trivialities during these troubling times should be cursed with whatever pox the cathouses can set upon them, ten times over."

"I've been keeping this place going for years," said Abram, "while you recline at Eclatant. I should have some say—"

"I've shown you my gratitude for your assistance, haven't I?" Dorian reached into his pocket, and then flipped a coin in Abram's direction. Abram snatched it out of the air. He colored and said something about the riggings on his boat. He joined the dockmaster at the ropes, but not before stuffing the coin into his pocket.

Eleanor watched Abram fiddling and fidgeting for a while before returning Dorian's tentative smile. "I didn't know you were coming," she said.

"I didn't plan on it this year...not with the...current mood. I've been at the Dragon Mines for nearly a month."

"I can see that." She put a hand to his face. A gash cut across his forehead. The pinkish scar stood out against his dark brow and pale skin.

He winced when her fingers brushed the wound, although it was too far healed to be painful. "I changed my mind. I've missed home. It didn't go well at the Mines."

Eleanor frowned as he explained the situation with the dragons. "No one knows what's troubling them? Not even Jones?"

Dorian shook his head, but he smiled a real smile. Eleanor caught her breath at its beauty.

"Nothing telling on the dragons, but we come closer to solving another conundrum. It's an interesting tale." He pointed at his own forehead. "I sacrificed an eyebrow."

Eleanor's own laughter sounded like birdsong in her ears. "You must tell me." His sudden burst of amiability encouraged her. "Dorian, a few weeks ago…did you…I thought I felt—"

"Uncle!" Nathan grabbed Dorian's hand and dragged him toward the skiff. Eleanor followed them.

"The race is starting. Hurry!" Nathan looked up at Eleanor with wide blue eyes. "Will you come?"

"Go, Mother," said Ticia.

Eleanor knelt before her daughter. "Are you sure, darling?"

Chou landed on Ticia's bonnet and spread his wings. "My eyes are sharp. I promise Ticia will not miss one oar stroke or shifting sail."

Ticia crossed her eyes and stuck out her tongue, but Chou was already commenting on the speed of the boats and the skills of each sailor. Eleanor laughed and kissed her daughter's cheek. She whispered in Ticia's ear, "Run along and find Ruby."

Ticia didn't need any convincing. She lifted her skirts and spun around. Chou slipped from her bonnet with a squawk. He flew beside her on her way to the barn.

Eleanor stood on the dock while Dorian adjusted the sail and Nathan clambered from one end of the skiff to the other. He offered Dorian bits of rope and tools. "Do we need this, Uncle Dorian?" he asked, holding up a fishing pole.

"No. The boats will scare away the fish."

"Can the fish hear the boats?"

Dorian offered Eleanor a hand. "They feel the water moving the way we feel the wind blowing. The race is like a storm to them."

Eleanor held onto Dorian's hand a bit longer than necessary. She blamed the rocking boat. Dorian steadied her. "Take care. Your skirts are heavy."

She sat on one of the bench seats. Dorian handed Nathan an oar. "Here, Son. Keep a hold on this. I'm sure we'll need to help our ship along."

Dorian let out the sail and it caught the wind. The sun struck it, and Eleanor had to shade her eyes against the glare. The skiff edged away from the dock.

Eleanor watched in silence as Dorian instructed Nathan on the ins and outs of sailing. "Here...now hold the oar like this...turn your hands down...pull with your shoulders, not your wrists, good! Can you tug this rope? Hard now! That's a good lad! That Desmarais strength...what a king you'll make! We need to go that way—is that port or starboard?"

"Starboard? That's what my sailing book told me, I think."

Dorian glanced at Eleanor. "There's a bit of your mother in you, too." He put a hand on Nathan's shoulder. "Let out this rope...now, be careful...when the boom comes around—"

"That means you must duck, Mother."

"Yes, captain." Eleanor leaned down and the boom swung over her head. The sail caught on the other side with a snap. The little craft turned toward the gathered boats. Eleanor listened to the soft smack of the hull against the dark blue water. Droplets landed on her bare arms and chest and sent pleasant shivers down her back. The wind lifted Nathan's hair, and Dorian's, and she felt more at peace than she had in months.

Dorian dropped the sail about two hundred paces from the line of boats. Nathan kept his eyes on the field by turning in a circle as the skiff spun in place. "Who has the fastest boat?"

"It's not the boat so much as the sailor. My brother Abram is a fine sailor. Would you bet on him?" Dorian laughed at Nathan's scowled reply. "Mayor Kebbits, then. Or Brother Paul-Peter."

"The Godsman?" Nathan asked.

"Wiley sailors, the Godsmen."

"Perhaps they pray the hardest for fine weather," said Eleanor. Dorian laughed again, and once again Eleanor's heart surged. "Look, Nathan! They're almost ready!"

The mayor's wife stood on the prow of the largest skiff. She held a handkerchief above her head. The racers gripped their oars.

Unfortunately, the wind had not changed course. The race would be run solely on the power of man. Eleanor imagined many wives would rub their husbands' aching shoulders this evening.

The mayor's wife tossed her hanky. It caught the wind and rose for a moment before opening and drifting downward. It touched the lake's surface and disappeared in the churn of a hundred oars. The sailing enthusiasts watching from the larger skiffs turned away from the spray. Everyone shouted, from the race participants to their wives and grandfathers to the circling gulls, who shot skyward with a collective squawk of annoyance. The line of boats headed toward the steeple of Holy Triumph Chapel and the village of Harper's Crossing on the far side of the lake. Eleanor could make out more cheering fans on the narrow beach beside the town dock. Most of them appeared to be jumping up and down, but it could have been the tossing water.

"Row, Uncle!" shouted Nathan. He slapped his oar against the waves. "Row! Row!"

"Remember," Eleanor said, "we aren't supposed to go get too close."

Nathan's tongue hung out of his mouth. His rowing only succeeded in turning the boat toward Laralee. Dorian raised an eyebrow.

"All right, just keep a goodish distance," said Eleanor.

"I'll row, Nathan," said Dorian. "You tell me who's winning."

Nathan ran to the prow of the boat. "I see the Mayor…and *Dragon's Breath*! There's the Godsman! I see his brown robes! My, he is a fast rower…I don't see Mister Abram…oooh, there's a fat man in the lead… Oh, Mother! The fat man fell out of his boat!" Nathan's foot slipped on the wet bench.

"Nathan, please! I shan't have you joining him!" Eleanor cried.

Nathan looked back at her with that unnerving wise expression. "You know I learned to swim in Solsea last year. Uncle Dorian would just haul me back in." He faced forward again. "The fat man can swim, too, although they're not able to get him into his boat. He's hanging on the side."

Dorian rowed hard, and soon their skiff passed the row of onlookers' boats. The women and children and servants aboard those bulky crafts curtsied and bowed. They called out blessings to Nathan, but he was too absorbed in his commentary to notice them, so Eleanor waved back for him.

The first boats reached the shore. The sailors leapt into the frigid, waist-high water. Eleanor caught a few curses as boats bounced off each other and the men themselves. Once the boats were firmly on the sand, the first man to pull a lily from the bucket on the beach would be declared the winner.

"HighGod," said Eleanor. "I think someone will break a leg."

"Casualties are part of the fun," said Dorian.

As Dorian steered their boat into shallow water Nathan went wild. "Ah! Uncle, it's Walter! And Mister Ransom, look!"

Eleanor leaned around Dorian. She caught sight of Ransom Tavish, Dorian's brother-in-law, and his son, eleven-year-old Walter, pushing their boat ashore. "Indeed!" she said. "Ransom! Walter! Push on, now! Oh, they're winning!" She shook Dorian's arm.

"Careful. We'll have a time returning to Laralee if I drop these paddles." He turned toward the beach. His eyes widened. "Damn! Good show, Ransom! On, boys!"

Eleanor covered her ears. "You'll deafen me *and* drop the paddle. Some sailor."

Dorian grinned. He grabbed both her forearms and made to push her into the lake. A drop of water ran down his nose and across his cheek. She had a sudden urge to lick it away. Her heartbeat pounded in her ears.

Dorian's eyes darted over her shoulder and Eleanor remembered their audience. He let go. "Good show, Ransom!" he called out, but some of the joy had left his voice.

Eleanor marveled at the sight of the finest men in Harper's Crossing pushing and shoving and grunting like beggars after a scrap of bread.

Ransom's stocky form broke from the crowd. Waves and sand sprayed up from a hundred thrashing legs. Eleanor felt a twinge of alarm. She couldn't find Walter's dark hair.

Ransom had lost a boot, but perhaps it gave him better purchase on the sand. He threw an elbow into the bouncing stomach of his nearest competitor, who happened to be a Godsman, HighGod forgive him. The Godsman doubled over and fell on his knees. Ransom knocked over the ceramic bucket, but when he turned around he held a long-stemmed white lily over his head.

"By the Bond," said Eleanor. "You Lake District boys spend too much time in the woods."

Dorian's didn't respond, and Eleanor's cautious happiness sank into the water below them.

"Where's Walter?" Nathan asked as Anne Clara burst through the crowd to congratulate her husband. Eleanor saw her scan the men and boys still clamoring onto the shore. Anne Clara shouted Walter's name over the curses and laughter.

"I saw him before they beached the skiff," said Eleanor, almost to herself. Most of the sailors were now on shore, but still no Walter. *Oh, dear HighGod, he was pushed under a boat, or crushed…*

"Where is he?" Dorian stood. "Walter! I need to go ashore." He tugged at his left boot.

Eleanor squinted at the line of boats. All of them the same, brown, white, brown, white…no. Something hung on the last boat's hull. A pale hand…and she could make out a bit of dark hair.

"Dorian—he's there—hanging on that boat!"

Anne Clara must have seen what Eleanor saw. She cried out, and ran toward the water's edge. Dorian swung a leg over the side of the skiff, but Eleanor took his arm. "You can't get there fast enough. Row closer."

He took up his oars and steered the skiff shoreward. Anne Clara was screaming. Ransom and two other men pushed the boats aside. Nathan watched in goggle-eyed silence.

"He's fine, Nathan." Eleanor said. "He swallowed some water."

Dorian's face was the color of the sail. She held out a hand, and they linked pinky fingers under the bench. The men took Walter by the sleeves of his waterlogged woolen sweater and dragged him onto the sand. Anne Clara covered her mouth with both hands. Ransom leaned into his son's face. The bystanders froze in a tense semicircle around man and boy, but the lake didn't care about Walter's fate. The waves continued chatting amongst themselves as they broke on the sand— *slurp-hiss-slurp-hisssss.*

Ransom sat back on his heels. "He's breathing!" he shouted.

Dorian slumped against Eleanor. Nathan climbed into Eleanor's lap. She squeezed him.

"Praise HighGod!"

The cheering crowd moved back as the shouting Godsman approached Walter. Eleanor's stomach tingled again. Walter hadn't moved, or opened his eyes.

"A miracle!" The Godsman knelt beside Walter. "Silence! Please! Let us give thanks." The people hushed again. "HighGod above us. You have saved Walter Tavish from the clutches of Lake Brandling, where so many men of Harper's Crossing have met their ends. Let this remind us, we must always respect the Lake as we respect all your creations."

The Godsman put his hands on Walter's thin chest, and then traced them along the boy's thick sweater to his shoulders. He finally touched the boy's forehead.

His hands shot away from Walter as if he had touched live coals. He fell backwards onto his rear end.

Dorian shaded his eyes. "What in the name of the Bond?"

The wind carried the Godsman's scream across the beach, the lake, and perhaps the entire town of Harper's Crossing.

"Hot! So hot! The Burning!"

Dorian handed correspondence to his courier via a crack in the stone wall, and allowed no one in or out of Laralee. He dismissed most of the servants. Less than a dozen chambermaids, cooks, and grooms were hard-pressed to manage even the simplified workings of the huge old house. Eleanor asked Pansy to help, and while she always made sure her children cleaned up after themselves, she gave each a list of extra chores.

"The king wouldn't approve," said Chou as Eleanor dusted a Fire-iron chandelier. He hung from his scaly feet.

"Blast him," she whispered into Chou's upside down face. "If he were here, he'd have to empty his own chamber pot."

Eleanor appreciated Dorian's attention to the children's safety. She longed to comfort him in his own worry, but he'd retreated behind an impassive face and halting pleasantries. She sometimes caught him spinning his spectite ring, but the dragon choker never burned red.

On the third morning after the race, with a tense peace hovering around Laralee, Eleanor invited Dorian and Orvid Jones to tea in the Leighward Parlor. The room clashed horribly with the rest of Dorian's tasteful new furnishings. Musty-smelling dock lines connected rusty chandeliers to brown ceilings. Hideous paintings of the lake, complete with dizzyingly inaccurate lines of perspective, covered the dark blue walls. A Fire-iron anchor graced the mantle and dozens of miniature anchors hung in a fishnet draped in a corner of the ceiling. Every couch and poufy ottoman wore white-anchors-on-blue-silk upholstery.

Eleanor sat across from Dorian and Jones. She handed each a cup of tea and a biscuit.

Jones cleared his throat. "What a…comfortable room."

Dorian's mouth turned up at the corners. "It's bloody hideous," he said as he sipped his tea, "but my grandfather had one just like it. Most great houses around here do."

"Tradition," said Jones. "Tell, how fares your nephew?"

"Not well, from what my sister's man shouted over the wall this morning."

"Dorian, I'm so sorry," said Eleanor. "Poor Anne Clara."

"Jones, we have much to tell the princess." Dorian set his tea and biscuit on the table. Eleanor blushed at his dismissal.

Jones and Dorian spent the next hour informing Eleanor of all their Ezra Oliver-related discoveries and adventures: the powerful combination of motivation and tone, the Buzzard call, the trek into the mountains, the discovery of Oliver's hideout and the new tone, and the cave attack.

"He worked a spell that set the very mountain against intruders," said Jones. "Exceptional and…unconventional…even by magical standards." He pulled a blue glass bottle from his cloak. Gray smoke leaked from the neck when he uncorked it. Eleanor heard the sound of a crackling fire, and something else.

"Ignore the fire," said Jones.

She closed her eyes, and focused on the other noises. *Creeeek— Thwack! Wacka-wacka-wacka…*

Jones corked and uncorked the bottle three times. Eleanor blinked. "A slamming door?"

"I thought so," said Dorian. "Unfortunately there's more than one slamming door in Maliana."

"It's the last part that's unique," said Eleanor. *Wacka-wacka-wacka.* "Maybe I have heard something…" She shook her head. "It's probably just wishful thinking."

"I'd ask around the Fringe," said Dorian, "but I doubt Gregory will allow it."

"Are you returning to Eclatant soon?" asked Eleanor.

"Gregory has granted me leave to see Walter's…illness…through until the—end—" He paused and she ached for him. "— and then I must go."

"Oh."

Jones seemed oblivious as the awkward silence stretched on. He slurped his tea. "A lovely meeting, but I have some conjuring to do—related to the Burning, you know—"

A fist rapped on the parlor door, hard. Pansy appeared in the entryway. She huffed and puffed as if she'd run from one end of Laralee to the other. Eleanor gripped the arm of her chair.

"Pansy—what is it—the children?"

"Fine, mum." Pansy rested her hands on her meaty thighs. "Fine—but I just heard—cook told me, and the groom told her—" She sucked in a few more gulps of air and straightened. "You know that girl—Jinnie—the chambermaid in the nursery?"

"Of course. What about her?"

"Pardon me, in this company, but she's a cheap slut, that one. A proper harlot. She's been sneaking over the wall to meet with Mister Ransom Tavish's valet. She didn't turn up for work yesterday morning or this. Her brother found her roaming the woods, babbling and burning up."

Eleanor thought she might lose control of her bladder. She wanted Dorian to rationalize it away. "She wouldn't disobey you, would she? These are your people—"

"Hardly," he said. "I don't know any of the servants. Gregory replaced every working hand I had on this estate before you arrived. I can't speak for their obedience any more than I can speak for their intimate proclivities."

"Jinnie is like a child herself," Eleanor said. "Nathan and Ticia love her. They're always hugging her. She pours their baths."

"I pray she weren't catching when last she tended them. I'm sorry to bear bad tiding unto you, Your Highness." Pansy wiped her eyes. She curtsied before Dorian and kept her eyes on his boots. "Or you, Your Grace, but a messenger called over the gate with news from Tavish's Fifth."

Dorian touched the white lace cap covering Pansy's thin blondish hair. "Tell what you must."

"Your brother-in-law, sir, he's ill. And your nephew, young Mister Tavish, he's gone on to HighGod."

CHAPTER 24

WILL I BE KING?

"Mother, my head hurts."

"No, darling," Eleanor said. "You're just hungry. You didn't eat much this morning."

"No. It hurts."

For two days a prayer had layered itself over Eleanor's every waking thought. *Please-High God-above-please-High God-above-please-please.* She made Ticia and Nathan stay in the nursery and permitted no visitors. She sat in a rocker and watched them eat, play, and sleep. She made excuses to touch their skin.

She knelt beside her son and his pile of dragons. His bright blue eyes and flushed cheeks told her all she needed to know. Her own eyes filled, but she smiled at him. "Are you sure you're not just tired, Nathan?"

"You should send Ticia away, Mother," he said in his high, matter-of-fact voice.

She touched his forehead, and the white skin felt like hot cobblestones under her fingers. She turned away from him and wiped her eyes. "Maybe you're right. You'll feel better with some quiet."

She helped Nathan to his bed. He trembled as he slid under the coverlet.

Ticia sat on a cushion in the picture window, a sketchbook in her lap. She squinted at the wisteria blooms creeping over the sill, and then bent her head over her paper. Eleanor crossed the room and gently took the charcoal pencil from her daughter's hand. "Tish, I'm going to ask Uncle Dorian to give you your own room."

"No thank you, Mother. I'd rather stay here with Nathan. We're lonely as it is, just us two." She peered over Eleanor's shoulder. "Why is Nathan in bed?"

Eleanor ran a hand over her forehead and found it blessedly cool. "He's tired."

"He's never tired during the day." Ticia jumped down from the ledge. "Nathan? Nathan!"

"He's resting. He doesn't feel well."

"Is he sick? Oh, Mother, he's sick!"

Eleanor knelt before Ticia. "Leticia Desmarais. You are nearly nine years old. You are a princess. You must be strong for your little brother."

Ticia bit her lip. "Must I go? I want to stay with him."

"I'll be with him every minute. I promise."

"Will he get better?"

Eleanor nodded emphatically. "Yes. He will." She led Ticia to the door and called for Pansy. As she gave Pansy instructions the maid's eye twitched, but the rest of her face was impassive as ever. Eleanor kissed Ticia. "I'll see you soon, when Nathan is feeling well."

Ticia nodded, but still she chewed her lower lip. Pansy took her shoulder, but before Eleanor could close the door Ticia put one small hand against it. "I love you, Nathan! Get well so we can play together! I'll even play dragons, if you wish it."

Eleanor turned back to her son in the bed. He suddenly seemed too small for it, as if the blankets and sheets and feather mattress might swallow him whole. She gathered a pitcher of water and a few cotton towels from atop the chest of drawers. The walk from the chest to the rocker between the beds had stretched from a few paces to a few miles.

She placed a wet cloth on his forehead. She took his hot hands, his fingers like dry straw. "Can you drink, love?"

"No."

"Please, just a sip. Please."

She helped him raise his head. The water dribbled over his chin and cheek. "Will Poppa come?" he asked.

Eleanor squeezed his hand. "Uncle Dorian will write to him. He'll be very worried." *How is it that I cannot promise his father will come?*

Pansy slid food under the door for the first two days, but gave it up when it became obvious neither Nathan nor Eleanor were eating. Chou brought flasks of fresh water through the window and made certain Eleanor drank a glass or two. Each morning she asked after Gregory, but Dorian had not head anything from Eclatant. She blessed him giving Ticia a room across from the nursery. Ticia sat in her own picture window, either drawing or dozing against the glass or just staring out into the courtyard. She waved and blew kisses and Eleanor smiled and waved back. On the fourth morning Dorian knocked on the door. "Eleanor, might I come in? I can help you."

Nathan slept soundly for the first time since the fever began. Eleanor tiptoed across the squeaky floor. "Thank you, but I'm fine," she said to the door.

"You should rest. Are you feeling—are you ill yourself?"

"No." *That I could be, in my child's place.* "How is Ticia?"

"Healthy. She never cries. She's a credit to you."

"Dorian—what of Gregory—"

"I'm sorry. Nothing. I'll write him again today. Please. Let me come in."

She pressed her face into the wood, as if she might touch him on the other side. "No. It's too dangerous. What news from Anne Clara?"

"Things are bad with Ransom, but so far no one else is ill. Abram has come to help me in the stables. The grooms ran off. Abram sent his wife and children south, to stay with her family in Sage."

"Kind of him. HighGod protect them."

Silence fell on both sides of the door.

"Take care, Dorian."

"And you, Your Highness."

Eleanor returned to the bedside. Chou landed on the arm of her rocking chair. "I suppose you're going to tell me I should have let him in," she said.

"No," said Chou. "You're right. It's too dangerous."

Eleanor waited for Chou to round off his comment with something snide, but the parrot just tucked his wings and hunkered beside her. She stroked his head, and then her son's. Her breath caught in her throat.

Nathan's hair was wet. His skin, cool.

Nathan woke two hours later and looked at Eleanor with clear eyes. When he asked her for water she nearly shouted for joy. Her hand trembled as she poured. Water splashed onto the sweat-soaked silk sheets.

She walked to the wardrobe. "A towel...no, he needs a fresh bed." Her voice trembled as she shook the wrinkles from a white sheet. A warbling voice drifted over her shoulder.

"Eleanor." Chou clung to her back. "You mustn't put too much stock in this recovery. Not yet. You know how it usually goes."

She selected a wonderfully soft cotton pillowcase. "It won't go that way, Chou."

"Most victims feel better for a day—"

"Some recover!"

"—and then fall ill again."

She spun around like a dog chasing its tail. The parrot held on, his wings flapping, red and blue feathers flying. She finally got hold of one of his legs. He whistled and let go of her dress.

"He will recover," she said. "He'll be fine."

Chou lit on top of the wardrobe. "I hope you are right, but you must be realistic."

"Always the doom and gloom with you! You've already written a proclamation of his—"

She couldn't say the word. The pause gave her time to take in Chou's yellow eyes, round with grief, and the patchy spots in his glorious coat of red feathers. She choked on a sob. "Oh, Chou, I'm sorry."

He shook his head. "I pray your hopefulness wins out."

Eleanor reached for him, and he climbed down her arm. She returned to Nathan's bed. He smiled at her, but he was still too weak to move. She set the clean sheets aside and took his hands.

"Will you tell me a story, Mother?"

She told him stories of her visit to the Dragon Mines with his father in those fabled days before his birth, and before even Ticia's. She started with his favorite, the tale he called Mother versus the Mean Mother Dragon. Halfway through the second telling, at the part when Eleanor and Teardrop leaped the rampaging dragon's spiked tail and returned to Gregory's side alive, Nathan asked Eleanor for a glass of pear juice.

"Why was the mother dragon so angry?"

"She wanted to protect her babies."

"Didn't she know the unicorns wouldn't hurt them?"

Eleanor smiled. "All mothers, dragons and unicorns and even mice, live in fear for the safety of their children."

They spent the rest of the afternoon reading, and playing with Nathan's dragons, and listening to Chou Chou's impressions. Chou added authenticity to Mister Abram Finley's wheezy Lake District drawl by stretching his neck to an absurd length and opening his eyes until they bulged from his head. A cough squelched Nathan's laughter.

"My head...I'm tired, Mother."

Eleanor pulled the covers toward his chin. "Of course, a nap."

"Love you, Mother." He slept soundly until just before dinner, woke, and asked for more pear juice. After an hour he once again heeded the call of sleep. Eleanor gripped his hands, marveling at their coolness. She hummed until he drifted off, and then rested her head against his thin arm. For the first time in nearly a week she fell into a deep sleep herself.

Nathan's thrashing woke her sometime in the darkest hours of the morning. She sat up and stretched to ease the stiffness in her neck. "Darling, are you thirsty?"

"Poppa! Poppa, where are you?" He threw back the covers, and his body heat blasted into her face.

She grabbed his hands. The fire had returned, and with a force she wouldn't have believed possible.

"Oh, no, oh, no, oh, no," said Chou. He tucked his head under his wing.

"Nathan—"

"Poppa! Poppa! Mother...Poppa! The dragon...dragon...Poppa!"

His fists hit the blankets and a thin line of spittle ran down his chin. She wiped it. "Nathan...darling...I'm here..."

He looked at her for a moment. "Where is Poppa? Mother...my head."

"He's coming—he's—"

"Poppa!"

Eleanor grabbed his arms and tried to force stillness into him. "Get Dorian," she said to Chou. "Ask him to come...please...if he will."

Chou disappeared out the window. Eleanor tried to coax some recognition out of Nathan, but whatever he saw was not in the nursery, and whatever he sought seemed to be back at Eclatant. He called for her intermittently, and she answered in a loud voice, hoping the part of him that fought the Burning heard her.

Dorian appeared over her shoulder, unshaven, in a simple gray undershirt, a pair of brown leggings, and bare feet. He rested his hand on her back. "What shall I do?"

"A man's voice...I thought maybe if you tell him...he doesn't seem to see anything..."

Dorian sat on the edge of the bed. "Nathan..." He glanced at her and she nodded. "It's your father...it's Poppa."

Nathan's limbs quieted. He stared at the ceiling for a moment. "You came."

Dorian swallowed. He took Nathan's hands. "I did. I'm sorry it took so long."

"Will you stay now?"

"Yes, I'll stay."

The boy's eyelids fluttered, and then closed. He gripped Dorian's hand. He moaned and shifted on the bed, but he didn't kick or scream. He whispered for his father again and again.

"I'm here, Nathan. I'm—" Dorian paused and Eleanor took his other hand. "I'm so proud of you. You are a true prince. A strong soldier."

"Will I be king?"

"You will be. The greatest king Cartheigh had ever known."

Eleanor stroked her son's dry red hair. She tried to hum, but grief had closed her throat.

When Eleanor opened her eyes she felt as if she'd been deposited inside a cloud. It took a moment to recognize the layers of white before her face as jumbled sheets and coverlets. Dorian was shaking her shoulder. She lifted her head and looked down at Nathan, peaceful and still on his back.

She touched the sheet covering his chest. "Oh...Dorian he's cool—he's..." The smile that had tugged at the corners of her mouth let go at the sight of Dorian's red eyes. She willed the tears tracking down his face to disappear. "Why are you—he's cool."

"He's cold, my love. Not cool, cold."

"No. You're mistaken."

"Touch him. His face."

"No."

Dorian took her hand. She moaned and tried to pull it away, but he spread her fingers

and pressed her palm against Nathan's icy forehead. "Cold, love. I'm so sorry." His fingers folded around hers.

She sat back in her chair and the small details leapt out at her. The bluish tinge to his lips. The stillness...too still. The tiniest bit of white peeking from beneath his not-quite-closed eyelids.

Her breath came in shallow gasps. She heard Dorian, but her tongue had fixed itself to the roof of her mouth. Her lips were glued together.

"I must take him, Eleanor. For everyone's safety. For Ticia's safety. Before the servants start screaming for a cleansing fire." He squeezed her hand. "I'll make a fitting burial for a Desmarais prince, I swear it."

She pried her lips open, but no sound came out. She managed a small nod, and then pulled her knees to her chest. She inhaled the sour smell of a week's worth of anxious sweat. Dorian lifted Nathan and cradled him like a basketful of cracked eggs. Nathan's head lolled, and Eleanor reached up to adjust it. A flash of green in the bed sheets caught her eye. She grabbed Green Pea, Nathan's forlorn stuffed dragon, and tucked it under her son's arm. She sat again, and watched Dorian leave the room with Nathan cradled in his arms. One bare white foot peeked at her from under his blue silk nightshirt.

"Your Highness?" Pansy's cracking voice drifted through the door. "Do you need anything? Should I call Chou Chou from Princess Leticia's room?"

Eleanor began rocking. Something burned in her stomach, but she'd become a blocked chimney. The smoke swirled through her veins and behind her eyes, searching for a way out. She held it in. Pansy let her be.

She walked to the window, with some idea of seeing Ticia, but her daughter's window was empty. Movement on the western side of Laralee's wide lawn caught her eye. Dorian and Abram stood among the dozen or so crumbling stone monuments in the Leigh family plot. Eleanor had passed the little cemetery fifty times in the past four months, but she'd never had reason to pay it any mind until now.

Dorian still wore his gray undershirt and old leggings, but he'd added a pair of stable boots to his grave-digging ensemble. She watched him for two hours as he disappeared inside the hole he was digging for her son's body. By the time the sun reached its noonday peak he'd sunk past his knees in the rocky earth. To his credit, it seemed Abram asked more than once if he could relive Dorian, but Dorian must have demurred. Abram stood watch over a white, boy-shaped bundle of sheets.

The day dragged on and Ticia did not appear at the window. Some part of her thanked Chou, or Pansy, for having the sense to keep Ticia from watching her little brother's internment. Eleanor listened to the sobs and screams of the few remaining servants echo through the empty house. The smoke inside her burned the back of her eyes.

As the shadows grew long she decided she was surely losing her mind. She watched Gregory walk across the lawn. Faster and faster he went, until he was running to the cemetery.

How clever of my insanity, for who could doubt the reality of such a detailed vision? His favorite purple tunic with the green tassels along the bottom…the one that always reminds me of a rug, haha! Those gray riding leggings with the holes in the knees…he's cut his hair…

She could see nothing of Dorian but the flash of a shovelhead and clods of flying dirt. The Gregory-mirage fell to his knees beside the bundle and shifted the sheets. He gripped his hair with both hands and looked to the graying sky above him. Eleanor could not hear his scream (for how can one hear the scream of someone who is not really there?), but she felt it, somewhere in the coals of the fire burning in her belly. She stood, too quickly, and turned from the window. The flames leapt up; yellow flashes before her eyes. Smoke filled her head. She couldn't breathe, or see her own hands before her face. Roaring yellow gave way to silent black.

Once more she awoke to a sight that made no sense. Black boots walking toward her across a pale green rug. The sound of her own name.

She pushed herself onto her elbows, and then sat up. The boots stopped before her and she stared at a pair of gray leggings. Bits of reddish brown hair poked through the holes in both knees.

Gregory knelt beside her. "Eleanor—sweetheart—" He bit his fist.

Her hand went to his wet cheek. He took it, and pressed his mouth against it. "You're real?" she whispered.

"What?"

Eleanor ran her dry tongue around her mouth. She pulled her hand from his and tucked her frozen bare feet under skirts. "You came," she said, in an imitation of Nathan's statement to Dorian.

Gregory sat down hard. "I did. I wanted to come sooner, of course. Father wouldn't hear of it. Too dangerous, heir to the throne—all that dragonshit." He grabbed her knees. "Yesterday morning I told him to go to the dogs. I left the Council Room—he was cursing me and screaming but I left anyway. Vigor and I—alone—all night across the country..."

Is he smiling?

She'd barely finished the thought before the expression in question left his face. His lip trembled, and he so resembled Nathan it pained her to look at him. "I thought I would get here on time—that he would survive. With his blood—our blood is strong—"

"You weren't here."

"I tried, Eleanor—"

"He called for you."

A small sound escaped the back of Gregory's throat.

"Over and over. But you weren't here."

"It's not my fault."

Eleanor felt nothing but a detached rationality. "You've never been here, really."

"Stop it. You're distraught."

Eleanor sounded very much like Rosemary questioning a student on philosophical theory. "I wonder...have you ever been here? Have we ever been together?"

"What are you blathering about?" He scooted away from her. "Our son is dead!"

"There must have been some truth in us. Sometime. But when?"

"Grief has driven you mad." He stood up. "I'll have Jones bring you a tonic."

"He called for you, Gregory."

"Stop saying that!"

"He called." Gregory's fist stopped just before her nose. She blinked at it. "You weren't here."

He backed away from her, tears rolling down his face. His eyes didn't leave hers until the door shut and broke the connection like a punch in the gut cutting off a scream.

Eleanor slept fitfully on the floor that night. The morning light found her on her side with her arms around her knees. She heard a ruckus outside the window and tried to sit up, but her left shoulder, arm, and leg were numb. By the time she'd coaxed the blood back into its proper channels the noise had stopped. It seemed a waste of effort to look after an extinguished commotion, so she lay down again and traced her fingers across the patterns on the rug. Her eyes fell on a wooden dragon under Leticia's bed. She forced herself to breathe.

She heard the door open and shut. Someone crossed the floor.

Eleanor knew the sound of his boot falls, and rolled onto her back. He sat beside her and crossed his legs. He still hadn't shaved. The dark circles ringing his eyes gave him the look of a gaunt alley cat. "He's gone. He took Ticia."

Something woke inside Eleanor. She sat up. "Where?"

"Back to Eclatant. He said she was no safer here than at home." Dorian rubbed his face with both hands. "I tried to talk him out of it. Ticia cried...screamed for you...but he forced her into the carriage."

"The noise this morning...Oh, dearest Ticia...why didn't I get up?" She slammed her fist against the rug. "No better use to my daughter than I was to my son."

"No. You couldn't have stopped Gregory. And you couldn't have done any more for Nathan. No one could have done any more." Dorian tucked a piece of hair behind her ear.

"Is he really gone?" she asked, in one last stand against reality.

"He is."

"Why can't I cry?" she asked. "I've been very capable of crying for most of my life." She gripped her skirts with both hands. He lifted her chin. The grief and compassion in his eyes finally allowed her an answer to that question.

Tears rained down on the flames in her stomach. She gripped both his hands in hers, and he pulled her into his lap. He stroked her hair while she sobbed and cursed and screamed her son's name and begged HighGod to have mercy and return him.

Dorian's face was beside hers. Their foreheads came together, as they had so many times. She closed her eyes. Their wet cheeks met. Her mouth touched his neck, her tongue tasted salt. His hands under her eyes. He wiped the tears into her hair and she did the same for him. One touch melted into another.

Somehow she was astride him, somehow he pushed her skirts aside and she loosened his belt. He slid inside her. She wrapped both arms around his head. He rested his forehead between her breasts, and they both went still. In those quiet moments something was whole inside Eleanor. She gripped his hair and squeezed him with both legs.

I will never let you go again, she thought.

He took her face in both hands. His thumb ran over her lips. "Eleanor, I—"

Snick! They both turned at the sound.

She pushed back from his lap. "The door?"

"Shh…"

The sound of feet running down the hallway.

"I shut it—" He scrambled upright and buttoned his leggings. He buckled his belt on his way out.

Dorian closed the door behind him. He went left, as the passageway ended in a floor-to-ceiling mirror ten paces to his right. He wiped his face and did his best to tidy his hair. He passed door after door on his way to the front hall.

He met Pansy huffing up the spiral stairway leading to the hall. Chou dropped out of nowhere and landed on his head.

"Your Grace," Pansy said, "good morning, how is—"

"Did you pass anyone on your way here, Pansy? Did you notice anyone coming from this wing?"

"No one but Mistress Jan, Your Grace. You just missed her. On the way to the kitchen, she said."

"Did she seem…in good spirits?"

Pansy looked at him as if he'd lost his mind. "Not a soul in this house is in good spirits, sir."

"Of course, you're right. Anyone else?" Pansy shook her head. Dorian stepped aside to let her pass. "See to the princess, please. Make sure she eats and drinks. Pour her a bath. Don't take no for an answer."

As she disappeared up the steps Dorian asked Chou to stay. The parrot sat on his shoulder. He whistled under his breath through Dorian's truncated explanation.

"You're sure someone was there?" Chou asked.

"Most positive. If it was Jan, well, she's already aware of the...situation. She has been for years, and she's held her tongue."

"It must have been her. We just saw her on the stairs."

"Your Grace?" Jones stood at the bottom of the steps. He wrung his hands like a nervous groom. "Your Grace...I'm to tell you..."

Dorian met him on the landing. "Out with it, Jones."

"His Highness commands you to be on your way to Eclatant before noon. You are to set out on unicornback immediately and catch the royal carriage."

"I can't just leave—"

"I'll stay on for two days. Leave me a list of anything you need brought back to Eclatant."

"The servants—the bookkeeping—"

"His Highness asked your brother to put things in order. The princess is to stay on."

"Dragonshit!" Dorian kicked the banister. "I'll leave when I'm bloody well ready."

Jones stepped out of boot range. "Please, Your Grace...lower your voice."

"Damn and blast him."

"Please! Heed him. You know he always regrets these outbursts. Give it a few days and you can intervene for the princess from Eclatant. We will need his good will if we expect to comb the streets of Maliana for Mister Oliver."

"He's right," said Chou as he landed on Jones's shoulder. "I'll give the princess your most affectionate goodbyes."

"I'll have the grooms bring Senne'," said Jones. He trotted down the passageway before Dorian could argue his case, or kick anything else. Chou landed on Dorian's shoulder for a moment, and then flew off to the nursery. Dorian was left in seething silence on the staircase.

CHAPTER 25

OUR MOST SACRED ASSOCIATION

FOUR GRIEF-HAZED WEEKS LATER, Eleanor returned to Eclatant at Gregory's invitation. Pansy seemed to hope familiar surroundings would improve Eleanor's appetite. "You're transparent, Your Highness," the maid said on their first morning at home.

"I can't Pansy." Eleanor sat at her desk. She hunched over a letter to Brother Marcus. "I just can't."

"I asked the cooks to make your favorite. Roast turkey. Baked apples."

Eleanor's stomach turned. Grief had turned her belly a permanent shade of green and shrunken it to the size of a pea. "It all tastes the same."

"How about these?" Pansy held up a tin of chocolate-covered almonds from Eleanor's favorite confectioner, Petti-Bonbons. "I've seen you eat an entire tin yourself."

Nathan loves them...Eleanor couldn't bring herself to think of her son in the past tense.

She pictured his face and hands covered in chocolate. She could almost smell his hair.

Pansy would not let Eleanor help with the unpacking. She moved to the couch by the fire and watched a chambermaid army rush between the wardrobe and the bathing room. She tried to read, but she had no more luck with words these days than she did with food. She put aside her book, *The Curious Magician's Guide to Curious Magical Theories*, and stroked Chou's shiny red back.

"Is my memory going, Chou?" She pointed at the frantic servants. "Where are Nellie and Daisy? And Perdita?"

"And Susan," said Chou. "She had the loveliest fingernails. Perfect for scratching my chin."

Pansy offered a glass of pear juice. Eleanor took a dutiful sip. "Sacked," said Pansy. "Cooks told me His Highness changed out all your personal servants just last week."

"Why on earth—"

The door opened. "Mother!"

Ticia raced across the pale blue rug. Her face crumpled with each step. She was in her mother's arms before Eleanor could stand. The servants froze in their curtseys like pose-able puppets. Pansy bellowed instructions over Ticia's noisy sobbing. "Out, all of you! Out! Their Highnesses need privacy."

The maids excused themselves in a shuffling flock of cheap gingham. Pansy followed them into the hall and closed the door behind her. Ticia cried for her baby brother for the better part of an hour before trailing off in a series of shuddering sniffles. She huddled in Eleanor's lap and stuck two fingers in her mouth. With the other hand she fingered the lace on the sagging bodice of Eleanor's gown. Eleanor rocked her and kissed her smooth forehead. If not for Ticia's legs dangling off her lap, Eleanor could have gone back in time eight years.

"She's needed your comfort." Gregory leaned against the closed door. "I've invited the Duchess and her mother to dinner. I trust you can be civil."

Eleanor brushed Ticia's hair out of her face. "Such a question is trivial in light of recent events."

Gregory's jaw jutted. "Eat something. You're too thin. How can you carry a child on such a frame?"

"Can you not lift me, Mother?" asked Ticia. Eleanor kissed her hair in response.

"You'll not ride, or dance, or entertain visitors," said Gregory. "Stay in your room unless I call for you. I'll have Pansy bring Leticia to you every day. If you seem too tired, she'll stay in the nursery."

Eleanor cringed at the meekness in her own voice. "As you wish."

"Dorian, Raoul, and I leave for Rabbit's Rest tomorrow morning. We return Sunday evening. I'll visit you then." He held out his hand. "Come, Ticia."

Ticia buried her face in Eleanor's bosom. Eleanor whispered in her ear. "Go now, Tish. I'll see you tomorrow." Eleanor smiled, and she swore she heard her jaw creak.

Ticia nodded and got to her feet. She curtsied before following Gregory out the door. When the door closed Eleanor's shoulders began shaking.

Chou dropped from his post on the Fire-iron chandelier onto the carved table beside the couch. He held a handkerchief in his curved beak. She gave him a watery smile. "Bless you." She wiped her nose.

"You must take more care...Jan seeing you and Dorian at Laralee... next time you won't be so lucky. It could have been anyone. We certainly can't trust these new maids."

"I know, Chou...but..." Eleanor pinched Chou's beak. "I've lost one of the three most important people in my life. I won't lose another." She went to her writing desk and lit three candles.

Two hours later she had a pile of ash and a letter. She'd burned half a dozen drafts until she finally found the right words.

Dear Sir,

HighGod forgive me, but my pride held sway even when my heart knew the justness of this apology. I beg you to pardon me my cruel words of this past winter. You have shown me the most profound loyalty these many troubled years. I recognize the need for subterfuge and the weight of your continued refusal to heed the call of commitment. What's more, it is unjust of me to fault you for your physicality when we are so long removed from one another. I swear, in the future I will put greater faith in the sincerity of our most sacred association, that which reaches beyond worldly delights, and less stock in my own juvenile insecurity. I am, as I have always been, yours in all ways.

She folded the letter into a tiny square and held it out to Chou. He took it in his beak, and then transferred it to one talon. "I'll tell him to burn it."

"You think he won't know?" With a whistle, Chou floated out over the garden, the letter clenched in his scaly feet.

Fear of losing her daughter drove Eleanor to obey Gregory for the first time in the history of her marriage. She stayed in her room. Over the next few days she removed and replaced her choker a dozen times. She vacillated between the agony of waiting on Dorian's call and fear of missing it if it came. By Friday morning her stomach had gone from the hollow pit of the last few weeks to a yawning chasm. Ticia arrived after breakfast, and Eleanor watched as she worked on her penmanship. Eleanor offered a correction or suggestion here and there, but even Ticia could see her heart was not in it. The child put her ledger to the side and took a small, worn volume of fairy stories from the pocket of her dress. Ticia had little patience for geography or mathematics, but she did love her happily ever afters.

Ticia sat in her mother's lap as Eleanor read the tale of Pearlymaid and the Little Men. Eleanor had always found Pearlymaid to be a simpering fool, so she took her usual liberties with the story. Pearlymaid refused to eat the evil witch's poison apple, and instead threw it at the old woman's head. It bounced back into Pearlymaid's face and chipped her tooth, spraying poison into her mouth. The prince found her asleep in the cabin. His kiss brought her back to life, and Pearlymaid took up her sword and joined him. Together they dispatched the evil queen once and for all.

"Ruby says Pearlymaid ate the apple," said Ticia. "She said the prince and the little men killed the evil queen."

"Our Pearlymaid wouldn't be so stupid, now would she?"

Ticia grinned a secret grin. "No. She's as smart as any boy. Smarter, I think."

"Girls, boys…some are smart, some are not."

Pansy came to collect Ticia at eleven o'clock, and Eleanor and Chou cast about for something to do. "I believe I shall read."

"You haven't finished a chapter in weeks."

"I'm trying something new." She held up a pamphlet.

"Martine's of Pettibone Lane—Collections for Spring—Bonnets, Slippers, and Other Necessary Accessories." Chou rolled his eyes. "Since when are accessories necessary? Doesn't the very term hint at their superfluous-ness?"

"Now, Chou, we all know a stylish bonnet is akin to water in the desert."

"Or a candle in a cave."

"Or bosoms on a whore." Eleanor sniggered, and put a hand over her mouth. "Excuse me."

"No—need—" Chou said, with a whistling chortle. "Bosoms are, in fact, the bodacious bonnets in a whore's arsenal of accessories."

Eleanor collapsed into the chair, her legs splayed out before her. She laughed until tears streamed down her face. Her stomach clenched and unclenched, the wilted muscles yowling in protest of her mirth, but she couldn't stop. The giggles finally trailed off, only to resurge with the mental image of a feathered bonnet perched on each of Pandra Tate's head-sized breasts.

Chou hopped into her lap. "It's good to hear you laugh."

She stroked his head and touched her choker. "I thought I'd forgotten how."

"He'll call," said Chou.

"Hmmm." Eleanor went to the open window and looked out over the garden. She inhaled the smell of freshly turned earth. The tulips were in their full glory, tiny bits of springtime sunshine trapped in overcrowded beds. She listened to the gardeners singing songs while they worked, some from the taverns, some from the chapels. One of them noticed her. He picked a tulip and held it up to her. She smiled at his small overture of deference, the first spontaneous act of its kind she'd been shown in months, and waved.

He returned to his work and Eleanor looked up at the soft springtime sky, the striated blues and shifting white clouds. For some reason the sun on her face made her shiver. She rubbed her arms and pointed at the clouds. "That one looks like a goose—do you see the long neck?"

"I see a raven."

"How can you see a raven in white clouds? A dove, perhaps, but—"

"No, a raven. There. Above the south wing."

Eleanor squinted, and picked out a bouncing black dot against the shining silver of the southernmost tower that housed the Council Hall and King Casper's receiving room. The dot kept coming, growing larger until Eleanor could just make out a sliver of white against the Frog's dark belly.

He flew past Eleanor and Chou and landed on her writing desk. He dropped a folded sheet of paper, but Eleanor saw he had another.

"Read it. Destroy it. My master sent me home with a letter to his sister. Goodbye." With that Frog took off again, leaving nothing but the note and a few black feathers in his wake.

For some reason Eleanor hadn't expected Dorian to write back. She'd assumed he'd either call or he wouldn't. The letter seemed to glare up at her from the dark wooden desk like a blind eye. Her pulse pounded in her ears as she unfolded the note.

Dear lady,

I hope you will excuse my lightness, but I must tell you the opening of your letter made me laugh.

Eleanor's heart sank.

Not because of the humor inherent in your sentiment, of course, but because it could have been written by my own hand.

And with that she exhaled.

Long have I wished to make amends, and yet somehow I did not manage it. You have my forgiveness for your outburst, not only because of your most sincerely given apology, but because I must admit to the truth in your accusations.

In light of our forced distance and the supposed necessity of removing suspicions, I allowed myself to justify any action on my part. Your words, although harsh, forced me to examine my motivations. I found them wanting. I bid you know it all meant nothing to me, and hope this brings you some comfort. I have never been so unhappy as when we are separated, and have never, in all these years, seen that unhappiness lifted until I found you again. I will try to keep that knowledge foremost in my mind through the long days and nights ahead of us.

While I hope that you will find another way to address your grievances in the future, and speak to me forthrightly of your concerns, I understand your anger. As I said to you many years ago, if my actions cause you pain I will cease and desist. Soldier's honor.

There is no wrong or right in any of this, my love. It is not black and white, or even shades of gray. The palette of our lives runs in bright rainbows and dark mud. I mourn what it has done to all of us. Could we have seen ourselves as such, ten years ago? In the days when we were so sure of our rights, and our rightness. I mourn your son, my most beloved nephew.

I see now that this letter is drifting into the realm of the incriminating, but I will continue anyway. If I could I'd write to you every day, so that you would know how I dwell on you and our most sacred association, as you so elegantly put it. If this is the only letter I ever write to you, know I send you my heart in every stroke of the quill.

Eleanor read the note again and again, committing the words to memory before she touched the paper to her candle's lit wick.

Sunday afternoon found Eleanor at Humility Chapel, in the first row of backless wooden benches. Eleanor hoped to speak with Brother Marcus after the service, for he hadn't answered her letter. Godsman or not, she found the idea of Marcus preaching an odd one. She thought of him as an educator, not a proselytizer.

She watched at the crowd around her, a mix of drowsy old ladies dripping with jewels, aristocratic parents and their well-dressed, fidgety children, and a few fervently muttering believers. Marcus glared at the congregation from his seat at the head of the chapel. Eleanor folded her hands and focused on the garlands draped over the altar. *Tulips. Roses. Daisies. Trumpetheads. Bluebellies. Irises. Wethervanes.* She matched blooms to the names she'd memorized from her botany encyclopedia. Sunlight streamed through the arched windows. The white fingers tickled new hues and textures out of the blooms.

The palette of our lives runs in bright rainbows...

The worshipers stood as Gregory, Dorian, and Raoul walked down the center aisle. The sharp sound of their riding boots on the limestone floors rebounded through the chapel, until it sounded as if a herd of horses had come in from the streets. Raoul took the seat to Eleanor's left, with Dorian on his far side, Gregory wordlessly slid in on her right. He smelled of sweat and road dust.

The congregation sat once more. Eleanor gripped her choker and prayed in the way dearest to her heart.

The tiny dragon warmed in her hand. She held out her hand to Raoul. She nodded at Dorian. His cheeks were flushed and his hair tousled from hours in the saddle. He tipped his head back at her. His ring threw flashes of blue her way as he spun it around his finger. He faced the altar again, and she saw his mouth turn up at the corners.

The warmth of the choker seeped from her chest to the tips of her toes, like the first sip of a hot drink on a cold afternoon. For the next thirty minutes her own disorganized prayers mingled with Marcus's Meditations on the new week.

"...will bear the fruits of our labors..."

Forgive me for my pride...

"...let us face each day with constant hearts..."

Nathan...Margaret...bless them...lost spirits...

"...and our Most Righteous Majesty..."

322

Thank you for my daughter…and for Dorian…but hold my sweet little boy close to you…

She hardly noticed when Marcus climbed to the pulpit, but his mention of the Abbey caught her attention.

"—Afar Creek. Yet some stay on. Although the citizens of this realm have made it clear they are not needed, or wanted."

Eleanor stiffened. Gregory squeezed her knee in warning as Marcus continued.

"Does anyone among us believe those who stay eschew magic? Of course not. The Oracle herself, the source of the most powerful magic on the Abbey grounds, remains. They deliberately stay and take up magical space. Space the magicians need in their search for a cure!"

The congregation muttered and nodded.

"I've worked closely with the witches in the Fringe. Perhaps they are not all malevolent, but we've all seen where their tactics lead." He looked at Eleanor and her face burned. "We've all witnessed the extent of their deception. Their twisting of supposed good works for profit. A profit of the most ungodly kind, if I might add. I will not speak of it here, in this house of our Most High."

Gregory squeezed harder, pinning her to the bench.

"HighGod wills us to humility. Here, in this chapel so named for it. But the witches will not heed his message. They stay on at the Abbey, conjuring and impeding the search for a cure, for the sake of their grudges and jealousies. Your children die, because they will not bend to the will of their sovereign and the magical superiority of the magicians." Marcus raised his voice. His broad face had gone beet red, and he pounded a mutton-sized fist on the Fire-iron pulpit. "Until the witches step aside and make way for a cure, His judgment will be upon them. And those that support them. I pray you will think on their pride, brothers and sisters, and find it not in your own hearts." He bowed to the altar and returned to his wooden chair.

"HighGod's praises," said the congregation. They stood to sing the final hymn.

Eleanor mouthed the words. She seethed through verse and chorus. Marcus followed two young Godsmen down the aisle. He sang at the top of his voice in a nasally baritone and handed flowers from the altar to the worshippers. *Pride indeed.*

The hymn ended and the worshippers waited in their seats for Gregory and Eleanor and their party to exit. She'd never been able to leave Humility Chapel on Gregory's arm without pondering her wedding day, but today the memory waltzed in and out of her mind like a cast-off dance partner. She hustled Gregory along.

They reached the chapel alcove, but Marcus was nowhere to be seen. She let go of Gregory and stepped onto the marble staircase leading to the chapel's small courtyard. She shaded her eyes and squinted against the glare of the HighSpring sun after an hour of candlelight.

Townsfolk bustled about on the street below her. As people recognized Gregory they bowed and curtsied and shouted blessings and condolences on the death of the young prince. Eleanor even caught her own name called out in sympathy. She waved and curtsied, but all the while she searched for Marcus's brown-draped bulk.

"There's your carriage," said Gregory. "We'll see you at dinner." He brushed her hand with his lips and descended the stairs toward his mount. Raoul followed him. Dorian paused for a moment on the stairs before joining them.

"Over there." He tilted his head toward First Maliana Covey, the hulking granite conglomeration of spindly turrets and skinny windows between Humility Chapel and Eclatant. Eleanor examined the little groups of magicians clustered on the Covey stairs in their gray and black robes. She found Marcus's broad back and stubbly dark head just before he crossed the magicians' threshold.

CHAPTER 26

THE BELFRY

ELEANOR'S BARE TOES TOUCHED dry dirt, not squelching mud, when she eased off her bed. She looked around the square, from the squat houses to the old well to the burnt out remains of Queen Camille's. Not a soul wandered the quiet streets.

"How odd," said Chou from her shoulder. "It's feels like the Fringe... yet it's not."

Rosemary stepped from behind the well. "Chou! It worked! I've never called a bird before. I wondered if you'd hear me."

"Like a banshee's cry, Rosemary."

"Dreams pass quicker in the waking world. Sit, please." The Oracle sat on her pillows beside the watching pool, wrapped in her usual timeless bearskin dragon robe. The smells of smoke and wet wood and burnt ink overrode the pleasant lavender that always accompanied the Oracle. Eleanor sat beside the pool. It reflected the scene around her, as if the square had fallen into the still water and rearranged itself upside-down.

Hazelbeth had always looked to Eleanor like the world's greatest great-grandmother, but now she resembled a week-dead corpse. She'd lost the last of her wispy white hair. Her face had caved in upon itself, from her cheeks to her forehead, as if she'd tried to swallow her own nose. Her eyes sunk so far back into her head that Eleanor wondered if she saw anything at all.

Eleanor cleared her throat. "You wanted to see me, Hazelbeth?"

"Yes, but I'm more interested in your bird."

Eleanor's eyebrows crept toward the crown her dreaming mind had set upon her head. "Chou?"

"I knew we could count on Chou for gossip," said Rosemary, "enchanted or otherwise."

Chou lit on the blackened ground. "I'm honored, ladies. What would you like to know?"

"Pray," said the Oracle. "What opinions have you heard on the streets? I listen to the pool, but so many voices are often jumbled. More so in these times."

Chou went puffy with his own importance. "Let me think...well, the strain of finding a cure is wearing on the magicians. They're pushing back against the king. Complaining about women's work."

"Women's work that they cannot master," said Rosemary.

"They don't have our centuries of healing knowledge," said Hazelbeth.

Eleanor thought of Marcus's sermon. "This whole endeavor has been an absurd folly, yet still the blame is laid on Afar Creek."

The Oracle nodded. "I would have a cure, no matter where it comes from. Those of us who remain try to refrain from excessive magic, but we cannot be but who we are."

Rosemary stood and stormed around the pool. Her gray dress flapped around her thin legs. "Excuses! It's not a matter of a bit more magical space. It's a matter of skill!"

"Abbotess," Hazelbeth said, "there is enough fire in Maliana. Our reciprocal anger will only stoke it."

Rosemary crossed her arms over her chest and sat, but a hint of pink touched her cheeks.

"You would think the people would riot in the streets," said Eleanor. "Demand the king reinstate Afar Creek."

"You heard Marcus, Eleanor," said Chou. "He's not the only Godsman preaching the magicians' cause from the pulpit."

"I thought Marcus a loyal friend."

"As did we all," said Rosemary. "I called on him at Larry's just last week, but he wouldn't see me. And every day he spouts the same message in one Chapel or another."

"His fascination with the Covey does not surprise me," said the Oracle. "It must have been traumatic for him, to think himself magical and then return to the mundane."

"But Marcus was always so kind—and keen to help at Queen Camille's. Why would he—"

A tolling bell snipped Eleanor's question in half. She put her hands over her ears. She'd never heard such a sound. Rich, full, heavy...the fudge tart of tolling bells. "The bells of Larry's!" she shouted at Chou. "Why are they so loud?"

She could just make out his reply. "It's your dream!"

Eleanor had to stop the sound before her head exploded. She ran across the block to Larry's. Rosemary called after her, but the dream shifted from magical meeting of the minds to average nighttime hallucination. If Rosemary, Chou, and the Oracle remained behind she ceased to hear them.

"Boys!" she shouted. "Stop the bells!" She ran through the open gate, up three chipped marble steps, and banged on the double wooden door. "Brother Marcus! It's too loud! Get those boys out of the belfry!"

The bells switched off.

The belfry.

The recital, years ago. Boys running into the library; coming from the belfry. The trapdoor slamming behind them as they climbed down the ladder.

Creee-smack! Wacka-wacka-wacka...

"Oh, dear HighGod…" Eleanor whispered. "He's at Larry's!"

The next day Gregory requested Eleanor's lunchtime presence in one of Eclatant's smallish dining rooms. As she approached the door she puffed out her chest. She hoped to create the illusion of cleavage.

"It's not use. You're as spare as a spoon," said Chou from her shoulder. "And you're missing an earbob."

"I must look robust." Eleanor stuffed the single earbob into her loose bodice and pinched her own cheeks. "Gregory will never let me accompany them if not."

"You've got the horn on the wrong end of the unicorn, as usual, darling. He hasn't agreed to let Dorian and Jones search the Fringe. Let alone you, his most sugared sweetmeat." Chou took off in the direction of the kitchens before she could swat him. He collided with a scurrying Jones. Man and parrot squawked at one another before each continued on his hurried way.

Dorian opened the door at her knock. Gregory sat at the head of the table, a quill clenched in his teeth. Documents and ledgers surrounded his untouched bowl of venison stew. His hair stuck up from his head as if he'd been struck by lightning. He glanced up, spit out the quill, and waved Eleanor and Jones into the chairs on either side of him. He clapped at the servants. "Food, wine. And move this rubbish to the far end of the table. The smell of ink destroys my appetite."

The servants fluttered around the table like a flock of hungry pigeons, adding and removing plates and glasses and shifting Gregory's books and papers. Someone set a bowl of steaming stew and a hunk of bread before Eleanor, and her stomach growled. She took up her spoon, and to her pleasure the soup tasted fine indeed. For the first time in over two months she ate with relish.

"You're feeling better, wife," said Gregory.

As it would be very like her to incite Gregory's anger when she most needed his acquiescence, and very like Gregory to become enraged by whatever she had the nerve to say, she simply nodded.

"So," said Gregory. "While I know the deep affection you each harbor for me, I assume you did not request this luncheon for the sole pleasure of my company."

Eleanor listened in silence as Dorian and Jones updated Gregory on the minutia of the hunt for Ezra Oliver. She expected her husband to laugh, or wave them off, but he just nodded and grunted and asked a few clarifying questions.

"...and so," Jones finished, "thanks to Her Highness we may indeed know where he is."

Gregory spoke as if Eleanor had left the room when she finished her soup. "A dream. It could be nothing more."

Dorian leaned across the table. "But you're willing to believe he's alive?"

"Not until someone lays eyes on him."

Jones shoved his bowl aside. Soup sloshed over the scalloped edges and onto the silk place setting. "Sire, in that cave—if you'd seen it—"

"You were attacked by powerful magic in a cave, Jones. Why must it be Ezra Oliver that set the trap?"

"Because none but him could conjure something like that!"

"Perhaps the witches are somehow behind it. A distraction to you—so you'll lose focus on the Burning."

Eleanor dug her fingernails into her hands until she was sure she'd drawn blood.

Dorian rushed on. "Greg, let us go to Brother Lawrence's. Let us try."

Gregory crossed his thick arms across his chest. "Suppose Ezra Oliver is indeed hiding out in the belfry at Larry's. How do you suppose to apprehend him?"

"Obviously we cannot knock on the belfry door and ask him to come with us," said Jones. "Dorian and I have decided to visit Larry's and examine the situation first, before bringing along soldiers or martials. We must take all precautions."

"And your martials did such a fine job dispatching him eight years ago," said Gregory.

"We'll need more," said Dorian. "A small army. That's why we need to go to Larry's. Determine how and when to make an attempt."

Gregory looked out the window. Eleanor could hear his boot tapping on the marble floor beneath them. "If I give my blessing," he said, "and you find nothing, then you must let it go."

"I—sire—I can't promise—"

Gregory narrowed his eyes at Jones. "You, sir, are obsessed. Perhaps if you spent more energy on the task my father set you and less on this wild goose chase, my son would still be with us."

"Your Highness." Orvid went a deathly shade of white. "I've put my heart into the cure. I swear it. I've not slept in two years."

"So why dwell on Oliver?"

Jones rested both elbows on the table. "Because he had so much to offer…more power than I could dream of…more respect than I'll ever have…I shouldn't be here, sire. It's his position. As long as he's alive, I'm an impostor."

"The king appointed you. No one thinks on Oliver anymore. To the world, he's dead."

"Magicians think on him. Still he holds sway in our minds. I have to find him. I can't live with the possibility that he will show himself and make me the fool for not finding him first."

"The Godsmen would chasten you for your pride."

"And I would deserve it. But I would also stand before Him and say I have not put my search for Oliver above my search for a cure."

Gregory exhaled. "Godsmen. If you're right, Brother Marcus will be praying for mercy, not offering meditations." Gregory drained his wine glass and called for another. "All right, boys. You may venture into the city with my blessing."

Jones cleared his throat. "Might the—uh—that is—would it be agreeable—"

"Damn, Jones! This conversation is boring me!"

"Might the princess come along?"

Gregory goggled at Eleanor. "You can't be serious."

She smiled. "Gregory—"

"We are," said Jones. "Please, sire. Princess Eleanor knows Larry's better than we. She knows the Fringe—she identified the bells."

"Fuck, no." He jabbed a finger at Eleanor. "You have some nerve."

"Please—"

"No!" He slammed both fists on the table. "With the Burning still on the streets—"

"I'll not touch anyone—I'll stay in the carriage until we arrive at Larry's. It's obvious I'm immune anyway, after Laralee—"

"Dragonshit!" Gregory's knees struck the heavy wooden table and his wine glass hit the floor. It shattered, spraying red wine over his ivory leggings. This time he pointed at Dorian and Jones. "Leave, both of you."

Dorian opened his mouth but Gregory didn't give him a chance to speak. "You. Get your ass out of here. Now."

Jones bowed and fled. Dorian followed him at a stiff-legged walk, as if someone had kicked him between the legs. Eleanor didn't know what was worse, Gregory's wrath or Dorian's dismissal.

Once the door closed behind them Gregory walked around the table. He stood behind Eleanor's chair. She felt his hands on her shoulders. His fingers crept up her neck and rested on the dragon choker. "Did you really think I would risk your safety?" He squeezed her shoulders until she winced. "Forget Ezra Oliver. You have one duty. To an heir."

He returned to his chair. She didn't know whether to stay or go. He called for the servants to clear the remaining dishes and return his paperwork. With the quill between his teeth once more Eleanor wondered if she'd slipped back in time an hour. Maybe the conversation about Larry's had not yet happened. Maybe she wouldn't have to see the humiliation on Dorian's face.

Gregory brought out a charcoal pencil and scribbled in silence for a quarter of an hour. He finally glanced up at her. "You may go," he said around his quill.

She stood and curtsied.

"By the way," he said. "Ticia won't be visiting this week. I've decided she should take up embroidery, and she'll have lessons in the morning."

"Embroidery," said Eleanor.

"Is there a problem?"

She shook her head.

"I, on the other hand, will be visiting you. Tonight. Be ready."

As Eleanor walked back to her chamber she came to a realization. The sympathy, the guilt, and the memories that had kept a warped fondness for Gregory alive inside her all these years had gone. She hated her husband.

Dorian traced his fingers over the Fire-iron doorknocker of the Brother Lawrence School for Boys. Some masterful craftsman had carved it in the shape of a book with the letters *BLS* emblazoned across the cover. A tiny inscription followed the monogram: *Welcome, Scholar.* He lifted the knocker, and then released it gently before it could make a sound against the scratched oak doors.

He turned to Jones. "You didn't say a word in the carriage."

"Nor did you."

Dorian had held his own tongue out of a singular desire to avoid mention of the conversation with Gregory. He couldn't think on it, for it resulted in simultaneous shivering mortification and boiling anger. For two days he'd felt as if he were in the clutches of some weird illness, an emotional case of the grippe.

Thankfully Jones was either too consumed with Oliver or too

socially inept to recognize Dorian's humiliation. Bits of creamy light puffed from Jones's nose with each sharp exhale. His right eye twitched. Dorian dropped his voice. "Remember, we're here to look, not fight. Expect a long road. If your emotions get the better of you—"

"What an absurd suggestion."

Dorian shrugged. "You're a powerful magician, Jones, but you're still a man."

Jones wiped at his nose, and then sniffed. The creamy light disappeared.

Dorian knocked, but the door didn't move. He pressed an ear against it. Jones shuffled his feet and plunged both hands into the pockets of his cloak, perhaps to hide enchanted evidence of his irritation. Dorian knocked again, harder.

A voice called from the other side of the door. "Peace, visitors... peace...I apologize for the wait—can I help—"

Brother Marcus's eyes widened with the crack between the door and the frame. "Your Grace...Mister Jones...ah—welcome!" He ran a hand over his stubbly head and tightened the horsehair belt around his waist. "Pardon—I didn't expect...please, come in! Planned or not... always a blessing!"

"Thank you, Marcus," said Dorian. He stepped into the small front hall and wiped his boots on the straw mat. "We were in the neighborhood, and thought a visit in order."

"Why?" Marcus asked, before throwing up his hands and grinning. "Why not? Jonathan!" A boy of about twelve peeked appeared in the passageway. "Take our guests' riding gloves. Leave them in my office—no, in my wardrobe."

They handed their gloves to the boy, who disappeared down the passageway once more. Dorian and Marcus took up most of the space in the hall, and Jones was fairly squashed against the door. Marcus simply grinned and blinked. Dorian had a clear view up his nostrils.

"Might we sit?" asked Dorian. "We'd like to discuss plague containment here in the Fringe."

It was as if someone had stomped on Marcus's foot. "Of course—silly me! How rude! We'll go to my—no it's a great mess—the study!" He strode down the passageway that had swallowed the boy. He made an abrupt left into the study, a dusty, forgotten-looking room not much larger than the front hall. Dorian peered down the passage before stepping over the threshold. According to Eleanor, the trapdoor leading to the belfry was just outside Marcus's office. Dorian knew the office to be in the back of the building, overlooking the rear courtyard. He and Jones would observe nothing of value from this vantage point.

Marcus sat on the edge of a worn ottoman. He didn't offer tea, or water. "So, how can I help you gentlemen?"

Dorian asked for news on the Burning in the blocks surrounding Larry's, and Marcus obliged with gusto. He rattled on about affected families and businesses, students who had sadly passed and a few who'd made miraculous recoveries. The clockworks on the wall behind the Godsman's head clicked out the minutes as Dorian nodded and asked for a clarification here and there.

"...and so..." After talking continuously for three quarters of an hour Marcus seemed to be running out of anecdotes. "...I've had some of the boys—those that seem immune, you know—delivering food to the sick—"

"Where might I find a chamber pot, Brother?" Jones had done nothing but sniff loudly through Marcus's dissertation.

"Of course...let me see you to my personal bathing room—"

"You must have a water closet in the kitchen." Jones stood up.

"Yes—but it's very small—"

Jones smiled and bowed. "I don't require much space. Excuse me." He turned left out of the study, in the direction of not only the kitchen, but of Marcus's office. Marcus stood and took a few steps after him.

"I noticed your visit to the Covey after Chapel this Sunday last," said Dorian.

Marcus sat on his ottoman once more. His small dark eyes flitted between Dorian's face and the open doorway. "Yes. The magicians have always donated books to Larry's. I peruse their library quite often."

"How generous of them."

"The wealth of their knowledge is astounding, and they always find room to share it with my poor boys. HighGod be praised."

"Inspiring sermon."

For the first time Marcus locked eyes with Dorian. "I seek to inspire the people of this city to the right path. All of them, from the Fringe to the palace. It is the calling of my kind."

"Indeed." Dorian rowed the conversation back into flat water by asking after the general health of the Godsman, but the topic of the Burning was wearing thin. Chunks of silence began to creep into the dialogue, each more awkward than the last. After fifteen minutes Jones's call of nature had obviously surpassed reasonable time limits.

Marcus fidgeted on the ottoman. Dorian had always thought if Marcus had not heard the call of the most HighGod he would have heard the call of the wrestling ring, but of late he had added a substantial layer of fat to his form, like a pat of butter on a lean cut of meat. His jowls brushed his chest when he looked down at his twiddling thumbs, and his belly rested squarely on his thighs.

"Have you any stories about...ah, the dockworkers?" Dorian asked.

Marcus grunted a no, and Dorian felt a twinge of desperation. *Horns and fire, what is Jones doing?*

He got his answer in a sound he'd heard at least a hundred times in the past month or so. *Creeeeaak—slam! Wacka, wacka, wacka...*

Dorian and Marcus were on their feet at the same time, but a marginal proximity and a nimbler figure allowed Dorian out the door first. He pulled his sword as he ran down the hall. He could hear Marcus's labored breathing a few steps behind.

Several small boys and the smell of baking bread drifted from the kitchen. "Go to your rooms, boys," Dorian said.

The children retreated at the sight of Dorian and his blade, but not before a high voice called out, "He's up the belfry, Brother Marcus!"

"Your Grace—I must ask you to stop—scaring the children—"

Dorian kept his eyes on the ceiling. He found the outline of the rectangular trapdoor, and tugged at a lumpy cord dangling a few hand spans above his head. As the door opened toward him it sang the first notes of its song. *Creeeak!*

A rope ladder fell through the opening. It began in the distant ceiling rafters, and the last rung hovered just above the floor. Marcus grabbed Dorian's arm. "Your Grace—"

"Do you have something to hide, Brother?" The tip of Dorian's sword brushed Marcus's multiple chins.

Marcus looked like a scarecrow in stone shoes trapped between a fire and a flood. He stepped away from the blade and leaned against the wall.

Dorian took the rungs three at a time. The ladder swung wildly under his weight. He grabbed at what he thought was a railing as he stepped onto the planked floor of the belfry. The smooth wooden bar cranked forward in his hands.

Creeeek—slam! Wacka, wacka, wacka.

The trapdoor flew shut behind him and some shifting mechanism sent the rope ladder shooting toward the ceiling. The door shuddered its way back into place, and went silent. Dorian took a few steps into the belfry. He pushed aside the ropes hanging from a dozen Fire-iron bells in varying sizes and shapes situated in the rafters above his head. The ropes smelled like wet saddle blankets.

"Another visitor! Mister Finley…Your Grace these days, isn't it?"

There was no mistaking that voice. Ezra Oliver always sounded as if he had a perpetual head cold. Dorian gripped his sword in both hands.

Oliver stepped out of the shadow of the largest bell. "You've always relied too much on that blade and not enough on the surprising amount of intellect HighGod gave you."

Nine years had not changed him one iota. The same lank brown hair and watery brown eyes. The same flat nose and receding chin. His clothes were the same. His boots the same ones that had slipped on the Council table and sent him ass over elbows into the Oracle's enchanted puddle.

"Good afternoon, Mister Oliver," Dorian said, as if they'd seen each other at breakfast. "Might I enquire as to the whereabouts of Mister Jones?"

Oliver pointed to the ceiling. Dorian peered into the dark cavern of the bell above his head and made out Jones's thin form, pasted against the curving Fire-iron like icing on a cake. Jones's eyes bulged. Creamy light mixed with gray in a magical soup around his head and arms.

Dorian swallowed. He was apparently on his own, with only a blade between himself and the most powerful magician ever to walk HighGod's green earth. He faced Oliver again.

"Bring him down."

"I think not."

"Why didn't you just kill him? And me?"

Oliver put a hand over his heart. "We've not seen one another in nine years! I'd not be so uncouth as to kill you both before a little catch up."

"Fine. What are you doing here? Where have you been all this time?"

"Ah, my boy…it would take nigh on as long as I was gone to explain, and while I give you credit for not being as big a fool as some, it's all quite beyond you. Your friend…the Chief Magician…now he might find it a compelling tale." Oliver shouted into the bell. "Would you like to hear about my journey, Jones? I've learned a thing or two, you know."

"You can't hide forever," Jones said, "the Desmarais won't allow it."

"The Desmarais…now there is a family that deserves, beg pardon, a collective fuck you." Gray light drifted from Oliver's ears and from each of his fingertips. "What a colossal mess good King Casper and his imbecile son have made in this country."

"You caused the very problems of which you speak," said Dorian. "Turning the people against the princess's school, and therefore the witches themselves. Hundreds dead from the Burning—for what? Your petty revenge?"

Oliver shrugged. "One man's pettiness is another man's peace. For example, I always found your incessant fucking and unrepentant kissing of the princely ass to be petty, but it must have brought you some satisfaction."

Dorian closed the space between himself and Oliver in three strides. Oliver's eyes widened. Dorian lifted his sword, but before he could strike the mist that had been leaking from the magician's hands poured out of his body in a silvery torrent. As Oliver's magic solidified into a gray wall, Jones cried out. Dorian spun around just in time to see him hit the planked floor.

"Peace, Mister Finley," said Oliver as Jones groaned on the floor behind them. "Lower your sword. I've something to say to you."

Dorian did as he asked and the gray wall retreated to a quivering shadow.

"You're a proud man," said Oliver. "Why do you grovel at the royal family's feet? I did it for a century. It got me nowhere. You don't have that long to figure it out. And you, magician."

Jones clutched at his leg. Dorian did not like the unnatural angle of his knee or the whiteness of his face. Oliver knelt down. "You have a measure of unusual talent. There's a reason I took you on as apprentice years ago. Jesting aside, I could teach you, boy."

He sounded so reasonable. Jones shifted and licked his lips. Oliver leaned toward Dorian. "I know what you want. What you can never, ever have, not matter how much money he gives you. With my help you could take it."

Dorian looked at his boots, and at the sword in his hand.

A smile touched the corners of Oliver's thin mouth. "Power. Control."

Dorian met Jones's eyes, and then turned back to Oliver. He smiled back. "You have no

idea what I want."

Dorian swung his sword. Oliver had no time for a wall, but he did fling a gray fireball at Dorian's ankles. Dorian jumped, and the fireball pinged off one of the Fire-iron bells. It split and no less than six fireballs ricocheted around the room. Dorian knew Fire-iron repelled magic, and that no magic was as dangerous to the conjurer as his own. Eleanor had used a piece of Fire-iron to turn Oliver's magic against him on the day he disappeared. Oliver had obviously not forgotten. He ducked the gray fireballs as if an army of martials were sending them his way.

"Jones, do something," said Dorian. "He's distracted—"

Jones's nodded through his mask of pain. His eyes filled with creamy light. Dorian touched his shoulder. He'd gone hot as any victim of the Burning.

The creamy light formed a watermelon-sized sphere in front of Jones's face. His head jerked in what looked like some kind of enchanted retching.

Jones's spell hit Oliver in the chest. He would have been knocked out cold had he hit one of the exposed beams lining the belfry walls, or one of the bells themselves. Unfortunately, alignment was not on Jones's side. Oliver sailed backward through one of the few windows in the belfry.

"Dragonshit!" Jones cried.

Dorian ran to the window. Oliver was getting to his feet on the front walkway of Larry's. A few chickens squawked around his ankles. Three goggle-eyed students stood on the stairs with baskets of broken eggs at their feet. A dozen Fringe folk in the usual varying degrees of slum rattiness gawked through the gate at the man who'd seemingly flown from the school's roof to the ground and landed in one piece.

"Mister Finley! Your Grace!" shouted Oliver as he brushed off his gray cloak.

Dorian dragged Jones upright.

"I'm so sorry," said Jones. "Stupid of me to come up here…but I panicked…I thought if he

heard us and disappeared…if we didn't lay eyes on him as His Highness said—"

"So nice to see you fellows," Oliver said, "but I must be going." He took a flattened

square magician's hat from his cloak pocket and adjusted it on his head. Shouts of "Magician!" and "The Covey!" rippled through the crowd.

"May we never again be parted for so long." Oliver bowed and raised both hands. His fingers opened and closed like the gills on a fish. Gray light left his head in a thin stream, and then traveled the length of his body. It seemed to be searching for a way back inside him. He grimaced as it congealed on his exposed skin and snuck up his sleeves and down his collar.

He didn't blink out as Dorian had imagined. He simply faded away, bit by bit, until only his snarling teeth and staring eyes remained. Lips wrapped around teeth. Eyelids closed. Oliver disappeared.

Gregory refused to allow Eleanor to sit in on the interrogation of Brother Marcus. She spent the afternoon sequestered in her chamber, as she'd spent every day since her return from Laralee. Chou landed on her head as Pansy handed her a short stack of letters. She flipped through the envelopes. Her old friends Anne Iris and Eliza. Anne Clara Tavish. Rosemary. Her regular correspondents. A pleasant distraction from the questions she'd hoped to ask the Godsman. The list ran through her head like a tune that would not be forgotten. She hugged the notes to her chest and walked to the open window.

"The weather is so fine, Chou," she said. She looked out over the gardens. The tulips still fought for space, but a few azalea bushes issued a pink and purple challenge. She longed for the feel of new grass on her bare toes. Nathan's boots would have not lasted five minutes on such a day.

"Let us walk," said Chou.

She wiped her eyes and shook her head. "I can't leave unless Gregory calls. If I argue with him, he'll keep Ticia from me. I know he will."

"So we're to rot in this room while the world blooms."

"He'll forget eventually. He always does. We'll have picnics with Ticia in the garden."

"I don't know, Eleanor." Chou whistled a sigh. "There's something different in his demeanor."

"All will be well, Chou." Eleanor ignored the hollowness in her stomach, and the tenderness between her legs that lingered two days after Gregory's last nighttime visit. She argued with Chou in her head.

He's always been brusque.

Something different in his demeanor...

No. Nothing.

She unfolded Rosemary's letter.

Dearest Eleanor,

Please pardon my shaky hand, but I write this letter with the paper in my lap, whilst sitting on a barrel outside the Palace Gate. The guards, who are merely following orders, won't let me pass. I pray my words find their way to you, for they are of utmost importance, to both yourself and your esteemed husband.

It is but three days since His Grace Lord Brandling and Mister Orvid Jones forced the traitor Ezra Oliver into the light, but all of Maliana is aware of his return. Sightings of him are rumored throughout the city. Of course, some of this is gossip, and some misidentification, but just this morning I am sure he did indeed show himself. In Smithwick Square, of all places! There are reports of a Godsman, his face covered in a cowl, speaking ill of our kind, and yourself, and even the king's majesty. So eloquent was he that a large crowd formed to hear him speak. Never did he reveal his face, but his words carried through the square as if through a golden trumpet. "The witches will not yield! The prince's harpy controls the king! The people must shout, and be heard!" All this and more, says he, and people crowd around him. But then this supposed man of HighGod is suddenly gone. Gone, as no natural man can be.

The people panicked, for they are much terrified of Ezra Oliver, and the Square became as empty as ever it is during a spring rainstorm.

This tale I heard from the dairyman who buys our extra milk, who was in attendance. He is an honest, HighGod-fearing sort, and I do not doubt the veracity of his story. I'm sure with proper examination the crown could find additional corroboration.

It is my hope to ever be useful to yourself, your husband, and His Majesty in this most urgent matter. Please do not hesitate to call on myself or Afar Creek if we may be of assistance in gathering further information.

With affection, as always,
Rosemary, Abbotess

Eleanor slid the letter into its envelope. "Chou, please take this to Gregory."

Chou took up the letter in his beak. "A delivery will get me out of this room, anyway," he said in a muffled voice. He floated out the window.

Eleanor set the other letters aside and sat on the window seat. She propped her feet on the cushion. As she did multiple times a day, she pushed sadness to the back of her mind, where hissed like a caged cat until she allowed it out again.

Of course Rosemary had wanted to inform Eleanor of the goings on in town, but her letter had obvious double intent of offering an olive branch to the king. Eleanor admired Rosemary's diplomacy as she contemplated the letter's contents.

Now that Oliver had been exposed, he seemed to have no qualms about making his presence known. He needn't fear apprehension in the city streets, for the capture of a man who could appear and disappear at will was hardly the domain of the local constabulary.

To what end? Eleanor wondered. *He wants the witches gone...and undermines the crown...to what end?*

Four gardeners traipsed up the low hill from the apple orchard. They stopped at the flowerbeds under Eleanor's window. She recognized the friendly one by his receding hairline and red neck scarf. She waved, and he bowed. His companions disbursed among the blossoms.

He's brought on a new man, she thought. She'd been watching the gardeners for days, and there were always three of them in the late afternoons. Her friend-from-afar, and his two portly companions.

The fourth man wore a wide-brimmed hat. He paced the rows of flowers. He picked up a trowel and dropped it again, and then took up a rake. The other gardeners knelt in the dirt, and tugged at the weeds.

A lazy fellow. He'll not last long with this troupe.

The new gardener tossed the rake across the flowerbeds. It snagged in an azalea bush and sent pink petals raining down on the grass. He wiped his hands on his pants, turned to the palace, and waved.

Eleanor started to lift her own hand in an automatic response, but her fingers closed in a fist somewhere between her stomach and her chin.

The man waved more energetically. He removed his hat and swept a low bow. Gray light followed the hat, creating a foggy rainbow from the top of his head to his black boots.

Eleanor clutched the window frame. Ezra Oliver smiled and waved madly. The other gardeners didn't notice as he faded away. The last Eleanor saw of him was a set of yellowing teeth, like the dismembered grin of an old lion.

CHAPTER 27

A BULL AT STUD

FOR THE FIRST TIME in memory the royal family did not take their summer holidays in Solsea. The king sought to avoid both the danger of travel and the appearance of excessive leisure. Most courtiers followed the king's lead and kept to themselves. With so many people writing letters to catch up on gossip that would normally have been discussed face-to-face (or behind-the-back, depending on the circumstance) the Papermans' Guild declared a shortage and promptly raised their prices.

Unfortunately for Eleanor, Sylvia Easton Fleetwood was never one to follow popular opinion or bother with trivialities like plagues. Or mourning for her departed sister, for that matter, although she did wear the requisite black gown (complete with scandalously low neckline). She arrived on the first day of MidSummer with her infant in tow. The child, a chubby boy of four months, was called John-Caleb. She brought him for the king's blessing, but Eleanor knew better.

The mysterious, fatherless babe drove the bored court ladies to distraction. No one spoke of anything but the child's resemblances. Eleanor's pride forbade her from looking closely upon him, but Chou reported him to be handsome, robust child, the spitting image of his mother and not a red hair upon his fuzzy head. Eleanor breathed a sigh of relief at that news, for with Nathan gone Ticia was now the sole heir to the throne of Caleb Desmarais. Eleanor cared not that a woman had never ruled Cartheigh of her own right. Unless a male child followed her, Eleanor aimed to see her daughter on the throne. A red-haired, bastard boy would do nothing for Ticia's cause.

Gregory was as mum as ever on the subject of Sylvia, and the child be might or might not have begotten. He did, however, use the Duchess's visit as a reason to release his wife from the forced seclusion of her chamber. Eleanor joined the few remaining courtiers at a small dance in honor of the Waxing Fest. The assemblage hardly took up a fourth of the Grand Ballroom, but Eleanor had not been in so much company in months. She squelched her natural standoffishness and made the rounds of female clusters. At a quarter to eight, she found her seat beside Gregory. He was in the middle of some raucous story, and didn't acknowledge her presence. She sat across from Dorian, and did her damnedest through five courses not to stare at him or reach her foot toward his under the table. When the servants cleared dessert, he closed his eyes for a moment, and her choker warmed her neck. He looked up at her from over the brim of his wine glass, and it was all she could do to keep herself from climbing over the table and into his lap.

"Sweetheart," Gregory said.

She dropped the red stone and it bounced off her collarbone. She rubbed the spot. Gregory took her hand. "It's good to see you out and about."

"Thank you for…inviting me."

He squeezed, just hard enough to cause discomfort. "You've been so amiable lately. I hardly know you."

She swallowed. "I only want to please you."

"Ticia has no talent for embroidery."

"She takes after me, then."

"She may come to you in the mornings again. Or you may walk with her in the garden, or visit the library. Whatever you see fit."

"Thank you, Gregory." Eleanor's mind added *for allowing me an audience with my own child,* but she stopped at gratitude.

Gregory started in with the tavern songs, and spilled a glass of red wine on his white tunic. Dorian rubbed his eyes. Eleanor was about to ask after his health when Gregory whispered in her ear. "Return to your room. I'll be along shortly."

Eleanor said her goodnights. Dorian didn't look up when she stood, but she felt his frustration as surely as if he had screamed her name.

There has to be a way, some way...

She mulled it over on her way back to her room, but nothing came to her. She didn't really expect some great revelation, as she'd thought on this predicament long and hard during endless days in her bedchamber. Her ruminations had brought her no peace on any topic. Dorian was still untouchable. Oliver still at large. Nathan still...

She shook her head, and thought of Ticia. At least she'd regained her daughter. She took the long way back to her room, past the nursery. With Gregory's improved humor she wanted to peek in on Tish.

She'd been going barefoot in her room, and her dancing slippers pinched her toes. No one was about but the servants, so she paused on a dim staircase to slip her shoes from her feet. Voices on the landing below her caught her attention. She peered around the corner.

Sylvia sat in a heap on the staircase with a glass of red wine dangling precariously over her pale yellow skirts. "Didn't you see him whispering in her ear?"

"No bother. He'll have time for you tomorrow."

"HighGod's eyebrows, Mother," Sylvia said to Imogene. "Are we to play a game of pass the princely parcel?"

"It is demeaning," said Imogene, with a sniff. "I don't see how you tolerate it. Alas, we do what we must."

At this Sylvia laughed and leaned her head against the wall.

Imogene tugged Sylvia to her feet. "Up with you. HighGod forbid someone see you mooning on the floor like a Fringe drunk on payday.

If the Duke of Brandling came upon us he'd be straight to his Highness with it."

"Don't worry about Mister Finley. I think he'll not always hold the prince's affections."

The shuffling of shoes and shaking out of skirts let Eleanor know they'd gotten to their feet. A few footfalls moved up the staircase.

"Gregory is watching him," said Sylvia.

"Why? How do you know?"

"I know more about the prince than anyone."

"More than his wife?"

"Her. She knows nothing. He's watching her, too."

Eleanor had no choice. She stepped around the corner before Sylvia and Imogene could find her pressed against the cold Fire-iron wall.

"Good night, ladies," she said as she swept past. Sylvia's eyes bulged for a moment, but before she could reply Eleanor clipped down the steps as if she'd not heard a word.

Gregory did not stay the night. He attended to his business without removing his tunic or his boots and with his leggings around his knees. Eleanor turned her face to the wall and closed her eyes, so she would not have to see the resentment build on his face with each thrust. He finished with a harsh grunt and pulled away from her. She watched his back as he straightened his hair and buckled his belt. A wet stream ran down her legs. A chill ran from the base of her neck to her tailbone. She rolled onto her side and tugged the sheet over her shoulder.

"Goodnight," he said.

"Goodnight."

Eleanor waited until he left the room before scrambling out of bed. She grabbed a towel from her dressing table and wiped frantically at her thighs, and then picked up a fresh towel and held it against her eyes.

She lit five candles. It was too hot for a fire, and she'd need considerable light to write a letter at this hour.

She sat at her writing desk, but she dropped the quill as soon as it touched the paper. Her hands shook.

What did Gregory know? Who could have told him something? She wracked her brain, and could find only one conclusion. She took a deep breath and picked up her quill again.

Dear Jan,

I trust this letter finds you and Ruby well. Ticia often asks after Ruby, and I hope to give a report of her good health and your own. The time we had together at Laralee, unplanned and fleeting as it was, will be cherished by myself and my daughter, despite the most tragic way in which it all ended.

I write today not only to confirm your wellbeing, but to thank you for keeping my trust for so long. I have reason to believe there is one among my close confidence who has not held constant. I'm sure you know I have always held your best interests in my heart, from the day I met you to the day you arrived at Laralee seeking asylum. If that trust were to be broken, I would beseech you to inform me, that I might better prepare for the ramifications of such.

I pray HighGod keep you and Ruby until we meet again.

Yours,
HRH Eleanor Brice Desmarais

Eleanor reread the letter, and found nothing specifically damning should it be intercepted. She inserted it into an envelope and closed it with her own wax seal of EBD. She rested her head against the desk and watched the candlelight flickering around the bedroom. She lifted her hand and curled her fingers into the shapes of bunnies and birds. Nathan had always loved those dark shadows, and the stories that went with them. She told herself fairytales and waited for Chou Chou to return with the sun.

She sent Chou back out the window as soon as he appeared, and he returned from Pasture's End before dinner. He lit on Eleanor's desk with his tongue hanging out like a black boot lacing. He trod across Eleanor's letter to Anne Iris and plunged his beak into her teacup.

"Chou, please," she said. "Don't drool on my letter. You know I detest sloppy

correspondence."

He slurped the tea with all the gusto and volume of a fallen teeto-taler in a wine barrel.

"So thirsty…it's dry these days…and the air in Pasture's End…pipe smoke and cheap perfume. Ugh."

"Did you deliver the letter? How is Jan? Ruby? Did you see the Madam?"

Chou gargled and spit back into the cup. "So many questions. Jan is well,

although one of the youngest whores recently contracted the Burning. Died in four days."

"HighGod."

"The girl was kept in seclusion, and Jan says Ruby seems healthy as ever. I could tell it rattled her. She's thin. Her hair is dull. I didn't see the Madam. Jan says she's terrified, and has refused to see even her best customers for months."

Eleanor pushed the cup, with its appetizing mix of cold tea and parrot spittle, to the edge of the table. "Let everyone else take the risk." She lifted Chou's left wing. "Where is Jan's response?"

"She thought it unwise to write. She asked me to bring you a message…" Chou's tongue wagged again, as if he were testing its flexibility. He spun in a circle. "I need…ah, your gloves!"

Eleanor held up one brown glove, made from a rabbit fur dragon robe. "Are your piggies cold?"

"No…no…put it on my head."

She raised an eyebrow.

"I must be in character!" he said.

She shrugged and humored him. With the glove on his head Chou appeared to have sprouted a full head of thick chocolate-y hair.

"Much more convincing," Eleanor said.

Chou tucked his wings close to his body. He opened his beak, and out spilled Jan's high voice, complete with the remnants of the Fringe accent she'd never been able to lose.

"Princess, I swear to you with my most whole heart that I have never betrayed your trust, in particular light of your most recent acceptance of my presence and Ruby's at Laralee. I know it to be no mean feat, and it added to the debt that I already owe you. Please know that it never once occurred to me to breach your confidence."

"Did she sound true, Chou?"

"Let me finish…Ahem…*I will pray for your safety, and for that of—*" Chou's yellow eyes rolled and he puffed out his cheek feathers.

"A blush?" asked Eleanor.

He nodded and went on. "*—your fellow conspirator.*"

Chou shook his head and the glove landed on Eleanor's letter. "That thing is bloody hot. My poor brains are fried. She finished with love and affection, et cetera, et cetera."

Eleanor sat back in her chair. "You believe her."

"She seemed genuinely emotional, but who is to know what emotions truly drove her words?"

"Do you think she's been in contact with Sylvia?"

"We know Sylvia has suspicions. We don't know if they come from her own spite or actual information. Who else could it be? Who else knows?"

"Rosemary. Pandra. The old witch who delivered helped Mercy Leigh deliver Ticia, but she died less than a year later. Mercy Leigh herself."

"Pandra would never tell. Gregory would kill her along with the two of you for lying to him."

"Rosemary, of course not."

"Mercy Leigh?" asked Chou.

Eleanor pictured the redheaded, ethereal witch who had assisted umpteen Carthean mothers through countless births. She shook her head. "No. Her loyalty is to the Abbey, and therefore to Rosemary. You know Jan's always fancied herself in love with Dorian, and if she saw us together at Laralee…as much as I hate to think on it…everything points to her." Eleanor's heart hurt at the thought, but try as she might, she couldn't come up with a more compelling traitor.

On a blisteringly hot morning in late MidSummer, Gregory decided to take Ticia on her first unicorn ride outside the Paladine. He demanded Eleanor and Dorian's presence as well, and although the thought of riding out with Ticia and Cricket thrilled Eleanor, the prospect of several hours sandwiched between her husband and her erstwhile lover did not. Her hands shook as she helped Ticia into her new riding leggings, and then later in giving her a leg up on Cricket's back. Ticia and Cricket's enthusiasm, however, soon overrode the heat and awkward company. Eleanor and Teardrop rode beside their daughters. They left Gregory, Dorian, and the stallions in their dusty wake. Ticia chattered about proper riding form and the few flowers that hadn't been baked to brown shells by the sun. Cricket capered and spooked at passing birds and butterflies. The ride proved to be the first truly pleasant outing Eleanor had taken since Nathan's death.

They stopped for a picnic lunch on the banks of Afar Creek, half mile from Eleanor and Dorian's old granary. The four unicorns stood hock deep in the sluggish water, while Eleanor, Dorian and Gregory listened to Ticia rattle on over her venison pie and dried fruit.

"I think Cricket will be as tall as Senne', don't you, Uncle?"

Dorian smiled. "She's a mare, Ticia. Mares are always smaller."

"Not always! Mother is like a mare, and she's taller than most of the men. Even Mister Jones, and he's a great magician. Even Grandfather."

"Hush, Tish," said Eleanor. She pulled a bit of grass from one of Ticia's red braids.

"Young ladies don't speak so about their grandfathers," said Gregory.

"Mother and Rosemary say I should always speak the truth."

"Tish, you know I've also told you there's a time for holding your tongue."

"Something Mama is just learning herself," said Gregory.

The innuendo floated over Ticia's head with the faint pulse of breeze. "Wind!" she said.

"You're getting red," Eleanor said. "Where's your bonnet?"

"Better to get her out of the sun," said Gregory. "Dorian, see the princess home."

"As you wish." Dorian whistled. Senne' trotted out of the water. Teardrop and Cricket followed him.

"Just the little princess," said Gregory. "Eleanor and I will stay behind for a while. We don't often have time to ourselves."

"Certainly." Dorian kept perfect control over his voice, but he turned his back on the picnic blanket. He tightened Senné's girth, and Cricket's. When he knelt on the blanket again he was all smiles. "Don't stay out here too long. You'll both melt and wash away down the creek. We'll be scooping you out of the Clarity in two days' time."

"Hmmm," said Gregory.

"Up, now, Ticia!" said Dorian.

Eleanor blew her daughter kisses. She sat on the blanket until both black unicorns disappeared into the woods.

Gregory stood on the sandy bank beside a crabapple tree and threw rocks into the creek. It felt like Eleanor watched his broad back encased in its purple tunic for hours before he finally turned around. "Come," he said.

She stood on shaky legs, for she knew what was coming. He'd not left off for more than a day in weeks. She hadn't even been able to turn him away during her flow this past month. She wanted to attribute his industrious attention to a strong desire to father another heir, but his curled lips and clenching, pinching fingers always brought back Chou's observations. *Something different in his demeanor…*

He's trying to fuck a reaction out of me. He's daring me to put him off. Her own crudeness shocked her, but once her mind had spoken the words they wouldn't be silenced. She shuffled toward Gregory with her arms crossed over her breasts.

On this warm afternoon Gregory took her against the tree, in full humiliating view of Teardrop and Vigor. He put a hand over her forehead and pushed. Bark drove into the back of her skull and her exposed tailbone. Her hair snagged in the bark's rough edges.

When he finished she tugged her leggings over her scratched and bruised bottom and swept the remains of the picnic up in the blanket. Teardrop and Vigor seemed as uncomfortable as Eleanor. Gregory whistled under his breath through the silent, agonizingly long ride back to the Paladine.

Gregory and Vigor broke for the bathing stalls without saying goodbye, but Eleanor and Teardrop stopped at the training barn. Cricket was asleep on her feet, so Eleanor led Teardrop into the shade under a willow tree for her rubdown.

Eleanor couldn't speak as she ran the currycomb over Teardrop's damp white hide. She didn't know what to say.

"I hate to see you used so," said Teardrop.

The comb fell from Eleanor's hand and disappeared in the long grass. She covered her face with her hands and inhaled the oddly sweet smell of unicorn sweat. "I wish him dead, Teardrop. If he died my problems would end."

"Some would, but more would show themselves."

"I don't care! Nothing could be as intolerable as this HighGod-forsaken situation. I can't...I just can't...what if we ran away—Ticia, Dorian, and me—"

"He would find you."

"He might not."

Teardrop regarded Eleanor with mild dark eyes.

"All right—I've always known that wasn't an option—but I can't help but—my wishes are my own!" Eleanor stooped to pick up the brush. "I don't have any reason to feel guilty. Nor does Dorian. He's served Gregory in every way, beyond the call of king and country, for years. Gregory uses him, and manipulates him, and treated him like a—a butler, or a martial magician. Juggle these fireballs, Your Grace, but don't you dare get singed!" She flopped onto the grass in a miserable heap.

"Your feelings are justified," said Teardrop, "but daydreams of a life without your husband...some fortuitous accident...such thoughts will do little to address your current concerns."

"I know."

"I would not dwell on them."

"I know, Teardrop!" Eleanor stood and resumed her brushing. Her arm swept over Teardrop's belly and haunches in manic, ever-widening circles until her shoulder ached.

"A soft brush now, perhaps," said the mare.

Eleanor's arm dropped to her side. "Of course. I'm brushing you raw. I'm sorry."

"It's forgiven."

Eleanor wasn't sure if Teardrop was forgiving her outburst as well as her rough grooming, but she wasn't asking for a pardon for her own sentiments. Teardrop always meant well, but today Eleanor found her wisdom wanting.

The unusual silence between Eleanor and her unicorn brought the workings of the Paladine into loud relief around her. Clopping hooves. The irritated squeal of a stallion at stud. Creaking wheels on a hay wagon. A hammer against a fence rail.

Just as Eleanor was about to make an attempt at mending a fence of her own and ask if Teardrop would like to visit the apple barrels behind the weanling barn, she caught the words of two junior Paladines. The boys panted past Eleanor and Teardrop with a full water bucket balanced between them.

"…Afar Creek…my da' told me…"

"No…I don't believe it. Watch me boots! You're splashin'."

"I'm telling you, Jimmy. I heard it from two other men, not just da'. Sick, it is. But it's the truth."

"There's whores a plenty in Pasture's End. Who'd force a witch?"

Eleanor forgot her argument with Teardrop. "Did that boy just say someone forced…a witch?"

Teardrop's ears pricked in the direction of the two boys. She nodded.

The first boy dropped the bucket. Water ran in rivulets over the dry ground. "Damn!"

"Boys!" Eleanor called. They blushed and grabbed for the bucket, as if they might catch the escaping water. "Don't mind the bucket. I'd hear what your father told you, young sir."

CHAPTER 28

A STEADYING HAND

THE HEAT DID NOT let up. Not at Eclatant, not in Smithwick Square, and not inside the thick stone walls of Afar Creek Abbey. Rosemary handed Dorian a cup of pear juice, and he accepted with gratitude. The shadows in the Abbey's dim front hall accentuated the dark circles under the witch's eyes and the hollows below her cheekbones. She said a few words over the cup before handing it across her ancient Fire-iron desk. Dorian inhaled the smell of pear trees in bloom as he put the cup to his mouth. The icy juice filled his chest on the way down. He shivered at the sudden cold.

"I thought to meet you in an office, Rosemary." Dorian's voice echoed over the bare walls and floor. "Abbotess and all."

"There are so few of us left. I moved into the hall so that I might see my charges. Sometimes I sit on the front steps. I don't need a desk, really. A lap will do."

"I came as soon as I could. I know you'd rather have Eleanor, but it wasn't possible."

"Your presence is her presence. I know that."

"Are the rumors true?"

The words seemed stuck in Rosemary's throat. "How I would that they were not...but...yes."

"A witch was—" Dorian waited until a few girls in simple gray dresses disappeared up the staircase, and then lowered his voice anyway. "Raped?"

"And as of this morning, you can add murder to the crime. Her injuries proved fatal." Rosemary's face glowed deathly white against the dark walls behind her. Dorian sat back in his chair for a moment. The thought repulsed him. Witches could be lovely...but their beauty was that of a deer...or a tree...of a mountainside covered in flowers. He could think of nothing more unnatural than forcing a witch into sexual relations.

"Tell me what happened."

"Mercy Leigh—"

"Not Mercy Leigh!"

Rosemary nodded. "She'd been visiting women in the Fringe. Helping with deliveries. Against the king's wishes, of course, but there's not much magic in babycatching, so I gave her my blessing. This Sunday past, she was walking home through the first light. The Outcountry Road was deserted. Too early even for the dairymen. Some men set on her—"

"How many?"

"She couldn't say for sure. Maybe five...they...well. You can imagine."

"No. I can't." Dorian leaned on both elbows.

"I've never heard of such an attack, Dorian. The Oracle says it's happened only twice. Twice in her centuries of association with Afar Creek."

"Why didn't Mercy Leigh defend herself?"

"Few witches dabble in martial sorcery, even the most powerful ones. We've always relied on the deference of the people for our protection." Rosemary let out a bitter laugh. "I shall be changing our girls' curriculum." She pressed her fingers to her temples. "You should have seen her when the constabulary brought her home. Her face...the blood...she told us the tale, and then spoke no more. She went on to HighGod just before dawn."

Dorian's affronted mind sought out the rational. "Perhaps a reward for the identity of the assailants will loosen tongues. I'll fund it with my own purse, and Orvid Jones has connections with the constabulary."

Rosemary's face hardened into an alabaster mask. "I have my own eyes and ears in Maliana, and they tell me that we may gain something from this tragedy."

"What do you mean?"

"The people are as shocked by this defilement as you and I. The magicians still haven't found a cure, and Oliver's rhetoric against us is feeling stale. Some think it's time to return healing to those who have long practiced it."

"The people's good will always extends to those who bring them results."

Rosemary nodded. "I have it that the head of the Butchermen's guild doesn't understand why the king can't apprehend Oliver. Why he didn't listen to the princess's warnings in the first place."

"How would the head of the Butchermen's guild know of the princess's warnings about Ezra Oliver?"

Rosemary sipped her pear juice. "All the Guildmasters know."

Dorian smiled. "Well done."

Rosemary leaned across the desk. White light leaked from her eyes and ears. It swirled in front of Dorian's face in hypnotizing loops. The edges bled to pink, and then an angry red. "We must take advantage of the tide of opinion. Eleanor must take advantage of it. The people's love is still there, buried under Oliver's vitriol."

Dorian grabbed at the white and red light. It warmed his fingers for a second before dissipating. "Don't worry, Rosemary. Eleanor will hear your message. I promise."

Beasts of all sorts frequented the Outcountry Road, day and night. Some walked on their own four legs. Horses, donkeys, and oxen walked on their own two legs. Chickens and pigs peered down from carts, sorry creatures that were most probably on the first leg of a journey that would end on someone's dinner table. The human travelers on the road where accustomed to neighing, squawking, oinking, and the occasional cock-a-doodle-doo. Unicorns are a different breed of beast, however, so Teardrop caused quite the spectacle when she gracefully broke through the woods. Carts skidded to a stop. At the sight of her silent shimmering, people pointed and dropped to their knees in the dust.

Eleanor heard her name on a few lilting voices. She didn't know whether to attribute the deference to renewed affection or simple shock at the sight of her, but for the sake of her nerves she clung to the former. Chou whistled a mining tune as he flew along beside Teardrop. Eleanor pushed her thick blond braid over her shoulder. It hung down her back, a steadying tail. She'd braided Ticia's hair in the same simple style before lunch that morning, for the child's hair still fell into her soup at times.

This will send Gregory into hysterics. The king won't tolerate it. She'll be lost to me.

Her fears accompanied her into Smithwick Square. A crowd fanned out behind Teardrop like the undulating train of an elaborate gown. Eleanor steered the mare into the center of the square, where puppeteers, jugglers, and balladeers fought for the people's attention and coins from atop a rickety wooden scaffold. A peddling magician retracted his display of dancing squirrels as Eleanor stepped from her stirrups onto the scaffold. The furry creatures ran up his sleeves and disappeared in puffs of orange smoke under his floppy hat. "'Scuse, Highness, 'scuse me," he said, with a crooked grin.

Eleanor faced the ever-growing crowd. Her heart hammered in her chest, and she searched the crowd for friendly faces. She heard nothing but muttering, saw only squinty eyes and pointing fingers. She waited for Ezra Oliver's magically magnified voice to roll over the square, or for Gregory and the king to appear with a bevy of Unicorn Guards and drag her back to Eclatant. Sweat ran down her back and dripped from the end of her nose. The sun itself seemed to be glaring at her.

She sucked in a breath of dry air. It smelled of ripe fruit and fresh bread, unwashed bodies and stagnant water. She looked down at the fountain she remembered from long ago bartering trips with her father. A dozen stone fairies capered around the edges, but the pool below them had gone still and murky in the summer heat.

Rosemary thought the people's love for Eleanor was still there, buried like clear water beneath the pond scum. She just needed to delve below the surface.

"People of Maliana! I say, good people! Your princess would speak to you, if you will hear me."

Teardrop snorted, and Chou flapped his wings from between the mare's ears. Ripples of conversation ran through the crowd.

"By now you've all heard of the latest tragedy to befall Afar Creek Abbey. Some of you knew the victim." Eleanor's voice caught in her throat at the thought of Mercy Leigh's calm blue eyes. "She may have seen you through the arrival of your children. She welcomed mine."

Women sighed and exchanged glances. They wiped their eyes and clutched at the hands and shoulders of their little ones.

"I'll speak of it no more. Not with so many of those children present. For I know every person here abhors it. As we should abhor the sentiments that brought the witch called Mercy Leigh to such a tragic end. The hatred set upon those who have done nothing but good for all of you."

The crowd shifted, a mass of squirming discomfort.

"Now, the assailants are the criminals. I'll not lay blame on those who have not cast a stone. But I will ask each of you to consider well. Would such a sacrilege have been possible in the Maliana of my childhood, or yours? In the city of five years ago?"

Heads wagged.

"We are in hard times. The king, HighGod bless him, wishes only to help you. To find a cure for this Great Burning that has plagued us these three long years. That has taken our—friends—and our children…"

"Bless you, Princess! Bless your poor son!"

Eleanor waited for the lump in her throat to slide into her belly before speaking. "Thank you, but I've not come for your pity. My grief is no different from the grief of any mother in this square. I understand your fears. Your frustrations. I know why the king gave the cure over to the magicians. The people of this city felt wronged by the witches. Wronged by me. What started out as an endeavor full of hope for your poorest daughters became a tragedy, but the witches never made a penny. Nor encouraged the girls who fell by the wayside. I swear to HighGod and on my son's grave."

"Peace on the soul of His Highness!"

"I have no quarrel with the magicians of First Covey. They are fine men—"

"Save Ezra Oliver!" The anonymous voice rang over the throng, and Eleanor saw people cover their heads, as if Oliver might appear and smote them.

"—but I ask you. If you were fighting a war, would you hire soldiers, or cobblers? If you needed a strong crop, would you see it tended by a farmer, or a bookbinder? Would you send foxhunters out to sea in a leaking boat to catch a whale?" Bursts of laughter from the listeners. "No, my friends! You would summon those most suited to the task. The most knowledgeable. The most experienced!"

"The witches!" shouted a young woman in a dairymaid's apron and kerchief. "The witches know curing like I knows cows!"

Heads wagged again, with gusto, as if this were some great revelation.

"There are those among you who will doubt my words. Cling to the useless rhetoric of the past few years. Words encouraged by a certain magician—" Eleanor scanned the crowd again for a figure in a hooded robe, or a pair of watery brown eyes and a grinning set of carnivore's teeth, but she saw nothing. She raised her voice. "A certain magician who calls forth such hatred for his own unknown ends. I say we won't hear those words anymore, nor act on them. I believe the thinking, godly people of this city will reopen their hearts to Afar Creek. I believe we will see a cure!"

Shouts went up from the crowd, and a few hats zipped through the muggy air.

"To Eclatant! Tell the king—"

"Bless you, Princess!"

"The witches will find the cure—"

Chou landed on her shoulder. "You convinced them. They'll be beating down the king's

gate, demanding the witches' reinstatement."

"I only hope he listens."

People reached up to take Eleanor's hand, but she stepped back from the edge of the scaffold. Although she assumed her own immunity to the Burning after her hours nursing Nathan, she couldn't be sure. She tossed coins into the crowd to distract from the self-imposed distance. Chou spoke into her ear again.

"I only hope he forgives you for causing another spectacle in the city streets."

"He's always wanted me to spread good will. This turned out as we wanted."

"The way you wanted," said Chou. "Whether it's what he wanted remains to be seen."

King Casper called for Eleanor before she had a chance to change out of her riding clothes, so she met him in his receiving room in dusty leggings. She folded her hands behind her back and wondered whether he could smell her fear along with her sweat. She pushed the soles of her boots into the marble floor to stop her feet from shuffling and tapping.

Casper regarded her in silence for what felt like several years. She assumed him to be waiting on Gregory's arrival before beginning his haranguing, so she jumped when he spoke.

"Cup of tea?"

"No thank you, Your Majesty."

"Of course not, with this weather. Pear juice!" A servant appeared at Eleanor's side. She took the glass and sipped politely.

"You must be thirsty after today's outing."

Eleanor felt as if someone had tipped the pear juice down her back. "Yes. It's dry in town."

"There's a reason anyone who can gets out of Maliana during the summer. Miserable. How I miss the Solsea breeze. Don't you?"

"Yes, Your Majesty. I do miss Solsea, but I have heard that place has not been spared by the Burning. I think it wise for us to stay here, given the circumstances."

"Yet you venture into the streets."

Eleanor swallowed.

"We are fortunate in that we can keep to ourselves somewhat," said Casper. "The townsfolk can't. They must trade, and sow, and sell their wares if they are to survive. And so their livelihoods push them together, and breed the disease that kills their children."

"I didn't touch anyone. Nor even come close."

"Why do some fall ill and some don't, Eleanor? Why do a few recover? What causes it? Is it an evil spirit? Impure thoughts? Some sin?"

"It cannot be the last, as so may children have died, and they are innocent of impurity and sin. As to your other speculations, I cannot know. No one does. The witches suspect diseases have varying causes. Some from outside us, and some from within. Perhaps some have a weakness that renders them more susceptible. Weak lungs...or—a sour stomach. Afar Creek has produced many books on such ideas, but they are only theories. Maybe future generations will better understand. Build on our knowledge."

She stopped talking, but still the king stared. She blushed, and waited for him to upbraid her for her babbling.

"Child," he said, "would that you had been a man, and my own son, instead of his wife."

Eleanor's mouth fell open.

"I know Gregory can be difficult. He doesn't appreciate your talents, or take advantage of them. If I had…in my youth…been gifted with such a partner…you must hold fast, Eleanor. He needs you. Cartheigh needs you. I'm old—"

"No, sire."

The king smiled. "Yes, daughter. When I'm gone Gregory will need a steadying hand. He has Lord Brandling, and Orvid Jones. Most of all, he has you. Do we understand each other?"

She nodded.

"You should not expect me to repeat these sentiments. Nor should you expect leniency if you disobey me in the future."

"No, Your Majesty. And yes…exactly."

"You went to Smithwick Square at my command. I decided to re-instate the witches and sent you to access the mood in town. Correct?"

Eleanor nodded again.

"Go change. I'll see you at dinner. And bring Leticia. She's too old to eat in the nursery. She'll sup with the rest of us from now on."

CHAPTER 29

CHILD-MINDING

AND SO THREE MONTHS later the Great Burning passed into history in the same way it had arrived, quietly. Within weeks of Rosemary's recall, the expelled healers and sorceresses concocted a cure. The winning combination included sixteen rare fungi in varying states of maturation, a newfangled enchantment that slowed blood flow through the veins, a cooling potion, and copious amounts of chicken broth. They tweaked the mixture as some victims lived, some lived longer and died anyway, and some recovered. By HighAutumn, the deaths had slowed to a sad trickle. The last recorded victim: the week-old son of the Dockmaster. Eleanor sent him a letter, along with five of Nathan's Fire-iron dragons for his remaining sons. Dorian delivered it for her, a sad gift on a beautiful morning.

Dorian kept his promise to fund the hunt for Mercy Leigh's assailants. With the witches returned to favor, the townsfolk were eager to help. Four carpenters and a cobbler's assistant met swift justice in a public hanging in Smithwick Square. While Dorian had always found such spectacles distasteful, he attended this one with a clear conscience. He cheered as loudly as any Fringe gawker when the trapdoors dropped from under the murderers' feet.

As for Ezra Oliver, he went quiet, but speculation about him did not.

Daily reports arrived at Eclatant. Someone claimed to have seen him at Chapel, or in the queue at Petti-Bonbons. An old woman camped out in front of the palace gate and refused to move. She swore the face of Ezra Oliver could be seen in the flaky crust of a stale mince pie, thus proving what the women had suspected all along: the magician was hiding in her potbellied stove.

Dorian thought himself accustomed to emotional peaks and valleys, but HighAutumn of the year Desmarais Three Hundred and Thirty exhausted even him. He vacillated between relief at the long awaited cure, obsession over Oliver's whereabouts, and an aching loneliness for Eleanor. Pandra's request for a private meeting did nothing for his already taut nerves.

He watched her flutter about the red sitting room like a giant, agitated, female version of Chou Chou. Each time she about-faced, red wine came dangerously close to sloshing over the edge of her crystal goblet. She planted her hands on her hips, and to Dorian's surprise, her eyes shone with tears. He offered her his handkerchief. She wiped her face, and then pushed past him. She sat on the couch. "He knows. I'm sure he knows! Why else would he have come?"

Dorian tried to rationalize with her, even as her distress threatened to engulf him like a bad odor. "Pandra, calm yourself—"

"Dragonshit!"

"So Gregory came here a few night ago. Hasn't he visited the Hussy for years? Just last summer, with me. And on is own, or so he's said."

Pandra blew her nose with a loud honk and returned Dorian's handkerchief. He gingerly set it on the back of the couch.

"Yes, yes, but this time he came to talk," Pandra said. "He didn't even lie with anyone!"

This revelation, more than Gregory's coldness and occasional double-edged comment, tested the soundness of the damn of rationalization that had long contained Dorian's fears. "What did he say?"

"He kept digging about that mysterious girl you loved all those years ago. He wanted to talk to the other girls about her. I made light of it. I said anyone but me who'd remember her was dead or retired."

"What else?"

"He asked when you come here…how often. Who you lie with. I panicked and said me, just me, like in the old days. That's one reason I needed to speak with you—if he asks, you must say we still fuck!"

"HighGod." Dorian set his glass of whiskey on the mantle. "Must you be so crass?"

"Crass my ass! I'm not talking pleasantries, Dorian! He wants to know what you're up to—who you're—" It seemed she searched for a more refined term, but came up with nothing. "—who you're fucking!"

"I'm not fucking anyone! I haven't been with her in months—god-forsaken, miserable—"

"Spare me your lovelorn blathering."

"I'm just saying we've been exceedingly careful." Dorian paced the room himself. Pandra watched him, as if hypnotized. He raked a hand through his hair in a passable imitation of Gregory. "He's been odd—strange—there's no doubt, and I'm sure that bitch of a Duchess—"

"Who?"

"Sylvia Fleetwood. She and Eleanor have been enemies since child-hood, and I'm sure she hates me, just for being close to Gregory. I once overheard her casting doubt on us—"

"And you continued?"

"No! We've kept our distance for two years." HighGod, had it really been so long? "Gregory can't possibly know for sure. We'd both be dead, or at least imprisoned."

"He suspects something of you. I have no doubt."

"Did he ask after Eleanor?"

She shook her head.

"Good…but who could be—" Dorian sat beside Pandra. She put a hand on his leg. "Pandra, I trust you wholeheartedly, but Jan…"

"She wouldn't."

"Call her, please."

Ten minutes later Jan sat in the chair opposite the couch. She wore a red dressing gown and her hair spilled loose over her shoulders. Her flushed cheeks hinted that she'd recently left a customer's embrace.

"I'm sorry to...disturb...you..." Dorian wondered if he'd ever feel anything but awkward in this young woman's presence.

She shrugged. "He'd just finished. Fallen asleep."

Pandra rubbed small circles on Dorian's thigh, and he fought the urge to throw her hand back into her lap. "Jan, I need to ask you—"

"The princess already asked me. I told her no. I didn't say anything."

"Are you sure? Never, to one of your patrons—"

"Don't talk to the patrons about anything but themselves."

"One of the other girls?"

Jan regarded him wryly. "We're not like the court ladies around here, Your Grace. Giggling about gossip and such."

"Of course," he said, feeling slightly stupid. "It's just...we're all fearful...and I can't figure out who might have..." He rubbed his eyes.

Jan wrapped her arms around herself, and for a moment she looked like the schoolgirl Dorian remembered. As if she knew the correct answer, but the teacher refused to call on her. "I told her. I swore. Why don't she believe me?"

"You've never said anything, to anyone? Not even Ruby?"

"No!"

He stared at her, and a deep blush leaked from her ears to the end of her nose. "Don't look at me so," she whispered. "Madam, might I go? He might wake up."

Dorian waved in the direction of the door. "Yes, go on. Thank you for answering my questions."

She muttered something that might have been a reciprocal thank you and stumbled over a half curtsy. When she was gone Pandra snorted. "She's never gotten over her girlish crush. I'm sure she sees your face when she mounts those old men."

Dorian pushed Pandra's hand off his leg. "Do you think she's telling the truth?"

Pandra lay back against the cushions. Her legs splayed out in front of her, and she rested her chin on her own white cleavage. "We'll find out, I suppose. When Gregory drags us all off to the dungeons."

There had been no proper fest for two years, and King Casper decided the Waning would be a celebration the likes of which Eclatant had not seen in all his long reign. Eleanor had known ten years of Fest planning, but she'd never seen Maliana so overrun with visitors. Eclatant reached full capacity, as did the townhouses of the Malianan aristocrats, the local inns, and the close-in country estates. Even the clannish nobility of far-flung Harper's Crossing arrived in droves. Anne Clara remained in the Lake District in deepest mourning for her husband and son, but Abram Finley had no such obligations. He hovered constantly at Dorian's arm, and followed behind him like a distorted reflection. Eleanor admired Dorian's tightlipped patience. She herself would have no doubt told him to bugger off and caused a permanent family rift.

Eleanor continued to battle her own familial tensions. Sylvia had become a semi-permanent fixture at Eclatant. Eleanor expected to find the her in the second row at the chapel service that marked the Fest's official commencement. She'd become accustomed the Duchess's eyes boring into her back as she stood between Gregory and King Casper. She did not, however, expect to find Sylvia in said place of relative honor with her infant son in her arms.

Cartheans considered it rude to distract a congregation with the cries and squeals of squirming babies and moody toddlers. Sylvia generally avoided caring for her own children at all costs, and Eclatant had no shortage of nursemaids and nannies. Eleanor could see no reason for John-Caleb's rosy, lace-bedecked presence.

The service droned on and John-Caleb, like any tired, hungry babe, began whimpering. Apparently he agreed with Eleanor's assessment as to the inappropriateness of his attending a long, loud chapel service. Sylvia bounced him and made little shushing noises, but Eleanor had bounced and shushed two babies, and a few glances over her shoulder told her the Duchess had no talent for it. She was about to offer to hold the poor child herself when Gregory turned and held out his arms.

Eleanor's stomach clenched as Sylvia handed the baby to him. Gregory, who had always had a surprisingly natural way with Ticia and Nathan, smiled into John-Caleb's round face. The baby smiled back. Gregory faced the altar. "Look at the flowers, lad," he whispered. "Blue, red, yellow..."

John-Caleb grabbed his pointing finger. He chewed on Gregory's Fire-iron wedding ring. Sylvia laughed into her hand.

The king stared unblinkingly at the altar, but disapproval emanated from his royal bulk like heat from a dragonrobe. Ticia peered questioningly around her grandfather, and Eleanor could sense the weighty interest of the entire congregation. When the music ended a few whispers were suddenly loud.

"Odd...why...baby..."

Gregory had slapped Eleanor in the face at a picnic two years ago, and now he did the same with this insidious recognition of Sylvia's son. Eleanor could already hear the consensus of the gossip mavens.

The boy must be his son...who can blame him when his own wife hasn't provided him another heir...Cartheigh needs a prince...

Eleanor wanted to scream at those imaginary, catty women before they could spread their poisonous message. *He has an heir in this row! Your princess!*

Gregory rested the baby on his shoulder and rocked him. John-Caleb's eyes drooped, and within minutes he was snoozing contentedly and drooling on the Crown Prince's shoulder. King Casper whispered in Eleanor's ear, "Tell him I said that's enough."

Eleanor spoke under her breath to Gregory. "Your father says that's enough."

"Enough what?" Gregory didn't look at her or slow his rocking.

"Child-minding, I assume."

Gregory snorted and the baby jumped in his sleep. Gregory patted his back and he quieted. He handed the child back to his mother. So content was he with Gregory's ministrations that he never noticed. He slept quietly in her arms for the rest of the service.

Not so long ago everyone called Sylvia a hussy and the child a poor bastard.

As for the hussy in question, she shared knowing smiles with the doting, complimentary onlookers around her.

"I've authorized the dungeonmaster to get answers out of Brother Marcus," said Gregory. "By any means."

Eleanor had no love for the Godsman. He had betrayed her, the Abbey, the good magicians of the Covey, and the Desmarais family itself. Hence, she deemed him a traitor to the whole kingdom. Still, Gregory's stony face and jutting chin didn't sit well with her. "You'd have him tortured?" Eleanor trotted to keep up with him. "You—after that debacle years ago, when Oliver tortured an innocent man? You were so angry—"

"This is different. We know Marcus is guilty."

"But why now? He's been in prison for months."

"And we have yet to find his co-conspirator. He's the only one who can give us insight into where Oliver might be hiding."

"Of course I want to find Oliver, but—"

"It's done, Eleanor. The king supports my decision. Although why he insisted you come along…" Gregory's muttered his irritation as if she'd gone deaf. "My wife in the dungeons interrogating a known traitor…"

"There has to be a better way."

"I used to think so," he said, "but I'm a different man these days."

Eleanor, Dorian, and Orvid Jones followed Gregory through a set of wrought Fire-iron doors and began the descent down several hundred moldy, slippery stairs. The glow from Dorian's torch and Jones's hands revealed damp walls covered in some furry substance. Here and there Eleanor caught movement in spiders on the walls and the odd centipede at her feet. She swiped at her neck. She couldn't shake the feeling that some of those creatures had flown or scurried into her upswept hair. She thanked HighGod Gregory had agreed to her request to wear her riding leggings. A dragging hem caked with all manner of dirt, mold, and squirming things might have sent her stripping to her stockings and corset, modesty and drafty dungeon air be damned.

The vibrating hum of Jones's magic followed them through the darkness. Eleanor rubbed her itchy nose. A whiff of her favorite peach-berry bath salts momentarily overrode mold and a hint of wet leather. She slipped twice, and had to steady herself on the slimy walls.

Eleanor was less suspicious than the average Carthean, but she still felt the weight of past pain and suffering floating up the tunnel from the chambers below them. She didn't fancy being noticed by whatever ill-mannered spirits lingered in the dungeon. She was about to ask Dorian to snuff the torch when the path widened out.

The dungeonmaster had arranged an office of sorts in a square chamber, with a desk and a table surrounded by six chairs. Several casks of wine and a beer keg rounded out the furnishings. Wall-mounted torches lit the passageways leading to the lower levels. Eleanor peered into the gloom as Gregory spoke with the dungeonmaster.

"The prisoners are housed on the lowest levels," said Jones in a low voice. "This room is mostly used for questioning…and…well—" He pointed to a room off the main chamber. Eleanor noted a wooden structure, something like a dining table crossed with a hangman's scaffold. Thick ropes and chains hung from it. More chains were strung against the far walls, and from the ceiling itself. Knives, picks, whips…as if a chef, a gardener, and a coachman had used the table to display the tools of their respective trades. Eleanor stepped behind Dorian, so his broad shoulders blocked the view.

A bustling along one of the passageways announced the arrival of the prisoner. His containment had left him much diminished, but it still took four guards to support Marcus. Shackles bound his ankles, so he did an odd hop-shuffle up the corridor. Small grunts that sounded like *eh, eh, eh*, kept time with the jingle of his chains.

Marcus wore a gray undershirt, and his leggings were torn off above his battered knees. His bound hands folded over his deflated belly like two dead fish atop a slack net. Eleanor initially mistook the dried blood covering his hands for gloves.

His stubbly hair was missing in patches, and Eleanor couldn't make out any of his features save for one bloodshot, open eye. Everything else ran together in purple bruises and half-healed lacerations. Traitor or not, she pitied him.

She crept closer to Dorian, and touched the edge of his tunic. He swayed in her direction. The guards thrust Marcus into a chair. Eleanor, Dorian, Gregory, and Jones took the others. The dungeonmaster, a tiny man with limited teeth and an even more limited vocabulary, joined his men in a gloomy circle around the table.

Marcus rustled his hands in his lap and muttered prayers. Jones opened his mouth, but Eleanor put a hand on his arm. She reached across the table and touched one of Marcus's swollen fingers. It darted away from her like a spooked mouse, but he looked up.

"Your Highness," he said, after a long pause. "Forgive my distraction, and my appearance, please."

At least they hadn't driven him completely insane. "Of course. I'm sure you're tired, but we must ask you some questions. If you answer us true, you'll live. If not—"

"You'll hang with the first light," said Gregory.

"Greg," said Dorian. "Peace."

Eleanor waited for Gregory to nod before continuing. "Might the prisoner have some water?" she asked the dungeonmaster. "A slice of bread?"

The dungeonmaster looked as if Eleanor had asked him for a roast goose and a bouquet of roses, but at Gregory's grunt of approval he nodded. One of the guards plunked down a water flask and half a loaf of brown bread on the table in front of Marcus. He swallowed the bread near whole and drained the flask.

"I'll start at the beginning," Eleanor said. "When did Oliver first come to you?"

"About six years ago. Before Queen Camille's burnt down. When the leaflets appeared. At first I didn't believe he was who he claimed to be. I'd never seen him, in the old days. But he kept coming back…and he showed me so much…" Marcus closed his eyes. "Magical."

"Magical what?" asked Jones.

"He could move things…from one place to another…easily. Take a paperweight off my desk and it would reappear in my chamber pot. Even living things. There was an old rat… scaring the boys, you know, although none would ever admit it. We'd tried to catch it—but even the knackerman's terrier couldn't kill that bugger. Jones took it by the tail and told me to go to the window. Damned if I didn't look out and see it running through the middle of the square."

Marcus's voice became more animated, as if he'd forgotten his pain. "I've done some study of magic…and I know a bit about it."

"Do you, now," said Dorian.

"I do, sir. Those kinds of enchantments, moving things from one spot to another without destroying them, aren't easy. And moving a living creature…like that rat…it hadn't ever been done."

"A magical scholar, you are," said Jones. Eleanor couldn't tell if he was encouraging Marcus or belittling him, but now that Marcus had started talking, he was like a cripple falling down the stairs.

"I had my own magic once…"

"I've heard," said Jones. "Perhaps the Covey was mistaken—"

"No," said Marcus with an emphatic shake of his head. "It was there. I remember the feeling—when I was a boy…red. My magic was red…but it went away."

"I'm sorry. That's rare, but not unheard of."

"Mister Oliver—he showed me things in my head, too. Things he'd seen. Places he'd been. I could almost feel my magic again."

"You were feeling the effects of his magic, Marcus, not your own."

"He said he might be able to help me find it…"

"And you believed him?" asked Jones.

"Why would I not?" Marcus glared at Jones. "Everyone thought it would be impossible for Mister Oliver to survive. Or for him to move from one place to another. To take others with him—"

"Take others with him?" asked Eleanor.

"He—sometimes moved people—not just himself—children mostly. He said they're easy to move, because they don't understand. The ones he took slept so soundly they never knew what happened."

"Why would he want to move—Dragon's breath…he didn't!"

"Eleanor, what?" asked Dorian.

"Children—just showing up! Those Mendaen children—in the first days of the Burning! How many were there, twenty? We thought them stowaways, but Oliver brought them here, didn't he? To spread the Burning in Cartheigh!"

Marcus nodded. "As time went by…I realized he couldn't bring back my magic. He only wanted my assistance."

"What sort of assistance?" asked Gregory.

Marcus wiped at his open eye. "I arranged meetings between the madams and the students at Queen Camille's. Encouraged them down the path toward whoring. HighGod forgive me—"

"My girls—Jan—the girl you took off the streets for me?"

"Not Jan—no, she was the only one who went on her own. I never spoke a word to her. It seemed too risky, what with her being close to you. I assume she saw the others and followed suit. She figured out the priciest house, and found herself a line of lucrative work, so they say."

"Her fate is your fault, just the same—you introduced the idea in her mind as sure as if you shook hands with Pandra Tate yourself!" Eleanor's fist hit the table.

Gregory closed his hand over Eleanor's curled fist. Marcus's voice was a rough whisper. "I'm sorry, Your Highness. I'm so sorry."

"All those years, the leaflets—and you knew where they came from? The people's hatred of the witches—the girls who died—and hundreds—thousands in the Burning—my son—"

"Why? That's what I'd know," Gregory said. "Oliver has always hated the witches, but it seems like a lot of effort for an old grudge."

"I have learning something of Mister Oliver these past years, sire. I thought he would keep me on, as his assistant, even when I knew he'd lied about finding my magic. I held my tongue for faith in him. I thought for sure he would deliver me from the crown's punishment. He could have appeared in my cell and taken me away. Healed my body with his great power. I called for him, when your DungeonMaster was working his savage will on me. Once I realized he would not come for me, I saw no reason to continue. HighGod used pain to open my eyes to my own sins. Greed and pride. In penance, I will tell you what I know."

Marcus lifted the water flask and a few stray drops fell on his swollen tongue. "Oliver wanted to undermine the witches, so that the king would drive them from Cartheigh. He knew of the people's love for them, so he crafted a long, slow demise. The fall of Queen Camille's was the first step. Sour the people against the witches. Raise suspicions. And then, set loose the Burning, a disease the likes of which we'd never seen in this country. Put forth the idea that the magicians could do a better job...stoke the anger until the king had to act."

"But the magicians had no luck with a cure," said Dorian.

"No, and it drove Oliver mad. He'd imagined an easy end to the

Burning with the cure in more capable magical hands, but nothing came of it. He even searched himself, but he came up with nothing. He hoped that if the magicians found a cure, the witches would be finished in Cartheigh. Afar Creek destroyed. He often spoke of the Oracle… how she claimed more magical space than any other enchanted being. It was all about space, really, in the end. He wanted to make as much magical space in Cartheigh as possible."

"Why?" asked Jones.

"I don't know the answer, Mister Jones. He never told me that part. As time went on and your magicians failed to find a cure, his rage grew. That's why he took to speaking in the streets. He knew the people would return to the witches. He was desperate to keep the ill will flowing… keep the witches weak."

"You're an intelligent man, Marcus," said Dorian. "Do you have any theories as to what he might have been up to?"

For a moment Marcus was a schoolteacher again, full of hypotheses. "I've imagined him planning an enchanted invasion. Something on a grand scale requiring large amounts of magical space."

"Interesting." Jones drummed his fingers on the table. "My librarian says you were hovering around the library. Talking to the young men. Thirty have left the Covey, sir. Thirty good magicians, vanished, one at a time, from their own chambers."

Marcus sighed. "I'm sorry. It's true. They've gone to Oliver. He needed magical assistance."

"Thirty apprentice magicians don't make a huge magical onslaught," said Dorian. "There must be more to it."

"I'm certain there is," said Marcus. "If I could tell you more, I would. I only know he hates the witches, and he wants them gone. He wants magical space…as much of it as he can get. He's obviously willing to sacrifice innocents to meet his ends." He rested his head on his hands. "What a fool I've been. Ahh, HighGod, forgive me—"

"You've been quite helpful, Marcus," said Gregory. "You'll live, for now, as long as you continue on this path."

"Thank you, sire. Your punishment showed me the extent of my degradation. The pain was in His plan. Bless you."

Gregory's face reddened, and he went for his hair. "Please—ridiculous—"

"It is of no consequence to me if I live or die. In this hole, or out of it."

"No need to discuss it now." Gregory stood, and the rest of their party stood with him. The guards hauled Marcus to his feet. Gregory couldn't seem to leave the dungeon fast enough, but before could escape up the passageway Marcus called out to him.

"Your wife, sire." Marcus stared at Eleanor, one white eye against a red face against a dark wall. "Princess, he does hate you as he hates the witches. You sent him into seven years of limbo. He called it magical agony. He will kill you, if he can."

Gregory put a hand on Eleanor's waist. He muttered under his breath as he steered her toward the passageway. "Bloody crazy—safe at Eclatant—"

Two hours later Eleanor was in a gown on Gregory's arm in the Grand Ballroom. She wore velvet, as tradition demanded. She smiled and curtsied and wished with all her heart to be in her room with a book on magical warfare spread out on her lap. She made a mental list of additional questions for Marcus.

She never had a chance to ask them. The next morning Chou brought word that Marcus had been found in his locked cell, as dead as a thousand victims of the Burning he'd watched Oliver unleash. The guards had not heard a sound, or seen anyone, but one reported that a gray light lingered around the Godsman until his body went stiff.

Dorian was so busy during the Waning, he hardly had time to

worry about Ezra Oliver or ponder the implications of Marcus's death. Gregory scheduled all his waking hours, from breakfast to contests to high tea with the ladies of the Desmarais Family Historical Society. Dorian nodded politely and sipped his pear juice while some biddy who resembled his late Grandpoppa in a corset rambled on about the placement of family pets in second century Desmarais portraiture.

Although Gregory kept Dorian on a tight rein, he had little to say. Dorian couldn't tell if Gregory was avoiding a discussion of Sylvia's child, or felt some guilt over Marcus's torture, or suspected Dorian was sleeping with his wife. The only way to ascertain an answer to any of those questions would be to ask him, and some questions were better left unanswered.

To Dorian's added irritation, Gregory was unusually solicitous of Abram Finley. Gregory had long teased Dorian about his awkward, gangly sibling, but when Dorian mentioned his intent to avoid Abram for the duration of the Fest, Gregory chided him.

"He's your bother, man. Your flesh and blood. Show him some respect."

So Dorian tolerated Abram's presence at his elbow through ten days and nights of social functions. With each day, Abram more fully embraced the role of erudite (and condescending) older brother. He interrupted Dorian, corrected him, and delivered several year's worth of unsolicited advice. When Abram suggested Dorian place a napkin in his lap before his ass had even touched the seat of his chair, Dorian considered stabbing him with a salad fork.

By the final night of the Fest, Dorian's nerves were as tattered as they'd ever been. For years he'd kept his drinking in check, but tonight his arm had a mind of its own. It reached out and took glass after glass of whiskey from passing servants, until his brain hummed between his ears. He wandered the edges of the party in a calculated round of meaningless chat that steered him clear of Gregory, Abram, and Eleanor.

He didn't trust himself beside her after seven shots of whiskey and a two glasses of wine, so he positioned himself where he could watch her instead. She wore a periwinkle gown; a color he'd always loved on her. It brought out the blue in her light eye, the fairness of her hair. The deep neckline, lined with tiny diamonds, complimented her white skin. These racy new fashions gave well-endowed women the appearance of overcompensation, but on Eleanor, the look was elegantly sensual.

He couldn't take his eyes off her as she laughed and sipped wine. He changed places in the ballroom, only to see her head turning, seeking him out. He pictured her in a thousand reclining positions in the granary and in the cave on the cliffside. His mind's eye traced every curve of her body. Remembered the taste of salt on her skin, the smell of peachberry bath salts. Her two-toned eyes looking up at him, from his lap when she—

"I need to speak with you."

Abram's voice jerked Dorian back to reality. He tugged at his tunic. Thankfully it was longish, and hid the physical result of his daydreaming.

"I've been trying to catch you for hours," Abram said in his most annoying fatherly voice. "It's half past one in the morning."

"There are a thousand people here. I've been saying my hellos." Dorian scanned the rapidly thinning crowd. "Where's Gregory?"

"He retired." Abram winked. "The Duchess of Harveston fell to sleepiness only moments later. How fortunate, to be the Prince."

"Hmmm." Dorian ran his tongue around his dry mouth. "I need some water."

"I just said I must speak with you." Dorian's pause gave Abram permission to continue. "I'm hosting the Lilies-on-the-Lake Ball this year."

"Wonderful."

"At Laralee."

Dorian handed his empty whiskey glass to a servant. "Thank you for asking me."

"It's the most celebrated party in the Crossing. The mayor asked me to host."

"You could host it at Floodgate Manor."

"Yes, but the mayor reminded me that we haven't held any large events at Laralee. It's time."

"We?"

Abram colored. "The Finleys are the most important family in the Crossing."

Dorian let the comment lie. "Take care of it." He started to walk away but Abram grabbed his arm.

"We'll need to make some improvements to the house—"

"Fine. Just be reasonable."

Abram cleared his throat. "I assume you won't—that is—you'll be busy—"

"What? Abram, for the love of the Bond, what?"

"I just mean there's no need for you to come back. For Lilies-on-the-Lake. I'll handle everything."

Dorian's brow wrinkled, and then he laughed. "You don't want me there?"

"Ah—it's not that—"

"It is precisely that. You want to throw a huge party at my house. You want me to pay for it. But you want me to stay away." Abram stepped back from Dorian's jutting chin. "You want to impress all the men who teased you when we were young—the women who spurned you. Play Duke of Brandling on my coin."

If Abram had had any chin to speak of it would have been just as forthcoming as Dorian's. "How dare you suggest—"

"The Finleys aren't the most important family in the Crossing, Abram. The Finleys are moderately aristocratic, as the Finleys have always been." He might not have finished his thought had he not been flying the whiskey banner, but out it came. "*I'm* the most important man in Harper's Crossing. It's not about our family, and it's most certainly not about you."

Dorian grabbed another glass of whiskey and bowed his goodbye. "Enjoy your party."

Something must have been in the air, for Eleanor had partaken of four glasses of wine herself, a goodly amount in the old days and a whopping indulgence for a woman who hadn't imbibed of anything but water, tea, and pear juice in public in years. She watched with rapidly blinking eyes as Dorian left the ballroom. She could see anger in the set of his shoulders.

Gregory had excused himself, quickly followed by Sylvia, nearly an hour ago. He never retired before his wife.

Maybe...just this once...

Eleanor handed her glass to a passing servant. She took a shortcut down the gloomy kitchen corridors toward the west wing and Dorian's chamber door. She'd never been inside his room, but she had walked every inch of Eclatant on cold winter days, just for a stretch of her legs. She knew the route as surely as if she took private tea with him every afternoon.

She alternated between a fast walk and a trot. Her heart pounded in her chest. The west wing was predominantly made up of guest rooms reserved for foreign dignitaries, and older courtiers who had no desire to be kept awake by Fest-time carousing. Dorian had told Eleanor years ago that he'd requested a room in the west wing, as the atmosphere was more conducive to study, and the library just below him. As the servants became fewer and far between she blessed his reclusiveness.

She made a final left turn, and there was his back, before her at the end of the hall. He turned at the sound of her footsteps. The door fell open behind him.

He stepped back into the shadows as she advanced, faster and faster until she was running. She crossed the threshold and fell into his open arms. He dropped his key. It pinged off the wooden floor as he pushed the door shut behind her.

"Eleanor—Ah…what are you doing—should we—" Her mouth against his muffled his words.

"Draw the latch."

He fumbled around behind her head as she kissed his neck. He groaned, but still some rationality lingered. "Maybe—"

She pulled away from him. "I'm here. Do to me what was written on your face all night."

Later it would have the feel of a dream, blurred at the edges. She'd somehow shed her blue gown; at some point he loosened her hair. His boots and clothes were strewn across the bedroom floor. When it was over she lay naked on top of him, spent and happy, aching and agonizing.

"What should I say now, Eleanor?" he finally asked.

She lifted her head from his chest. "Don't say anything, and I won't have to leave.

Morning won't come."

Dorian kissed her, long and slow and deep, with his hands in her hair. He helped her dress,

and checked the hallway. She clung to him, but he eased her out the door. "Go now, my love. Ticia will be looking for you in a few hours." She pressed a fist to her eyes. He removed it. "I must know you're safe. Please."

She nodded and stepped into the passage. The wine had long since worn off, but

jumbled thoughts accompanied her back to her room. Dorian's words, flashes of their lovemaking, fear that someone had seen her going or coming…she looked up to find herself facing Gregory's chamber.

She'd only stayed with him a handful of times in their ten years together. He always decided the hour of their conjugal association; it was Eleanor's duty to wait for him. She'd knocked, however, on many occasions. Usually late in the morning when he'd missed breakfast or a visit with the children. She'd grown accustomed to the delays. His frantic voice shouting, "Just a moment!" or Melfin's long face peeking from around the door and declaring the prince to be indisposed.

She stopped before his door. The Fire-iron *GD* mounted on the thick wood winked at her in the torchlight. The guard cleared his throat. "It's late, it is, Your Highness. His Highness has been asleep a few hours."

Eleanor chuckled. "Oh, we both know he's in there, sergeant, and we both know he's not sleeping." She banged on the door.

Why am I doing this?

"Your Highness! Please, don't!"

Still baffled by her own behavior, she knocked again. "Gregory?" Bang. "Gregory!"

Shuffling on the other side, and the lock jiggling. Gregory's face appeared in the crack. His eyes widened. "Eleanor—what—" He closed the door, and she heard his muffled voice. He cracked the door again and slid into the hallway in his leggings and bare feet. He rubbed at the scruff on his face as he closed the door behind him. "Horns and fire, why are you still awake? Is Ticia all right?"

"I stayed late...had a lark."

He glanced at the guard, who seemed hypnotized by the torchlight. "I'm glad you enjoyed yourself. It's late—I was sleeping—"

"I wanted to see you," she said, although she'd had no such intention until three minutes ago and Dorian's sweat still covered her body.

I need to be certain....

She almost pitied him the smile that crept around the corners of this mouth. "Ah...I'm glad...but—tomorrow, or I mean tonight—it's so late—"

She took advantage of his fumbling, grabbed the door handle, and stepped into his chamber.

Eleanor knew how long it took a Carthean noblewoman to dress without the help of servants. The sight of Sylvia Fleetwood in her petticoat, her glorious bare breasts pointing at her lover's wife like two well-aimed arrows, did not surprise Eleanor. Sylvia pulled her long dark hair over her chest and lifted her chin.

Eleanor smiled. "Good evening, Sylvia."

Gregory took her arm from behind. "Eleanor—it's not what you think." Panic and a bizarre hopefulness churned his features.

She laughed. "It's just what I think, Gregory. What I've thought for years. Now I know. Thank you. I do so like to be well-informed."

"You've nothing else to say?"

Eleanor walked out of the room. She paused on the staircase and looked back at him. He clenched the open doorframe.

"Goodnight, Gregory. Sleep well."

CHAPTER 30

THE DRAGON IN SMITHWICK SQUARE

PREDICTABLY, GREGORY RETURNED TO Eleanor's bed the next night. Perhaps he assumed she'd rediscover a gnawing jealousy. Eleanor knew she should give him what he wanted, but she felt nothing but relief. She had no mind to pit Gregory's remaining affection for her against whatever he felt for Sylvia.

The palace emptied of Fest-goers and a chill settled into Eclatant's Fire-iron walls. Eleanor relished the free hours with her daughter. On the last Tuesday morning in Midwinter, Rosemary joined them in Eleanor's room for hot chocolate and biscuits.

"Must you go back to the Abbey?" asked Eleanor. She stood by the fireplace with one hand on the mantle. "We've only had a few hours."

"You'd be amazed at what can come to pass at the Abbey in the span of an afternoon."

"How do you keep track of all those little one?" Eleanor asked.

"I should like to have so many friends," said Ticia. She bent over a sketch of her mother.

"You must visit the Abbey, little love," said Rosemary. "Watch the girls conjure." The witch peered over Ticia's shoulder. "Beautiful, child. Eleanor, she's quite talented."

"I don't know where it comes from," said Eleanor. "Certainly not from me."

"Poppa showed me some of his old drawings. From when he was a boy," said Ticia. "He said he would draw all day when he wasn't practicing riding or fencing."

"Well, that's nice. From the Desmarais side, then." Eleanor had no idea Gregory enjoyed drawing. He'd never mentioned it.

She admired Ticia's sketch. The child had smudged the pencil marks with her finger to add roundness to her mother's arms and cheeks.

"Your dress is pretty, Mother...but what if..." Ticia erased the sleeves and sketched them off the figure's shoulders. She added some brushy feathering from shoulder to elbow. "Lace—and lace on the hem..."

Ticia looked up at the two women with earnest enthusiasm. "Dresses are important. They make a lady feel beautiful, and everyone looks beautiful in different things. And if you add a nice bonnet..." She bent over her paper again.

Eleanor squeezed Ticia's shoulder and walked to the window. Rosemary followed her.

"I should bring on an art teacher..." Eleanor said. "Maybe I could find her a book on—"

"What's that?" Rosemary pointed out the window.

A dark cloud hung over the city, as if a summer thunderstorm had come back early from holiday. "Not a cloud," Eleanor corrected herself aloud as she examined the growing plume of darkness. "It's too thin—and going up—it's smoke!"

"Over Smithwick Square?" said Rosemary. "A fire in one of the stalls?"

"No stall fire can produce that much smoke. And look, there are two other plumes. That one looks to be over the Fringe—"

At that moment Pansy opened the door. "Mister Orvid—"

Jones pushed past her.

"—Jones. Magicians!" Pansy said. "All spells and no manners! Come, Your Highness…" She hustled Ticia and her drawings out the door.

Jones joined Eleanor and Rosemary at the window. He tapped on the glass. "You must collect Teardrop. All unicorns are needed in town."

Eleanor's eyebrows lifted. "All unicorns? To fight a fire?"

"The king commands it. He's coming himself, with Fortune. Gregory and Vigor—Dorian and Senne'…they're already on their way."

"HighGod, Jones. What is it?"

"Three dragons."

"What do you mean?" asked Rosemary. The columns of smoke had met above the city, giving the impression of a slowly shifting black lightning bolt.

"Someone set dragons loose in Maliana," Eleanor said, as grim comprehension dawned on her. "I'll give you one guess as to who."

The scene in Smithwick Square made the burning of Queen Camille's seem like a campfire. Flames bounced from the wooden stalls to the thatch-roofed houses. People ran in and out of shops, their arms loaded with boxes and barrels, trying to salvage their wares and belongings. Panicked livestock bumped against soldiers and unicorns. The smell of scorched hay made Eleanor sneeze. Over the screams and braying and crackling came the intermittent shriek of an angry dragon.

The temperature was that of a summer afternoon. Eleanor broke a sweat. She wiped her stinging eyes and urged Teardrop toward the center of the square. A dark shape, roughly the size of Humility Chapel, shifted behind a wall of smoke. A blast of wind granted Eleanor and Teardrop a moment of relative coolness and an unrestricted view.

A dragon emerged in the clearing haze. It flexed its neck, and the golden scales lining its back stood on end like angry icicles. It took three plodding steps toward the fountain— the same one Eleanor remembered from her childhood— and grasped the carriage-sized basin in its jaws. The dragon flung the chunk of carved marble across the square with all the ease of a two-year-old child dumping a soup bowl. It hit the wall of Bertram's Best Bakery. Shingles and a few stray loaves ricocheted back into the street.

The dragon stepped through the fountain. The water evaporated and disappeared in puffs of steam around its scaly feet. It crunched through the smiling fairies on the fountain's edge and made for a pen of pigs. The animals squealed and ran up against the fence rails. The dragon's tail whacked the ground as it scooped up pig after pig in its jaws. It swallowed each one in two gulps.

It was hungry, Eleanor thought. *Now it will calm...we can subdue it.*

The dragon belched black smoke. It shifted and trembled. The green flanks twitched. It let out a pitiable whistling cry, and with a horrible retching it vomited.

Eleanor clapped a hand over her mouth at the smell of burnt pork and bile. The two remaining pigs screamed and sobbed in porcine horror as they were covered in the smoking remains of their companions.

The dragon shrieked and backed away from the pigpen. It sprayed fire in blinding, impartial destruction. It plowed across the square, ripped open the roof of a mason's shop, and blew a blast of heat into the building. Flames shot from the windows.

"Eleanor!"

She turned from the hypnotic carnage to find Senne' and Dorian, with Vigor and Gregory behind them. "How do we stop it?" she asked.

Dorian dismounted. "The unicorns must stop it. We manage the townsfolk."

Eleanor and Gregory joined him on the ground. She turned to Teardrop. "Stay with me—you have no experience with dragons. It's too dangerous—"

Teardrop shook her head. "We're all needed."

"No! Please. Help me with the people." Eleanor threw her arms around Teardrop's neck.   Teardrop nibbled her hair. "This is the work of my kind. I know it in my soul, even if I have not worked the Mines as a Vigor and Senne´ have. Let me do this."

Eleanor crumpled a handful of silky mane between her fingers before she let go. She slipped the bridle over Teardrop's ears. "Be careful. Be strong."

Teardrop shook her head and stretched her jaws. Eleanor thought she had never looked more beautiful, or powerful. Senne´ nipped her shoulder, and the three unicorns joined twenty or so others in a huddle by the ruined bakery.

"What are they doing?" Eleanor asked.

"Strategizing, I assume," said Gregory. "Blondie—"

"Blondie?"

"The dragon," Gregory raised his voice as Blondie caterwauled his frustration. "He's never left the Mines in his life. Out of one cave, into another. He's confused. Frightened. Subduing him won't be like leading a transfer."

"Can they do it?"

"I hope so. Nearly all these unicorns have experience in the North—Arrow, he's very good—and Cedar...besides, Teardrop is right. Whatever grace is in the Bond, it's in all of them." Eleanor heard wonder in his voice, and the calm practicality that had so impressed her during their month together at the Mines.

"Where did it come from?"

"It just appeared, along with two others," said Dorian. "One in the Fringe, one by the Dockworks."

"I can't see how Oliver does it. The heat, and a dragon must weigh—"

"There's no time for speculation on magical theory," said Gregory called over his shoulder as he strode into the smoke.

"Stay with him," Dorian said.

Eleanor wasn't sure if Dorian wanted Gregory to watch out for her, or vice versa. She followed Gregory around the edge of the square, and soon found ways to be of use. She carried water buckets, and held the hands of lost children until their parents appeared in the smoke. She joined Gregory in helping an old woman calm her panicked donkey. Eleanor stopped hearing the noise of the dragon, and the smoke no longer bothered her. She moved from one need to the next, and kept Gregory's broad back before her.

As they approached the Pasture's End side of the square, Eleanor tripped on a cast-off water bucket. He ankle rolled and she stumbled. A little girl ran into her path. They collided and the child cried out.

"Eleanor? Eleanor!" Gregory shouted.

"Peace, Gregory. Where's your mother?" Eleanor asked the child.

The girl, who looked to be about five, shook her head. "Grandma, in the bed." She pointed at the burning building behind her. "In the shop."

Flames crept over the building, which Eleanor vaguely remembered as a furniture store.

"She can't walk," said the girl, "but it's hot, and she's thirsty. Do you have water?"

Eleanor turned toward the flames, but Gregory stopped her. "It's about to go up hard. We can't take the risk for one bedridden old woman."

She glared at him. "You'd let her burn up?"

"Some will die today. Some already have. We can't save everyone."

"You sound like your father after Queen Camille's."

Gregory yelled his response over the whooshing flames behind them. "He was right! Those girls died anyway—and the risk...I don't have an heir, Eleanor!"

She looked at him incredulously. "You have Leticia!"

"I need a boy. Not a girl."

"Just because there hasn't been a Desmarais queen doesn't mean there can't be!"

"I won't risk the Bond to find out." He took her arm. "Do you think Ticia could stand losing you? So soon after Nathan?"

His words had more heat in them than the flames behind her. She tugged at his grip, but it was half-hearted.

"Come—bring the child," he said.

Something inside the furniture shop exploded. Embers rained down on Eleanor's back and burned through her cotton tunic. The girl screamed. Gregory put an arm around Eleanor's shoulders and tugged the child into his shadow. They stumbled away from the building. Gregory pushed Eleanor to the ground. She huddled under him, with her arms around the shrieking child, and inhaled the smell of singed hair.

Gregory spoke in her ear. "Take the girl. Witches—seeing to the wounded by the bookbinders." He pulled her to her feet and kissed her roughly before pushing her in the direction of the bookshop.

Eleanor tiptoed among the wounded with a water flask. She offered sips and comfort. The witches loaded the injured into open-air carts. Eleanor looked over the huddled, moaning crowd. It would take the witches hours to transport them all to Afar Creek. They ministered to the most desperate cases on the spot, but the lack of supplies and bad air hindered their efforts.

The dragon rambled from one end of the square to the other. It yelled, blew fire, and thrashed its tail like a spoiled debutante in the midst of a good foot stomping. The unicorns repeatedly approached it, in large groups and in trios and couples, but each time the dragon greeted them with howling rage and spewing flames. Eleanor was glad she couldn't tell one white unicorn from the next. Only Senne' stood out from the crowd like a puff of hard smoke.

The day dragged on until the shadows lengthened through the smoke. The dragon refused to give in, and it drifted down the alleyways. It had destroyed the walls of buildings around it.

"We can't let him leave the square," said a voice over Eleanor's shoulder. She turned to see Orvid Jones, his white eyes staring from his soot-covered face. "Senne' suggested—I came to tell you—that is—"

"Does Dorian need me?"

Jones shook his head. "We're going to send one unicorn to the dragon."

"I saw a single unicorn calm a dragon once. Tremor—the lead stallion at the mines. It was amazing."

"Sometimes they react well to an individual. We need a mare. Teardrop is the only one."

"No. I won't allow it."

"It's a male dragon…he might respond better to a female."

A unicorn stepped from the crowd, and suddenly Eleanor couldn't believe she'd missed Teardrop's delicate head and slim legs among the crowd of taller, bulkier stallions. She dropped the flask and sprinted across the square.

Gregory intercepted Eleanor and wrapped his arms around her waist.

"Teardrop!" she cried. The mare had almost reached the dragon, but she jerked her head and paused.

"Shhh, don't distract her."

"It will kill her, Gregory—please, call her back!"

"It won't. You know her. She wanted to do it."

Eleanor went limp in his arms. He held on, but his grip softened.

The dragon followed the mare's progress with one yellow eye. The grind of its growl became louder, until it sounded like every bee in the world had descended on Smithwick Square. Teardrop stopped before the dragon. Eleanor couldn't hear Teardrop's voice, but she could make out her intent in the set of her ears and her tail. All the complexities of a unicorn's speech in the shake of her head and a few hard blasts of air from her nostrils.

Tired...frightened...home...

The dragon's tail hit the ground in three bangs.

Help you...home...

The dragon shot a blast of fire into Teardrop's face. The flames glanced off her horn and her hide. Her whiteness glowed orange. Eleanor hid her face against Gregory's chest, but she couldn't look away for long.

Teardrop's mane lifted, and then settled on her neck. She stepped closer to the dragon. *Fire...no more...home....*

The dragon lowered its snout, and wrapped its thin forearms around its head. To Eleanor's disbelief its shoulders shuddered, as if in great scaly sobs. Three horns poked from between its talons.

Teardrop's ears pricked. Eleanor gripped Gregory's forearms as the mare snuffled at the dragon, as she had over Cricket when the filly took her first steps. The dragon groaned as Teardrop's muzzle danced over its golden mane and down to its thick rear legs. The swishing tail went still. It flopped onto its side and rested its head on its forearms. Eleanor read exhaustion in every spike.

"I'll be damned," said Gregory.

Eleanor realized he still had his arms around her waist, and she still held onto him herself. As she stepped away Gregory brushed her sweaty hair off her neck.

The king and his contingent of unicorn guards rounded the corner from the direction of the Dockworks. Eleanor ran to meet Casper and his stallion, Fortune. "What news from the Clarity, Your Majesty?"

"It's not good," the king said as he dismounted. "The dragon has burned up the docks, five warehouses, and at least twenty ships. It's so hot the water has dropped. The steam...it's like the Tallassee jungles." He pointed at Teardrop and the dragon. "You're having more success."

Gregory joined them and explained Teardrop's unexpected role.

A grim smile crossed the king's sweaty face. "A woman's touch. She must come with me to the Dockworks. The unicorns there need her assistance."

"Let her have a drink, at least," said Eleanor.

"Quickly," said the king. "The Dockworks, the Fringe, and I've just heard word of another dragon in the West End."

"Near my father's house!" said Eleanor.

"Oliver's wrath doesn't discriminate between rich and poor. There are manors burning up and down the West Hundred Herald's."

Eleanor started to excuse herself to attend to Teardrop, but quick hooves on cobblestone made her pause. A witches' cart careened toward them. The driver waved a long whip in one hand. "Your Highness!"

The witch, a healer Eleanor had met on some visit or another, leaned back against the reigns and the carthorses came to a wheezing halt. "Afar Creek—Oliver—magicians—an attack—"

"Oliver is at Afar Creek?"

"We tried to close the gate, but he blasted it off the hinges. A horde of martials rushed the Abbey. Some are dead…children, and the wounded townsfolk in the courtyard…" Bright purple tears shot from the witch's eyes.

"You need help," Gregory said, with surprising eagerness. "I'll take Vigor—Jones, you retrieve more martials from the Abbey—"

"You're right, Gregory. Someone must stop Oliver. But not Vigor, and not you." The king turned to Dorian. "Take my personal guard— there are two dozen of them, on horseback. Jones, gather as many martials as you can find at the Covey."

Gregory's face was a storm cloud in the slowly clearing smoke. "I want to go, Father. I want to fight him."

"No. You must stay here."

"He disgraced us, and yet no Desmarais will go after him? You send Dorian—do you think he'll stand a better chance?"

"Don't be a fool. You're not going for the same reason I'm not going."

"I've already towed that line today! I've not taken stupid risks—but this isn't carelessness, it's altogether different!"

"Eleanor, go with Dorian," the king said. "You know the Abbey better than the rest of us."

"Your Majesty—" Dorian didn't get a chance to finish the thought before Gregory exploded.

"Fuck, no! She's staying here. She's *my wife!*"

The king advanced on his son with a speed that belied his advancing age and his ample girth. "I am your father, and I am *your king!* Your duty is to your throne. Try to remember that, and the dignity that should come with it."

Gregory's chest rose and fell. Eleanor had never seen his eyes so wild. Dorian hesitated.

"Mount up!" the king shouted. Dorian did as Casper asked, and the king included Eleanor in what came next. "Once the dragons are subdued, I'll send the unicorns to the Abbey. Don't be afraid to take a risk—not with the soldiers, and not with the martials. Help the witches, but above all else, you must keep Oliver there until Jones and his martials arrive."

"Yes, Your Majesty," Eleanor said. She looked at Gregory, but he was staring into the empty space above her head, so she took Dorian's outstretched hand. It was warm and dry.

Senne' shifted his weight as she settled onto his back. Eleanor wasn't sure what grip would be most offend Gregory, so she rested her hands lightly on Dorian's hips.

"Your Majesty. Your Highness," said Dorian.

"HighGod-speed," said the king, but Gregory said nothing.

"On, Sen," said Dorian. "The Abbey, fast."

Senne' lunged forward. Eleanor had to grab Dorian's waist to avoid being tossed over the stallion's tail. She looked back at Gregory, in the hopes it might somehow reassure him of something…even something false, but his expression did not change one iota. As they raced toward the Abbey, Eleanor inhaled the smell of Dorian's tunic and exhaled smoke and worry. She tightened her arms around him and pressed against his back like an extra layer of clothing. He transferred the reigns to one hand, and gripped one of hers in the other.

CHAPTER 31

FALLING DIRT AND SPINNING LIGHT

SENNÉ'S HOOVES WERE TOO loud in the Abbey courtyard, like jaunty music at a funeral. Overturned barrels and carts spewed produce and medicinal herbs over the dusty ground. Spilled tonics pooled in brightly colored puddles of drying mud, and burst flour sacks gave the impression of recent snowfall. The scent of trampled melons added an inappropriate sweetness to the smoky air. The only movement came from a few sheepish, skulking chickens. Their pea brains had somehow conveyed the need for silence to their beaks.

Witches and townsfolk dotted the courtyard in prostrate lumps of gray and brown cotton, as still as boulders at the bottom of a steep hill. Some might have been cut down in place, some as they fled. Eleanor rested her head on Dorian's back. His heartbeat thumped in her ear.

Dorian asked the captain of the king's guard to look for survivors. He dismounted and reached for Eleanor. She allowed him to lift her down, just for the feel of his hands on her waist.

Senné raised his muzzle and sniffed the air. "I smell fear."

"Inside the Abbey?" Eleanor asked.

The stallion nodded and walked toward the brick and wood-planked chapel. Eleanor and Dorian followed him.

Senne´ sniffed the chapel's sun-shaped door handle, his front legs on the landing and his back legs on the dirt. Eleanor and Dorian climbed the four steps between. Dorian reached for the handle.

"Wait." Fear filled Eleanor's chest and crept up the back of her throat, like too much soup in a small pot. She hadn't seen her teacher's white hair among any of fallen witches, but surely that luck couldn't last.

Dorian squeezed her shoulder. Years of communicating without speaking made words unnecessary. He waited until she nodded and opened the door.

The chapel seemed as lifeless as the courtyard. Even more so, as there was not a chicken in sight. Eleanor stepped across the threshold. "Is anyone here?" Her voice evaporated among yesterday's drooping flowers on the carved Fire-iron altar.

"Eleanor?"

Rosemary appeared in lines of weak sunlight streaming through the soot-covered windows. Perhaps a dozen people followed her, a mixture of young witches, a few healers and some injured townsfolk. Eleanor ran down the aisle and embraced her teacher. "Thank HighGod, you're safe."

"For now," said Rosemary, "they might not be so charitable if they come back."

"Who?" asked Dorian.

"Oliver's martials. He left them to dispatch us, but they bade us hide in here. Maybe they couldn't do it...boys, really..." Rosemary leaned on the altar. A raised welt marred the side of her head. Purplish red against her white hair. "There's no bolt. We can't even lock them out..."

"Rosemary, sit down." Eleanor eased the witch to the first bench. Dorian handed Eleanor a handkerchief. She dabbed at Rosemary's head. "Oliver is gone? Did he disappear?" Eleanor asked.

"No...he's heading for the Oracle's cavern. A few of the sorceresses

followed him and his men across the fields. To try and hold them off."
Rosemary laughed. "Our most powerful conjurers cannot defend us. No
locks on our doors, or our gates. How trusting we've been. How stupid."

"Rosemary—"

"No more," said Rosemary, with an adamant shake of her head. "I
am Abbotess, and the women of this Abbey will learn to protect themselves under my watch."

Eleanor touched Rosemary's cheek. "We've come to help you. We've
brought soldiers, and Orvid Jones is on his way with help from the
Covey. The unicorns are coming."

"It won't be soon enough. Oliver might have trouble finding the
entrance to the cavern, and the sorceresses will provide a bit of distraction, but if he finds Hazelbeth..."

"She's so weak," said Eleanor, picturing the wretch she'd seen in her
last dream vision.

"There's no replacing her." Rosemary's eyes finally came into their
usual sharp focus. "She is Afar Creek, and we are her. If ever this Abbey
existed without her, we've long forgotten how. He knows all this. He
understands us. You must stop him."

Eleanor didn't fully comprehend Rosemary's fear, nor did she think
anyone but a witch of Afar Creek Abbey could, but she did have her
study of Abbey history and the observations of years of visits. Hazelbeth
was more than the oldest witch at Afar Creek...or the wisest, or the
most powerful. She connected the witches to each other, and to their
history, and even to their future.

The final blow, Eleanor thought.

Senne' splashed through the shallows of Afar Creek, crested a low
hill, and pounded across a meadow of eternally blooming lavender.
Eleanor peered around Dorian's shoulder at a stand of oak trees. The
woody behemoths loomed behind a bramble thicket, one so dense

rabbits would need pruning shears to navigate it. A lone sorceress with short black hair huddled before the gray and green tangle. She looked up when Senne' stopped.

"They've all gone to Hazelbeth," the witch said in a dull voice. "We couldn't stop them. All dead…" She pointed at her friends lying around her, as if Eleanor and Dorian needed some clarification other than crooked bodies and glazed, staring eyes. She seemed amazed at her own uselessness. "They didn't think me enough of a threat to finish me off."

The king's soldiers crested the hill, but the site of them brought Eleanor no reassurance. What good could men with swords do against so much magic?

"We must go after him," said Dorian. "At least slow him down, until Jones arrives."

"Slow him down…" Wheels spun in Eleanor's head, dislodging the bogged down carriage of her mind.

"I'll go in," Dorian said. "Take the soldiers. Most will surely die, but the king said we must be bold."

She called him away from the witch as the soldiers dismounted and drew their weapons. "We must go. You and I. Leave the soldiers here."

"I'd rather you stay out here. You could tell me your plan. I'll carry it out. I swear it."

She smiled weakly. "I have no doubt that you would, love, but Ezra Oliver and I are long overdue for a chat."

Senne' cleared a swath through the brambles, so Eleanor reached the entrance to the Oracle's cavern with fewer scratches than on previous visits, but the stallion could not fit through the narrow entrance. He paced in a circle. Thorns glanced off his shiny black coat as if he were made of Fire-iron. "Hooves-be-damned," he muttered. "Shit-in-a-bale."

Eleanor had never heard a unicorn curse. She whispered so to Dorian.

"He couldn't enter the cave in the Scaled Mountains, either," said Dorian. "Put off them, I suppose. Although…" Dorian peered into the dark passageway that seemed cut out of the thicket itself. "It's not really a cave, is it?"

Dorian insisted on walking in front of Eleanor. He held her hand in one of his and his sword in the other. They had no torch so they navigated the blackness by the feel of the cold, prickly walls and Eleanor's memory.

The magical light of Oliver's martials leaked back through the passageway, illuminating their way. Dorian's tan tunic appeared to have been dragged across a wet rainbow. Eleanor dragged her fingers across the Garden's complex, living architecture; a web of gnarled tree roots in the ceiling, floor, and walls. Some hung down like wooden chandeliers, while still others grew out of dirt floor and reached for her ankles.

The martials filled a wide grotto, like a swarm of multi-colored ants. Eleanor recognized the short path to the Oracle's personal chamber by the Fire-iron sunflower hung above the entryway. *A watchful flower*, Rosemary had told a ten-year-old Eleanor on her very first visit to this cave, on the eve of her father's death.

Dorian stopped. "What now?" he whispered.

She kissed him. "Do you trust me?"

He pulled back just enough to answer her. "You know I do."

"Then follow my lead."

Dorian watched Eleanor step into the magician's circle of light. Reds, browns, greens, and dark blues were as vibrant against her blonde hair as they would be on any blank canvas. As he'd promised, he followed her.

"Mister Oliver?" she called out. "Am I disturbing you?"

The martials spun around like well-drilled soldiers. The magical reflection blinded Dorian. He stepped in front of Eleanor and raised his sword.

It seemed the martials could only act collectively, from their light to their voices. Gray mist smothered the rainbow, and their warning shouts switched off. Dorian blinked, but he couldn't dispel the flashes of color that lingered before his eyes.

"Her Highness and His Grace!" said a familiar nasally voice. "We're blessed with a royal visit!"

Eleanor curtsied.

Ezra Oliver stepped from the shadow of his own power. "How polite, Mistress Brice—you don't mind if I call you by your maiden name, do you? I've never been able to think of you by any other."

"Of course," said Eleanor. "Mister Oliver...I...that is... I've been curious..."

"Have you something that needs saying?" Oliver said, with his own poorly concealed curiosity.

"You cannot kill the Oracle."

"Now why would I want to do that?"

"I don't know, sir. But you seem bent on it, so we couldn't just let it happen."

Oliver's face fell. "How uninspiring. I honestly expected more from you, Mistress Brice." He nodded at one of the martials. "Finish them."

"He can't," Eleanor said.

Oliver looked mildly interested again. "I'm the prince's wife," she continued. "Lord Brandling is—well, he's Lord Brandling. If that martial kills us, he'll be hanged."

"He left the service of the Desmarais, and any worry about their retribution, when he joined me."

"All of Cartheigh is in the Desmarais's service."

"Bah. I'm the one doing this country a service, even if no one sees it." The gray mist gathered over Oliver's head in rolling thunderheads. "The people are too stupid to know when a change is needed."

"And you'll bring it?" Eleanor covered her giggles with her hand.

"Of course—I—stop laughing at me! I command you to shut up and listen!" Oliver planted his hands on his hips like a frustrated chef haranguing the kitchen staff. "You have no idea what I've suffered—years of pain—not knowing myself, or where I was. In this world, and in some other, trapped between the two for a while—then wandering the Scaled Mountains for six months with nothing but the clothes on my back…" Oliver strode across the passageway, and his martials gave him wide berth. "I have seen places and things the likes of which you could never imagine—"

"Yet you always find your way back to Cartheigh. Why come home, just to kill off large portions of the populace?" Dorian joined in Eleanor's questioning, and the needed minutes ticked by as Oliver agreeably rambled on.

"Innocents always die in a revolution! The Burning was not so bad, really, most were so delirious they felt no pain, and the banshees hastened them on quick enough. Necessary sacrifice, even those Mendaen children—"

"How did you bring them here?" asked Eleanor. "I still can't believe it."

Oliver swelled at the admiration in her voice, and Dorian assumed him only too happy to brag about his own power to the woman who had sent him into exile. "The same way I brought the dragons. With me." The magician smiled. "Oh, I know centuries of sorcerers said it couldn't be done, but they were fools. Anything can be done with power and will. I practiced, in the mountains, first on my own. Then with rabbits. Those children were easy—pop off to Mendae, find some waif with red eyes and a hot forehead. The streets were crawling with children and the Burning—and dip back to a downtown Maliana corner. Children dead before anyone could find someone to translate for them, but not before they handed off the sickness. Once I could transport humans, I saw no reason to limit myself. Practiced on those hideous giant buzzards."

"Is that what I smell?" asked Dorian.

"And I moved on to dragons, Your Grace." Oliver shot a gray fireball at Dorian's knee. Dorian deflected it with his sword, but it clipped his elbow before disappearing. Pain flowed down his arm, and a red patch bloomed on his sleeve.

"Quick, as always," said Oliver. "I admit, your appearance at the Dragon Mines last year gave me pause. I wondered if you'd interfere with my practice."

"I don't believe you got in and out of the Mines," Dorian said. "Impossible. You must have had help on the inside."

"Please. I just appeared and disappeared inside the caves—"

"In the heat?"

"A powerful cooling spell. Magicians have always used them in the North. They last only a minute, but that's more than enough time to transport a dragon." He held up hands covered in thick dragon robe gloves. "I've gone through dozens of these."

"No wonder the dragons have been agitated," said Eleanor.

"Noble, stupid beasts," Oliver said, "but not as stupid as the miners. What a lot of buffoons. Any one of them would have been a hindrance, not a help."

"You needed help in Maliana," said Dorian.

"Oh, Marcus," said Oliver, and Dorian was sure he'd not had such an intent audience in years. "Another buffoon, but a malleable one. That fool did everything I asked without question. Sent your girls to the whorehouses. Set your school on fire. Spread my message and hid me in the belfry. All under the assumption I could return a power that probably never existed."

"I'm sure you would have found it if it was there to be found," said Eleanor, and for the first time Oliver looked suspicious.

"Your flattery is a waste of time. I'm going to kill you no matter how subtly you kiss my ass. Both of you—Gregory Desmarais's brains and brawn."

"Eleanor bested you before," said Dorian.

The sarcastic good humor left Oliver's voice. "She did not. A freak accident. And I—I emerged more powerful than before. Perhaps I should thank her. She showed me worlds that I never would have seen without her."

"Worlds?" asked Eleanor. "What world is there, but this one?"

"Or, perhaps that is all your sheltered mind can comprehend. You are a smart girl, but you still have the limits of the mundane." Oliver tapped the side of his head like a patronizing grandfather, and then addressed the martials. "Move back. Mistress Brice has been a worthy opponent, and Lord Brandling has had his moments of brilliance. I'll do them the honor of killing them myself."

Dorian was desperate to keep Oliver talking. "Did you know it was Eleanor who uncovered the hidden magical residue in your spellwork, not Orvid Jones? Did you know she led us to you in belfry? She's never stopped besting you."

"Liar. She has no magical powers."

"She has something more powerful. A keen mind."

Ribbons of gray smoke shot from Oliver's ears, and he resembled a human kettle. *Jones,* Dorian thought, *for the love of the Bond, where are you?*

"She's a meddling bitch who's never known her place, just like meddling bitches of this HighGod forsaken Abbey."

Eleanor touched Dorian's back. Her hand trembled, but her voice was strong. "Mister Oliver, for years you have been intent on destroying me, and in light of our previous interactions I suppose I don't blame you. But why the witches, still? Did someone here do you some great evil?"

The streams of light coming from Oliver's ears abated, as if someone had dampened the fire under the teapot. "It is as it has always been, Mistress Brice, a matter of space. There is not enough room in this world for all I want to accomplish."

"But witches and magicians have conjured side by side for all of human history."

"And magical learning has been at a relative standstill for most of that time. Look what I accomplished in my freedom."

"Forgive me, sir, but I cannot believe this is all about magical learning. You must have another motive for needing to control all the magical space in Cartheigh. You have plans beyond destroying the witches and far beyond taking revenge on me."

Oliver smiled. "You, child, should have been a man."

"And a prince, or so I've heard."

"No, not a prince. A magician. I could have made use of you." He waved his hands, and another gray fireball joined the one already floating above his head. Both swelled to the size of meat platters. "Unfortunately, as it stands you will not live to see what I'm planning. Nor your handsome duke. This conversation has been quiet stimulating, but it's over."

Dorian stepped in front of Eleanor again. The warmth of her hands seemed to spread up his back, and over his shoulders. His hair lifted, although there was no breeze. Eleanor tugged at his tunic.

The cave lit, bright as a Solsea summer morning. Orvid Jones and his martials pushed past them, one color tumbling over the next like waves rolling toward a rocky shore.

Dorian flattened Eleanor against the wall, but she caught glimpses of the battle raging around them from under his arm. Whizzing fireballs pinged off one another, splitting and multiplying until she was sure no one knew who was killing who, or which side anyone claimed. The magicians wore the same dark cloaks and flattened Covey hats. Aside from the differentiations in color of magic one man reflected the next.

Eleanor and Dorian crawled to a thick tree root. It arched out of the ground like the hunched back of a kamelcow. "Stay here!" he shouted as he drew his sword.

Eleanor swallowed a scream as Jones's hand clamped on her boot. "The sorceress said you'd been in here for nigh on an hour," the magician yelled. "How are you still alive?"

"Oliver wanted to boast, and we let him."

Despite the chaos the edges of Dorian's mouth twitched. "He was keen to impress Mistress Brice. If he were a normal man I'd call him infatuated. He thought us fascinating."

"I was," said Eleanor, without thinking. Orvid scowled and she tried to explain. "Oliver may be a lunatic, but he's an interesting lunatic."

A purple fireball crashed off the dirt wall above their heads. A hunk of tree root bounced off the top of Eleanor's head. She rubbed the spot and spit dust from her dry mouth.

Eleanor peered over the root as Dorian and Orvid joined the fight. Her eyes followed Dorian through layers of falling dirt and spinning light. His sword deflected the magicians' projectiles and sent them spinning back into their conjurers' faces. She tried to track the source of the gray fireballs, but being of average height and build Oliver stood out no more or less than any of the magicians.

She searched for a pattern in the colorful madness. Most of the fireballs flitted around the cave before splitting into smaller spheres, disappearing, or returning to their owners. The larger gray ones circled the edge of the battle. They caused little havoc. *It's almost as if they're waiting for something...or perhaps keeping watch...*

Eleanor's eyes widened. The entrance to the Oracle's personal chamber had always glowed faintly blue, a reflection of the watching pool. This afternoon, blue had darkened to gray.

She crept away from the sheltering root in a monkey-ish combination of hands and feet. The floor vibrated under her hands, and her knees bashed off the floor-bound roots. She prayed no one would notice her through the clashing colors on the filmy air.

She reached the Fire-iron sunflower, ducked down the passageway, and ran toward the Oracle's chamber. The ruckus behind her faded, as if miles separated her from the fight. The passageway dipped down and the watching pool came into view.

Ezra Oliver had his back to Eleanor. Gray light shone from his hands in two muted beams, only to be stopped by a glowing blue wall. Gray and blue met in the center of the pool. The dark water below the opposing colors churned and chortled like soapsuds spinning down a drain grate.

"Because I can, that's why!" Oliver shouted at a pile of robes across the pool.

The kind of voice one would associate with a stern teacher cut through the blue light. "You have a power the likes of which I have not seen in all these ages. I admire it."

The gray beams shivered. "Don't you flatter me, too. I've listened to enough of that dragonshit today."

"Powerful or not, you're a fool. Perhaps you were not at one time, but this endeavor proves it."

"You're the fool." He closed his hands in fists and gray struck blue with a thunk, like two mountains colliding. "You sit in this cave, wasting your HighGod given talent on daydreams. I act with mine, and you mock me!"

"Your power is your own. You decide the course upon which to set it."

"You're jealous—and afraid of me—"

The Oracle's face emerged from the dragon robes. Eleanor felt something splat against her forehead, as if someone had thrown a pat of uncooked dough at her face. She touched the spot, but found only sweaty skin.

Distract him, said a voice in her mind that sounded nothing like the voice of her own thoughts.

"You could stop this, Mister Oliver," said the Oracle.

Eleanor touched her spectite necklace. She stepped out of the shadows. "The king would forgive you!" she shouted.

"HighGod damn you!" Oliver flung a fireball at Eleanor. She jumped, but it clipped her boot and her foot shot out from under her.

"You could have your old position back," she said. "No king would turn away the most powerful magical alley in the world!"

"Shut up, both of you!" said Oliver, but the light wavered again. "He—did he say he would?" His arms trembled.

The Oracle stood. She was no taller than Ticia, with the arms and legs of a born-too-soon-baby. Her gray witches dress fluttered like a bunch of trapped autumn leaves around her bony knees. Her eyes went azure. She flung the blue light across the pool.

The force of the Oracle's power knocked both Eleanor and Ezra Oliver off their feet, two landlubbers on a tossing ship. Eleanor hit the wall behind her and slid to the ground. Oliver landed on his stomach by her feet.

Eleanor's hands went to her neck as she stood, to the stabilizing solidity of her spectite necklace. She always reached for it, whether in grief or pain or confusion.

Her eyes widened. It was gone. She shook her tunic, the pain forgotten. Oliver groaned as he got to his feet in front of her. "You bitch—bitches—"

Grumbling from above cut him off. A chunk of root encrusted dirt the size of a donkey cart broke from the ceiling. It crashed into the watching pool. Cool water landed in droplets on Eleanor's face and hair. A few fell into her mouth and fairly sizzled on her parched tongue. Dirt poured from the ceiling in an unnatural rain of earth on water.

Oliver seemed to forget about destroying Eleanor and the Oracle in his desperation to save his own ass. He scrambled down the passageway, slipping and sliding in the oozing mud. Eleanor fumbled around the edges of the pool until her foot struck something yielding. Hazelbeth peered up from her pile of robes with the same confused face Eleanor remembered from her last dream visit. "What are you doing, child?" the Oracle asked. "There is rough weather about."

Eleanor yanked the blankets off the old woman. She squealed like a modest girl, but Eleanor scooped her up as easily as she'd ever lifted Ticia or Nathan. She ran to the entrance to the passageway.

Dorian flung his sword aside as he climbed over a fallen boulder. "Drop that—what—" He peered into the bundle in Eleanor's arms. His eyes widened. "No, Let me." He took Hazelbeth from Eleanor's arms. The old witch moaned and covered her face with her hands.

"Be careful," Eleanor said, her hand on his arm. She pushed him toward relative safety. The cave shuddered, like the collapsing hull of a sinking ship. Eleanor ran into the passageway and spun around. Something glowed red, then blue, on the cavern floor. The dragon choker disappeared under a thousand tons of dirt.

Dorian carried Hazelbeth back to Afar Creek. Eleanor walked beside him, lost in thought. According to Orvid, Oliver had returned to the scene of the battle. He shouted that the Oracle was crushed and called his martials to his side. The martials clung to him and one another like ivy on an old house. All disappeared in a slow fade of gray cloaks and vibrant magic. Jones's men were left with nothing but open mouths and their own sputtering fireballs.

"I suppose he meant crushed in both a literal and figurative sense," said Orvid, when Eleanor told him about the cavern collapse.

They reached the Abbey at sunset. Four healers met them at the chapel door and relieved Dorian of his burden. Rosemary offered quick kisses, said something about the sick rooms, and followed the healers into the Abbey. The rest of the surviving witches trailed behind, sobbing and praying. Their keening crawled under Eleanor's skin and joined the headache pounding between her ears. She sat on an overturned bucket and Orvid handed her a water flask. She drained it in one gulp.

She set the flask on the ground as Vigor and Fortune charged through the Abbey gate. Dozens of the Unicorn Guard followed them, and Eleanor spotted Teardrop near the front of the battalion. The unicorns joined the jumble of martials, mounted soldiers, and a few wandering townsfolk.

King Casper and Gregory dismounted. "What news?" called Casper.

Eleanor, Dorian, and Orvid Jones took turns telling the story. "...and so here we are," said Jones. "Half of Maliana in ruins, scores of dead and injured...Oliver—who knows?" He kicked a squashed loaf of bread and creamy sparks flew from his boot.

"Once more we have no idea where he is...or what his next move will be," Casper said. "At least this time we won't fool ourselves into thinking him dead."

Gregory stood behind Eleanor. His knees brushed her back. "What now, Father?"

"Jones must find him."

Jones nodded, and from the eager look on his face Eleanor thought he'd start as soon as the king gave him permission to return to the Covey.

"We must assume the worst," said the king. "He as much as told Eleanor and Dorian he was planning something. We will shore up our allegiances. Go to the Tallassees."

"I'm sure we can count on their loyalty," said Dorian.

"And the Svelyans," said the king.

"We haven't received them in ten years," said Gregory.

"It's time we did. We need them, and Kelland, and where goes one nation goes the other."

"But Svelya—"

"Is the only country that poses a true threat to Cartheigh, and it sits just over the mountains. If we are to face some unknown magical invasion, I'd rather count them our friends."

Gregory touched Eleanor's head. She looked up at him. "You must be tired," he said. "The Unicorn Guard will see you home. I'll call on you later this evening."

Eleanor found the strength to haul herself onto Teardrop's back. Woman and mare engaged in mutual fussing. "You're burned," Eleanor said.

"It's nothing. Our muzzles are tenderer than the rest of us. You've been…" She neighed. "Clobbered, walloped, and generally trod upon."

As the mare turned toward the Abbey gate, Eleanor realized Dorian and Gregory had not spoken a word to one another. She put a hand to her throat, to the spot where the dragon choker should have been.

CHAPTER 32

BRIGHT RAINBOWS
AND DARK MUD

ELEANOR TOOK A BATH, ignored the dinner Pansy set out for her, and climbed into bed. She checked the clockworks on the bedside table. Half past seven. Plenty of time to doze off before Gregory showed himself. She curled on her side with her arm under the pillow.

She awoke to bright sunlight through the blue bed curtains. Her arm felt like a piece of cold beef. She shook it. Once the blood flowed freely she reached for the clockworks. Ten in the morning! She hadn't slept so long in years.

Pansy shuffled into the room with a white and purple checked gown across one arm and a plate of toast balanced on the other. "Look who's joined us!"

"Good morning, Pansy. I must have been more tired than I realized. I hope you apologized to His Highness?"

"When, my lady?"

Eleanor took a bite of toast. "Last night, of course. When he came to see me."

"He didn't come last night, Your Highness." Pansy laid the gown on the bed and shook out a petticoat that had seemingly been stored in her apron.

"Oh, well…something must have come up. Let's hurry, please. Ticia will be here any minute."

"Princess Leticia ain't comin' this morning. Prince Gregory's man brought me the message."

Eleanor's toast got stuck on the way down. She swallowed, and it scraped along her smoke irritated throat. "Did he say why?" she asked in a croaking voice.

"No. Just said not to expect her this morning. His Highness also wants you to stay here. In your room, until he calls for you."

Still the toast could not find the proper path. "Water, please, Pansy?" Eleanor said. She sat at her dressing table. "Where's Chou Chou?"

"With the princess. She was missing you yesterday, and when he came to the window late last night I sent him back to her, what with you so tired."

Eleanor nodded, but she kept glancing at the window's reflection in her mirror, in the hopes that Chou would appear. Gregory's failure to turn up last night and his grounding of both Ticia and herself unnerved her. She longed for Chou's whistling reassurance.

Her agitation grew as Pansy fixed her hair and helped her into her gown, and her mind was made up before her coiffure. As Pansy fastened the last button she spoke. "I'm going to the library."

Pansy frowned. "But His Highness said—"

"I'll be back directly." She walked out her bedroom door with Pansy's flummoxed protests ringing in her ears.

The library was empty but for Monty the librarian. Eleanor ran her fingers along the military history volumes. She pulled anything that seemed to have a magical angle. *Watchful Sprites: Fairies as Spies. Caleb Desmarais and Unicorn Strategy. The Army of a Thousand Martials. An*

Anthology of the Ogre Wars. While Eleanor loved history, she'd never seriously studied war craft. Regardless, each title brought the twinges of excitement that always accompanied a new academic fixation.

I'm sure Gregory won't mind if I read for a time...perhaps I can find something of use to the king...or Jones...

She hugged the books to her chest, spun around, and nearly collided with Sylvia Fleetwood.

"Gregory told you to stay in your room," said Sylvia.

"I came to find some books—I was just leaving—" Eleanor stopped herself. "How do you know what Gregory asked of me?"

Sylvia shrugged. "He told me. I saw you cross the Great Hall, so I followed you. Go back. I don't want you upsetting him."

The book on ogres slipped from Eleanor's grip and hit the floor with a smack. She stooped to retrieve it, and seriously considered knocking Sylvia across the face with it on her way up. "My husband is fortunate to have you to look out for his wellbeing."

"Someone has to do it."

If Eleanor had been a witch magical light would have shot from every pore. She bent over her petite stepsister like a tree in a high wind. "Spare me your asinine attempts to convince me you care sincerely about anyone but yourself."

Sylvia stood on tiptoe. "You don't deserve him," she hissed.

Eleanor laughed. "The two of you really are perfect for each other—you're both convinced of your own virtue!"

"He loved you! He still does!" Sylvia's eyes shone with bright tears, and Eleanor's teeth clicked shut on her tongue. Sylvia backed away from her. "I've listened to him—all these years—trying to make you forgive him for whatever ills he did to you. But you wouldn't."

"What—I—" Eleanor sputtered, looking for words in what was quickly becoming a surreal conversation.

"He's the crown prince! It's his right—to do whatever—and with whomever he chooses. Any proper princess would know that—accept it."

"I never claimed to be proper."

Sylvia shook her head. "Of course not. Mother spent years training me—while you emptied shit pots and scribbled essays for Rosemary. But he chose you anyway." She wiped her eyes.

"I'm sorry," Eleanor said, "but what's done is done."

"He needs a male heir!"

The morsel of solicitude in Eleanor's voice melted. "He has an heir. His daughter."

Sylvia blinked, and her reddened eyes sharpened again. "He knows. He has proof. Just last night."

"Proof of what?" Eleanor couldn't control the tremble in her voice.

"Someone told him—I'm not at liberty to say whom, of course, but let's just say I'm shocked at the disloyalty of some people! Gave me quite the lesson in fidelity, for sure."

"I've no idea what you mean."

Sylvia smiled, once again a shark in petticoats. "We've suspected for years…or I have. Gregory didn't want to believe it, but…haven't you noticed? He and dear Dorian haven't been so chummy lately."

Eleanor tried to push past Sylvia, but her stepsister hopped into her path.

"You've been fucking Dorian Finley, haven't you?"

"That's absurd." Sweat ran down Eleanor's back, but she could think of nothing else to say. "Absurd."

"You thought you were so careful…the two of you—always standing close, but not too close. Laughing, but not too loud. You must know it was your eyes that gave you away." The grin fell from Sylvia's face like a dropped brick. "I could see it because I've spent the last ten years in want of someone I could not have."

The books slipped again in Eleanor's sweaty grip. "I'm leaving now."

Sylvia stepped aside. "By all means, don't let me stop you obeying your husband's command."

Eleanor walked to the exit on quivering legs.

"He has proof, Eleanor!" Sylvia sang out from behind her. "Proof!"

Eleanor burst through the library door. She made a hard right and for the second time in a quarter of an hour she ran into an unappealing someone.

Abram Finley grabbed her arms. "Your Highness, take care! You shall fall!"

She excused herself and kept going. *I fear I already have.*

Eleanor approached the dark silhouettes framed in the neat white and purple barn's entrance. A Fire-iron unicorn weathervane swirled cheerfully on the pitched roof. She stopped in the entryway for a moment. She inhaled the smell of hay in shallow breaths and listened to the sound of her own skirts shifting in the dust. She watched Dorian's back as he rubbed Senné's legs with a piece of gray linen.

Senné pricked his ears in her direction and whickered his curiosity. Dorian turned around and smiled. "Good morning. Are you feeling better? You looked so tired—" As his eyes flickered over her face seriousness settled onto his own. "Has something happened?"

She stroked Senné's nose and told him of Sylvia's revelation. His face paled until he looked as if he'd spent the last few years devoid of sunshine, perhaps trapped in the depths of the Dragon Mines.

"She could be trying to make you admit to something."

Eleanor shook her head. "She's never been so candid in twenty years." A lump rose in her throat.

"I should—we could—" Dorian leaned on Senné, and his black tunic melted into the unicorn's dark hide. "I don't know."

"Sylvia thinks she loves him."

"Maybe she does."

"She wouldn't know how."

"Everyone loves differently, Eleanor. Think of how Gregory loves you."

"He doesn't love me. I certainly don't love him. I'd see him die, and free us both."

Dorian looked at her with pleading eyes. "Please, don't say that."

"We face HighGod knows what punishment for our love for one another. Yet still you cling to your affection for him."

"He's given me everything I have. All of my hatred of him comes from his ill use of you. His possession of you."

"You can't have it both ways, Dorian. He's one person."

Dorian stepped under Senné's neck. She should have backed away and put space between them, but at this juncture there seemed little point. "To you he is. To me he's like different members of an extended family. The man who holds the woman I love when I should be holding her. Who hurts her"—he choked on the words—"in the vilest ways. But he's also a boy I taught to fence and a man with whom I've shared more laughter than I can remember. He's the heir of Caleb Desmarais. He's my future king."

Eleanor crossed her arms over her chest and hung her head.

"He does love you, Eleanor. The truth has come home, and we have no choice but to let it in." He took her hand. "I envy your certainty, but please, don't begrudge me my confusion."

She listened to the muttering of the barn doves and several long breaths on Senné's part before speaking. She touched his cheek. "You always show me the other side of any argument, and I'll not deny my own dishonesty. For years I carried it with me, like a bag of rotten fruit, but I had to set it down to keep going. Too much has happened between Gregory and me. But whatever you feel is yours. The three of us—wrongs—rights—bright rainbows and dark mud."

"Lord Brandling?"

Eleanor jumped at the sound of Orvid Jones' voice. "Jones…good morning."

Jones didn't smile, or acknowledge Eleanor's presence. "Prince

Gregory asks that you retire to your chamber, Your Grace, until he sees fit to call on you."

The hint of color that had returned to Dorian's cheeks bled away again, but he bowed. "Certainly. As soon as I've finished with Senne′—"

"Now, Your Grace."

"Is something wrong?" Eleanor asked.

Jones turned mild brown eyes on her. "What could possibly be wrong?"

Eleanor's panic led to babbling. "I found some books—on war craft—perhaps we could look at them together—"

"You, too, are to retire to your chamber. I'm surprised to see you here, since that message was already delivered today." The whites of Jones's eyes darkened to creamy yellow. "It will be a long time before I hasten to your side again, Your Highness. For I do not tolerate disloyalty to my prince, even in those I assumed to be the truest of friends."

"I'll go now, Jones," said Dorian. He turned his back on the magician and looked at Eleanor with desperate eyes. "Peace, lady."

She had to swallow three times before she could return his sentiments. Her hand darted out, of its own accord, and brushed his spectite ring. "Peace, my lord."

Dorian did not leave his chamber for two days, and Gregory joined him in seclusion. Eleanor couldn't eat. She couldn't sleep. Ticia didn't visit. She received one message from Gregory, telling her to attend Sunday evening chapel. She simultaneously hoped to see him and dreaded it. She knew one look at his face would tell her everything.

He was not waiting for her in the carriage, nor did he appear at Humility Chapel. She couldn't concentrate on the service. Chou repeatedly nipped her ear to elicit singing from her or remind her to stand with the rest of the congregation. After the service, her fellow worshippers asked after Afar Creek and the search for Ezra Oliver, but she demurred and hastened in the direction of her carriage. She stepped over the chapel's threshold, only to have her senses assaulted by bright sunlight, the smell of too many flowers, and the shouts of hundreds of gathered townsfolk. They tossed blossoms at her and called out her name. Two Unicorn Guards paced the cobblestones at the foot of the stairs. The unicorns snorted at the crowd. Their riders kept up a steady volley of "Keep back! No nonsense!"

Eleanor froze. She blinked at the happy mob.

"It appears they have forgiven you your past transgressions," said Chou. "Well…go appease your admirers." He took off from her shoulder as she walked down the steps. She clasped hands and accepted flowers until the pile grew unmanageable. She handed the blooms to a soldier and started a new mound. She tried to respond to her subjects' shouted sentiments.

"Thank you—I—"

"Brave princess! A credit to His Highness—"

"Ezra Oliver is gone once more—praises!"

"Well—he's not really gone—we just don't know where he—"

"Will you return to the Fringe, Princess? The children need to see your lovely face—"

"Of course, as soon as I can—"

Chou landed on her shoulder again. Eleanor backed away from the people to prevent anyone from losing an eye to a spiky red feather. "Eleanor, over there—someone wants to speak to you—"

"I'm coming, Chou—there are so many—"

"No, you must come now—it's Jan!"

Eleanor turned in the direction of his outstretched neck. A flash of red at the collar of a dark floor-length cloak caught her eye. Jan stood on the edges of the crowd, near the Covey gate. "Tell her to meet me in the Chapel," Eleanor said to Chou.

He flew off, and Eleanor turned to the lieutenant in charge of her escort. "I've forgotten something." She ran up the chapel steps before he could offer to retrieve it for her.

Anger burned behind her eyes as she approached the hooded figure at the foot of the altar. She didn't stop until she saw Jan's chest rising and falling under her cloak. "How dare you come to me," Eleanor said.

Jan pushed her hood away from her face. "Pandra told me Lord Brandling has been confined—"

"How did you know about that?"

Chou landed on Eleanor's head and cleared his throat. "I, uh—went to see Pandra. Last night."

Eleanor reached up and grabbed him. He belched a squawk.

"If Gregory finds you flying about," she cried, "you'll be tomorrow's lunch!"

"I hoped to garner more information. Find something of use."

"Chou Chou is safe, Your Highness. His Highness hasn't been to the Hussy in a week."

Eleanor squeezed Chou, as if Jan might try to snatch him away. "He visited a week ago? Is that when you told him?"

"I never told him anything! I swear it!"

"Stop lying to me!" Eleanor said. "I know you told him about—what you saw at Laralee!"

"I don't know what you're talking about!"

Eleanor laughed. "We heard you! The door, shutting—we heard it!"

Jan's brow wrinkled and two tears spilled over her eyelids. They made dark tracks in her white face paint. "I swear—what door? Your Highness—what do you think I saw?"

"Dorian and I—together—after Nathan's death—"

Jan put her hands over her mouth and blushed a brilliant red under her makeup. "I never—oh, dear HighGod. If someone saw you two in a—an improper way—it wasn't me."

Something in the shock and embarrassment on Jan's face told Eleanor the girl was telling the truth. "You haven't been dropping hints to Gregory when he visited the Hussy? Or—or maybe met with Sylvia Fleetwood?"

"Prince Gregory don't see me when he comes. He always asks after the blonde girls. And I've never talked to the Duchess, Your Highness. She'd not stoop so low, I don't think."

Eleanor sat heavily on the first bench. "I thought for sure...if it wasn't you." She turned to Chou. "Who?"

"A servant? They were all Gregory's people," said Chou.

"Maybe it doesn't even matter." Eleanor rested her forehead on one hand.

Jan tentatively touched her skirt. "I'm sorry, Your—Eleanor." Eleanor closed her eyes as Jan continued. "I was so jealous of you—with your two handsome men and your castle. But now...I wouldn't be you for all the gold in the world."

CHAPTER 33

OTHER HEARTACHES

ON MONDAY MORNING GREGORY requested Dorian's presence in his study at nine o'clock. Dorian arrived at half past eight with the assumption of waiting on Gregory, but Melfin let him in directly. He found Gregory seated at the card table before the fireplace. He'd turned it into a desk of sorts in the past few years, as his responsibilities increased and his card-playing time did the opposite.

Melfin announced Dorian, but Gregory didn't look away from the fireplace. He didn't move, a stone prince carved into a plush armchair. Dorian took a matching chair beside him. He turned his own eyes to the fire. A thousand memories pressed in around them as a wordless half-hour ticked by. The fire shrank and began to sputter. Gregory did not call for Melfin, or make a move to stoke it himself.

"Unburden yourself," Dorian finally said.

"I didn't give you permission to speak."

"I've never needed it before."

"No. We have a long history of familiarity."

"A privilege I recognize."

"Fuck you!" Gregory exploded out of the chair, surprising even Dorian. "You treacherous, lying motherfucker!"

Dorian watched Gregory's mottled face and bloodshot eyes as he raged before the fire. "You've been fucking my wife—you—my best friend! After everything I've done for you!"

"Gregory—"

"Don't give me your fucking denials! You were seen. The two of you. Her astride you like a—" Gregory gasped for air. "—well-trained whore—" A maniacal giggle escaped him. "She always did like it that way—fucking bitch—"

Dorian stood. "This is about you and me. Leave her out of it."

"Defending her again, are you?" Gregory attacked his hair with both hands. "It's been there—in front of my face. Sylvia was right—but I didn't believe her—I couldn't. All this time—how long?"

"It started her first summer in Solsea. But it was there, before that. It's always been there."

Gregory sat in his chair. "I've been that stupid...for ten years?"

Dorian pressed his fingers to his eyes. "Gregory—I can say I'm sorry ad nauseum. I would take your pain from you a thousand times. But I'm not sorry for loving her. It's the only good thing in my hypocritical, deceitful existence."

"How can you say that to me? I made you a duke. I gave you a unicorn. You have riches and a beautiful home and the respect of everyone in my kingdom. My father loves you like a second son."

"And I will always be grateful. But I would give it all back to you, even Senné, for a life with her. I'm telling you the truth. Finally, after all these years. I pray you go easier on her, for she's the mother of your children, but do with me what you will. I'll not argue with you, or try to convince you otherwise. I know the penalty I deserve."

More quiet minutes crawled by. Gregory's nostrils began twitching, and he tapped one boot on the purple rug. "You should be drawn and quartered."

Dorian's stomach clenched, but he said, "You're my prince. It will be as you wish it."

"You should visit the dungeonmaster first. He can determine if you've been lying to me about anything else."

Dorian nodded. He spun his spectite ring around his shaking finger. *I'll be able to call to her.* The thought comforted him until her remembered she'd lost her choker.

"She's all you want, is she?" Gregory said, in a thoughtful tone. "Riches...unicorns...they mean nothing?"

Dorian stiffened. The hairs on his arms stood on end. A frightening smile played at the corners of Gregory's mouth. He leaned in close, his voice a hissing whisper. "I know you. If I kill you, I've let you off easy. No. Everything will be as it has been. But she's still mine. She's mine as much as the clothes on your back, and that big house in the Crossing, and that black beast you ride."

Gregory spoke through barred teeth. "I'll not go easy on her. I'll do with her what I please. Morning, noon, and night if I choose. Every night, you'll watch me take her to my room and know I'm inside her and she's screaming and crying and begging for mercy but you won't be able to do a fucking thing about it. If I see you talking to her, I'll kill her. You'll be watched, all the time, and if anyone else sees you talking to her, I'll kill her."

Dorian exhaled, and realized he hadn't drawn breath since Gregory started talking. Red lights flashed in front of his eyes.

"You'd do better not to deceive one who knows you so well, Lord Brandling. Those who know you, know best how to punish you. You'll be my man. Mine, as you always have been. You're both mine, to do with as I choose. I choose to let you live, and let you suffer."

The floor pitched as Dorian left Gregory's study. He opened one of the double doors, stepped into Gregory's bedroom, and leaned against the closed door.

Gregory's sentence ran word for word in his head like a terrible hymn. His hand clenched at one of the Fire-iron doorknobs, as if he was searching for purchase on the edge of a cliff. The knob was slick with his terrified sweat. *I'll not go easy on her...inside her...screaming and crying and begging for mercy...*and the last. *I'll kill her.*

Those three words were a mental smack that woke him from his fear-induced daze. As he let go of the slippery knob he heard something from the study. He peered through the crack between the two doors.

Gregory's head rested on the card table. He covered his face with his arms. His shoulders shook, and chuffing, gasping noises floated across the empty air to Dorian on the other side of the door. Dorian caught a few muttered words. "Please...no..." and "Ah...HighGod...why...why."

"Lord Brandling?"

Dorian whirled around. Melfin waited to escort him from the Prince's presence. Dorian wiped his face with his handkerchief as he fled into the hallway. His spectite ring slipped off his sweaty finger and hit the marble floor with a *ching-cha-ching!*

Dorian lunged after it, both hands on the ground, like a little boy after a loose marble. He'd nearly caught it when it struck a pair of polished brown boots.

"Dorian, stand up. How undignified."

Dorian straightened and looked into his brother's miffed face. He replaced the ring and started to walk around Abram. "Excuse me—" Dorian paused. "What are you doing?"

"His Highness asked me to bring him the mayor's report on tax revenue in the Lake District." Abram swelled with is own importance.

"I'd come back. I've just seen him, and he's in no mood for visitors."

"You've seen him?" A stack of papers shifted in Abram's arms. A few white sheets escaped his grasp and floated to the floor in lazy sweeps, like petals from a wilting flower.

"Yes. Just now."

"Oh—ah—oh."

"I don't think I'll be at dinner. I'm not feeling well, if anyone asks."

"Of course. I'm sure you have many things on your mind...but don't...don't worry about Anne Clara, Dorian. Or Laralee."

"I'm not."

"It's just—well, you know I'll take care of everything. Back home."

"Of course, Abram." Dorian walked three steps, and then stopped. He faced his brother again. "You'll take care of everything."

Abram nodded.

"If I'm gone, you mean?"

Abram's face paled. "Not that you're going anywhere—"

Dorian grabbed him by the shoulders. "Should I be going somewhere? To scaffold, perhaps?"

"Dorian—I don't know—"

"It was you. You saw us at Laralee. You told him." Dorian's frenzied whispering threw spit in Abram's face. "What did he promise you? To betray your own brother?"

Abram's eyes bulged, and his nose almost touched Dorian's. Anyone passing by might have mistaken them for two lovers locks in a passionate embrace. "Don't take the high and mighty road with me! You're the one who sinned! When I saw you—taking her like a proper husband—you're the one committing treason with the prince's—"

Dorian clapped a hand over Abram's mouth. "Don't you dare say it. Never again, or so help me HighGod I'll cut out your tongue with our father's knife."

Abram's head thrashed and Dorian let go. "You've always gotten whatever you wanted," Abram said. "From the time we were children. You thought you could have riches and the prince's love and fame and even the princess, but you can't. I won't let you. Soon you'll be dead, and I'll be living at Laralee in your place."

Dorian shook his head. "Do you hate me so much?"

Abram answered with his silence.

"He's not going to kill me, Abram. He says he wants to torture me. I'm sure he does, but I know him as well as he knows me. HighGod knows I'll pay for my pride, but he's just as guilty of that sin. He doesn't want anyone to know about this. The shame would be too much."

Abram's left eye twitched, and Dorian saw the beginnings of grim comprehension. "If you know, you're in more danger than I am. I'd hold your tongue from now on."

Dorian stepped away and bowed. "Good day to you, Brother."

"Close the door."

Eleanor did as Gregory asked. She walked across the blank expanse of the king's receiving room, toward her husband seated on his Fire-iron throne. Dark-eyed, redheaded men stared down at her from the oil paintings covering the walls. Desmarais kings from Caleb to Casper. Someday Gregory would join them, as Nathan would have, had HighGod been more merciful.

The room seemed to stretch away from her, as if her footfalls took her farther from Gregory rather than bringing them together. She only stopped because her foot struck the edge of the green and gold rug under his throne. Her gaze traveled from his polished black boots to his powerful legs in their black silk leggings. He rested his elbows on the armrests. The Fire-iron reflected the intricate jewelwork on the sleeves of his purple tunic. Tiny rainbows danced off the marble floor below him. In King Casper's absence, Gregory was larger. More imposing. More like his ancestors on the wall behind her.

"I've met with Lord Brandling," he said. "All is revealed."

"I see," she said.

"You are concerned for our daughter, are you not?"

"Always."

"So you say, yet you could not have been thinking on her security while engaged in"—his voice caught—"the actions which have recently come to my attention."

"On the contrary. Her safety was paramount in my mind."

"Your greatest fear should have been your husband's retribution." He laughed. "It's my fault. I've let you run wild. You're only a woman, after all, with a woman's weaknesses."

Eleanor didn't respond.

"I've spoiled you." He stood and walked toward her. She folded her hands behind her back and looked at the floor. He stopped just out of striking range. "Am I not speaking the truth? Say something! You're never short on commentary."

He slammed his first into his hand. "Beg me for forgiveness! Or tell me I'm a terrible ass! But don't just stand there."

"There's nothing to say. I'll not rehash years of ills against me. You know them. Just as you now know my sins against you."

He crept closer, and the redness of his eyes came into stark relief. His voice cracked. "Of all the men in my kingdom, why him?"

"Oh, Gregory. You don't have to ask that question." Her heart had crept up into her throat, and she spoke haltingly around it. "It could have been only him. No one else."

Gregory swiped his hands over his eyes on the way to his hair. He turned away from her and walked to his father's throne. He rested one boot on the seat cushion and one elbow on his knee.

She waited, unsure of how to respond. For all she knew Dorian was already in the hands of the Dungeonmaster. She drove her fingernails into her palms at the thought.

Gregory straightened. His face resettled into its regal mask. To her surprise he took her hand. "It's my duty as your husband to bring you back into line. If you have not the strength to resist temptation, I'll do it for you."

"Gregory—"

"You're my wife, Eleanor. HighGod joined us, and nothing can change it. Anything that comes between us will be permanently removed. For the safety of your virtue."

He put a hand on the spot where her shoulder met her neck and squeezed. "If you refuse to forget him, if your memory will not obey me, I will have to distract you with other heartaches."

"What will you do to him?" she whispered.

Gregory changed the subject. "I think it's time Leticia saw a bit of the countryside, don't you?"

"She's been to the Lake District."

"Harveston is lovely in the springtime. The Duchess has offered to host her at Buckhill. She'll be a fine playmate for little John-Caleb. It will encourage her maternal nature."

Eleanor couldn't breathe.

"We'll have plenty of time to ourselves. To sort all this out. Hopefully we'll see her in Solsea." He led her to his father's throne. He placed one of her hands on each armrest and stood behind her. She felt him rustling her skirts.

"I've always wanted to do this," he whispered in her ear. He wrapped one arm around her waist and lifted her petticoats with his free hand. He pressed against her, and her suddenly bare knees banged off the cold Fire-iron. "In this room. It's exciting isn't it?"

When she didn't respond he transferred his arms to her neck and his pelvis hit her bottom, hard.

"Yes, exciting," she said.

Poking, prying, between her legs. She bit her lip until she tasted blood. Tears fell onto the embroidered *D* on the purple cushion below her face.

And so they were reunited, in Gregory's mind, anyway. Hers was far away, in a cave on the side of a cliff...and then in a granary. Green eyes, dark hair, a sparkling blue ring on a gentle hand.

CHAPTER 34

WHAT WE SHALL
MAKE OF IT

"...AND THEN THE CLOCK struck midnight. Bong! Bong! The girl ran from the prince. The hem of her lovely gown turned to rags around her feet, but her glass slippers gave her speed. She took the stairs like a bird in flight, light and graceful, but so swiftly did she flee that her tiny feet ran right out of her shoes. She reached the landing, and turned to see the prince pick up her

slipper—"

"Why don't they ever remember about how you fell down the stairs?" Ticia asked. She leaned across Eleanor's lap and pointed at the drawing in her book of fairytales. "And here—it shows you waving to Poppa with the slipper, but you told me you never saw him pick it up."

"It's true. I didn't have time to wave. I barely escaped, as it was, what with landing on my bottom and cutting my foot when the slipper cracked."

"Can I see it? The cracked slipper?"

Eleanor nodded, and Ticia retrieved the slipper from its place in Eleanor's music box. She sat in Eleanor's lap and cradled the shoe in her own. The colors swirled and shifted, like clouds before a thunderstorm, just as they had ten years ago on the night Rosemary conjured them and sent Eleanor off to the Second Sunday Ball. Flashes of color rose to meet Ticia's dancing fingertips.

"Tell me about Chou."

"Don't you want me to finish reading?"

Ticia shook her head. "Your version is more interesting."

Chou landed on the rug in front of Eleanor and Ticia and spread his wings. "I'll tell this part, thank you. Ahem, so...I stood in the court-yard—on two legs! And wearing pants! An odd feeling, I'll tell you. The damnable goats—the horses were goats, you remember. It drives me mad when the books bring mice into the equation—were arguing and dropping turdies all over the palace driveway"—Ticia covered her mouth and giggled—"and your mother, nowhere to be seen! What's a parrot disguised as a coachman to do? So I—"

"Leticia. How goes your packing?" Gregory closed the nursery door behind him. "The Duchess wants to leave this afternoon."

"Must I go, Poppa?" Ticia asked. Her voice trembled.

"We'll see you soon. Mother and I have much work to do. You'll find more diversion with the Duchess."

"She doesn't like me. Why does she want to take me with her?"

Her questioning was turning up the heat under Gregory's pot of patience. "Tish," said Eleanor, "have Pansy and Chou take you to the library. You'll need a book for the journey."

"Reading in the carriage makes me ill," said Ticia, but she obeyed. Chou landed on her head. Eleanor watched her go with burning eyes.

The door closed behind Ticia. Gregory held a black silk bag in his hand. She eyed both the man and the bag with suspicion. "Come. The light is better here."

She joined him at the window, and looked out over the same drive-way where goats in the guise of carriage hackneys had once driven Chou Chou to distraction. The courtyard bustled with its usual chaos. People yelling. Animals braying and squawking and lowing. Not a creature, man or woman or beast, was still, yet one figure stood out in the commotion. A tall man tightening the girth of a bay gelding.

Eleanor watched as Dorian moved around the horse. He lifted the animal's feet and ran his hands down its legs. He handed off a few bags to his valet and the man loaded them into a small but ornate traveling carriage. A dozen mounted soldiers milled around the coach.

Dorian straightened. He looked up at the nursery window, as if he could feel Eleanor's eyes upon him. She balled her hands into fists to keep from banging on the glass.

"Rosemary sent this," Gregory said. "The witches found it in the rubble." He took the dragon choker from the black bag. "Lift your hair."

She did so and he hooked the clasp. The choker settled into the hollow of her neck, its familiar weight cool against her skin. She touched the spectite. It glowed dark green, and then melted to purple. She squeezed it, and said a prayer of thanks.

"It's not even scratched," said Gregory. "You'll be glad to know the Oracle is well. The pool is dug out and restored."

"Praises," said Eleanor, and then in a whisper, "Where is he going?"

"He's escorting the rogue dragons, north to the Mines."

"On horseback?"

"I've retired Senne' to the stud barn. We need black unicorns for breeding." Gregory rested his hand on her shoulder. Eleanor wondered if Dorian could see him past the reflections and shadows. If he did he gave no indication. He watched the window, and spun his spectite ring on his finger. He touched his own throat, and Eleanor was suddenly sure he could see the necklace.

"He'll travel north past the Mines once the dragons are safely returned. Through the Scaled Mountains. Into Svelya."

"Svelya?"

"I've given Lord Brandling a great honor. He's to be our new Ambassador at the Svelyan Court, in Nestra. My father thinks we need to rebuild our alliances. He'll be our mason."

"I see," said Eleanor, trying to keep her voice as neutral as possible.

"He'll be gone for a few years, at least. If he performs well, he might just take up permanent

residence."

A small sound tried to escape the back of Eleanor's throat. She pounced on it before it could become a scream, like a cat landing on a quick mouse.

"Wave goodbye to him, sweetheart," said Gregory. "It's all right. Wave goodbye."

She lifted her hand. Dorian swept a low bow in return, mounted, and cantered through the palace gate with the soldiers and the carriage trailing behind him.

An hour later, on Outcountry Road, Dorian had added a small herd of unicorns and four irritable dragons to his retinue. Blondie puffed and blew at the weeds lining the drainage ditches. The scrubby plants went up like little birthday candles. Dorian pulled a dragon robe tighter around his shoulders and called out to one of the unicorns. "Arrow, that's a good lad. Try to keep him on the road."

He patted the neck of the bay gelding and the animal muttered his thanks. Dorian faced north, toward the Dragon Mines and Svelya, and breathed deep of the HighWinter air.

The truth.

He closed his eyes, but he could still see the sun in yellow flashes against black. It lit a memory in golden light. He folded his hand over his ring.

Gregory left Eleanor at the window ledge. Chou returned from the library and crouched on the cushion beside her.

"Rosemary delivered the necklace herself," he said. "Gregory wouldn't let her visit, but I heard her telling him about Hazelbeth's recovery. Apparently she's just as powerful and full of mystical brouhaha as ever. They both look forward to seeing you soon."

Eleanor toyed with the choker. "The king sends missionaries to find friends for Cartheigh, but we must fight our own enemies."

"Casper will support your part in the effort, but will Gregory? Perhaps…now that you have the people's love again."

She looked Chou in his bright yellow eyes. Something swelled inside her, and for the first time in months, it wasn't grief or fear. "I'm grateful for it, Chou. HighGod knows I am, but I'm going to carry on, whether Gregory or the people of Cartheigh like it or not."

"I'm here, of course, if you need extra brains."

"My daughter needs me." She squeezed the spectite. "Ezra Oliver must be stopped. I'm alive. Dorian is alive. He said the truth has come home. Let us see what we shall make of it."

She stood, and warmth coursed through her hand. She looked down. The dragon choker blazed crimson against her neck.

What happens next?
Turn the page to read the first chapters of the finale,

THE GLASS RAINBOW

CHAPTER 1

A LONG ROAD
AHEAD OF YOU

AFTER FOURTEEN YEARS, ELEANOR Brice Desmarais knew the passageways of Eclatant Palace like she knew the patterns of her own thoughts.
She took turns and stairs and ducked low-hanging tapestries without
pausing; an unusually tall, unusually blonde woman, with unusually
straight carriage. The servants were accustomed to the sight of Eleanor
rushing about the castle. They bowed and asked for her blessing, for
they'd long since overcome their fear of her mismatched eyes. Eleanor
had twice vanquished the most feared magician in the history of the
kingdom of Cartheigh. Her eyes— one robin's egg blue, one reddish
brown— could not possibly be as unlucky as everyone once thought.

Eleanor lifted the skirts of her ivory gown as she climbed the last
staircase on the way to King Casper Desmarais's receiving room. White
dress against white skin and the marble steps made her all but invisible,
until a flash of crimson besmirched the colorless tableau. A red parrot
dropped from the chandelier onto her head, a jaunty kite let loose from
a high wind. She tapped his scaly feet. "You'll ruin my coiffure, Chou."

"I've never liked you in braids, anyway." Chou flapped about on her head. His wings were like a matched set of elegant feathered fans, the sort the older ladies carried to chapel on hot summer days.

"Thank you for the breeze. It *is* warm for LowAutumn."

"Don't bore me with talk of the weather. I want to know why his majesty wants to see you."

"If you couldn't find out, no one can. We'll know soon enough."

Chou left Eleanor's head as they approached the Fire-iron door to the receiving room. She picked a stray red feather from her hair and shook out her skirts. Chou landed on a suit of armor. "I shall stand guard, my lady." He tucked his beak under his wing and promptly went to sleep.

Eleanor's nerves did a jig in her stomach as she waited before the door. Colors swirled under its silvery surface, barely perceptible, like a whispered riddle. She panicked whenever the king formally requested her presence. The same refrain rang through her head, an overused chorus in a bad opera.

He knows. He knows. He knows.

For over four years the secret had held, but she could not be sure of its safety. She never knew when, or how, King Casper would discover that Prince Gregory's wife, the mother of his grandchildren, had conducted a ten-year-long affair with his son's dearest friend.

The door opened and Orvid Jones, the Chief Magician, announced Eleanor's arrival. No camaraderie touched Orvid's brown eyes, nor did he show his buckteeth in the flash of a smile. He'd treated Eleanor with all the warmth of a snuffed candle since he learned the truth about her relationship with Dorian Finley, Duke of Brandling. She had long since given up trying to make amends.

Eleanor crossed the room and stopped before her father-in-law. Casper sat on his Fire-iron throne, a stout man with thick auburn hair that was finally going gray, like clouds giving in to sunset.

"Eleanor, good day," said Casper, as she curtsied. "Gregory, offer your wife a glass of wine."

Eleanor turned to the refreshment table. She'd been so focused on the king, she'd not noticed her husband skulking in the corner. His lack of welcome was unsurprising. Husband and wife rarely spoke, except during public appearances. They didn't say much in the nursery, or at meals. They were even silent on the frequent, unfortunate occasions when Gregory visited Eleanor's bedchamber and attempted to plant a male heir in her belly.

"Eleanor doesn't drink wine before dinner. Do you, sweetheart?" Gregory took a seat in his own Fire-iron throne beside Casper. Both men crossed their ankles and rested their elbows on the armrests. They so resembled one another, aside from a few layers of fat, a mustache, and Casper's graying hair, that Eleanor might have been looking into a distorted mirror.

"Correct, husband. I like a clear head when I'm managing the children's affairs."

"It is certainly wise to be alert to all affairs."

Thankfully, the innuendo floated over King Casper's head. "Speaking of the children," the king said, "I have some news. About Leticia."

"She's to be wed," said Gregory, before Eleanor could open her mouth.

At first the comment didn't register. "Who's to be wed?"

"Leticia."

Eleanor shook her head. "She's twelve years old."

"The Duke of Brandling has had great success repairing relations with the Svelyans," said the king. "Not that I doubted he would."

"Dorian has always been a charmer, as we all know," said Gregory.

Oh, Gregory, how clever you think you are, with your veiled insinuations. Under other circumstances, Eleanor may have thrown a reciprocal double *entendre* his way. Something so subtle as to be beyond his recognition, for safety's sake. Not enough to stoke the dragon's fire, but sufficient to soothe her own smoldering pride. In this critical moment, with both men's judgment and authority bearing down on her, she only had conversational space to fight for her daughter.

"He convinced King Mangolin to consider my daughter as a bride for his son, Crown Prince Samuel."

"Gregory, you can't be serious. Leticia? Married to the Svelyan prince? Dorian loves Ticia, he would never—"

She stopped herself, and shut her teeth around her opinion. In their unspoken agreement to avoid one another as much as a royal couple feasibly could, they eschewed the subject of Dorian above all others. Before today, Gregory hadn't so much as spoken his name to her in years. Sweat beaded on her forehead. For Dorian's sake, she must not goad Gregory with reminders of their former familiarity.

"They honor Ticia with their consideration," said Gregory. "Samuel will someday be the second most powerful king in the known nations. She'd do well to be his wife."

Eleanor pictured Leticia, her sunshine child, trapped in a drafty Svelyan Castle. Locked in a gray mist, beyond the Dragon Mines. A hundred miles of jagged mountains between Ticia and her family, a barely passable field of battleaxes turned sharp side up. Married to a Svelyan lord she didn't know, surrounded by a language she would not understand.

"She's *twelve*, husband." Eleanor clung to the rational. "A child, not a wife."

"High time we settle on plans for her," said Gregory. "I'm heading north in four days. King Peter has invited me to visit. Meet his son. Tour the kingdom. A gesture of friendship unthinkable five years ago."

"Is it safe?" Eleanor asked. Casper always hesitated to send his only son and heir into danger.

"A battalion of the Unicorn Guard will escort Gregory," the king said, "and our finest magicians. Orvid Jones himself will accompany him. This is a mission of goodwill. Leticia's betrothal will help secure an alliance with our old enemies."

The room sunk into silence. Both men watched Eleanor, as if they knew what was coming. She tried to hold her tongue, HighGod knew she did, but it slipped from her grasp like a slippery fish.

"Please, Your Majesty. Ticia is too young to be married. And sent away—to Svelya? She'll be so frightened—and we don't even know this Svelyan prince. What if he's cruel, or stupid, or a drunkard—" The Svelyan prince took shape in Eleanor's mind. A hulking blonde man with squinty eyes, bad breath, and heavy hands. "Please. Don't do this. Your own granddaughter—and the next heir—"

"Leticia is not my heir," said Gregory. "As of this moment, I have no heir."

The king laced his hands over his belly. "Leticia's importance to the crown lies in her marriage. As for an heir, you produced a son once. You can do it again, with prayer and effort."

Eleanor was too distraught to be mortified by the king's reference to carnality. "You can't. It's not right. She's *my* daughter!"

Eleanor's words tinkled off the Fire-iron chandelier over their heads. Casper rubbed his mustache, and stood. Eleanor dropped a curtsy as he approached. She expected a reprimand, but his voice was soft, as if addressing a babe himself. "Do you think I have no care for my own granddaughter?"

"I cannot imagine, sire, that if you did you would send her away."

Eleanor stared at the king's belt. The Fire-iron *D* embossed on the buckle rose and fell with his labored breathing.

"Go with Gregory," he said.

"Sire?"

"Go to Svelya. Meet with the prince. Report your estimation of him to me. I will take it into consideration in my final decision."

Eleanor rose. "Oh, Your Majesty, thank—"

"I'd not planned on her coming along," said Gregory, as he stood. "I've decided."

Gregory raked a hand through his hair. "Father, I don't want to take her."

"I won't be any trouble on the journey, Gregory," Eleanor said. "I promise."

"I'm sure Dorian will be pleased to see you both after four years," said Casper. "Now, you're dismissed. Go prepare. You have a long road ahead of you."

"Must you go?"

"Yes, darling," Eleanor said to Leticia. "Your father needs me."

"No, he doesn't." Ticia shook her head so adamantly that her auburn plaits slapped her cheeks. "He'll have Vigor and the rest of the unicorns and Orvid Jones. He'll see Uncle Dorian. We need you. Natalie and I."

"You must take care of Natalie for me. You're the older sister."

Natalie danced around Eleanor's skirts, grabbing for her mother's waist. Eleanor picked her up. "Heavens, love," she said as she kissed Natalie's silky hair. "You're getting so big. I shan't be able to pick you up much longer."

Natalie grinned and gently bopped Eleanor's nose. "Mama, you should stay," she said.

"I won't be gone long, sweetheart. I'll be back before you miss me." She set Natalie on the ground. She wrapped her skinny arms around Ticia's waist, and Ticia kissed the top of her head. For a precious moment, Eleanor marveled at her daughters' beauty. Ticia with her dark red hair and reddish-brown eyes, even features, and long, slim form. As for Natalie, from portraits, Eleanor knew her to be the spitting image of her aunt, the Princess Matilda, who had died in childbirth before Eleanor came to Eclatant. Matilda's beauty was legendary: strawberry blonde hair, large greenish-hazel eyes, and a smile that could light up a dark room in the heart of MidWinter. Natalie even had a dusting of light freckles over her nose, just like her aunt. Like Eleanor and Ticia, she was tall for her age, and slender.

Despite being quite familiar with the signs of human reproduction, Eleanor hadn't recognized them during the anxious chaos proceeding Dorian's expulsion from Eclatant. Low and behold, Natalie entered the world only seven months after he went north, a welcome blessing in those long months of acute mourning. She continued to surprise and delight Eleanor every day. At three and a half years old, she could already read simple words, and write her name. She spent hours pouring over storybooks. In that vein, she reminded Eleanor of her poor son, Nathan, gone five years now. Nathan, however, was a serious and somewhat reserved child, while Natalie charmed everyone. Like Ticia, and truth be told, like her father. While Eleanor adored her children equally, she sometimes thought little Natalie inherited the best of her parents.

"You're coming back tomorrow, mama?" Natalie asked.

"Not tomorrow."

"The next day?"

"Not the next day, either." Eleanor sighed. Natalie always understood more than she should. Her mother would find no respite from guilt in the child's obliviousness. Eleanor offered her a stuffed unicorn. She cringed at the thought of how Natalie would grow during her absence, but not as much as she cringed at the thought of Ticia married to an unknown Svelyan.

As usual, Ticia would not be deterred. "I still don't understand why you have to go—"

"I told you. Poppa needs me." Eleanor felt no need to inform Ticia of her potential matrimonial fate.

"—and why you must take Chou Chou!" Tears filled Ticia's eyes.

"Darling, Chou and I have been together since I was Natalie's age. Younger, even. He'll never let me go without him."

The wooden nursery doors opened, and Gregory strode into the room. Ticia ran to him. She pelted him with questions about the journey, but he steered her in the direction of her easel. Like most children, she was distracted by an opportunity to impress her father.

"It's very good, sweetheart." Gregory ran a finger along Ticia's portrait of her unicorn, Cricket. "Try a darker gray around the muscles in Cricket's haunches. Think of the shadows."

Ticia's brow furrowed. She took up her charcoal pencil and a smudging rag. "Shadows..." she whispered, and set about following her poppa's advice.

With Ticia occupied, Natalie dropped her toy unicorn and jumped into her father's arms. "And you, little one. Or—" He lifted Natalie above his head. She squealed in delight. "—maybe not so little. Perhaps Pansy feeds you too many sweetmeats."

"She's perfectly healthy," said Eleanor.

Gregory laughed. "Of course she is. She'll be as graceful as Ticia, and my darling Matilda. Not like me as a child. So round! In those portraits in father's study I look as if you could roll me down the hall. Do you need help with your packing?"

Gregory's chatty mood and solicitousness unnerved her, in light of his usual abject distaste for company. Eleanor kept her own tone light and pleasant for the girls' sake, but she watched him out of the corner of her eye as she folded a blanket. "I'm nearly ready. Since we're going on unicornback, there's not much to be done."

"I've written to King Mangolin. He shall have his finest seamstress at your disposal when we arrive. Your new gowns will be the height of Svelyan fashion."

"Thank you. And thank you for allowing me to accompany you."

Gregory set Natalie in front of her dollhouse, where she started a lively conversation with the figurines. He walked to Eleanor and took her hands. His whispery voice was as smooth as a ream of the Svelyan silk he'd promised her, but his gripping fingers cut into hers like blunt sewing shears. "That was the king's decision, not mine. Just know that if I catch wind of any impropriety, I'll cut off his manhood and serve it to the dragons on a Fire-iron platter."

And with that he was gone. Eleanor sat on the edge of Ticia's bed. There was little question as to who's manhood risked removal from his person. The sun slid behind a cloud, and Eleanor's shadow faded on the woven rug below her skirts. Her trembling fingers danced over the Fire-iron and diamond chain around her neck. She touched the dragon choker's center stone. Even if she raised the memory in her mind, the one that magically united the dragon choker with Dorian's ring, the distance between Eclatant and Svelya had proved too far for the Rosemary's spell. She could not make his ring glow with comforting blue fire. He would not feel her heartfelt attempt to remind him she was still here, and she still loved him. Regardless, she thought of the broom closet anyway, as she often did. When the red stone warmed her chest, the room didn't seem so cold.

The day of Eleanor and Gregory's departure dawned gray and drizzly, as if HighGod were preparing them for the North Country weather. Eclatant's formal courtyard spread out before Eleanor, in all its imposing glorification of the Desmarais family and the Great Bond. A thousand purple and green banners flapping in the wet breeze gave the impression of so much polite applause, and the rose bushes clung stubbornly to their blossoms, as if dropping a petal would be sacrilege. Eleanor stood next to her unicorn, Teardrop, beside the larger than life statue of Caleb Desmarais. The first Desmarais king peered down at his descendants and their subjects from the back of his own stone unicorn, the great stallion Eclatant. Both man and mount wore expressions of benevolent tolerance. Eternal patience with those to whom they'd handed their collective legacy three hundred years ago.

Eleanor tucked her hair into her cloak. She inhaled the scents of wet livestock and baking bread. Chou yawned in her ear. "Always so early with these northern voyages. The sun is barely awake. The chickens are peaceful in their coop."

"Look a long journey in the face, as the witches say." Eleanor kissed Teardrop's silky muzzle. The mare snuffled her neck. Her ears pricked and her white lashes blinked over her liquid eyes like the wings of excited dragonflies. She shifted her mighty haunches, and Eleanor felt anticipation flowing beneath her ivory hide. "Not quite time to go, dearest. We're to have a formal send away."

"The air is so clean in the North," Teardrop said in her breezy voice. "I remember the taste. Like water from a deep spring. And the smell of the dragons. Burning rocks."

Chou landed between Teardrop's ears and nibbled on her forelock. "Do you remember so well the smell of Giant Buzzards, carried on a cold wind?"

"Hush, Chou," said Eleanor as she hauled herself into the saddle. "We'll not have you complaining."

Chou whistled. "Sarcasm is complaining at its highest form. A sign of intelligence."

Eleanor laughed and patted Teardrop's twitching neck. Eleanor had not been to the North Country in over thirteen years, and she'd never left Cartheigh in her thirty-two years of life. Despite agonizing over leaving her girls, she shared Teardrop's excitement. Her own eagerness, however, went beyond a long ride, clean air, and a herd of dragons.

She had not seen nor heard from Dorian since he quietly left Eclatant to serve as the king's ambassador to Svelya. She often wondered if she'd ever lay eyes on him again. The crushing grief over his absence had become part of her persona, as much as the birthmark in her left eye or her tendency to break into a sweat under duress. It sat, deep in her chest, through parties and chapel services. It was there during Ticia's lessons and on evenings when she rocked Natalie to sleep. Between his loss, and the deaths of Nathan and her oldest friend, Margaret Easton

Delano, sadness was Eleanor's constant companion. She pictured it as a black cat with pale green eyes, purring along with her own heartbeat.

"Fare thee well, my darling girl!"

Rosemary's voice rang across the cobblestones. The witch clipped toward Teardrop on feathery legs, with no hint of her one hundred years of life her easy stride. Eleanor smiled at her teacher. "Abbottess, you didn't need to make the journey from Afar Creek to see us off."

"The Abbey will carry on for a few hours without me." Rosemary looked up at Eleanor with dancing dark eyes. "How long in coming, this journey."

Eleanor squeezed Rosemary's hand. The witch was, other than Chou Chou, her oldest companion. Rosemary had schooled Eleanor in secret through her years of imprisonment in her father's house. Eleanor clung to Rosemary's letters and lessons, slivers of hope under the harsh rule of her stepmother, Imogene Brice. Fourteen years ago, when Imogene refused to allow Eleanor to attend the Second Sunday Ball, Rosemary conjured Eleanor's romantic notions into existence with a lovely gown and a pair of glass slippers. When the dream fell apart, shattered by the twin realities of her dismal marriage and a passionate, forbidden love, Rosemary kept Eleanor and Dorian's secret for ten years. No one had shaped Eleanor's life like the Abbottess of Afar Creek Abbey.

Rosemary squeezed back. "Promise me you will take care." The witch glanced at Gregory, mounted on his white stallion, Vigor. "There will be many eyes upon you."

"I hear you well," said Eleanor. "The girls will have their regular tutors from the Abbey, of course, but perhaps you can find time to visit?"

"Of course. Leticia and I will write to you. Soon Natalie will be writing her own letters."

"Help Leticia with her penmanship. I fear the artist in her makes for sloppy correspondence. And don't let her play with the cracked slipper. She likes to show it to Natalie." Eleanor's heart hurt. "I will miss them so. Perhaps I should have woken them."

"No, let them sleep. I will personally see to them this morning. Ah, here is the Godsman." Rosemary's brows lifted. "That one isn't much more than a child himself."

A young man in brown robes joined King Casper beside the statue of Caleb Desmarais. He looked to be less than twenty years old, slim and slight. Eleanor only took such measure of him because he so clashed with her memory of Marcus, the Godsman who'd turned traitor five years ago. She couldn't help but compare the young man's nervous piety to Marcus's hulking arrogance.

He wasn't always such, she thought. *He was a good man, until Ezra Oliver twisted him about. Marcus helped us as well as he could, in the end, and lost his life for it.* Anger simmered between her ears. *Damn Oliver. Murdering, manipulative disgrace to magic.*

The king said a few words about the growing friendship between Cartheigh and Svelya. His secretary scribbled the speech on a piece of parchment. The next few days would find printing press copies of the king's good intent spread over the capital city of Maliana and beyond. Casper turned to the young Godsman. "I ask for the blessings of HighGod on my son, his wife, and their party."

The young man cleared his throat. His voice was high, but louder than Eleanor imagined it would be.

"HighGod, we ask that you protect His Highness, Crown Prince Gregory Desmarais, on the long road ahead. In him, you've entrusted the power of the Great Bond. The mystical gift to Cartheigh. The intertwining of unicorn, dragon, and the Desmarais family. As he travels North, he will venture into the heart of the Bond itself, the Dragon Mines. From whence flows all the wealth and peace you've bestowed upon this kingdom for three centuries. Like the Fire-iron that the dragons create with their breath, like the numinous calm that exists in the touch of horn on scale, like the undying love between prince and king and these most noble steeds, all elements of the Great Bond are connected. We pray that you will watch over Gregory, the keeper of this gift, and aid him in his quest to continue the work of Lord Brandling, far across the Scaled Mountains. May the friendship between Cartheigh and Svelya become a bond in itself, for the mutual benefit of both nations."

Eleanor watched Gregory throughout the Godsman's speech, and despite her bitterness toward him, she saw him as he appeared to everyone else in the courtyard. A powerful man of thirty-five with a ramrod back, a broad chest, and a chin like a sawed-off tree trunk. The light rain darkened his red hair to brown. It clung to his neck, and only accentuated the strength in his shoulders. He held his head high throughout the young man's prayer. When the Godsman finished, he offered this, with a simple elegance: "You do me honor, and you honor the Bond. Might that I am worthy of HighGod's protection, and the privilege of my station."

Eleanor knew Gregory at his worst. His most drunken and childish, slovenly and vindictive. But even she couldn't deny that there was a great king inside him somewhere.

CHAPTER 2

GREAT CHAINS SET IN MOTION

THE EXPEDITION PUSHED NORTHWARD for two days. Villages on the outskirts of Maliana gave way to country estates. As the land coarsened the settlements became fewer and farther between, until only a few secluded farmhouses dotted the greenish gray landscape. The Clarity River shrunk to a glorified creek. Hunched hills straightened into the beginnings of the Scaled Mountains. Eventually, signs of human habitation disappeared. Eleanor hoped for a sight of the wild unicorns that lived in the marshes south of the Mines, but they encountered only hawks and wild donkeys. Eleanor's fingers went numb in her riding gloves. The wind kept up a constant whistle in her ears and brought with it a progression of smells and sounds like a sensory map of the voyage: lowing cows, rank peat moss, and finally, the acrid smell of Fire-iron dust.

They passed through the tiny hamlet of Peaksend Village and crossed the road to Peaksend Castle, the northern stronghold of the Desmarais family. Eleanor had never been inside Peaksend. She eyed the granite fortress with morbid interest. Her mind's eye had created a

picture of a matching Svelyan monolith skulking in mountains, awaiting her daughter.

Gregory called a halt at the entrance to the Dragon Mines. Chou
emerged from Eleanor's hood. "Smashing! We're here. It looks the same.
Probably has for three hundred years."

Eleanor stroked his head as the Dragon Mines churned before
her. Miners pushed bockety handcarts loaded with hunks of meat and
chunks of glistening raw Fire-iron. They shouted and cursed one another, but the working unicorns went about their business with their
usual tail-swishing tranquility. They came and went from the seven
dark holes in the mountainside. Some of the caves spewed sparks,
some leaked smoke, and one accepted human and unicorn visitors in
complacent quiet.

"Only one cave at extraction?" Eleanor asked Gregory.

Gregory nodded. "Yields were less than expected this summer." He
didn't elaborate, but Eleanor read his mood in his squinting eyes and
the hand that raked his hair.

Eleanor and Teardrop followed Gregory and Vigor down the narrow path into the Mines. The Unicorn Guard trailed behind them, a
wedding procession of white hides and silver horns. Eleanor's boots
squelched in the mud when she dismounted, but she didn't care. She
stretched her arms above her head, happy to have both feet on solid
earth.

Matt Thromba, the mine boss, made his bow-legged way toward
Eleanor and Gregory through the chaos. He bowed to Gregory and
kissed Eleanor's hand. She hugged him, and he blushed under his three-
pronged beard.

After chatty exchanges about the weather and the journey, Gregory
went to business. "When will cave five be cool enough to begin
extracting?"

"In three days, sire," said Thromba. "But the yield in cave six has
been a fine one. Dragons went deep this summer, they did."

"Still, one cave isn't enough."

Orvid Jones joined the conversation. "Has the mood improved down below?"

"Some," said Thromba. "Not as keen as I'd like them to be, honestly. Only two litters this year. The bulls spatting, and the does on the cold side."

Gregory's hands went to his hair again. "What's the matter with them? I fear to say, it reminds me of Oliver's meddling."

Thromba shook his head. "Nothing so bad as that, sire. When Oliver was snooping about it drove the beasts mad. You remember, how we had to chain Blondie in the courtyard to keep him from killin' himself and maybe a few others? No. This is just a bit o'irritation, like they've all caught a cold or summat. I'm thinking it might be the groundwater."

"Ah, that makes sense," said Gregory. His hands returned to his pockets.

"Groundwater?" asked Eleanor.

"A river runs through the caves, so it does. Dragons don't drink much, but they do need a drop here and again. They wade in the river once a season. Tremor told me it's a right sight. The dragons burn so hot, you know, the water level sinks below 'em. Poor creatures have to chase it with those long oul' jaws while it's evaporating right before their eyes."

"How awful," said Eleanor.

"Ach, they manage, your highness. A good swig or two can hold a bull over for three months. But you see, that swig must be clean. Fresh. Dragons can eat just about anything, but they're temperamental about their water."

"Perhaps wine?" said Chou. Eleanor hushed him. The thought of a herd of dragons wading in an evaporating river fascinated her.

"Anyhow," said Matt. "Every ten years or so, when the summer rains get too heavy in the mountains, some filth gets sent down the river. Filth from up north."

"What kind of filth?" asked Eleanor.

"Ach, your highness, you with your questions. It's not a proper topic." Thromba's face flamed again.

"Tell her, Matt," said Gregory. "She'll only dig it out of me, or Orvid, if not."

"If you say so, sire, but it's right unpleasant. You see, there's a small Ogre Camp about a hundred miles from here—"

"Ogre Camp?" Eleanor's mind went to the myriad lessons she'd had in her youth on ogres and the Ogre Wars of five-hundred years ago. She knew there were three camps. The two largest in northern Svelya, and a smaller one somewhere on the Carthean-Svelyan border. "Svelyan magicians manage the ogres, do they not?"

Thromba nodded. "They do, but even magicians can't control the rains. When they get so heavy...it washes the...Oh, HighGod, sire. I can't say it."

"It washes the ogre piss and shit into ground water. It goes sour," said Gregory. "Ogre offal is quite harsh. Fouler than Giant Buzzard droppings."

Eleanor blushed. "Oh, well. That does indeed make sense."

Thromba scrambled on. "We're hoping once the next watering comes around in fortnight or so, all will be well."

On that pleasant note, they broke up to allow the travelers time to sup and wash as best they could. Orvid joined the Unicorn Guards in the miner's tents. Eleanor and Gregory retired to the two-story wooden cabin that served as lodging for important guests. She climbed the stairs to the simple bedroom, but Gregory remained in the sitting room before the fire. He poured himself a tankard of ale and sat on a rough bench with his bow across his lap. He chewed on a hunk of dried beef.

The sun slipped behind the mountains as Eleanor changed into a cotton nightdress. She touched the pile of dragon robes spread across the bed. Fox, wolf, rabbit, bear. She recognized some of them from her one trip to the Mines with Gregory, thirteen years ago. Her heart hurt, for although she already knew she was in love with Dorian on that long-gone journey, she'd enjoyed Gregory's company. She'd held out some hope that their marriage could somehow be salvaged.

The door creaked open behind her and she slid under the robes. Gregory blew out the candle. He didn't say anything as he pulled off his boots, but Eleanor could hear his belt sliding thought its calfskin loops. She clenched her teeth.

Gregory lifted her nightdress and rolled her onto her stomach. He pushed one of her legs aside and worked his way inside her. She wasn't ready, or willing. Her body had no response, and the friction between them was like sanding paper on a rough board. Eleanor buried her face in the fox-fur robe. It pulsed with a dragon robe's weird living warmth beneath her nose. She inhaled the scent of musty fur and waited for Gregory's latest attempt at impregnation to come to a merciful end.

He pulled away from her, his breathing loud in the uncomfortable silence. He'd not slept beside her in over four years, but on this night, there was nowhere else for him to go. The space between them was an overgrown garden of awkward resentment. A thorny hedgerow that poked Eleanor's back even as she squirmed to the edge of the bed. She curled on her side and shut down her mind. HighGod was kind, and within a few minutes the exhaustion of the voyage and two night's fitful rest on the hard ground claimed her. She fell asleep.

A restless dragon's cry woke her sometime in the wee hours. She rolled onto her back.

Bad water. The thought swam through her fuzzy mind. It joined the remnants of a dream about a burning thirst and a receding river. She opened her eyes.

Gregory had left the bed. He slept upright, in a wooden rocker, with his chin resting on one elbow and his tankard in his lap.

Two days later the travelers set out again, into the heart of the

Scaled Mountains that separated Cartheigh from Svelya. At times the mountains blocked Eleanor's view, only to have the gaps between them open up to an endless line of sight. Rows of spiky granite stretched beyond her eyes' ability to find an end to it all. Eleanor alternated between claustrophobia when the mountain walls closed in and terror at the unfathomable emptiness when the cliffsides below them plunged into dark nothingness. Always the wind was in her way. It surrounded her on all sides, as tenacious as a cloud of gnats. It blew into her nose and lifted her hair. It set her eyes to water. It so seared her nostrils that by the second day she no longer smelled anything. It was just a wind smell, cold and damp but otherwise anonymous. It yammered at her in its monotonous, whistling voice, and she wished the path would widen out. The single file line provided little space for conversation, but plenty of room for uncomfortable thoughts.

Anticipation still flavored most of her ruminations, but fear had crept into the recipe, like a pinch of pepper in a sweet soup. She couldn't keep her hands off the dragon choker.

It's been over four years. What if something has changed? Perhaps he's found a lover. She bit her lip. *Does he know I'm coming? What shall I say when I see him?* She'd undoubtedly be limited to innocuous, milquetoast salutations. *Hello, your grace. How nice to see you. You're looking well.*

The fear grew through a hundred miles of mountain peaks, and three nights' sleep in a rough tent with Chou Chou snoring contentedly beside her head. On the morning of the fourth day, she whispered her worry and doubt to Teardrop as she tightened the mare's girth.

"Unfortunately, no amount of contemplation will ease your mind. Only he can give you the answer you seek. You have no choice but to wait and see."

Eleanor kissed Teardrop's nose. As usual, the mare was gallingly rational. And exasperatingly correct.

Their party slogged through another long day and uncomfortable night. On the fifth morning, the steep drops disappeared, and the path morphed into a road encased between two rock walls. An ancient artist had carved intricate designs into the granite. Birds, wolves, mountain goats, even the odd dragon. Skinny Svelyan letters spelled out messages that no one in Eleanor's party, save possibly Orvid Jones, could decipher. A three-story wooden gate appeared as the sun rose above the travelers' heads. Armed sentries peered down at their foreign visitors, human and unicorn. The guards shook their lances and shouted instructions. The gate to Nestra opened with the grinding of great chains set in motion.

Eleanor caught her breath at the Svelyan capital's strange beauty. The city leapfrogged the Gammon River. Houses, shops, and chapels perched on a freshwater archipelago interconnected by stone bridges. The Gammon pooled in superficial calm in sheltered nooks between five wooded islands. Along the straightaways, rapids raged around jagged boulders, as if the river might shake the rocks loose and hurl them at the city above. The citizens of Nestra, blonde dots draped in dark furs, crisscrossed bridges and steered long canoes through the Gammon's calmer harbors. The stronghold of the Svelyan kings braced itself across the river on the city's north end. Instead of solid land, Gammonreil Palace rested on a Fire-iron bridge. The span's arched and buttresses reflected the churning currents. Beyond the castle, a waterfall cascaded over the nearest mountain in a never-ending liquid curtsy. The falls kept up a low, rumbling growl, like a captive lion, bored in its cage.

"The ground hums below my feet," said Teardrop.

"HighGod's eyebrows," said Chou. "What a place."

Eleanor couldn't have said it better herself.

Gammonreil Palace had no courtyard. There was no space for one. The western bridge lead directly to four sets of Fire-iron doors.

"Leftover from the days when Svelya controlled the Mines," whispered Chou.

Eleanor nodded. Teardrop stepped across the threshold into the largest hall Eleanor had ever seen. Even Eclatant's Great Hall couldn't compete with this cavern, which could surely house half the dragons of the Mines, with room left over for a smallish ball. Six marble fireplaces encircled the room. Eleanor looked up, past the mounted heads of giant northern elk. Stone chimneys met a ceiling of iridescent glass windows. Prismatic light rained into the hall, like the many-hued spells of a hundred magicians.

"Is that roast pork I smell?" asked Chou.

"You don't eat meat." With a gurgle, Eleanor's stomach reminded her that she did not share her parrot's herbivorous tastes.

"But with pork comes rosemary bread. And pear pudding." Chou sniffed and licked his beak.

"Don't count on it. Don't you remember Christopher Roffi's rabbit stew?"

The Svelyan courtiers whispered in their guttural language and pointed at the unicorns. Teardrop snorted at their rudeness. Lords and ladies in clusters of dark blues and greens quietly compared their impressions of the visitors amongst themselves. Even the younger women showed little skin beyond their bare necks. Thick fur lined every bodice, as if the ladies had sprouted winter coats to cloak their modesty. The men, heavily clad in their own furry garb, resembled the bested animals peering down from the fireplaces. Above the neck, however, all traces of ruggedness disappeared. Their eyes were icy snowflakes, frozen in their pale, elegant faces. Eleanor caught a dark head here and there, but for the most part, her white blonde hair would finally be commonplace.

Bugle blasts—three short, one long— silenced the crowd. The caller announced Gregory, Eleanor, and their Chief Magician, Orvid Jones. They dismounted and approached the winding staircase at the end of the hall. The Unicorn Guard waited behind them at a respectful, watchful distance. Vigor's wide hoof slammed a protective warning against the marble floor, overriding the soft click of Eleanor's boot falls.

A small welcome party waited for them in the center of the hall.

A short woman with chin-length white hair and pixie-ish features unabashedly examined Eleanor. Her wide eyes gave her a look of perpetual surprise. When she moved, a greenish light followed her. It hovered around her head like grassy fog. Her fur trimmed gown resembled those of the other ladies, but Eleanor immediately surmised her to be a witch.

The second figure was a young man, not yet twenty years old. He was tall, but even his thick robe could not hide his slightness of frame. A mop of black hair framed his babyish but pleasing face.

"Prince Samuel?" whispered Chou.

"I hope so," whispered Eleanor. While the lad didn't have the look of a conquering hero, he had potential. He couldn't have been less like the husky, grizzled northern liege of her nightmares.

The third man wore a hood, but as he stepped forward to greet them his height and ambling walk gave him away. Eleanor's pulse blasted against her temples, a trumpet fanfare of her fear and desire.

Dorian pushed the hood back from his face. She first noticed the beard. It accentuated the already strong angles of his face. From ten paces away she could see hints of gray in his thick dark hair. Unlike the Svelyans around him, he still wore it past his ears, as if he'd chosen that bit of cultural milieu to cleave him to his homeland.

"On behalf of King Peter Mangolin," Dorian said, "I welcome my prince, Gregory Desmarais, son of Casper and heir to the throne of Cartheigh, to Gammonreil. Praise HighGod for your safe journey."

"HighGod's blessings on you, old…friend," said Gregory. He put a stiff arm around Dorian's shoulder and stepped away.

"King Peter would have been here to greet you himself, but he is indisposed. He sends his Chief Sorceress, Agnes, and his son, Prince Samuel of Svelya, in his stead."

For a moment the designation of Chief Sorceress distracted Eleanor from her inspection of Dorian. She touched Chou's scaly foot with one hand, communicating her surprise and interest with the brush of a finger in the lifelong language of their avian-human partnership.

She hadn't realized Peter Mangolin put his highest magical faith in a woman. She'd never heard of such in any nation, or read of it in any history book. From what she knew, Svelyans hewed close to traditional notions of masculine and feminine. Closer even than the average conservative Carthean. Chou chortled his mutual curiosity in reply.

Gregory stepped forward to greet the Svelyan prince and the witch, and Dorian turned to Orvid Jones. A hostile cream-colored light seeped from the magician's nose as they embraced, as if Orvid exhaled dirty frost. Apparently, he'd no more forgiven Dorian's disloyalty than he had Eleanor's.

Once he'd left Orvid's chilly embrace, Dorian turned to Eleanor. He gazed past her shoulder, as if he anticipated another visitor, then bowed and took her hand. She'd hoped to touch his skin, but he wore leather gloves. "Your highness," he said.

Eleanor could feel Gregory's eyes, and Orvid's, crawling over her like a plague of locusts. "Lord Brandling," she said. "How nice to see you." She cringed inwardly, for the greeting sounded as lackluster as she'd predicted.

"And you," he said. "Welcome." He met her eyes as he straightened, ever so briefly, but she saw nothing in his gaze. She felt nothing. He was a bearded man in a heavy cloak, an elegant diplomat, a beautiful stranger.

CHAPTER 3

EVERYONE HERE
HAS A SECRET

ELEANOR'S BEDROOM AT GAMMONREIL did not quite meet expectations after the fabulous Great Hall. It was half the size of her room at Eclatant, with dark stone walls that looked inclined to hold the damp. Two solid blue tapestries trimmed with brown fringe hung on either side of the room, like rugs in a painting with skewed dimensions. The tapestries lorded over a simple wooden desk, two chairs and a small table, a simple fireplace, and a low-slung wooden bench covered in furry cushions. Only the bed impressed. Carved from a chunk of solid granite, its four thick posters bore sculptures of battling angels and demons.

"I shall sleep with my head under my wing," said Chou. "Lest I wake to those fellows and think myself trapped in a nightmare."

Eleanor laughed. She didn't mind the coziness. The linens smelled clean and the bearskin dragon robe across the bed was certainly inviting. A Svelyan maid drew her bath and laid out a nightdress, and within an hour she crawled into bed. She pushed her worry over Dorian's aloof greeting to the side.

He's being careful. Tomorrow he will smile at me, and I'll know all is well.

462

She closed her eyes on that happy thought. She woke to a brown velvet gown trimmed in white rabbit hanging from one of the bed posters, a plate of buttered toast, and a message from the Chief Sorceress. The magical lady in question appeared at Eleanor's door promptly at nine o'clock, as promised, just as Eleanor's Svelyan maid finished her hair. Eleanor joined the tiny witch at the wooden table with a cup of tea.

"How are you finding your space? I am hoping you are liking it well." Agnes's high, wispy voice clashed with her harsh Svelyan accent, but at least Eleanor understood her. She felt a pang of nostalgia, as Agnes's idiosyncratic tweaking of Carthean grammar replicated her old friend Christopher Roffi's take on the language.

"Very nice," said Eleanor. "Although, the maid and I did have a time. Our language barrier is as steep and thick as the mountains between your country and mine. I think I frightened her, poor woman."

Agnes laughed, and her tiny nose crinkled. A pretty thing, she was. If she were not a witch, she'd have attracted many male admirers. "I'm sure she has been hearing of your story for years. Poor, pretty girl becomes a princess with the help of a magic spell. We are all knowing of the glass slippers in these days."

"Ah, well." It always surprised Eleanor when people spoke of her story with such reverence. Surely, she was not the first person of lean means to find herself unexpectedly elevated. Perhaps Rosemary's magical intervention made for a particularly interesting tale. "That was a long time ago." She took Agnes's hand. "I'm so thrilled to meet you. A Chief *Sorceress.*"

Agnes colored, but Eleanor sensed her admiration pleased the witch. "My king does honor me with his faith."

"Pardon, but I did not think Sevlyans were so forward thinking."

"As a group, we are far from it," said Agnes. "But the former Chief Magician was an unusual man. He formed a deep friendship with the Abbottess of C'adda. The Abbottess, bless her, was seeing some measure of talent in me. She asked him to take me on as his apprentice. So he did."

"And your talent blossomed under the nose of the king."

She nodded. "The old magician passed on three years ago, HighGod's blessings on him as well, and he recommended me to take his place."

"Amazing. King Peter agreed with his choice?"

"Surprisingly, yes." Agnes's delicate features darkened for a moment. "The lords were not so keen on my elevation. I fight for my position every day."

Eleanor shook her head. "Why are men so frightened of powerful women, magical or common?"

"What will they do with themselves if women no longer need rescuing?" This time Agnes squeezed Eleanor's hand. "I am so pleased to have you here, your highness. I am hearing you are a woman of learning and strong opinions. It can be lonely, here at court. The lords might dislike me, but their wives and daughters—what is the word—they *detest* me."

"I have known many such women. I probably don't hide my contempt as well as I think I do. I'm afraid my persona has never leant itself to popularity at court."

"Then we shall be detested together." Agnes waved her hands, and two green birds shot from her fingers. They circled Eleanor's head and disappeared in a puff of verdant smoke.

Chou raised his head from under his wing. He stretched and left his perch for the table. "Have we some feathered company?" he said with a yawn.

"None so handsome as you, Master Parrot," said Agnes. "Nor so exquisitely plumaged."

Chou went all puffy at the compliment.

"Agnes," said Eleanor, sensing an opening. "Speaking of handsome, what can you tell me about Prince Samuel? He seems a likely lad."

Agnes abruptly retreated into formality, her face bland, and her hands folded on the table before her. "He is a blessed young man, our esteemed prince."

"Yes, but what is he like? You know he's to marry my daughter. Is he kind? How does he pass the time? Riding, or hunting, or maybe—"

"I must be going. Surely you'll have time to get to know his highness yourself during your visit."

"Of course—I'm sorry—"

"I shall be seeing you at the dancing tonight." The witch smiled. "Promise me we will talk of literature and history? I am having a strong desire to drive the Lord High Chancellor mad with academia."

"Certainly!" Eleanor hadn't had such an appealing invitation in years.

Agnes took her leave, and Eleanor and Chou flopped in a comfortable heap on the huge bed.

"What a fascinating woman," said Eleanor. "I shall enjoy getting to know her better."

"Indeed," said Chou. "But for one so frank about her own tribulations, she certainly wasn't eager to discuss her prince."

"Perhaps they value the privacy of the royal family."

"Or perhaps Prince Samuel has some corpses in his cupboard."

"Chou, that's morbid." She rolled onto her back. "He's not even a grown man yet. How many secrets could he be hiding?"

"This is a palace, Eleanor. Everyone here has a secret or knows a secret or is looking for a secret." Chou stretched his wings. "Which reminds me, we've been here an entire day. It's high time I take a turn about the castle and—"

"And see what you can see."

He whistled and took off. Eleanor stared at the thick beams that crisscrossed the ceiling above her. She pictured Samuel's pleasant face and his tentative smile when he'd kissed her hand. Of course, Agnes was simply showing respect, and Chou was simply seeking gossip to take back to Eclatant. She sat up and reached for the printed schedule beside her bed. She perused a list of the day's events. Surely some function would put her in the same place as Dorian. *Ah, an afternoon strike stick league.* It sounded terribly boring, but Dorian was a celebrated strike stick player. She could stomach an hour of pipe smoke, clacking balls, and whiskey drunk courtiers. To look upon that loving smile she so longed for, she could tolerate almost anything.

Eleanor had never been overly concerned with fashion, but even she found her new Svelyan wardrobe to be a dull affair. The dress she donned for dinner was a replica of the one she'd worn during the day, with slight variations in color (dark blue) and fur (red fox).

"Do I smell like a smoking lounge?" She asked Chou as she spritzed herself with peachberry perfume. She'd flittered around the strike stick hall for an hour, but Dorian hadn't shown. "What a waste of time."

"I get a whiff of pipeweed when I land on your hair," said Chou, "but since no one else sits on your head, your olfactory anonymity is secure. You'll smell as fresh and flowery as all the other ladies."

"I wish Anne Iris were here. She could do something to liven up this dress." She winced as the silent Svelyan maid twisted her hair into a painfully tight knot at the base of her skull. "Or Pansy, to fix my hair. I fear if this good lady pulls any harder my eyes shall migrate to the sides of my head."

Chou waddled along the mantle, in his version of a seductive sashay. "And so the princess entered the ballroom, resplendent in boring blue, like a furred river flounder."

Eleanor sprayed him with her perfume.

An hour later Eleanor, her stretched scalp, and her peachy parrot joined the rest of King Peter Mangolin's court in the ballroom. She determined the ostentatiousness of the great hall to be purposeful, to make up for the lack of decoration in the rest of the palace. A larger replica of her own bedroom, the ballroom had dark walls, hung with bland tapestries, and small fireplaces. No granite bed, but otherwise, she felt relatively at home. Agnes added a bit of flair with lovely magical touches. The sorceress circled the edges of the ballroom, directing schools of enchanted silver fish. They swarmed the ceiling, turning *en masse*, like dancing mirrors. She'd also enchanted the floor tiles. As the guests' boots and slippers skipped over them, they flashed in time to the dance steps. A trio of fiddlers plunked away in the corner, and the ever-present smell of roast meat hung in the air. A pleasant scene for an evening's socialization, but Eleanor's nerves came back with a vengeance as the servants passed wine and bits of cheese. She felt Dorian's absence just as keenly in this strange castle as she had within the familiar walls of Eclatant. Perhaps more so. Here, there was a chance he was purposefully avoiding her.

She longed to visit with Agnes, but with the witch otherwise occupied, she had little choice but to cling to Gregory. He introduced her to various Svelyan lords and ladies. Some of the men spoke Carthean, but the women just nodded and smiled and looked her up and down with their frigid blue eyes. She tried to focus on the faces before her, but she still couldn't find Dorian. Her insubordinate eyes searched for him over fur bedecked shoulders and around hands outstretched in greeting. An hour ticked past, and he did not appear. Of course, Eleanor could not ask after his whereabouts. Finally, Gregory presented her with someone compelling enough to hold her attention.

"Prince Samuel," she said to the young man. "I'm so pleased to have a chance to speak with you."

He took her hand, gingerly at first, before he seemed to remember what he was supposed to do. He gave it a firm squeeze and a kiss. She took measure of him at close proximity: his thin frame, thick black hair, and dark blue eyes. He had pale skin and a full mouth.

"I'm also pleased to speak with you, Your Highness. You are very lovely, as everyone is saying you would be." His cheeks flamed, until his face matched his rosy lips.

"You flatter me, sire," she said. "I've borne three children, and nursed them through long nights. I can see it in my face these days."

"Surely you adopted your children, madam, so lithe and lovely are you."

Eleanor's mouth hung open for a moment, and then Prince Samuel chuckled. He exhaled, as if relieved to have landed a successful first compliment. Eleanor relaxed herself. *This lad does indeed have potential.*

"Remember, Eleanor, princes will say anything to win a smile from a lady."

Eleanor ignored Gregory's jab and focused on the boy before her. "How old are you, Samuel?"

"I'm nearly nineteen, your highness."

She tried to hide her surprise. With his slight frame and fey voice, she'd assumed him closer to sixteen. Still, better than the man of thirty-something she'd imagined on the journey.

Gregory excused himself to get a drink. Eleanor and Samuel chatted about the voyage and her lodgings for a time, before another young man, this one blonde and strapping, called him away.

"It *is* odd that Agnes was so evasive in discussing his character," said Eleanor, when Chou landed on her shoulder. She perused the room again, but still no Dorian. "He seems a pleasant sort, once he gets comfortable. Charming, in fact. His Carthean is excellent."

"You can try to ask the lady herself," said Chou, as Agnes eased through the crowd. Narrowed eyes and a few pointing fingers followed her. She grasped Eleanor's hand. Green smoke puffed between their fingers.

Eleanor complimented her on the magical entertainment and Agnes professed admiration for Eleanor's earbobs before they turned to more intellectually stimulating topics. Eleanor mentioned the trouble with the dragons and her fascination with their watering habits. "Those poor creatures chasing water that forever evaporates before them. There's something tragic in it."

Agnes sighed, and Eleanor sensed the weight of her position in the green light behind her eyes. "It is sad, but life is hard. Why should dragons be immune to challenges?" She pointed across the room. "Uncouth it may be to speak of such before dinner, but you did mention the Ogre Camps. Those magicians in the corner? They're part of the Ogre Watch."

A cluster of magicians sat around a high table. They wore black robes trimmed in black fur. They kept to themselves, and no one seemed bothered by their seclusion, or inclined to infringe upon it.

"I'm surprised to see such men among polite company," said Chou.

"It is true," said Agnes. "They rarely leave the camps. But a few are visiting once a season to give their report. Of course, they are an unsavory lot. No faulting of their own, for how can one be cultivating manners when surrounded by ogres through day and night?"

"They keep watch at all times, do they not?" asked Eleanor.

"It is quite a trying job. The—how are you saying it? The walls—the Restraints—must be maintained. A complex spell."

"That's why they are so well paid, those magicians," said Chou. "All the kingdoms in the known nations tithe the Ogre Camps."

Agnes tapped the little purse hanging from her waist. "The magicians of the Ogre Watch earn their coin, for sure."

"I should like to see an ogre," said Eleanor.

Chou rolled his eyes. "Of course you would. Just like you'd like to examine the mouth of an angry dragon, just to see if you'd be burned."

"Tsk, your highness," said Agnes. "I doubt very much you will see one, nor should you wish it! Few women are allowed to visit the camps."

"Women aren't allowed to visit the Dragon Mines either, but I've been there. Twice."

"Of course, that would be up to Prince Gregory. But thankfully, if he refuses, you will—as we like to say— eat your luck for supper, and get no seconds. HighGod willing, no one will ever be seeing an ogre outside of the camps. In this lifetime, or your great-grandchildren's."

Two days later, Eleanor finally met the elusive King Peter Mangolin, the Mountain Lion of Svelya. She took an audience with him in his receiving room, a circular chamber on the palace's top floor. Many small windows created a pretty patchwork view of the river valley. The view of Peter himself, however, could not be described so kindly.

She had heard he'd been suffering from an illness the past year or so, some manner of wasting disease. The old man who sat on the Fire-iron throne before her did not appear strong enough to stand, let alone lead a great nation. She guessed his age at somewhere in the realm of eighty years. He had not a hair on his head, although he did have copious white eyebrows. His blue eyes had faded to a nothing color. He rather reminded Eleanor of a male version of Hazelbeth, the Oracle of Afar Creek Abbey.

As was the case with Hazelbeth, King Peter's voice did not match his decrepit frame. It was sonorous, with all the rich intonation of a long-practicing Godsman at the pulpit. He spoke with only a hint of his native accent.

The old man greeted her and smiled, revealing two remaining front teeth. An ancient, grinning rabbit. "Come closer, child. My ears are tender. All of you, closer." He waved to Dorian, Gregory, and Prince Samuel. They formed an attentive ring around him.

"Does your daughter fancy you, your highness?" asked the old king.

"I'm afraid Leticia takes after me in the face, Peter," said Gregory. "Although she's shaping up to have her mother's fine figure."

"She's beautiful," said Eleanor, both in defense of Ticia and in mortification at Gregory's sexualization of the child.

Peter laughed. "Surely she is. Do you hear that, Samuel? A pretty flower. New blossom."

Eleanor blushed. The old king's salaciousness made her skin crawl, as if she were watching a rat drool over a piece of spoiled meat. The young prince had even less luck controlling his embarrassment. He shuffled his feet and mumbled something unintelligible.

"What color are the girl's eyes?" Peter squinted into Eleanor's face.

Eleanor blinked, in an old shield against such scrutiny. "Brown. Both of them."

"Good. One less reason for my Council to oppose."

"Who would oppose my daughter?" After discussing Ticia like a fine brood mare, Gregory was suddenly the protective father.

"Some would prefer a Svelyan match for Prince Samuel," said Dorian. "Or possibly a Kellish princess."

"Samuel's own mother was a Talessee duchess." Peter scowled. "Hence that mop of black hair, that he insists on keeping so girlishly long." The rabbit teeth reappeared. "Not that you Carthean gentleman look the least feminine. No accounting for custom, is there?"

While Eleanor tentatively liked Samuel, the conversation seemed to be heading in the direction of a signed treaty. "Let's not get ahead of ourselves, sirs. Leticia is but twelve, and we're here to discuss a possible match to benefit all parties."

"That's not the impression Lord Brandling gave me," said the king.

So it *was* true. Dorian, of all people, was pushing a match between her daughter and the Svelyan prince.

"We must ensure that everyone is agreeable," said Eleanor.

"I'm in no rush," said Samuel.

"Wise." Eleanor tried to catch Dorian's eye, but his darted between Gregory, Samuel, and King Peter. Damn his impassive face and refusal to look at her. "The pitfalls of rushing into marriage are many. Once the deed is done, it cannot be undone."

"Do you see some problem with my son? Something wrong with him?" asked Peter. "He's a fine young man. A strong stallion. Any woman in the world would be blessed to have him!"

"We're not speaking of a woman, sire, but a child," said Eleanor.

"Eleanor, watch yourself," said Gregory.

"It's fine, father—I'm in no hurry—we can wait as long as—"

"Silence, boy," said the king, and Samuel's comely mouth snapped shut. "I'll set the time, and the date, and the lucky partner." He smiled at Eleanor, but it didn't touch his eyes. "Let us end this discussion now, and think on it, all of us. Lord Brandling, princess, you are dismissed. I'll keep my son and Prince Gregory here with me for a time. We shall speak freely, as a king and kings to be."

Gregory ran a hand through his hair, but he grunted a goodbye. Eleanor thought she heard a warning behind it.

He needn't have worried. Eleanor followed Dorian from King Peter's receiving room. As the door closed behind them she rounded on him.

"How could you?" she asked. "Push a marriage match for Leticia, at her age? Send her away from me, from her sister? From Cricket and Eclatant and everything she knows?"

Dorian opened his mouth, but Eleanor cut him off.

"You, of all people, who knows the misery of those trapped in a loveless marriage! After everything we suffered!"

"HighGod above," he said. "Keep your voice down."

"Did you hear how that old pervert spoke about her?"

He leaned toward her and spoke in a harsh whisper. "I've been writing to Casper and

Gregory about this for over two years."

"What?" said Eleanor. "I've not heard one word about a marriage until two weeks ago!"

"Exactly. They won't consult you. Leticia's hand is a bargaining tool, nothing more. She'll have no say in whom she weds. Princesses—princesses of the blood, that is—never do. Gregory's sister Matilda married a Talessee duke twenty-five years her senior when she was thirteen."

Eleanor paled. Matilda had died in childbirth only a few years later.

"Casper and Gregory will marry her to whom they choose, no matter what I or anyone else says. When I met Samuel I thought, here is a nice young man. Relatively close to her age. Better she be married to the son of an old pervert than the pervert himself. I'm trying to make the best of it."

Make the best of it, thought Eleanor. *That's what I've been doing for fourteen years.* She crossed her arms across her chest. "No," she said. "I won't allow it."

"*You* won't allow it?"

"I will *not allow* it."

Dorian turned in a circle, shaking his head. He chuckled, or sniggered—she wasn't quite sure how to categorize it— the kind of condescending, exasperated laughter that turned Eleanor into a spooked cat, hackles raised and claws drawn.

She planted both fists on her hips. "Ticia will choose her own husband, when she's ready. Perhaps she'll be queen herself."

"Eleanor, you're not being realistic!" Dorian threw up his hands.

"I've never been realistic. Not about love." She stalked down the varnished staircase. Her skirts tangled in ungraceful clumps around her legs.

"Eleanor. Damnit. Eleanor!"

She nearly tripped twice, so she grabbed the layers of thick cloth and hoisted them almost to her knees. A passing chambermaid gasped at the sight of her scandalous woolen stockings. She didn't care. Her eyes burned.

He smiled at her, yes, but it hadn't been loving or reassuring, only patronizing. He said her name, but it wasn't a gentle expulsion of tenderness. Instead, he'd vented his frustration at her perceived unreasonableness. She'd felt a distinctly inimical inclination to punch him. In short, their first private conversation in almost five years was an unqualified disaster.

Find out the conclusion to the *Cracked Slipper
Series* in the last installment,

THE GLASS RAINBOW

ALSO BY STEPHANIE ALEXANDER

The Cracked Slipper Series
The Cracked Slipper
The Dragon Choker
The Glass Rainbow (Coming in Spring 2020)

Also coming in 2020: *Charleston Green*, set in Charleston, South Carolina, the story of a clairvoyant mom of three, who uses her paranormal talents to solve a century-old murder mystery while rebuilding her life after a devastating divorce.

ACKNOWLEDGEMENTS

The *Cracked Slipper Series* has been a ten-year labor of love. Since I began the first book in 2009, my life has changed immeasurably. I've been through the hardest times in my life, and come out the other side with an outcome that is beautiful beyond anything I thought it could be. Too many people have been a part of this process to name them all, but a few require special recognition. On a practical note, thank you to Kathy Meis and Shilah LaCoe and the rest of the team at Bublish for their creativity and knowledgeable insight. The Bublish model is a unique platform for authors and a great addition to the ever evolving publishing world. As to the ones I hold dearest, first, to my sister-cousin, Haley Telling, thank you for always cheering me on, and coming up with wonderful ideas for ways to get my work out into the world, and helping me keep my chin up when the process beat me down. This is a hard business, and your eternal optimism helped me remember that the stories are the heart of it. Thank you to my mother, Dianne Wicklein, who I admire above all other women, and who is a testament to the redemptive power of tenacity and faith. Thank you to my three wonderful children, who have gone from babies to teenagers while I labored on this project and rebuilt my life. They are my reason for pushing myself on good days, and my reason for getting out of bed on bad ones.

Lastly, thank you to my husband, Jeffrey Cluver. I would call you my Prince Charming, but as this book has tried to illustrate, Prince Charming is overrated. Instead, I will call you my best friend, my closest confidante, the rock I cling to when I'm floundering in a sea of writer-ly self doubt. You read my first drafts; you give me feedback I didn't know I needed; you spark my imagination when it's feeling about as combustible as a wet match. Thank you for being you.

There are so many others, but I will have to thank them all in person, lest I risk running on for another hundred thousand words. But lastly, thank you to my readers, who fell in love with Eleanor, her journey, and the enchanted universe she inhabits. I hope I've done justice to her story, and your imaginations.

— Stephanie

ABOUT THE AUTHOR

Stephanie Alexander grew up in the suburbs of Washington, DC. Drawing, writing stories, and harassing her parents for a pony consumed much of her childhood. After graduating from high school in 1995 she earned a Bachelor of Arts in Communications from the College of Charleston, South Carolina. She returned to Washington, DC, where she followed a long-time fascination with sociopolitical structures and women's issues to a Master of Arts in Sociology from the American University. She spent several years as a Policy Associate at the International Center for Research on Women (ICRW), a think-tank focused on women's health and economic advancement.

Stephanie embraced full-time motherhood after the birth of the first of her three children in 2003. Her family put down permanent southern roots in Charleston in 2011. She published her first novel, *The Cracked Slipper*, in February 2012. Along with two sequels (*The Red Choker* and *A Ring in Blue*), the series has sold over 40,000 copies. *The Cracked Slipper* has made multiple appearances on Amazon's fantasy bestseller lists, and peaked at #11 in all genres. Stephanie has appeared on local and national media, been a contributor on many writing blogs and in writing magazines, and regularly joins with book clubs for discussions of her work.

In addition to her personal writing, Stephanie returned to the College of Charleston as an Adjunct Professor of Sociology and Women's Studies, and launched her freelance ghostwriting and editing business, Wordarcher, LLC. She has ghostwritten dozens of books, from novels to memoirs to academic theses. Beginning in the Fall of 2015, as a single working mother, she attended law school on a full academic scholarship, earning her juris doctor with honors from the Charleston School of Law in December, 2017.

She currently practices family law in Mount Pleasant, South Carolina, the Charleston suburb that is the setting of her latest novel, *Charleston Green*. Her personal experience rebuilding her life after divorce inspires both her legal work and her fiction.